BALTHAZAR

CLAUDIA GRAY

HARPER TEEN
An Imprint of HarperCollinsPublishers

HarperTeen is an imprint of HarperCollins Publishers.

Balthazar

Library of Congress Cataloging-in-Publication Data
Gray, Claudia.
    Balthazar / Claudia Gray. — 1st ed.
        p.   cm.
    ISBN 978-0-06-196118-2 (tr. bdg.)
    [1. Vampires—Fiction. 2. Psychic ability—Fiction. 3. Love—Fiction.
4. Horror stories.]   I. Title.
PZ7.G77625Bal   2012   2011024243
[Fic]—dc23   CIP
                                                                 AC

    12   13   14   15   16   LP/BV   10 9 8 7 6 5 4 3 2 1
                                        ❖
                              First Edition

BALTHAZAR

Chapter One

THE DEAD WERE WATCHING.

Skye Tierney gripped her horse's reins in her gloved hands as she shut her eyes tightly, willing the sensation to go away. It didn't matter, though; whether or not she could see the actual images, she knew what was happening near her—the horror of it was as tangible, and real, as the gray winter sky looming overhead.

Not watching somehow made it worse. Taking a deep, shuddering breath, Skye forced herself to open her eyes—to see the woman fleeing for her life.

She thought he wouldn't follow her up here. He hasn't been the same since his fall two months ago; it was as if the goodness in him left when his head was cut open, and something else—something darker—flew in. She'd thought he wasn't paying attention, but he was. He is. He's here now, his fingers digging into the skin of her arm as he talks about how she has to be stopped.

This is different from his other fits. He's scaring her so badly

that her throat goes dry and she wants to just fall on the ground,
play dead like some kind of witless animal, so that perhaps he'll
walk away in one of his dazes. But she can't pull away from him
even to fall; he's too large, too strong. Voice shaking, she tells him
he's not thinking clearly, that he'll feel sorry for this when he comes
to himself again. Her desperate lunge away from him makes his
fingers sink so deeply into her flesh it seems as though her skin will
tear. Her feet slide in the fall leaves as she hits at him with her one
free hand.

He's smiling as if he'd just seen something beautiful as he pulls
her around in one long circle, just like a child twirling a friend, the
way he twirled her when they were little together, except that he
slings her over the side of the cliff and lets go.

She screams and screams, arms and legs kicking at the rushing
air, all of it futile, and the fall lasts so long, so long, so fast—

Skye stumbled backward against Eb, her veins rushing with adrenaline and her throat tight. The image faded, but the horror didn't.

"It's still happening," she whispered. Nobody to hear her but the horse, and yet Eb turned his massive black head toward her, something gentle in his gaze. Her parents always said she gave him credit for feelings he couldn't have or understand. They didn't know anything about horses.

Leaning her head against his thick neck, Skye tried to catch her breath. Despite the warm gray coat and thick teal sweater she wore, cold air cut through her skin to deepen her shivering. The wind caught at the locks of her auburn brown hair that hung from beneath her riding helmet, reminding her that soon night would fall and the wintry beauty of the riding trails on state land behind her house would turn to bitter, even savage, chill. And yet she couldn't bring herself to move.

Their words to each other had been spoken in a language Skye didn't speak, didn't even think she'd heard before. Their clothing and hair made her think they must have been Native American. Was what she'd seen something from five or six hundred years in the past? Did the visions take her back as far as that? Further? It felt like there might be no end to them.

As impossible as it seemed, the visions of past deaths that had surrounded her for the last five weeks—ever since the fall of Evernight Academy—weren't going away. She never doubted for a moment that the deaths she'd seen were real, no mere nightmares. This . . . psychic power, or whatever it was, had become a part of her.

It wasn't as though she'd never believed in the supernatural before this winter; the home she'd grown up in had been haunted. The ghost in her attic had been as real to her as her big brother, Dakota, and about equally as likely to hide her favorite toys to tease her. She'd never been frightened of the girl-ghost upstairs—understanding, somehow, that it was playful and young. Its pranks were gentle and funny, things like taking her pink socks and putting them in Dakota's dresser, or knocking on the bed frame just as Skye was drifting to sleep. Dakota had "known" the ghost first, and he was the one who had told her it was nothing to be scared of—that ghosts were probably as natural as rain or sunshine or anything else on earth. So she had never doubted that something existed beyond the world everyone could see.

Despite that, Skye had never suspected just how much closer, and more dangerous, the supernatural could get.

Since her sophomore year, she'd been a student at Evernight Academy—which, so far as she'd known, was an elite boarding school in the Massachusetts hills, like many others; sure, there were some odd rules, and some of the other students sometimes struck her as definitely older than their years, but that wasn't so weird . . . she'd thought.

No, she hadn't suspected anything out of the ordinary about Evernight. When her good friend Lucas told her it was dangerous—a school for vampires, no less—she'd assumed he was joking.

Until the freaking *vampire war* broke out.

Eb nudged her with his nose, as if willing her back to the here and now. Skye decided he was right. Nothing helped her as much as riding.

She steadied herself on the snowy ground before slinging one foot up into the saddle and hoisting herself into her seat. Eb remained motionless, waiting, ready for her. To think she had him because her twelve-year-old self had told her parents she only wanted a black horse with a white star on its forehead.

(*That's silly*, Dakota had said. He was sixteen, maddeningly superior by then, and yet somehow still the person she wanted to impress more than any other. *You don't pick horses by colors.*

They're not My Little Ponies. But he'd smiled as he said it, and she had forgiven him right away—

No. She wasn't going to let herself think about Dakota.)

Well, okay, she had been silly. Back then she hadn't known what to look for in a horse: sureness, steadiness, the ability to know the person on its back as surely as any other human being ever could or would. Eb had all that, and the star.

I should hurry home in case Mom and Dad check on me, she thought. Even in her mind, the words rang hollow. They would be in Albany, working hard. Supposedly this was because their jobs were so demanding—which they were. Skye knew that. But she also knew that the real reason they'd buried themselves even deeper in work during the past year was because they didn't want to let themselves think about Dakota either. Skye hadn't quite realized how far they'd taken it until she moved back from boarding school five weeks earlier. She also hadn't realized how badly she'd wanted them to be home.

But they all had to deal with this in their own way. If that meant she had to deal on her own, okay.

Clicking her tongue and bringing in her heels, Skye got Eb moving, his hooves crunching through the snow. Only about six inches of it on the ground at the moment, which was as good as it got in upstate New York in early January. Soon it would be falling a foot or two at a time, maybe more. All around her, the stark branches of leafless trees stretched up to claw at the low gray sky.

"Now we know to avoid the cliff," she said aloud, her breath making clouds in the crisp late-afternoon air. "That's one more place we won't go. Soon we'll have figured out a nice long track in the woods to ride on every day, one where nobody ever died, and I won't have to see anything scary at all."

But already Skye felt as if she would never again be able to escape the presence of death.

It had begun at Evernight, during that last terrible day. As the vampires fought among themselves, some tribal battle she'd never understood, ghosts trapped within the building had been set free. One of them—Lucas's dead love, Bianca—had remained imprisoned. Skye's loyalty to him had led her to make a spontaneous offer—to take Bianca inside herself, to be possessed by her—in order to help her escape.

What Skye hadn't counted on was how it would feel to share a body with a dead person—how terrifying it was, even when it was someone she instinctively trusted. And she definitely hadn't realized that being possessed would leave her open to the spirits of the dead *forever*.

As Eb took her through the heavy woods, Skye wondered if anybody besides her had ever seen these visions. If anyone else understood that throughout Darby Glen, on the streets, in the buildings, even out here in the forest, the world reverberated with the echoes of death after death—

A snapping sound nearby startled her, but only momentarily; it wasn't unusual to see foxes darting among the snow or deer foraging for what little food remained this time of year. Skye almost welcomed the break from her thoughts—better to lose herself in the moment, in the warmth of Eb, the rhythm of his stride, the beauty in the woods around her. So she looked toward the sound with more relief than alarm—

Until she saw that the snap had been caused not by an animal but a man.

He stood there in his brown coat, staring at her. If he had smiled, waved, or called out hello, Skye wouldn't have found it unusual; this was state land, after all, and though she and Eb often had the trails to themselves this time of year, she wasn't the only one who found the forest in wintertime beautiful.

But he didn't do any of those things. He just stared at her with a flat, almost haughty gaze that felt unnervingly familiar.

"C'mon, Eb." Skye urged her horse to go a bit faster, still only slightly shaken. This guy, whoever he was, didn't look good to her—but as a rider, she was faster than he could ever be.

Or so she thought.

Eb's steps quickened further, and the muscles in her body tensed to hold her steady in her seat. Twigs snapped beneath his hooves, and ice crunched—and yet she could hear more than that. She could hear footsteps behind them.

Skye glanced over her shoulder and saw the watcher in the brown coat, walking after them now, unusually sure-footed on the treacherous terrain. His unnerving expression hadn't changed at all, but his hands were no longer in his pockets. He was clenching and spreading them, over and over, as if preparing for some kind of strenuous task. Like, say, strangling somebody.

Which was probably completely paranoid of her, she decided;

she couldn't allow her visions to bleed over into her every waking thought. But she looked back at the trail ahead and wondered if she dared to urge Eb to move faster. Rocky—snowy—but not too bad. She jabbed her ankles into his sides, not too roughly, just hard enough for him to know it was time to move.

Eb shifted into a brisk trot, or as brisk as he could manage given the undergrowth, but it was enough to leave behind any human who wasn't running to keep up.

Again, Skye looked over her shoulder. The guy was running after her. And more than keeping up.

This was real. It wasn't paranoia, or a supernatural vision of death, or some hysterical hallucination cooked up by what she'd been through at Evernight. That man was real, and he wanted to hurt her, and he was coming after her as fast as he could.

Skye dug her heels into Eb's sides and snapped the reins, the signal for him to gallop. Treacherous as the ground was, Eb responded immediately by breaking into a run. She leaned forward, the better to avoid being smacked in the face by the tree branches now rushing by her. Her breath quickened, the air so brutally cold that her throat ached. Fear lanced through her, but anger, too—fierce enough to almost overcome the fright. How dare this jerk try to come after her? He was a disgusting creep and she wished she could take a horsewhip to him, but she knew that instead she had to get the hell out of here.

Above her, she heard a strange thudding in the trees. Her eyes darted upward, and despite the blur of motion overhead she could make out his shape. He was above her. Twenty feet up.

And leaping ahead of her as if he were weightless.

Oh, my God, she thought. *It's a vampire.*

This one wasn't like the vampires at Evernight. He wasn't trying to hide what he was. He was moving faster than Eb. Coming for her. Coming to kill her.

Eb stumbled so suddenly that even Skye's expert seat couldn't hold her in place—she went tumbling in front of him, hitting the frozen ground so hard the breath was sucked out of her.

Dazed, Skye stumbled to her feet. A fragment of her helmet lay shattered against the snowy ground; but for the helmet, that would've been her skull. Her left hand was scraped badly enough to drip blood, and plenty of it. For one moment she looked at her horse, who hadn't budged since the stumble, as though he were stuck in place—if his leg was broken, he'd have to be put down, oh, God, no, not Eb—

But then the vampire landed only a few feet away, and she had to run.

Skye went as fast as she could, but he was faster. He leaped ahead of her, making her skid to a stop. Desperately she ripped off her helmet and held it in front of her chest—it was the only shield she had—but he began laughing.

Laughing at her. Toying with her. And there wasn't a damned thing she could do about it.

"Are you cut?" he said. His voice was smooth and pleasant; he spoke as if he'd just found her there, injured, and wanted to be of assistance. Of course he wasn't fooling her and he knew it. This was just a game he wanted to play.

Well, she'd be damned if she'd play along. "Get lost."

The vampire stooped down and dipped two of his fingers in the small red puddle her blood drops had made in the snow. "It looks beautiful against the white, doesn't it?" he said dreamily. "Like red roses in a bridal bouquet." Then he lifted his fingers to his lips and licked her blood away.

Then something happened to him—his gaze seemed to dim, and his jaw went slack, and his entire body became still. It was completely bizarre, but it was a chance and Skye meant to take it.

She bolted back toward Eb. If he was injured then—no, she couldn't think about that. If he wasn't, she might be able to get back on him and ride out of here still. Head whirling, Skye pushed herself faster and faster, seeking Eb's black form amid the deepening afternoon shadows—nightfall would be on them soon—

Until a hand closed over her elbow, jerking her back so sharply that she cried out. Skye turned back to see the vampire no longer distracted. His grip was so strong it hurt, and though she pulled back there was no freeing herself.

"Let's make red roses in the snow," he whispered.

She thought, *I'm going to die.*

And then someone else reached from behind her, grabbed the vampire away from her, and threw him—physically threw him, farther and harder than any human could have done—so that he thudded into a tree trunk two dozen feet away before landing on the ground.

Skye turned to see her rescuer—and then gasped. There, his strong profile outlined against the dim glow of sunset, was another vampire—one she knew.

His name escaped her lips as a whisper: "Balthazar."

Chapter Two

BALTHAZAR HAD COME HERE LOOKING FOR Skye Tierney. Thanks to Lucas, he'd known she was in trouble. But he hadn't expected to walk right into a fight against another vampire.

Then again, neither had his opponent, who was about to get one whether he liked it or not. Balthazar intended for him not to like it one bit.

"Balthazar." Skye was wide-eyed with fright and astonishment. "What are you doing here?"

"Right now? Kicking this guy's ass. Stay back and get out of here if you can." Thankfully, she did what he asked, stepping farther away toward safety. That meant he didn't have to worry about protecting her and could concentrate on making this vampire sorry he'd ever decided to feed on a helpless girl in the woods.

His opponent righted himself, no more than dazed by the throw. Balthazar had expected as much. He bolted toward the guy as fast as he could. The element of surprise was all he had going for him. He didn't drink human blood often, and obviously this one did, plus something about him told Balthazar that this one was older than he was. Stronger. More powerful.

Surprise paid off. He was able to tackle the vampire solidly, taking him down to the ground. Balthazar grabbed for a nearby branch, a short one that could serve as a stake. Though he disliked killing his own kind and avoided it whenever possible, the alternative here meant leaving behind a threat to human life. No way. But as he lifted the stake overhead, readying the fatal blow, something happened that he hadn't expected.

He recognized the vampire.

"Lorenzo," he said. Knowing him was more reason to stake him, not less, but the astonishment of seeing this vampire—from the most terrible moments of his past—froze Balthazar half in place, stake still clenched in his fingers. "What the hell are you doing here?"

"I might ask the same of you." Lorenzo's shock was similar to his own; this meeting was a horrid coincidence, no more. Immortality seemed to increase the probability of coincidence. Given enough time, paths would inevitably cross—even the ones you least wanted.

"Leave this girl alone. Why are you after her?"

"Because she is human and we are vampires—something you too often forget. Now, ask what you really long to know," Lorenzo said. "Ask me if I came here with Redgrave."

He said the name so sweetly, as though it were a father or

a lover. For all Balthazar knew, it was some of both. The name never ceased to send a chill through him—part dread, part hate. *Redgrave.*

"Where is he?" Balthazar demanded. His voice was almost a growl now.

"Not near enough to watch you die."

The blow slammed into Balthazar's chest—both hands, spread broadly, nearly enough force to crack ribs. It sent him flying backward, not far, but enough for Lorenzo to skitter free. Within an instant they were both on their feet, facing each other. Balthazar still clutched the stake; it was as close as he would get to an advantage from now on.

Lorenzo de Aracena, of sixteenth-century Spain, a would-be poet and a dirty fighter. Often subservient to his sire—Redgrave, the darkest vampire Balthazar had ever known or hoped to know—but just as often renegade. Sometimes his sire pushed him away for his own reasons; Lorenzo always went limping back eventually, eager for someone to tell him what to do, what to think, whom to kill. He would always be someone's slave. Most vampires were, in the end.

Balthazar wasn't. He didn't know if he was strong enough to kill Lorenzo, but he was damned sure going to try.

"Do you want the girl for yourself?" Lorenzo smiled, almost politely. "That's impossible, I'm afraid."

"She's not going to be yours," Balthazar replied. He kept his voice even as well. Inside, though, he was uncertain—it was strange of Lorenzo to challenge him about Skye in particular.

For the two of them, just seeing each other was reason enough to get into it. But why claim possession of Skye? She was just a girl, just a convenient victim chosen at random.

Wasn't she?

"So many possibilities," Lorenzo said. "So many opportunities. Too rich to waste on a battle with you."

And then he vanished. As if he'd disappeared into thin air—a gift some few vampires aged into, but only after a couple of millennia. Lorenzo didn't have that talent; he'd just streaked into the night without a sound. Balthazar turned and ran in the direction Skye had gone.

He hadn't learned what the guy was up to, only that it wasn't good—and that Skye still needed his protection.

Balthazar caught up with her not far away; she'd stopped by a large dark horse, evidently hers, and kneeled by its front hooves. Lorenzo was nowhere to be seen, and the woods around them were silent. The danger seemed to have passed for the moment, but she couldn't have known that. He said, "You'd have done better to run."

"If you won the fight, I didn't have to run. If you lost, it wouldn't have done any good. The other vampire was faster than me."

Which was a good point, actually. He liked her steadiness in the face of danger. "Is your horse hurt?"

"Eb's okay, I think." Skye sounded as relieved as though she were talking about a good friend, not an animal. "But I want to be sure—and I'm so freaked out I can't tell if he's shaking or I am."

"Let me check." Balthazar clucked his tongue—an old habit, one he'd almost forgotten, but it still worked. Eb allowed him to run his hands along his legs, which were sound. "You were right. He's not hurt. Only startled."

Only then did Balthazar really look at Skye. Her long hair—deep brown, if memory served—looked almost black as night drew on. Although her breaths still came quickly, she was surprisingly composed given what had just happened to her, and how much worse it could have been. Her cheeks were flushed from the exertion of her headlong chase.

"We need to get out of here," she said. "Do you know how to ride?"

"It came in handy before the invention of the car."

"Oh. Right." That caught her off guard for only a moment. "Eb can carry us both as far as the stable. Come on." Skye looked up into the darkening air as if another vampire might come plummeting toward her at any second. Though Balthazar didn't sense any others nearby, he thought she had the right idea about leaving this place as soon as possible.

So when she swung up into the saddle, Balthazar didn't hesitate. As soon as she had her seat and Eb was steady, Skye offered him her left arm. The reins remained in her right hand; her control of the horse was such that she was able to slide her feet out of the stirrups and hold him steady just through that mysterious communication between human and animal. Balthazar put one foot in the stirrup and mounted easily—he hadn't done this in a long time, but his muscles retained the memory, and then he was next to Skye. They were sitting so close that they touched, thigh to thigh and shoulder to shoulder, and for one moment he couldn't help noticing how warm she was. How fast her heart was still beating.

"Hang on," she said, readjusting her feet so that she had the stirrups—taking command again.

"I'm ready."

With that, she spurred Eb back into action, and the horse began taking them back toward civilization. Back toward safety, Balthazar would've said—but he wasn't totally sure of that at the moment.

Her breath made clouds of fog in the bitterly cold air. His didn't.

The stables turned out to be not some major commercial enterprise, the way most of them were in twenty-first-century America, but a smaller structure built of wide planks of wood not far behind Skye's home. Though the lighting was electric instead of candles, it ran through heavy black lanterns that conjured up old, pleasant memories. The scent of hay took him back.

As they approached, he said, "Will your parents come outside? Do we need to cover who I am, what I'm doing here, anything like that?"

"They're in Albany. Lobbyists, and their bill is under discussion, so—I've hardly seen them for more than ten minutes a day since Christmas."

"That's not much."

"They have their reasons." There was humor in Skye's gaze as she glanced back at him. "And why wouldn't I tell them the truth? You're an old friend from school who's come to say hi."

"Do they know about Evernight? What it really was?"

"Nope. I figured I'd rather close out my senior year at my hometown school than a mental institution. Though I'm not sure I see any difference." She sighed as she dismounted.

"Is anyone else at home? Do you have a sister or brother?"

Skye stiffened at the question, and he hesitated before getting off the horse, unsure why this was such a sore subject. Then she said, shortly, "My brother died last year. It's just me."

"I'm sorry. I didn't know."

"It's okay. I'm on my own, but I can take care of myself."

Clearly, this wasn't something she wanted to discuss. So he dismounted without another word.

Balthazar led Eb into the warm stable and began unsaddling him. One other horse, a mare with a reddish coat, whickered as if welcoming them inside. Skye didn't interfere, just watched him put up the tack and brush Eb down. Only when she appeared satisfied that Balthazar really understood how to care for a horse did she speak. "Okay, so, how did you know to show up in the woods like that? Do you just go around finding people in trouble like . . . Vampire Batman or something?"

He had to smile. "I wish. No, Lucas told me you were having some trouble and asked me to drop in on you, check things out. He didn't mention any vampire attacks, though."

"There haven't been any. Not before today, I mean. I only

wrote him about—" Clearly this was difficult for her to talk about. "About the visions. The deaths."

"So, you're still seeing them." Lucas had said that she was being overcome by what appeared to be wraiths; instead of being haunted, however, Skye was witnessing deaths in vivid, graphic detail—constantly. First they needed to find a pattern. "Is it happening more frequently now? Does it happen at night, during the day, after you've done something or not done something . . ."

Skye shook her head. The lantern light burnished her dark hair, bringing out the hint of auburn beneath the brown. He'd hardly ever allowed himself to notice before, but she was a strikingly beautiful girl. "It's not about anything I do or don't do. It's only about where I am. If I'm in a place where somebody died, I see it. But it's more than seeing—I know how everyone felt. The victim and the killer, if it was a murder."

"They aren't all murders?" Wraiths were created only by homicide; if she was seeing other kinds of deaths, then wraiths had nothing to do with it.

"Sometimes they are. But sometimes they're just—sudden. Violent. None of them are peaceful." Skye folded her arms in front of her, unconsciously shielding herself. "The first one I saw was on the drive home from Evernight. We got caught in traffic on the interstate, and while we were idling there I saw this car crash—the aftermath of one—and this crumpled body . . . I thought I must be going crazy. Or that all that weird stuff at Evernight had me, I don't know, not in my right mind. But when I watched that crash over and over—watched that guy die, heard it, even *smelled* it—I knew it had to be real." A shudder rippled through her. "Did you know you can smell blood in smoke? You can."

"Yes, I knew that." Best not to get into how. "So you see the visions whenever you're near the site of a sudden death."

"It's like the dead want me to pay attention. Like they want me to go through it all with them. When it's happening, I have to fight to remember who and where I am. I want to snap out of it, but sometimes I can't. Is this—did Lucas send you because you know a lot about this kind of thing?"

"Unfortunately, no." Balthazar kept brushing Eb; he'd forgotten how much this simple, repetitive act helped him concentrate. Working on cars was fun, but it had nothing on caring for a horse. "Lucas and Bianca would've come themselves, but Black Cross has been giving them trouble lately."

"Black Cross?"

"Oh. I forgot you didn't know." For the first time, it occurred to Balthazar that Skye was still an outsider in the world of the supernatural. Despite everything she'd seen and done, much of his world remained a mystery to her. "Vampire hunters. Don't worry; Bianca and Lucas are fine. But they wanted me to find out more about what was going on with you, and make sure you were okay. Instead you're being hunted by a vampire."

Skye tucked a lock of her hair behind one ear, obviously trying hard to concentrate, though this had to be overwhelming for her. "Okay. Vampires are . . . everywhere, then. Not just at Evernight."

"Not just at Evernight. A lot of us try hard to live normally and get by, but there are dangerous ones out there. And the one you ran into tonight, Lorenzo—he's bad news."

Bad news: What an understatement. But telling her the full truth right now was something Balthazar didn't want to do unless it was necessary—it would only panic her. Above all, he didn't want to get into the labyrinthine complications of his own long past.

"Will he come back?" she asked. "Or was that just . . . random?"

"I don't know." And he didn't like not knowing. "I'm going to hang around for a few days and make sure he's cleared off. So don't worry too much. But no more riding alone in the woods at dusk, okay?"

"Don't worry. I'm not exactly in a rush to repeat the experience." Her eyes met his, only for a moment, almost shyly. He didn't understand why; after all, they'd known each other for almost three years. Granted, they'd never shared more than a few words of conversation, and he'd borrowed her Twentieth-Century History notes once to get some modern perspective, but they weren't strangers. And she'd always struck him as outgoing, forthright . . . even bold.

Balthazar finally got it when she said, "All right, I know the answer to this question, but still, I have to ask. You're—you're a vampire. Right?"

"Right." He studied her face carefully in search of her fear or revulsion, but she didn't turn away. "Does that bother you?"

"Not as much as it probably should." She laughed at herself. "I mean, I already knew. Sort of. But I guess I needed to hear it from you."

Perhaps Skye distrusted him now; he wouldn't blame her if she did. "I don't feed from humans. You're safe with me."

"I know that. If I hadn't known it before today—I would now."

"Anything you need to know about any of this, you can ask me. I might not know the answer, but if I do, I'll tell you. So you don't have to stay in the dark any longer."

"Okay. Good to know." As she ran one hand through her hair, Balthazar could see that she still trembled slightly. Despite the brave front she was putting up, Lorenzo's attack had shaken her.

Placing one broad hand on her shoulder, Balthazar said, "Listen. Go inside and warm up. Get some sleep if you can. I'll be outside all night, and we'll talk it over tomorrow."

"Tomorrow." She grimaced. "It's the first day of school—I'd forgotten all about it. I mean, I was dreading it up until now. But the whole vampire-attack thing kind of put it all in perspective."

"See, it won't be *that* bad. And I mean it—you don't have to be afraid tonight. He won't bother you again."

"Do you want to come in? My parents won't get home for hours yet, so they won't know or care. And it's cold out here."

"I can watch the house better from out here. Don't worry. Vampires don't feel the cold as badly as humans do."

Skye looked up at him, and her face revealed more of

her vulnerability, and her gratitude, than words could. For a moment, he felt a surge of protectiveness—and something else besides—

No humans, he thought. It was an old rule of his.

"Thank you for rescuing me," she said. "I ought to have told you before."

"That's what I'm here for." Balthazar meant it as a sort of joke, and yet it was a good way to think of himself. Better than most of the other reasons he had to exist, anyway.

He remained outside, watching the warm glow of the window that must have been her bedroom, for another hour. No sign of the parents—but, more to the point, there was no sign of Lorenzo, either.

They've hunted this area before, Balthazar told himself, arms wrapped around himself, his black cloth coat poor protection against the deep chill of upstate New York in January. *Yeah, it was at least a century ago, but still—this is ground Lorenzo knows. So he could just as easily have come here alone. Skye might simply have been in the wrong place at the wrong time.*

That was the explanation Balthazar liked best: It was the one that meant Skye was already safe. Lorenzo had been thwarted, and he knew Balthazar was around to interfere with his hunting plans. He'd move on somewhere else. She wouldn't be in danger again.

But it might not be that easy.

He looked up toward Skye's window, and for one moment

he glimpsed her silhouette, graceful and quick. Even the fall of her thick hair over her shoulder was clear, and surprisingly tantalizing. Just as Balthazar began to feel guilty—as if this were spying rather than watching—she snapped off the lights.

Immediately he went on higher alert; if Lorenzo returned, this was when he would strike—when he thought he had her off guard. Balthazar circled the house, a large, modern structure apparently on the outskirts of town, and listened carefully, not only with his ears but with all his senses, including the ones that told a vampire when another was near. Nothing.

Finally, he decided he could risk getting himself something to eat. Though he would never have said this aloud to Skye— nor to almost anyone else, even other vampires—being near her while she was bleeding had sharpened his appetite.

How he hated that. Looking at a beautiful young girl, liking her, wanting to help her, and yet being unable to forget that one part of him saw her as prey.

Balthazar moved into the woods just off her home's property, sniffing the wintry air. Pine, dirt, any number of birds (mostly owls and sparrows, too hard to catch and not much to enjoy), the horse's sweat from earlier, a hint of Skye's delicate perfume, but something muskier, gamier—*there*. Deer. Close by, too.

Hunger whetted, he walked into the forest—then began to run, moving as silently as possible so as not to startle his prey. Already he could imagine the thick blood filling his mouth, heating his core, giving him again the shadow of life he wanted so badly—

✢ 24 ✢

But he couldn't smell the deer's blood within its body, and he should've been able to by now.

He came to a stop a few feet short of the deer, its still form all but invisible in the midnight blackness. It lay on the snow, its neck twisted at an unnatural angle. There was no heartbeat to be heard.

Despite his natural predator's disappointment at losing prey, Balthazar knelt by the dead deer to investigate. Its throat had been ripped open, probably hours ago; only the severe cold had kept decomposition slow enough that he hadn't yet been able to smell it. Every single drop of its blood had been drained.

As his hand ran over the deer's coat, he felt the bite marks: dozens of them. It had been devoured—by vampires, several of them. And the blood had been drunk through the bites. Ripping open the throat had been unnecessary. Just something the killer enjoyed. Something he'd done many times before.

Balthazar's hands clenched into fists as he thought of the vampire who had led this pack, whose signature he saw written before him in torn flesh: *Redgrave.*

He's here.

Chapter Three

AS USUAL, SKYE AWOKE TO THE SOUND OF HER phone's alarm chiming at her. Not at all as usual, just rolling over to swat the phone into silence made her whole body ache. At first her groggy mind only supplied, *I'm really sore.*

Then she remembered why, and she bolted upright in bed, clutching her white sheets to her chest.

Skye breathed in deeply in an effort to steady herself against the rush of adrenaline that flooded into her, the memory of the vampire's attack almost as unnerving as the attack itself. Could that really have happened? And was it possible that Balthazar More had showed up to rescue her? That seemed more like one of her old study-hall daydreams than reality.

But the scrapes along her arms and soreness of her muscles didn't lie.

She looked down at her phone to see that she had two new text threads. One was from her best friend from Evernight, Clementine Nichols, whom she'd messaged about the craziness last night. Her reply:

OMG r u serious? More vampires? In Darby Glen? R they every-where? BE CAREFUL. Balty rescue sounds hot don't drool on him.

Just like Clem to somehow combine dire warnings about staying safe and a joke about Skye's old crush on Balthazar.

She didn't recognize the phone number that had sent the other message, but her eyes widened as she read it:

Skye, I did some investigating last night. The vampire presence in your town may be more dangerous than I previously thought. Don't panic—there's no reason they should be after you. But be cautious. I'll be staying around a while looking into this. Stay safe, and good luck on the first day of school.

Some interesting facts there:

That was Balthazar's number. (Add to contacts—clicked.)

Balthazar was the kind of guy who used totally correct spelling and punctuation even when he was texting, which was sort of bizarrely hot. She was in serious trouble if commas could get her going.

Not only had she not imagined the vampire attack, but she also apparently had to look out for a whole infestation in town or something like that. Not good.

Balthazar was going to be sticking around, for reasons scary enough that she shouldn't have felt a small thrill at the idea.

Last and most depressing of all: She had to go to school.

She started to rise, grabbing for the old clothes she kept nearby for her morning muck out of the stables—only to recall that she hadn't put them out. Their neighbor Mrs. Lefler mucked the stables now, in exchange for ample riding time on Eb. They'd set up that arrangement last fall, when she made the heartbreaking choice to leave Eb at home instead of bringing him to the Evernight stables; at the time, she'd thought Mom and Dad might take some comfort from riding him.

Well, that hadn't worked at all, and now that one simple task—which, though gross and tiring, had anchored her world most mornings of her life since age twelve—was gone. And it was a really bad sign of how much fun you *weren't* having when you actually missed shoveling horse poo.

Skye groaned and covered her head with her pillow. Better to face a vampire attack than Darby Glen High.

She'd thought the first day back at Darby Glen would be bad. It turned out she'd been too optimistic.

Someone she'd barely known (Kristin? Kirsten?) back in middle school hardly glanced at Skye as she said, "Looks like someone got kicked out of her snob school. Back down with the little people? Must suck."

"My school . . . burned down," Skye said, figuring that was as close as she could get to "it was destroyed in a ghost apocalypse" without sounding like a crazy person. But then she realized, too late, that correcting that assumption made the rest seem true— like she looked down on Darby Glen High and the kids who went there. Did everyone else think that? Probably.

Every hallway was hung with composite portraits of differ-ent graduating classes, and she happened to glance up just as she went by Dakota's senior year. There he was in his tux, grinning and unaware. He'd been the same age then that she was now. For the first time she realized that, eventually, she'd be older than Dakota had been when he died.

(*I'm catching up!* she used to joke with him on her birthdays, when she was briefly three years younger than him instead of four. *See, I'm getting closer!* It wasn't funny anymore.)

Skye quickly looked away, pushing Dakota to the back of her mind.

Then she had a bottom locker with a cranky lock. Just great. After struggling with it for what seemed like five straight minutes, she wrenched it open, piled in all her books except for her first two subjects, and stood up to see Craig Weathers.

Her boyfriend for more than two years, until he'd dumped her three months ago.

With his arm around his *new* girlfriend, Britnee Fong.

The girl he'd dumped Skye for.

Skye felt like a bucket of cold water had been dumped over her head—both shocked and humiliated, the two forces combining to freeze her in place. Craig looked amazing, as always: tall and slim, with full lips and gorgeous eyes, his dark skin warm against the white sweater he wore beneath his letter jacket. Every inch of him was familiar to her—too familiar. It was Britnee who surprised her, someone who'd moved here after Skye had gone to Evernight and whose Facebook profile photos were all, frustratingly, pictures of her cat.

And Britnee was even cuter than she'd dreaded: stylish

boho clothes, a pixie haircut that framed her face perfectly, and the same chunky-heeled boots Skye had been secretly coveting for weeks. She was a little heavier than Skye had imagined her being, but the pounds had gone to all the right places, boobs and butt—a girl might complain about the weight there, but a guy never would.

It would've been bad enough even if she'd been able to duck away before they saw her, but she wasn't. Craig stopped in his tracks, and Britnee looked up at him in confusion before staring at Skye and saying, "Ohhhh." Like it hadn't occurred to either of them that she'd be showing up today. The gossip mill in Darby Glen must have fallen down on the job for once.

Craig smiled at her, a stiff imitation of his usual handsome grin. "Skye. Hey."

"Hey." She shunted the books over to her hip and looked past him, down the hall, trying to make it clear that there was somewhere else she had to be. As in anywhere else that was not here.

"Um, hi? I'm Britnee?" Just great. Britnee Fong was one of those girls who pronounced every single sentence like it was a question. Proof positive that she was both irritating and an air-head. "I've heard lots of awesome things about you?"

Oh, so Craig made sure to compliment his ex-girlfriend to his new girlfriend. Super classy. "That's nice. See you later." Skye stalked past them toward her first class, or at least where she thought her first class was. The buzzing in her head that was half anger, half pain muted the noise in the hallway around her.

At least you're safe here, she told herself, thinking back to last night in the snow and the vampire's strange smile as he'd watched her. It wasn't exactly comforting.

Her first class was the Colonial History Honors Seminar, which meant that would be her homeroom, too. She tried to orient herself within the school building, but the sheer boringness of it struck her all over again. After two and a half years at Evernight Academy—with its centuries-old stone building, stained-glass windows, carved wood banisters, and arched ceilings—Skye found Darby Glen High so ugly that she wondered if it had been built this way on purpose, as a kind of punishment for its students. Cinder block walls with murals that hadn't been painted recently or well, lockers the color of asphalt that somehow looked like they belonged in a jail more than a school, drop ceilings and harsh fluorescent light: Every single bit of it was depressing.

It hadn't seemed that way to her back when she was at the middle school next door—an identical building. But after Evernight—

After the school filled with ghosts? And vampires? Skye reminded herself. *You should be grateful for a little normal, even if it's dull.* Maybe she'd find it a refreshing change . . . after a while.

Finally, only a couple minutes before homeroom was supposed to start, Skye managed to find her classroom. Craig and Britnee were already in there, in the front row, side by side. Of course. She managed not to make eye contact again as she hurried to a desk in the back.

A girl with long, curly red hair who sat in front of her turned and whispered, "Hey. What's with the drama?"

"I'm sorry?" Skye said.

"You and Craig and Britnee? I saw that standoff in the hall-way. It was like a shoot-out in a Western or something."

It wasn't any of this girl's business, but the description made Skye smile a little despite herself. She'd needed a smile today. "Craig and I used to go out. He dumped me for her. We just hadn't seen each other since, is all."

"Oh, so *you're* Skye." The girl nodded, as if satisfied. Obviously the Darby Glen gossip mill wasn't totally out of commission after all. "Well, I'm Madison Findley. We just moved here last summer. Listen, if you ever need anybody to run interference between you and your ex, or that fat cow he's with, just let me know."

Britnee was no cow, but Madison was just trying to make her feel better, Skye figured—and she did, a little. "Thanks."

The chatter in the room stilled as their teacher came in—a man at least six and a half feet tall, and seemingly nearly as wide. His bristly beard created the illusion that his jaw jutted out like a bulldog's. His dark eyes swept the room like a SWAT team member's laser sight for a rifle.

On the board, the teacher wrote his name: *STERLING LOVEJOY.*

He was so intimidating that nobody laughed at that name. Nobody even smirked. This was not a guy you wanted to catch you in the act of texting.

After that, the normal humdrum high school crap got started, and Skye felt herself relaxing a little bit, particularly when it turned out that she knew exactly nobody in her calculus class and could sit in the back, enjoying the relief of solitude.

Okay, so, Craig and Britnee were in her homeroom. She didn't have to sit near them or talk to them, and she already had a new friend to distract her, so that was all right. Maybe she'd get lucky and they wouldn't be in any other classes with her. Some people had it in their heads that she was a snob, but they'd probably forget about that soon enough. Probably.

Anyway, high school wouldn't last forever. Sometimes it seemed like it would, but watching her first high school crumble into destruction had made it clear to Skye just how temporary all that stuff was. Five and a half months: She could do it.

If she could just not be attacked by any more vampires.

When the bell rang for third period, she checked her schedule to remind herself what came next: human anatomy/sex ed with Ms. Loos. Skye thought sourly that she'd already educated herself about sex, for all the good it did her, but whatever. Then she walked in to see that Craig and Britnee were both in this class, too.

Fantastic. She'd have to listen to sex ed lectures while watching the only guy she'd ever had sex with flirt with the girl he was having sex with now.

But only after class began did Skye realize the worst of it.

"We're moving into more sensitive subjects now," Ms. Loos said. She was sort of attractive, at least for a teacher, with her blond hair and her leopard-print skirt, and she perched on the edge of her desk like she didn't know it would make the guys stare at her legs. "I've had most of you all year, and I know you're mature students. So I'm calling on all of you to be on your best behavior."

The janitor walks in, his face gray, his eyes unfocused. Something's horribly wrong, but he doesn't realize it yet. He only thinks he's tired—tired of cleaning up after stupid kids, tired of pushing around that broom, tired down to his bones.

Stop it, Skye told herself. *It's not real; you know it's not real!*

But his death already surrounded her.

Pain lashes through him, snaking out from his chest down his leg, along his arm. He opens his mouth to scream, but his lungs won't take in air. Suffocation hurts. The blood vessels in his eyes are starting to burst.

"You, in the back?" Ms. Loos stared at Skye, who realized the entire class was staring right along with her. She'd clutched the top of her desk as if it were a life preserver in a stormy sea, and the janitor's dying agonies still washed over her. She could see him, crumpling to his knees behind Ms. Loos, there and yet not there. "Is there a problem?"

Skye swallowed hard, attempting to keep her attention on the here and now. "No, ma'am."

Ms. Loos folded her arms, the hint of a smile around her dark-lined lips. "If you find the subject of sex distressing, come and talk with me later, mmm-kay?" A few people in the class giggled, and Skye turned red. She couldn't help feeling like Ms.

Loos was more interested in making a joke at her expense than offering help. Fabulous.

She also couldn't help noticing that Craig was now staring at the floor. Did he think he'd ruined her for having sex with anybody else?

And did any of that matter while this man was dying, right there in the classroom?

Skye closed her eyes tightly, then opened them again. The janitor had vanished. His death hadn't lasted that long.

But she was going to have to relive it every single time she came into this room, which was going to be every single morning.

Five and a half months suddenly seemed longer than it ever had before.

As Ms. Loos kept talking, Skye let her mind wander far away from school, all the way back home to her stable. She imagined the way Balthazar had looked in the lantern light, how he had been there to protect her when she needed him most. Then her imagination traveled even further back, to Evernight in the days when she thought it was more or less normal, and Balthazar was her favorite eye candy as he walked down the hall. In the days when she had this other, better life, and she was just another teenage girl.

The days she'd never see again.

When the school day was finally done, Skye decided to skip the bus home and walk. It was cold as hell—enough that her throat stung anytime she breathed through her mouth—but she didn't care. Riding home on the bus would just make the school day seem longer. What she wanted now was to be alone.

However, it crossed her mind that being alone was maybe the opposite of being careful in a town that might be infested with vampires. So instead of taking the quick way home—which led down a winding country road—she decided to go the long way on Garrett Boulevard. Traffic would be busy, and there would be the occasional cyclists and joggers around. She'd just be alone in spirit, but that was enough. She'd get home in plenty of time to spend a long, enjoyable evening with her head under a blanket, screaming in pent-up frustration and anxiety from one of the worst twenty-four-hour periods in her life.

But the Garrett Boulevard path was longer than she'd counted on, and her cheeks and nose were frozen numb long before her home was in sight.

Why didn't I buy that car last summer? Skye thought as she trudged along the side of the road, hands jammed in the pockets of her long down coat. Her reasons had seemed good at the time—she could afford only a junker, she couldn't have taken it to Evernight, and her parents had hinted that they'd buy her a nicer car as a graduation present. At that moment, though, with the temperature hovering around ten degrees, Skye would've given a lot for some old junker car with a working heater.

Maybe I ought to have asked Balthazar for a ride home. But could vampires get driver's licenses?

Just as she was beginning to get lost in a stupid but delicious daydream of Balthazar sweeping up to her high school on Eb, wearing a long black cloak or something similarly Darcyesque and romantic, extending his hand to her in front of Craig, Britnee, and everybody, Skye glimpsed her first jogger—a diehard who was out despite the chill. She raised her hand in a wave—and then stopped.

That wasn't a jogger.

Even at this distance, she recognized it as Lorenzo.

Chapter Four

TRACKING A VAMPIRE WAS DIFFICULT WORK.

Usually, Balthazar liked it that way, because that made it difficult for anybody to track him. Whether he was evading Black Cross or his own disturbed sister, Charity, he valued the ability to disappear if and when he wished.

When he was the one doing the tracking, instead of the one being tracked—not so much fun.

All day he'd worked his way through the woods, painstakingly searching for evidence of animal kills. A forest hid its secrets even at the best of times, and in such cold weather, with snow thick on the ground, the bodies were hard to find by either sight or scent. After long hours of combing through the underbrush and checking the trails, Balthazar had found only one other vampire kill. It, too, bore the vicious bite marks but not the throat gash that would've marked it as Redgrave's; he thought the fox had died within the hour.

Lorenzo is alone right now, Balthazar thought. Redgrave had been in this area with him earlier, though, and probably some others—his tribe waxed and waned over the years, sometimes as few as five or six, but sometimes as many as twenty-five. Whom might he meet with again? Constantia? Charity?

Don't think about it. Focus. Lorenzo was on his own for now, and that was all that mattered.

Balthazar leaned down close to the carcass, breathing in deeply. Lorenzo's scent lodged deeply within his predator's mind. It felt good to have an excuse to be a hunter again, to let those powerful instincts claim him.

He squinted at the ground; the snow cover was too patchy here for him to track Lorenzo by his footprints, but scent alone would do it. He began walking along the path, moving faster and faster as he became surer of his route. The path led up the hill, toward a public space of some kind—the rushing of cars came closer, became louder than the wind through the bare branches of trees.

Then he rounded the hill, saw what lay past it, and breathed in sharply: a school. The sign at the front of the drive proclaimed it DARBY GLEN HIGH SCHOOL.

Skye's school. Lorenzo was pursuing her after all.

Balthazar began running as fast as he could—faster than most humans would be able to match, but if he was seen, to hell with it. Skye was in danger, and it was late enough in the afternoon that she'd almost certainly have left school by now.

Was it possible she'd taken the bus, as she had this morning while he watched from a distance? He hoped so. For now he kept running, kept following Lorenzo's scent along what appeared to be a main road, busy with traffic. Even if Lorenzo had been unable to find Skye, Balthazar was dead set on capturing him now.

But as he ran, he began to detect Skye's scent as well.

Balthazar had a sudden vision of Skye crumpled and bloody like the fox he'd found in the snow, and the mere image sickened him. His inhuman speed wasn't fast enough.

Lorenzo's path took him off the main road, away from Skye, which didn't encourage Balthazar at all. Lorenzo would have quit following Skye only to get ahead of her, to stand between her and the safety of home. Balthazar hesitated for only a moment, deciding—then followed Skye's path. As badly as he wanted to catch Lorenzo, Skye's safety was more important.

Finally, as Balthazar ran around another curve of the road he saw her—alive, well, upright—but staring ahead, at Lorenzo, who stood in her path and closer to her than Balthazar was to either of them.

"Skye!" he shouted, but an eighteen-wheeler roared by at that moment, its engine drowning out his voice. Skye started running, not into the road or back toward Balthazar, but slightly up the hill toward a building, a gas station from the looks of it—

—but one that looked long deserted, with a dusty, faded sign that proclaimed gasoline was for sale at ninety-seven cents a gallon. Not good. A public space would've given her some protection, but an abandoned building wasn't shelter. It was a trap.

Lorenzo dashed after her, his eyes only for his prey. Balthazar pursued them both, anger and battle heat flooding through him. He gave way to those emotions so seldom, and yet they felt almost as hot and real as being alive.

The door had probably been pried open by vandals years ago. Balthazar ran inside just after them; old, rusty bells on the handle jingled. Skye, against the back wall with nowhere else to run, saw him and shouted, "Balthazar!"

Whirling around, Lorenzo saw him; his smile had a curiously glazed quality, as though he were drunk or drugged. "You're still protecting her," he said. "You can't for long."

"Won't have to for long." Balthazar grabbed the nearest thing at hand—the end of some abandoned metal shelves, where snacks or motor oil had once been—and shoved it forward hard. The other end of the shelf slammed into Lorenzo's side, sending the vampire staggering back.

Skye turned toward Balthazar, but he gestured toward the door. "Get out of this place! Get back out to the road!"

She didn't argue, didn't hesitate, just ran through the door like he'd said. Thank God she had some sense.

Balthazar rushed toward Lorenzo, but he was already up, and the punch he aimed at the guy's face only swung through air. Lorenzo shoved him back, growling, "You *do* want to keep her for yourself. Admit it."

That didn't merit an answer. Balthazar glanced around the old gas station, with its moldy drop ceiling and dusty walls. There were few potential weapons, and no wood to fashion a stake. The old freezer doors still had their glass, though, and while it would make for a messy beheading, he'd done worse.

"We'll drink her dry," Lorenzo said, and it wasn't mere taunting anymore; his words sounded more like a promise to himself. "Nothing's going to stop me from tasting her again."

One booted foot through the freezer door made the glass shatter. Balthazar went for the largest section, which was still connected to the metal frame—that made a sort of ax, if he could pry it loose—

"Balthazar!" Skye came running back in with a jingling of bells, and how could she be so stupid as to run back into a fight between two vampires?

Then he saw the three other vampires just behind her. Two were unknown to him—disheveled, young, vicious, the usual—but the tallest of them, in the back, looked tantalizingly familiar . . .

Lorenzo leaped at him, but Balthazar dodged, pulling his makeshift ax free and running toward Skye. The first of the other vampires came in through the door just in time for Balthazar to slash at his neck with the glass for a swift beheading. Skye screamed—yeah, it was messy, and the vampire was new enough that it fell like a dead body to the floor—but the bigger problem was that the glass dislodged from the metal frame and shattered against the floor. No more ax.

As the other vampires came in, bells on the handle jingling, Skye pulled Balthazar backward; almost before he'd realized what she was up to, they were through the door that led to the gas station attendant's booth. She slammed it shut and locked the door—a pitiful knob-only lock that wouldn't hold for long, but it was better than nothing. They were pinned together in a space hardly big enough for one person to stand in, much less two. He could feel the fast rise and fall of Skye's frightened breathing against his chest.

One of the vampires slammed against the glass wall of the booth, realizing too late that it was bulletproof. Balthazar put one hand against the far wall and tried to think of what to do; the building was so old, so run-down, that the wall felt almost soft against his hand. And there was a cold draft coming in, too.

The tallest vampire stepped closer, and for a moment, Balthazar's mind froze. Almost without his realizing, he whispered, "Constantia."

"Hello, darling. Long time no see." Constantia smiled the same possessive, arrogant smile she'd always had for him. Her burnished gold hair hung long and straight as ever, and he had somehow managed to forget how tall she was—at least a couple inches taller than him. Even in the plain gray coat she wore, Constantia was a striking figure: like a statue of some avenging Teutonic goddess, beautiful beyond belief but hard as stone. "You ran far and fast last time, Balthazar. But now you've run in front of something we want."

"Are we trapped?" Skye whispered. "I trapped us, didn't I?"

"You bought us time," he said to her, refusing to answer Constantia. Long-ago memories of the 1950s came back to him—he'd worked at a service station in Montana for a while, fixing up cars mostly, but occasionally pumping gas. This station had used the old-fashioned pumps; the switches were still on the wall. Because they were manual, not computerized, they probably still worked.

Would any gas fumes still be lingering in the tanks all these years later? They might have to find out. He snapped the switches to ON with one swipe of his hand.

Constantia slammed her foot into the door; the old wood bowed and splintered immediately. Two more kicks and she'd be in.

Balthazar said, "Cover your face. I'm going to break through the external wall."

"With what?" Skye looked around, and he couldn't resist a smile.

"With me."

No cinder blocks, please no cinder blocks—

With all his vampire strength, he threw himself at the rotten, drafty section of the wall, which thank God was not reinforced with cinder blocks, and broke through. It hurt like hell, but Balthazar was able to stumble free of the jagged gap; Skye followed him instantly, grabbing his arm as he staggered to walk off the blow. "They're coming," she said as he dragged her toward the front of the station and, behind them, the bells on the gas station's door jingled again.

"I know. Come on."

As they ran toward the pumps, a car pulled in—long and silvery, with the weight and gleam of expense. A Bentley, maybe. Balthazar knew many vampires with a taste for luxury like that, but he also knew which of them was going to step out even before he did.

Redgrave stood up. His dark gold hair was slicked back, almost the same color as his perfectly tanned skin. The camel-colored coat he wore was tailored perfectly to his lean, angular form, and a heavy golden watch shone on one wrist. As he saw Balthazar, his hazel eyes glinted, avaricious and cruel, much as they'd been the first day they ever met—one of the last days Balthazar would ever be alive—

Skye pulled them ahead faster; at least one of them wasn't so easily distracted, Balthazar thought. He grabbed his old lighter from his pocket, snapped it into flame, and dropped it into the pile of papers and debris in front of the old station just before pulling loose one of the pumps and turning it on.

"What are you doing?" Skye cried. "We have to move!"

"We do now." Balthazar grabbed her hand again and ran almost as fast as he could, towing her after him though he knew it had to almost hurt her to be dragged along at this speed. But they got to the very edge of the road before the pumps blew.

The explosion slammed into them, a wave of heat as solid as rock, shoving them both off their feet and into the snowy drifts at the side of the road. Balthazar saw the wall of flame blazing up brightly and felt a deep, irresistible terror well inside him. Fire—fatal to vampires, one of the only things that ever could destroy him completely—

Get over it. You're in a snowbank. The only vampires burning alive right now are the ones who killed you.

Tires screeched, and Skye flung herself against his side as a car on the nearby road—its driver apparently startled by the explosion—ran off the pavement into the ditch so hard that the entire hood crumpled. For one moment Balthazar looked up at the gas station, just in time to see Redgrave's car speeding past them, back on the highway.

Well, he hadn't finished off the bastard, but at least he knew the old crew remained as afraid of fire as he was. And Skye was safe from further vampire attacks . . . for the moment.

"Are you okay?" Skye called toward the driver of the wrecked car as she stumbled through the snow. "Hello?"

Balthazar pushed himself up to follow her. The driver of the car looked dazed, and on his forehead—

Blood. Lots of it. He stopped in place, not trusting himself near such weak prey at such a moment; it was too soon after the fight, too soon after he'd let himself be a hunter again.

"Mr. Lovejoy!" Skye got the car's door open to lay one hand on the injured man's shoulder. He was apparently too weak to answer her. "It's okay, Mr. Lovejoy. I'm calling nine one one right now." As she pulled out her cell phone, she said to Balthazar, "It's my history teacher. He's hurt. Are you all right?"

Desperate for blood. Bound to protect her from a danger he didn't understand.

"Yeah," Balthazar said. "I'm fine."

Weary, dizzy, he knelt in the snow and lowered his head, thinking only to collect himself. But on the snow was a small cluster of blood droplets—those of the man from the crash. Mr.

Lovejoy. Or Skye's cut hand. Maybe even his own, if he'd gotten banged up worse than he realized.

But Balthazar soon lost the capacity to think about them in any rational way. His mind focused on only one thing: blood.

Just a taste, one taste, you'll get your strength back—

He dipped his fingers into the stains on the snow. The blood had already chilled. But he slid his fingers between his lips—even cold blood would be glorious to him right now—

And then the world went away.

Replaced by a better one.

Chapter Five

Massachusetts, 1640

BALTHAZAR BREATHED IN DEEPLY. IT HAD seemed to him, for a moment, that there was something strange about the fact that he needed to draw breath—but why should that be? They had just walked up a steep hill, which was enough to make anyone pant.

That brief oddness was quickly forgotten, replaced by a rare, deep satisfaction. According to his parents, and to the rest of their community, one's best was never good enough—no life was industrious enough, virtuous enough, ever. But right now he was alone, save for his sister and his dog, neither of whom judged him. At market in Boston, he had sold the cow for fifteen strands of wampum, three more than his father had expected him to get, which would surely make his parents happy. Good-man Cash had even given each of the Mores an apple—a rare treat, for free, out of nothing but kindness.

As Fido bounded ahead in the high grasses, Charity leaped after him. Her natural exuberance was too great for the strict rules under which they lived, but try as he might, Balthazar could see nothing sinful in it. Perhaps it was not prudent for a young girl to dance around in the sunshine in front of others—that could be seen as immodest, he guessed, though he understood Charity had no such intention. Here and now, though, with nobody else to watch, his little sister could be free, and she knew it.

"Why can't every day be market day?" Charity said, holding out her hands as if she wanted to catch the sunlight in her palms.

"Because we don't have something to sell every day, just as nobody needs to buy something every day."

"I wish we could."

Balthazar had a flicker of a thought about markets that really were open all the time—even at night—but the peculiar daydream faded in an instant.

"If it were market day every day, then we could have jugglers and singers every day, too."

"You've never even seen a juggler in your life."

"Mama told us, and she even tried to show us with the potatoes before Papa came in that time. I think it would be fun."

Their mother made life back in England sound much more enjoyable than life in Massachusetts Bay Colony, Balthazar thought. Their father often reminded them that they were building a city greater than London could ever be—the city of God on earth—but that was poor comfort in winter when the snow piled high, the wind whipped through the crevices at the corners of their two-room house, and there'd been nothing to eat for days but deer jerky and root vegetables. Then their mother's stories of London—with shops that sold a fragrant hot drink called "coffee" every day and singers that performed in the marketplace for anyone to hear—well, it sounded closer to heaven than Massachusetts Bay Colony was likely to get.

"You like market day, too," Charity said. "Because you get to see Jane."

In front of his parents, Balthazar would have denied it; for his sister, he had only a smile. "She looked well today, didn't she?"

"A green dress. Green!" Charity—who had never worn any color dress but black or brown, and was surrounded by women who considered colorful clothing a sign of pro-England sympathies at best, immodesty at worst—couldn't get over it. Truth be told, Balthazar himself had understood for the first time just how bright colors could inspire lustful thoughts.

Or maybe that was just Jane. Her sweet face, heart-shaped because of the widow's peak to her lustrous dark hair, the deep shade of her skin, the lines of her slim waist sheathed in that beautiful green, the way she smiled at him—above all, the way she smiled at him—

Don't think of it, he told himself. *It can never be.*

Jane was not from a family among the Godly, the only group with whom Balthazar's father wanted him to associate. Though they were not currently members in good standing with the church, due to his mother's dangerous flirtation with the heresies of Anne Hutchinson, his father knew they could regain that acceptance and respectability. Jane never would. She traveled about with her father, an itinerant merchant who peddled his wares up and down the coasts of the colonies. They certainly were not members of the church, and only a special act by the governor allowed them and their kind to be in Massachusetts at all.

Rumor had it they were papists. Among the Puritans, this was beyond redemption—far worse than the heathenism of the Natives who dwelled nearby.

But Balthazar could not see sin embodied in anyone as good as Jane. Though they had only ever spoken at market days, he knew that he cared for her, and that she thought well of him, too. The way her eyes lit up whenever she saw him made the whole world seem to melt—

It can never be, he reminded himself.

"When I grow up, and Mama doesn't make my dresses any longer, I'll wear green, too," Charity said. "Green dresses, green caps, green aprons, even green shoes. Every day."

"You'd look like an asparagus."

His little sister stuck out her tongue. "A *beautiful* asparagus." He jokingly swatted at her, so she dashed ahead, beyond his reach.

Charity might have fared better in London, Balthazar thought. There her dreamy, unfocused temperament might have been seen merely as eccentricity, or even creativity. Their mother's family, a warmhearted, friendly group to judge by their annual letters, might have shown her more acceptance, and that might have made Mama strong enough to stand up to Papa on her daughter's behalf.

Instead, here she was looked at as peculiar at best, wicked at worst. He'd heard the occasional ominous whisper—*witch*—but he suspected her troubles would be far more ordinary than any trial for consorting with Satan. Though only fourteen years old, Charity was already widely considered unmarriageable, even in a country where men outnumbered women. The few talents allowed to ladies—cooking and sewing—were too meticulous for her, with her wandering attention, to master. Nobody else saw her as she was now: bounding through the grass, sun painting her fair curls with light as she whipped off her cap, beautiful not in spite of her strangeness but because of it.

I will always have to look out for her, Balthazar thought. It wasn't a new realization, but the weight of it felt heavier somehow.

As Charity rounded the hill, skipping down faster ahead of him, he stooped to pet his dog. He noticed again the cracking in the leather of his boots; they were worn thin, and really they'd been made for him too early—he'd still had a little growing to do, and so the toes of the boots were too tight. Might his father consider using the extra wampum to buy him some new ones before winter? Unlikely, but it was worth asking.

He heard Charity laughing and saying something—it wasn't unusual for her to talk to herself.

But this far from the road, it was odd to hear someone else reply.

Balthazar rose to his feet and hurried over the hill, where he saw Charity standing beside a wagon driven by two people—a man and a woman—neither of whom was known to them. They must have come to market, but he hadn't seen them there; two people like this would have stood out, dressed in brilliant colors, the woman's hair loose and free like a small child's. Like Charity's.

Strangers were rare in this part of the world, the only part Balthazar had ever known; perhaps that was why he became suspicious so quickly. He hurried down to Charity's side.

"You would look enchanting in green," said the man holding the reins. He was a handsome man, and Balthazar would've known it even without Charity's adoring gaze to guide him. His hair, his skin, even his eyes all seemed to be touched with gold, and he had a fine, patrician profile. His clothes seemed well made, and the new, uncracked leather of his boots shone. "Ah, and who have we here?"

"My older brother, Balthazar More." Charity went up on tiptoe to confide, "He's not as strict with me as my parents."

"Then perhaps he will not mind an introduction," said the blond-haired woman, whose locks would have looked lustrous if she had not been sitting next to the strangely dazzling man. Perhaps they were brother and sister as well. She was beautiful in her statuesque way, but there was something avid about the way she looked at Balthazar. It was the way some of the ruder men looked at women whose hair was not partly covered, or girls just leaving childhood whose skirts were not yet fully long. He hadn't known women could look at men this way, too.

If it had been Jane looking at him so hotly, Balthazar thought he might have liked it. But she wasn't Jane.

"Good day to you, sir," Balthazar said, turning his attention to the man. "Forgive my sister. She is eager to make friends."

"How wise of her," the man said. "Call me Redgrave. I think we shall be very good friends indeed. Don't you agree, Constantia?"

"Oh, I do," Constantia whispered, leaning past Redgrave's shoulder to peer at Balthazar again, the sunlight catching her hair—

"Balthazar?"

He tensed as the phantasms of the past vanished, leaving him back in his own mind, in the here and now. He still knelt in the snow, the taste of blood fading on his tongue. Skye's face was pale with worry.

"How long?" His voice croaked as though he hadn't spoken in months. "How long was I . . . out?"

But Skye said, "Maybe a minute and a half? I don't know. Are you okay?"

"I think so." What the hell had just happened to him?

The smell of smoke and gasoline reminded him where they were; at the sound of distant sirens, she looked past him. "I don't want to leave Mr. Lovejoy—we have to stay—but how are we supposed to explain this?"

"Leave it to me." Balthazar summoned all his strength of will to stand upright again. "I've got a lot of experience in covering this stuff up."

The police were told that Skye had been walking home from school, and that Balthazar was headed toward downtown, when they separately saw the explosion. Mr. Lovejoy's car had then jumped the curb; no doubt he'd been startled. Another car had sped away afterward, but they couldn't say what it had to do with the explosion. They were bewildered, innocent bystanders, no more.

"I still can't believe they bought that," Skye said as they walked away from the scene, smoke still thick in the darkening sky overhead.

"Why not? It's actually more plausible than the truth." Balthazar glanced back at the police cars behind them. None of the officers suspected they had any greater involvement. It was frightening how good he'd become at lying over the past few centuries.

"I just—I feel awful. Mr. Lovejoy's all banged up, because of me—"

"It's not your fault." He spoke so forcefully that she stared at him, but it was important that she understand this. "What happened is not because of you. It's because Redgrave and his crew came after you. All of this is their fault. Nobody else's. Never forget that."

"Redgrave?" Skye frowned. "I thought you said his name was Lorenzo."

"The one hunting you last night and this afternoon is Lorenzo. The one who drove up at the end, the guy with gold hair? That's Redgrave. He's much older and much more powerful. Almost anything Lorenzo does, he does because Redgrave wants him to."

"But why?" Skye breathed out in frustration, her breath creating a little cloud in the frosty air around them as they continued toward her house.

"I'm not sure." Though he was beginning to consider a disquieting possibility. Skye was holding her injured hand. She had reopened the cut on her hand during their escape. If that was her blood he'd tasted on the ground—if that was the reason for what he'd just experienced—

But that was impossible. Nobody's blood had that kind of power. Surely some of what had happened in his mind had more to do with the fact that he'd just had to face Redgrave for the first time in more than thirty years. He'd been injured and dazed; he'd had a hallucination. He couldn't be sure of more than that.

Balthazar forced himself to focus again on Skye's situation. "I don't know what it means yet, but whatever it is about you that Lorenzo responded to—it's made Redgrave curious. Once he's curious, there's no stopping him."

"Is this the reassuring part of the speech? Because I'm starting to get worried."

"There is no reassuring part of the speech." His eyes met hers, and he could see Skye's effort at a joke was her way of trying to be brave. Good: She'd need some bravery to get through this. "This is bad. This is real. And until we figure out what to do—I'm staying with you."

For the first night, at least, this meant staying in her room.

As he punched out a text message—hey, he was getting pretty good at this—Balthazar said, "Your parents really aren't going to notice the guy staying in their house?"

"They'll probably get home after midnight and leave before six A.M. Usually they don't even look in here," Skye called from her bathroom closet, where she was changing into her nightclothes. He ought to have offered to stay downstairs, in some room her parents wouldn't enter, but if one of Redgrave's tribe tried to get in through the windows of her bedroom—no, it was too dangerous. For tonight, he was staying close. "They work really hard ever since—since Dakota." From the tightness in her voice, Balthazar knew that must have been her brother's name.

Although Balthazar knew he was no expert in dealing wisely with grief, he said, "They shouldn't leave you alone so much."

"That's how they cope. When they get hurt, they work harder. Since last summer, they've been working harder than they ever have in their lives." The depth of her understanding surprised him; he'd been on earth a lot longer than Skye before he'd been able to look past his own pain to somebody else's. "They leave me little notes and treats. I know they love me. It's okay."

Her room was a colorful place, with lavender walls and a bright quilt on the bed, and a shelf laden with gleaming equestrian trophies and ribbons. A couple pieces of homemade artwork hung on the walls: a collage made mostly of magazine cutouts that seemed much too angry to be Skye's own work, and a framed, blown-up, artistically Photoshopped photo of Skye with another girl he remembered from Evernight, Clementine Nichols. And yet there was something a little bare about the room—maybe only because she'd been at boarding school the past two and a half years.

Or maybe not: On one slightly dusty shelf, Balthazar could see the imprints where framed photos had once stood. They'd been removed from this shelf not that long ago. Pictures of Dakota, he thought. Skye's parents weren't the only ones in the family who reacted to pain by pushing it away.

She continued, "Besides, my parents never had tons of free time, not after they started lobbying in Albany. Thus boarding school." Skye stepped out of the closet, and Balthazar glanced over at her briefly—or that was the idea. Instead, he couldn't look away. She was dressed in a black T-shirt and leggings, but both of them hugged her lithe body, breasts to waist to hips to thighs—

No humans, he reminded himself, thinking of Jane. But the old rule seemed very far away.

Skye couldn't quite meet his eyes, as if she knew what he was thinking. Then, when she glanced up at him again, he felt the impact—heat coursing through him, as real as blood. "So, if you're really staying in here until morning . . ."

"I'd better," Balthazar said, though he had just dramatically downgraded his chances of getting any sleep. This was going to be a restless night.

"Well, the window seat might work. But you're a big guy; it might not be comfortable for you."

He glanced at the window seat, the last corner of the room that still seemed to be part of a child's room rather than a young woman's. "I wouldn't want to disturb the sanctity of the stuffed animal graveyard."

"They're just my old toys." Skye looked a little embarrassed, as well she might, but he noticed how carefully she picked up the stuffed bears and dogs to put them on the floor. "See how it's a daybed, too? My friends used to sleep over on it. But if you don't think you'll fit, I could take it. You could stay in my bed."

That conjured up all kinds of dangerous thoughts. *Stop it*, he told himself. *Her teddy bear is in this room. She was a child not long ago.*

She's not a child now—

Stop it.

His phone chimed at the same moment hers did, covering his momentary awkwardness, he hoped. "Excuse me," Balthazar said. As he read his message—good, that was a relief—he heard Skye gasp. "What's the matter?"

"The school sent out an email. Mr. Lovejoy's alive and every-thing, but—he's going to be in traction for weeks. He really got hurt today." Skye's fingers tightened around her phone. "It's still sinking in how dangerous this is. Do you think Redgrave's going to try coming after me again?"

"I know he will."

"So I just have to—go around tomorrow knowing they might come after me?"

"Not tomorrow." Balthazar glanced out her window, wondering if they were already staring back. "They'll be here tonight."

Chapter Six

OMG, BALTHAZAR IS IN UR BEDROOM RIGHT NOW?

Skye kept her phone cupped close to her, so there was no chance Balthazar would read Clementine's message. *It's kind of an emergency. Tell u about it later. OK?*

She hadn't been able to bring herself to text Clem about the second vampire attack or the fact that she had apparently attracted the attention of some vampire clan that was even worse than the others. So little of it made any sense to her yet: Which vampires were evil? Which weren't? How did Balthazar know any of them? Were they really going to come after her again, tonight?

It was all confusing, and scary, and so she'd told her best friend only about the one thing she did understand for sure, which was that her biggest crush over the past two years had decided to spend the night in her room.

Under any other circumstance, it would've been awesome.

"Assuming they don't leave Darby Glen tonight, they'll start tracking your movements." Balthazar kept peering out her window, ever on the watch. "We'll have to work out some way for you to get to and from school safely. No more wandering out on the road."

Embarrassed, Skye said, "It seemed safe at the time."

"I realize that. I didn't mean to make it sound like—"

"Like you thought it was stupid." She folded her arms in front of her, trying to make a point, but then it occurred to her that this T-shirt was a little tighter than she'd remembered. Without a bra—yeah, the arms in front felt more comfortable. Definitely. "Which it was."

"You didn't yet know they were after you specifically." When he wanted to be reassuring, Balthazar's voice became so warm. Almost soft. Coupled with his imposing, broad-shouldered frame, it made for an intoxicating combination.

"I knew vampires were on the loose in town, which is bad news . . . no offense."

"None taken."

"But I still rushed out of school, just because I wanted to be alone, and I wasn't thinking. Obviously I can't make any more mistakes like that until—until we get this taken care of."

But what did that mean, in this context? How were they supposed to get the vampires to leave her alone? Kill them all? She remembered seeing vampires lying on the grounds of Evernight, stakes buried in their chests, and wondered if that was what they'd have to do. Skye had never asked herself if she could kill anyone or anything except for Eb, in some nightmare scenario in which he'd broken his leg.

Maybe she wouldn't have to attack anyone. Balthazar would keep her safe. After seeing him today—swooping in just when she thought she was dead, wiping the floor with that vampire, smashing through that wall to get her to safety—Skye could believe that there was nothing he couldn't handle.

Her phone dinged one more time, signaling a final text from Clem: *Use protection.*

As Skye silenced the phone, hoping desperately that she wasn't blushing, Balthazar said, "Why did you want to be alone?"

"Huh?" She had to backtrack past her overheated thoughts about Balthazar to remember what they were actually talking about. "Oh, this afternoon. My first day back at school just—it wasn't good. Although now that I compare it to getting repeatedly attacked by vampires, it doesn't seem so awful."

"Why was school so rough?" He frowned, looking genuinely concerned, like bad times at Darby Glen High could possibly compare to the situation they now found themselves in.

Then again, she was going to have to go back tomorrow, wasn't she? Unless she was dead by then. Skye sighed. "Someone died in my anatomy classroom."

"What?"

"Not today! Long ago, I mean. But I can still see it." The horror had been buried under the sheer panic of the afternoon, but now it welled up again, cold and bright. "I'm going to have to watch this guy die of a heart attack every single day."

"Can you transfer out of that class?"

"Maybe. I'll have to check." Evernight Academy hadn't allowed transfers; she had no idea what the rules were here.

"The effect could stop over time, or lose power, maybe."

"Maybe," Skye said doubtfully. "I've been avoiding every . . . death place I've found, so I haven't tested that. It feels like it's always going to happen. You're right, though. I don't know. I guess anatomy class is where I'll find out."

"We might still figure out a way for you to manage your—psychic gift."

"That would help," she admitted. "But it's not the worst part about school. The rest sucks, too. I mean, I fell out of touch with most people back here while I was at Evernight. Now they all think I'm some kind of stuck-up snob who doesn't want to have anything to do with Darby Glen."

"They'll see past that," Balthazar said gently. "And there must be some people from before that you were glad to see."

A lump formed in Skye's throat as she thought about the only person from before who had really counted. "Well, I saw my ex-boyfriend, Craig. With his new girlfriend. So you can imagine how much fun that was."

"Ouch." Balthazar made such an exaggerated face of pain that she had to laugh despite herself. "This is the guy who dumped you right before the Autumn Ball last year, right?"

"How did you know about that?" She hadn't thought Balthazar More paid much attention to her at Evernight Academy, much less that he was keeping tabs on her love life.

"Lucas told us. He was nervous about asking you to the ball

just as a friend. Sounds like this Craig guy has rotten timing."

Remaining her constant boyfriend for two and a half years, then dumping her for someone else only a couple months after they'd had sex for the first and only time—and not even half a year after her brother's death: Yeah, that counted as rotten timing. "To say the least."

"Forget him," Balthazar said simply. "I know—easy to say, hard to do. But any guy who doesn't appreciate you isn't worth keeping."

Which sounded like maybe Balthazar appreciated her. No—she was reading too much into it, surely. Balthazar glanced away, no longer meeting her eyes. Skye didn't know whether to feel awkward or elated; she knew only that it was impossible to look away from Balthazar, his handsome profile outlined against the dark, frost-rimmed glass of the window—

Wait. The frost was—growing. Lacing over the entire window—on the inside of the window, too, turning everything white, blinding out the night.

The sudden chill in the air made Skye's skin prickle, and she wrapped her arms more tightly around herself as the cold became almost painful. Her lamp flickered, the electricity failing, but the light didn't die out. Instead it changed into an eerie blue-green color that seemed to shimmer, almost as if they were underwater.

She remembered one of Dakota's last photos from Australia, a scene from an underwater cave, and she wondered if this was what he'd seen before he died. Terror and sorrow seized her at the same time, paralyzing her.

At least, until the ceiling started to move.

"Oh, my God." Skye backed toward Balthazar; she didn't know what was happening, but knew she wanted him close. "What's going on?"

"We just got a lot safer."

Startled, she looked up at him. Balthazar's face was alight, like he'd just been given the most marvelous gift in the world.

The rippling on the ceiling broke free, came forward, took shape. First it was a swirling, glittering shape, like a cyclone of snowflakes, but then it acquired the form of a young woman with flowing red hair and wide, gentle eyes—but not just any woman. Balthazar said her name first: "Bianca."

"I like your room," Bianca said. "It reminds me a little of the one I had back in my hometown."

Skye, still not sure she was able to speak, nodded. Bianca seemed to understand her shyness; at any rate, she didn't press Skye for more, just turned back to Balthazar, who hadn't stopped grinning at her. He said, "I'm glad you could make it. I didn't really have a plan B."

"You usually come up with something," she said, folding herself up on the window seat beside Balthazar. Bianca seemed more at ease in her pajamas than Skye was in hers—and more comfortable with Balthazar, too.

Dim memories of Evernight Academy gossip floated back to her, stuff she hadn't paid much attention to at the time. Skye had known that Balthazar was dating someone during her second year at Evernight. She was still in love with Craig at the time, so Balthazar was just a hot guy for her to get a thrill out of walking past in the hallways. It hadn't mattered which girl he was with. But now, as she watched them together, Skye was pretty sure Balthazar had been with Bianca.

As in Bianca, girlfriend of Lucas, the single best guy friend Skye had ever had.

As in Bianca, the ghost Skye had saved at Evernight.

How was it possible for her day to get even weirder?

Skye asked the first question that came to mind: "Where's Lucas?"

Though Bianca had already been smiling, her expression took on a greater light, a greater tenderness, than before. Any doubts Skye had about Bianca's loyalty toward Lucas faded in that instant. "He's up in Maine with some friends. We're lying low for a while. Taking some time to just be together. These past few months were hard." A shadow seemed to dim Bianca's unearthly translucence, but only for a moment. "Lucas says he doesn't care about the cold or the snow or anything. He's enjoying being alive. And I'm enjoying being with him."

"That's good," Skye said. Lucas had been so angry and wounded last year; it was a relief to hear that he'd found peace.

"He says hi, by the way," Bianca added. "And he's sorry he couldn't get here himself. I travel faster than most people."

"Yeah, looks like it." Which was as close to a joke as Skye could manage. Growing up with a ghost in her house had been one thing; sitting around in her room calmly chatting with one was another. Plus there was a vampire on her window seat. Her whole definition of *weird* was changing fast.

Bianca's face shifted into delighted surprise, and she disappeared from Balthazar's side—only to reappear across the room. "You have one of Raquel's collages!"

"Oh, yeah. Right! I saw her making this in one of the arts rooms at Evernight our first year there, and I raved about it so much she ended up giving it to me. Mostly to shut me up, I think." Talking to a ghost was feeling more natural all the time. Skye joined Bianca by the collage, which showed several guys making dramatic gestures or big faces, with a ticked-off girl in the center. "Raquel titled this *Save Your Drama for Your Girlfriend.*"

"I love her stuff," Bianca said. More quietly—not hiding her words from Balthazar, but making it clear that she was speaking only to Skye now—she added, "Lucas told me about the visions you've been having."

"Do you know what it is? How to stop it?"

Bianca shook her head. "You're unique, so far as any of us know—which isn't that far."

Skye hadn't really expected any other reply, but the disappointment hit her harder than she would've thought. Maybe it was only that so many bizarre, frightening issues were piling up on her at once; she would have been so relieved to get an answer to any one of them.

"You probably had some innate ability to begin with," Bianca continued, "but when your mind was opened to the world of the dead for so long, when I possessed you—something profound changed inside you."

"Something profoundly awful," Skye muttered.

Gently, Bianca added, "What I do know is that this happened to you because you saved me at Evernight. I know that's not a risk you meant to take. I just wanted to say . . . I don't even know what to say. That I'm sorry, I guess. And that I'm more grateful than you can ever know."

"I knew it was a risk. I took my chances. We all got out of there, so it worked." Somehow, putting it like this made Skye feel better. It was better to consider the death-sight as the natural result of something brave she'd done, instead of scary visions from out of nowhere. She decided to always try thinking of it that way from now on.

"It's getting late," Balthazar said. His attention was fixed outside the window now. Had he seen something? "After midnight. Sometimes that's when Redgrave likes to strike."

"Who is Redgrave, exactly?" Bianca asked.

"A vampire I know. Not someone you ever want to meet."

So—Balthazar clearly cared about Bianca, but he hadn't told her everything about himself. Not even the few snippets of his past that Skye had learned the last couple of days. That was interesting . . . Wait. Had he said Redgrave was about to strike?

Skye said, "Are they coming right now?"

"They'll be more likely to come after they think you've gone to bed." Balthazar went to her lamp and snapped it off. Instantly, her room went from cheerily bright to shadows, illuminated only by Bianca's faint aquamarine glow.

"Hold on—we're *trying* to get them to come in? Is that really a good plan?"

"They're going to come," Balthazar said. "Better now, when

we're expecting it, than later when we aren't."

Which was logical, if terrifying. Skye slowly nodded. "We ought to get it over with now, before . . . before my parents get home. I don't want them in the middle of this."

"Don't worry," Bianca said. She was fading into transparency, her glow hardly more than a shimmer now. "Balthazar's here if I fail."

Bianca was their first line of defense? What exactly were they planning?

The last of the blue-green glow faded. Though Skye knew Bianca must still be there, she was now invisible and silent. Moonlight off the snow provided enough light at the window for her to see Balthazar's outline, a broad, reassuring shadow. She stepped toward him, seeking both safety and comfort. He remained utterly motionless.

Her entire house had never seemed so quiet. Though Skye knew two others were in the room with her, neither of them was breathing. No wind was blowing, so even the usual rushing sound of the breeze through the trees was absent. The silence surrounding her was complete—

—so much that, from one floor up, Skye was able to hear a faint scratching, then a pop of metal on metal. And, as her heartbeat sped up and her breathing became shallow, she even heard the soft creak of the back door being opened.

The Time Between:
Interlude One

December 29, 1776
Trenton, New Jersey

IN ALL HIS MANY YEARS IN NEW ENGLAND,
Balthazar had never known a winter as bleak as this. The snow
lay on the frozen ground, nearly two feet thick, soft even weeks
after falling because the sun had not provided enough warmth
to melt any of it, however briefly, and create ice. It muffled
sound and made the terrain unfamiliar. Roads and towns he had
known for over a century were strangers to him now.

Redgrave disliked the snow. Bloodstains showed too easily,
as did their tracks.

"And yet there's nothing like a war for business," Redgrave
said for the thousandth time that winter. He lounged in front
of the fire in the small inn where they'd taken up residence.
Between the foul weather and the nearby hostilities, Redgrave

and his tribe were the only guests—and thank God. "You'll never eat your fill as often with less trouble than you will during wartime, I promise you that, my little darling."

Redgrave's long fingers stroked through Charity's fair curls as though she were his pet cat. Balthazar's gut churned; watching Redgrave touch his younger sister in that way had never ceased to disgust him, though at least—after nearly a century and a half—Charity no longer flinched.

"We should head south," Constantia said, leaning her head back against Balthazar's chest. He resisted the urge to push her away—that never worked, not for long, and defiance created more trouble than it was worth. Her gown was the height of fashion—broad-skirted and bedecked with ruffles—and she'd even powdered her hair. In this modest inn, with its beaten wooden benches and plain stone hearth, she looked as out of place as an emerald amid riverbed stones. "Washington won't move again so soon. I'm sure of it. We'll have to travel farther afield if we want to keep feasting."

"Ready to see a bit more of the world?" Redgrave crooned to Charity, who nodded obediently. Her stare was unfocused, and the sleeve of her dress had fallen off her shoulder.

Lorenzo's feral grin widened as the barmaid came in, carrying a tankard of ale for them. The barmaid was young and pretty—coal-black curls and plump, rosy cheeks—but no slattern meant to service the male guests upstairs for a few coins exchanged quietly on the back stair. Perhaps she was the innkeeper's niece, or the daughter of a friend, Balthazar thought:

a girl here to earn a bit of extra money for her family during a hard winter, pretty enough to cheer guests who otherwise might grumble about the cold rooms or poor food.

But that meant she was pretty enough to tempt the cruel. Balthazar had seen that wild light in Lorenzo's eyes before. It meant pain, and death, and the crumpled bodies of women thrown to the floor like rags.

"Will you be wanting dinner?" the barmaid asked, acting more nervous than she ought to have been. She understood something was wrong about this group; she was more perceptive than most, Balthazar thought. This stirred in him nothing more than pity. It would have been better if she hadn't known what was coming. The girl continued, "We've a fine stew tonight. Right filling."

Lorenzo ran one finger along her forearm as she poured him more ale. She jerked back, sloshing suds onto the floor and making the other vampires laugh. "We'll eat our fill soon enough," Lorenzo said, to even louder laughter. "You, my dear—I wish to write a poem about you."

Oh, God. The subjects of all his vile poems were his worst murders. Balthazar wished he hadn't seen the vulnerability or innocence in the young barmaid's face. Then he would not have pitied her. He tried to deaden himself to pity—it would make this bitter existence of his slightly less cruel—but he hadn't succeeded, not yet.

"What is your name?" Lorenzo asked. "I must know your name, you see. I must learn what rhymes."

The poor barmaid, obviously longing to escape but unable to, replied, "I'm called Martha, sir."

"Martha?" Lorenzo started cackling. "What in the world rhymes with Martha?" His Spanish accent hardened the *th* sound into a *t*.

"Thank you, sir. Good evening." The barmaid dropped a quick curtsy and hurried out. No doubt she lived in a room on the premises. No doubt Lorenzo would find her.

You could find her. You could warn her.

Balthazar closed his eyes tightly, trying to silence the voice of compassion in his own heart.

For the past 136 years, he'd drifted along in Redgrave's wake. He'd never stooped to Redgrave's level—murdering and drinking from innocent humans for sheer pleasure—but little remained of the proud Puritan boy he'd been in life. When he found humans worth the killing, whether they were brigands or mercenaries or rapists, Balthazar killed with all the righteous vengeance he could muster; he knew, however, that the pleasure he felt when he drank their blood was not righteous. It was purely carnal. During wartime, when they found the mortally wounded, he dispatched them quickly to the afterlife for what he tried to think of as their mutual benefit. When he could find no one wicked or dying, he ate animals, hunting deer in the forest just as Redgrave had taught him. This was as much virtue as he could claim—because he lived among murderers and did not move to stop them.

He'd had his reasons, at first. Exposing Redgrave meant

exposing himself, and Charity, which was worse. Charity murdered indiscriminately, as if she had no idea left of what was right or wrong—Redgrave's countless brutalities had wrenched the very concept of evil from her mind. Balthazar had rationalized that he had to keep his silence lest he destroy Charity even more completely than he already had.

But for the last several decades, he'd found it harder and harder to care.

"Come with me," Constantia whispered, her hand tracing down the length of his chest. "The hour is late."

When she took his hand, Balthazar didn't resist. He let her lead him upstairs to their room, to their bed.

How he hated her, but he couldn't resist her. The first woman—the only woman—he'd ever lain with, with no love or tenderness between them. Her kisses tasted like poison, and he kissed her more deeply for that, hoping that one day the poison might finally finish this life that wasn't life and let him truly die. Every time she took him to bed, he felt another shard of his human soul crumble into dust.

Balthazar only wanted it to be over.

A few hours later, as Constantia slept by his side, Balthazar lay awake, tormented by thoughts of the barmaid.

Let it go. It's no different from the other times. You aren't the one killing her. So that means it's not your concern.

I know it's going to happen. If I know and I don't stop it, that's as bad as if I drank her blood myself.

Finally, unable to bear it any longer, Balthazar slipped from beneath the bedcovers. He set each foot on the floorboards carefully, wary of awakening Constantia—but she was a sound sleeper, and tonight was no exception. For a moment he stared down at her, with her lustrous hair splayed across the pillow and her exquisite body outlined by the sheets that had covered them both, and wondered how a form so beautiful could hide a person so monstrous.

Enough. He had work to do.

Balthazar slipped into his trousers, shirt, and boots; the rest of his clothes were unnecessary. In the hallway of the inn, far from the modest fires in the rooms, the air was almost colder than it would have been out of doors. No candles lit his way, but one of the few undeniable advantages of being a vampire was the ability to see in the dark. Sure and swift, he found his way down the stairs. His sharp hearing caught the sounds immediately—he'd come just in time.

"Sir—you should return to your room, sir."

"But I wish to be here."

He navigated the passageways of the old inn as well as he could, making his way to the very back. There, just in front of a doorway that must have led to the alley, was the barmaid's room. She stood there, wrapper around her as she shivered, while Lorenzo held a candle too close to her face.

"I have written my poem," Lorenzo whispered to the trembling girl. "Do you not wish to hear it?"

"Nobody wants to hear your poems," Balthazar said,

stepping into the dim hemisphere of light the candle allowed. "They're abysmal. Go to bed and leave Martha alone."

Martha brightened; Lorenzo scowled as he said, "This is none of your concern."

"And none of yours, either. Leave her. I won't go until you do." Balthazar folded his arms in front of his chest.

Lorenzo remained still a moment, as if unable to believe that anyone so depressed and passive as Balthazar would take a stand—much less here and now, for the sake of a young woman none of them had seen before a few hours ago. Balthazar could feel the anger within Lorenzo, the frustration of a denied kill, and the certainty that he would pay for this defiance later.

But not now. Now they needed shelter in the middle of town, and fighting in the middle of the night would awaken too many humans. Drinking from the girl would no longer be a clandestine, unknown act. It had become too dangerous to risk.

With a scowl, Lorenzo swept past Balthazar. He stomped his entire way up the stairs, like a spoiled, thwarted child. Martha slumped against her doorjamb in relief. "Thank you, sir. He was most insistent, sir."

"I know they tell you to be kind to the guests," Balthazar said. "But you don't have to put up with that. You shouldn't. It's not safe. You must take care of yourself. If anyone ever makes you . . . frightened, or unsure—then be wary. Take whatever precautions you must. Do you hear me?"

Martha nodded. A curl of her dark hair fell across her rosy

cheek, and for a moment Balthazar remembered what it had been like to feel desire—real desire, human need, not this shadow of lust that Constantia demanded of him time and again. Not that he would ever endanger another human through showing affection for her. Not after Jane.

The girl was more innocent than he was, of course, suspecting nothing of him but noble motives. "Why do you travel with such people? They're not—they're not gentlefolk. Unlike you, sir."

"I have nowhere else to go."

"Anywhere else would be better, I should think." As if afraid she'd overstepped her bounds, Martha flushed, stepped backward, and gave him a quick nod before shutting her door soundly.

Anywhere else would be better.

More than that—Martha had called him a gentleman. He had saved her from Lorenzo, and even if there would be consequences for his action, this girl would not be the one to bear them.

Was it possible there was a place for him in this world? People who might accept him as something other than a monster?

It seemed impossible—yet less impossible than it had always been before.

Then he went back upstairs, returning to Constantia's bed and the wreckage of his existence. He lay beside his lover, blankets pulled up around his shoulders, and shut his eyes tightly.

But he did not sleep.

* * *

By dawn, Balthazar knew what he had to do.

He rose and dressed fully, stockings and breeches and coat and hat. Constantia still did not stir. For a moment he looked down at her beautiful face and tried to think how to bid her farewell—if he could ever divide himself from her entirely, which at that moment seemed impossible. She was poison, but poison that flowed within his veins. She would be a part of his vampire self forever.

And yet it was easier than he would have thought to walk out of that room, hopefully never to see her again.

Charity was awake. Balthazar had known she would be; even in life, she rose before anyone else, before the sun itself. She sat in the great room of the inn, huddled in her bedraggled clothing before the lingering embers of the fire. The glowing coals and the dim light of dawn from the one window provided the only light. Her eyes lifted to his, but she did not rise to greet him, nor speak.

She'd had very little to say to him since the day she died.

"Charity," Balthazar whispered. "Is Redgrave asleep?"

"Yes." Her place in Redgrave's bed was as assumed, and as unnatural, as Balthazar's place beside Constantia.

"Very well. That gives us a chance to go."

"Go?" It was as if that were not a word in English, so flat was her incomprehension.

After a century and a half of captivity, who could blame her? Balthazar reminded himself to speak slowly and clearly.

Sometimes Charity failed to understand, but this—this she had to understand. "We're leaving them. The vampires. We're going this morning. Setting out on our own. You and me."

Charity's brows knitted together in consternation. "Leave Redgrave?"

"Yes. Charity, this is our chance. We can leave them behind. Let them follow the war. We'll make our own way. Maybe—maybe on the outskirts of a city, where we can hunt animals in the woods and nobody will bother us." Balthazar knew she would resist this—Charity liked human blood far too much—but surely it would be worth it to her, if it meant escaping the murderer and rapist who had held her captive so long. "Just us. As it should have been. You understand me, don't you?"

Slowly, Charity nodded.

Balthazar smiled. Thank God. Why had it taken him so long to see just how simply, how quickly, their long nightmare could end? He had no idea where creatures like he and his sister could find peace in the world—they were unholy, damned, no part of God's creation—but they could look, couldn't they? They could try. Together, they might find a way to exist without Redgrave, without Constantia, without the bloodshed. It was just possible that he and his sister might have the chance to be . . . happy.

Then Charity said, "You want to take me away from Redgrave."

"Yes."

"Away from him. Away from all the blood. Away from everything." Charity's body trembled now, shaking almost as strongly as a convulsion.

"Charity, listen to me." Balthazar took her shoulders in his hands. "This isn't how we should be living. You know that, don't you? Don't you feel it, deep down?"

A tear trickled from the corner of Charity's eye as she nodded. The glowing embers pinked her pale cheek. "I do. I know how it should be. And I know who took it from me."

The shove hit him as hard as a blow, sending Balthazar sprawling across the room until he landed flat on his back on the stone floor. Charity stalked toward him, her fragile hands balled into fists.

"Come with *you*? Trust *you*?" Charity shook her head. "Not you. Never you!"

"Charity—"

She reached into the fire, pulling out a superheated pair of tongs that glowed red in the early morning light. Metal near melting cast pinkish-red light onto her face, onto her unearthly smile. "Get out. Go away. Or I'll behead you myself."

"Come with me," Balthazar pleaded. "Charity, please. This is our best chance."

"You didn't choose me!" she screamed, so loudly that he knew at least one of the vampires would wake.

So Balthazar pushed himself up from the floor, drew his coat more tightly around him, and ran out into the snow. As it sloughed into his boots, chilled him head to toe, he continued hurrying away from the inn—from Redgrave, and Constantia, and the only life he'd known since his death.

He still had no idea what kind of existence a monster like himself could expect.

He knew only that he had to find it—and face it, alone.

Chapter Seven

BALTHAZAR REACHED INTO THE INNER POCKET of his long coat, taking hold of the bone handle of the wide-bladed knife he'd put there. This would do for a beheading if he got the chance.

Not that it was likely. Redgrave wouldn't invade Skye's home with anything less than full force. Lorenzo, Constantia, and the rest of the crew he'd acquired since they'd last met—they would all be with him. That meant Balthazar had to stick to the plan and put off his ultimate revenge until later. Even though there was nothing he wanted more than to make Redgrave pay for what he'd done to him, what he'd done to Charity—

—his eyes sought Skye, her form visible in the darkness, young and frightened but trying so hard to be strong—

—because of what Redgrave was doing to Skye, too. Because of every foul, selfish thing Redgrave had done these past four centuries. It was more than enough reason to take off a guy's head.

Not tonight, Balthazar reminded himself, though he followed it with an inner promise: *Soon*.

The footsteps reached the stairs, heavy against wooden floorboards. Skye jumped slightly, and Balthazar could see that she was trembling. He laid one hand on the small of her back, and she steadied herself immediately. It was humbling to think that she would rely on him so completely, given how he'd failed with Redgrave in the past.

Starting, of course, with the day of his death.

The tribe was in the hall now, mere steps from the door. Skye's breathing had become as fast and shallow as a deer's at the moment of slaughter. Balthazar pressed his hand more firmly against her back, just for an instant, before he took it away to step in front of her, between her and the danger.

So faintly that Balthazar could barely make it out, Redgrave laughed.

He thinks it's funny. Funny that Skye's scared to death, funny that I'm up here waiting for him.

We'll see how funny he thinks it is in a minute.

The door swung open. Redgrave stood there, framed by darkness, as though he were alone. Skye gasped, but Balthazar forced himself not to turn back to her. Redgrave would see that as weakness.

"Well, well," Redgrave said. "I always knew we'd meet again, but I hardly thought it would be in a girl's bedroom."

"Get out." Balthazar didn't expect Redgrave to do this, but it was all he had to say to him.

Redgrave just grinned. "You were making a pet of her, weren't you? Can't say I blame you, Balthazar. She's quite lovely. You never did indulge enough. But I hope you've already had your fill."

"You're seriously disgusting," Skye said, but Redgrave didn't even glance at her. To him, she wasn't a person, merely a vessel for the blood he craved.

"I said, get out. Turn around and walk out of here," Balthazar said.

"You don't really expect me to do that, do you?" Behind Redgrave, at the edges of the doorframe, a couple of the other vampires appeared, as if to prove to Balthazar just what he was up against. They might have been any other set of young people—college aged, perhaps, one of them still wearing her hipster horn-rimmed glasses—but Balthazar could sense the ferocity behind their bland faces.

"No, I don't expect you to go," Balthazar said. "But I thought I should give you fair warning."

Redgrave grinned, his smile refined, even beautiful, despite the evil heat in his eyes as he looked past Balthazar to Skye. "Do you even know what you've got there?"

The flickers of the intense flashback he'd experienced that day lit up within Balthazar's mind, reigniting his anger. "You're the one who doesn't know what he's dealing with."

As Redgrave stepped forward—stalking turning into attack—the room's temperature plummeted to a chill so deep that Balthazar felt as if he would go numb. Skye's human breath created a small cloud of vapor in the darkness of the room.

Redgrave hesitated only a moment, but that was long enough.

Brilliant, aquamarine light flooded the room as ice began to coat the windows, the walls, and the ceiling. In the center of the light, Bianca took shape, spinning from something not unlike a wavering candle flame to herself, red hair streaming around her.

As Redgrave lifted his head to see her, Balthazar could tell the ancient fear still held sway over him—that he, and all of his tribe, were still violently repelled by one of the only things that vampires dreaded as much as fire.

One of the vampires behind Redgrave whispered, "Wraith."

Bianca swept forward, sliding horizontal, somehow turning herself into a blade that slashed through Redgrave, the wall, the door, all the vampires. Balthazar knew from having seen her in battle that this wouldn't kill any of them, but it apparently hurt like hell. Half doubled over, Redgrave hissed something in his old language, the one Balthazar had always refused to learn, and the entire tribe fled.

The only sound for a moment was the thumping of the back door as they went out the way they'd come.

Then Bianca laughed. "Wow, some vampires scare easy."

"You're telling me vampires are so terrified of wraiths that they'll steer clear of this house just because they saw Bianca?" Skye, who had already scooped out most of the ice from her room, shouted over the whirr of the hair dryer she was currently using on her bed quilt.

"It's an old superstition that goes deep for us." Balthazar himself didn't care for being around wraiths who weren't named Bianca, and even that had taken some getting used to. "Deeper for Redgrave than for most—he always had a particular horror of the wraiths. I'd seen him panic at the sight of one before. Trust me, he won't come back to confront Bianca again. From now on, at least, you can spend time here and sleep without worrying about being attacked every single second."

Bianca reappeared in the room; Skye jumped only a little bit. She was making progress. "I've searched everywhere," Bianca said. "Where's your ghost?"

Skye blinked at her. "How did you know I used to have one?"

"That's the only way humans got admitted to Evernight Academy," Balthazar explained. "A connection to the wraiths. Ghosts. Haunted houses, that kind of thing."

"Like Clementine's haunted car," Skye said thoughtfully. "The house I grew up in, in the center of town, that one was haunted. It was a little girl who sat by the fire with me sometimes. She never said anything; she just seemed to want somebody to sit with. I liked her. Thought of her as, like, an imaginary playmate who wasn't imaginary." Her expression was fond, even warm; Skye's ability to deal with the supernatural continued to surprise Balthazar. "But we moved here two years ago. New construction. No haunting here that I know of."

Bianca frowned. "That's not good. I'd hoped I'd be able to talk to your ghost and make sure you were protected all the time. I can't stay here permanently."

"We should be all right," Balthazar said. "Relatively few vampires know the ways to trap or repel ghosts. He won't try this house again. It's the rest of town we've got to worry about."

"You really know how to cheer a girl up," Skye said, and he smiled at her apologetically.

Bianca, who now had a very odd smile on her face, said, "You know how to call us if you need us. Skye, thanks again for everything. You're in good hands. Balthazar—it's nice seeing you like this."

Like what? Balthazar wondered, but it was enough to bask in her approval. Though his old love for Bianca had finally shifted into something simpler and less romantic, he thought he'd always have a weak spot for her smile. He lifted one hand in farewell as Bianca faded slowly from sight—returning to Lucas yet again.

Skye tucked a lock of her thick brown hair behind one ear as she said, "I'd forgotten you two used to go out."

"That was never—Bianca was always with Lucas, really. Our relationship was more about hiding their romance." And if he'd been fool enough to forget that for a while, he thought, he had no one but himself to blame.

"But you liked her, didn't you?" This girl had seen right through him. "Do you still?"

"No. I mean—of course I care about Bianca. I always will.

But she never wanted what I wanted. It took me a while to accept that, but I have."

Why did it feel so strange, talking about that with Skye? It felt like . . . like talking about one girlfriend to another. Bad form. Though of course Bianca had never really been his girlfriend, and Skye—that couldn't happen, for her sake.

They'd cleared the last remnants of ice from her bedroom, and he'd double-checked the entire first floor and fixed the locks—though Redgrave's phobia of wraiths meant that the doors probably could be left wide open from now on without the tribe returning. Tonight's crisis was taken care of: time to look toward the future.

"You're going to take the bus to school in the morning, right?"

Skye gave him a look across her darkened bedroom. "Of course. I'm not going to walk along the road again by myself. But what do we do after that? If they came after me on one of the main streets in town, they'd come after me in school."

"I'm working on that," Balthazar said. He didn't want to make any promises before he knew for sure. "I'll see you tomorrow."

"Wait—you're leaving?" She looked stricken.

"I promise you, they aren't coming back tonight."

"But you could still stay here. My parents wouldn't see you."

"There are a few things I need to take care of. If I did that here, I'd keep you up."

"Like I could sleep after this." Skye sighed, but more in

tiredness than frustration. Balthazar disliked leaving her, but for the moment she was safe, and he had to think about protecting her in the long term.

"Just go to school tomorrow and trust me, okay?"

He tossed the words out lightly, a phrase and nothing more. But Skye's expression became solemn as she said, "I trust you."

She really meant it.

He hadn't realized, until that moment, how badly he'd wanted to hear her say that.

That night, he returned to the cheap hotel room he'd rented on the edge of town, when he'd believed he would be here for only a handful of days. Obviously he'd need a longer-term solution, with Redgrave on the scene. The danger to Skye wouldn't go away in a day, or a week. This required long-term thinking. This required commitment.

Balthazar went to bed around midnight. Though he, like most vampires, preferred to remain awake at night and rest during the day, he knew that behaving this way separated him too completely from human society. There were times he'd allowed himself to drift into a vampiric existence; those were the times when he'd looked up to see that a year or a decade had come and gone without his having had a single meaningful experience. No more, he'd decided.

Besides, if he wanted to help Skye, he'd need an early start.

And he did want to help her—more strongly than he could have imagined he would after only a couple of days—

Refusing to think about it anymore, Balthazar went to sleep. And dreamed.

1988.

How long had he been out of synch? Five years? Closer to ten, maybe. Balthazar's jeans and T-shirt weren't quite right— everybody wore jeans washed out pale now, and the stripes on his shirt's sleeves had gone from ubiquitous to unfamiliar. But he could pass. He could manage.

It wasn't like he hadn't left the house in Chicago for ten years. He'd made trips to the hospital blood banks and the butchers, to get the blood he needed. He'd walked to the nearest bars and walked back. Sometimes he went to the store for cigarettes. But depression hung a kind of veil over everything—clouding it, making it more distant than it really was.

Now that Balthazar was pushing himself out again, that veil was gone. In its place was a world transformed.

Like cars. When had cars become so dull? Everything was white or gray, boxy and boring.

Women's fashions were interesting—sort of like the 1940s on acid. Big hair, big shoulder pads, brilliant neon colors: It would take some getting used to, but he'd give it points over the 1970s.

And the storefronts all seemed to have gone away. Maybe this was because of those "malls" he'd heard about. He'd have to see one.

"Look at this," said Redgrave, falling into step beside him. "Balthazar's revisiting his glory days."

Balthazar stopped where he stood, staring at Redgrave, trying to understand how he could be here. It made no sense—he hadn't seen Redgrave in at least—in at least—

"You tried to destroy my tribe. To destroy me." How was Redgrave in his mind? Everything around them was changing now. The twilight Chicago street seemed to be shimmering—no, melting, not vanishing but melting the way candle wax did—taking on new shapes.

The shape of a dance club in the late 1970s.

He'd been here once. No. This was the first time. Balthazar's confusion only increased as Redgrave became more and more gleeful, clapping his hands as he circled Balthazar. A haze of smoke from cigarettes—and other smoked substances—made the blinking lights around them seem almost eerie.

"I've only just begun finding ways to hurt you," Redgrave said. "Take this dream, for example. I'd never have done anything so rude, if you would only mind your manners. But Charity says you haven't minded yours at all."

Charity. His baby sister. Balthazar looked across the club and saw her—

—Charity and Jane in their dresses from the 1600s, with Constantia standing between them—

"Do you want to live it all again? I'll make sure that you do." Redgrave leaned closer to Balthazar, his feral smile bright in the gloom. "Unless you get out of town now. Leave Skye to me."

Skye—Skye didn't belong to this place, to this time—

Balthazar sat upright in bed, startled awake. That dream had been a vivid one.

Too vivid.

Any vampire's dreams could be invaded by that vampire's sire. Normally it was an affectionate gesture—which was why Redgrave had always left him alone. Balthazar had hardly thought of this skill before last year, when Charity had taken to invading Lucas's dreams during his time as a vampire. She had tormented him psychologically all night long until Balthazar had stopped her—by invading her dreams in turn. It had been a savage business, one that sickened him to think of.

But not as much as it sickened him to realize that Redgrave was following their example. From now on, any given night could see his dreams turning into a torture chamber. The dreamer never understood the true nature of the dream until it had ended; until then, all the fear, confusion, and pain was quite real.

Balthazar thought once again of seeing Charity and Jane standing side by side. He remembered the last time he had seen that, and he never wanted to return there.

If the only way to stop the dreams was abandoning Skye—

—then let Redgrave do his worst.

Balthazar knew how to look twenty-one years old if he had to.

He'd mastered that art long ago, though these days it mostly came in handy when he needed to buy a beer. (Whose idea had it been to raise the drinking age that high anyway? As someone who'd grown up in an era when fifteen-year-olds were considered adults, he found the modern prohibitions on marriage and alcohol consumption ridiculously Puritanical—

and he'd *been* a Puritan.)

At any rate, he knew how to appear older than the age he'd died at, nineteen. Allowing a shadow of stubble to grow on his cheeks got him partway there. Wearing expensive, well-cut, conservative-looking clothes helped a lot, too.

Now, looking twenty-four years old—that was tougher.

His suit appeared right. The stubble was scratchy without making him look unkempt. Balthazar studied himself in the mirror before dispensing a considerable amount of hair gel— "Infinite Hold," it promised, somewhat rashly—and combing it through, so that his curls vanished into a hard, slicked-back style. Then he pulled out a pair of tortoiseshell glasses with the modern rectangular frames. The lenses were merely glass; he'd heard these were fashionable these days and had bought them just to experiment. But hopefully they'd work as part of his disguise, too.

Double-checking his phone, he saw that Lucas had sent the fake documents he needed. Supposedly there was a twenty-four-hour copy center in town; he'd be able to print those off, and he knew that Lucas and his other friends would provide the phone verifications necessary.

This could work—if he played his role right. It was all up to him.

"It's lucky you showed up today," said Principal Zaslow, across the desk in her cozy office at Darby Glen High. "There was a car accident last night; we lost our history teacher for at least two months. I had no idea where we were going to find a qualified substitute who could work that long, starting immediately."

Balthazar gave her his best, most confident smile. "I'm your man."

Chapter Eight

"DO YOU REMEMBER THAT THING THAT WENT around about how gang members were going to beat up people at random, for, like, an initiation? And if anybody flashed headlights at you then you had to get out of there because they'd picked you? I bet that's what happened to Mr. Lovejoy."

"That's so stupid. He was in a car accident."

"I heard he was driving drunk."

"He'd be fired already if that were true. Maybe the person who hit him was drunk and that's what you heard."

"You're awfully quiet, Skye." Some girl looked at her with narrow ferret eyes. "What, feeling guilty? Were you the one who ran him down? The rich think they can get away with anything."

People laughed. Skye flushed with shame; the taunt struck too close to the truth. What had happened to Mr. Lovejoy was, however indirectly, because of her.

And it was one more reminder that school was not just unbearable now—it was also unsafe. If Redgrave or any of the other vampires came in here, who was going to stop them? The elderly school secretary who sweetly asked visitors for their ID at the front door? Not likely.

Maybe it was ridiculous to think that vampires would come barging into Darby Glen High, but she didn't know how far they'd go, or what they would or wouldn't risk. Surely they wouldn't want to kidnap her in public. But who knows?

She'd gotten up early enough in the morning to walk to the bus while her parents were going to their cars. That wasn't much protection, but it was something. Here at school, she was totally exposed.

To everything, including Britnee Fong.

"Should we be quieter?" Britnee was perched on the edge of Craig's desk; he'd hitched two of his fingers through a belt loop at the waist of her denim skirt. "Because, like, won't they come in here? And tell us to shut up? Then we'll get a substitute?"

Madison glanced at Skye, like *My God, that girl is stupid*, before she said, "Do you seriously think that we're not getting a sub? Is your big plan for us to just sit in here silently all semester and hope they don't notice Mr. Lovejoy is out?"

"It's weird they haven't gotten anyone in here already," Craig said quickly, obviously trying to stand up for his dimwit girlfriend. "The other teachers are probably pissed off by now."

Probably this was true, Skye thought—in the absence of Mr. Lovejoy, her homeroom had gone from hushed voices to the verge of anarchy. So far, the drawings on the dry-erase board weren't obscene, but they'd probably get there in five more minutes. Wasn't it bad enough that she was going to have to go through every school day in fear for her life without everybody being completely obnoxious in the bargain? She slumped down over her desk.

Madison said, "Be careful, Britnee. You don't want Craig's desk to collapse under the weight."

Skye looked up, startled by how seriously bitchy that was; it was nice that Madison stuck up for her, but that had been *mean*. Britnee chewed on her lower lip as she slid off Craig's desk. Craig gave Madison his most searching stare—and he could really do that, look at you like he was looking into your soul. Madison didn't seem to notice or care. Then he glanced at Skye, and she knew exactly what he was thinking: *This is the kind of person you want to be friends with?*

Which was judgmental of him. Madison's jokes were only meant to make Skye feel better, even if they were a little out of line. Plus, what right did Craig have to judge anybody? He was the one who had dumped her while she was still grieving for Dakota, and only a short while after they'd slept together for the first time.

Skye deliberately turned to Madison and said, "So has anybody come up with anything interesting to do in Darby Glen since I left? Or is Café Keats still the only game in town?"

"Pretty much." Madison tossed her coppery ringlets as she frowned at a chip on one manicured nail. "But, hey, basketball's started back up. We can go to the game tonight. That's something, anyway."

Craig was the basketball team's star forward, so Skye figured the game was the last place she wanted to be . . . even if it weren't exposed to vampire attack, which was definitely reason enough on its own to say no. As she started to make an excuse, though, the door to their classroom opened and Principal Zaslow walked in. Everybody fell silent at once as people dove for their desks.

Skye gaped as Balthazar walked in after the principal.

He'd brushed his hair back and put on glasses, which made him look older, but no less hot. Instead of the dark jeans and long coat he'd worn yesterday, Balthazar now had on pressed slacks and a tweed coat over a sweater vest—and somehow he made even that look hot.

The hush in the room took on a different quality the minute Balthazar walked into it, signaling the rapt attention of nearly all the girls and at least a couple of the guys. Madison leaned closer to Skye and murmured, "Oh, my God. This semester just started looking a whole lot better."

Taking her glasses from the beaded chain around her neck and putting them on her nose, Principal Zaslow said, "As all of you know, Mr. Lovejoy is looking at a long hospital stay and recovery. Luckily, we've already arranged for a full-time substitute. Mr. More will be taking over both homeroom and history teaching duties from now until Mr. Lovejoy can return to us. I trust you'll show him a warm Minuteman welcome, and your full attention and respect."

"That's not all I'd show him," Madison whispered, and a couple of girls nearby sighed as if to say, *Me too.*

Skye could hardly do more than stare as the principal walked out and Balthazar wrote his name on the board. "Hello, everyone. As you can see, it's More with one *o*, not two—pet peeve of mine."

"More as in *give me more*." Madison's crush was clearly already in full swing.

Balthazar had to have heard that—he had powers and abilities nobody else in this room could guess—and it hit Skye all at once: *Nobody knows the substitute teacher is a vampire.*

She put her hand over her mouth, trying not to laugh. Although Balthazar looked reasonably confident to anybody who didn't know him well, Skye knew him well enough to realize that, six weeks ago, he'd been on the other side of the classroom and now had no idea what to do. "I know we're all thinking of Mr. Lovejoy and hoping he'll recover soon. I was called in at the last minute, and I admit, I'm going to need some time to get up to speed. For today, you should treat this class as an extra study hall. We'll dive in again tomorrow."

People glanced at one another—the girls in open delight—as they took out their books and started pretending to do homework. Skye palmed her phone, angling it behind her notebook even though she doubted Balthazar would chastise her for using it. Quickly she texted him, *OMG WTF are you doing?*

The pile of books on top of Lovejoy's desk . . . now Balthazar's desk . . . apparently let him hide his phone, too. *You were exposed at school. Too dangerous. I needed a way to watch over you here.*

Since when do you teach history?

Since today. But I've lived through a lot of it. That's got to count for something, right?

It won't count when Zas checks your credentials and finds out you don't have any.

Thanks to some hacking—by our mutual friend Lucas, by the way—she'll find that I'm fully accredited. Apparently I got a master's in education from the University of Mississippi. Who knew?

Skye turned her phone over, lest she start laughing out loud. Or screaming. Her life was more and more like a supernatural roller coaster all the time.

Within two hours, she definitely felt more like screaming.

"Miss Tierney?" Ms. Loos gave her a look across the anatomy classroom. Skye could barely hear her over the drumming of her heart as the poor man collapsed in front of the room—again—his death drowning out everything else. "You look terrified. Are you well? Do you have some kind of *condition* I should know about?"

Snickers came from around the room. Skye braced her hands against the desk, her stomach churning. "No, ma'am. I'm fine."

"This classroom isn't the place for your personal drama, people." Ms. Loos pretended to be talking to the whole class, but her sharp eyes remained focused on Skye. This woman got off on picking on the weak—like she was in high school instead of teaching it. "If you're not capable of handling the subject of sex with maturity, then you should reconsider being in here to begin with. Transfers are still available."

Skye just hung on. The death began to fade, though the cold sweat trickling down her back and the cramps in her muscles told her the aftermath would be with her for a long time to come.

So, that was zero percent better. She definitely needed to check on transferring out of this class.

As Ms. Loos resumed her talk about how sex differentiation evolved millions of years ago, with mollusks or something, Skye put her head in one hand. This morning, for a brief hour, everything happening to her had seemed like a kind of adventure. A roller coaster. Balthazar's sudden appearance in her classroom had suggested that everything could be solved quickly and easily.

That had been a brief illusion, though. Now her problems loomed large and dark around her.

Skye took a deep breath. Before jumping competitions, she had gone through a checklist in her mind, making sure every single thing about Eb's tack was perfect, or if not, how she could handle the difficulty. It couldn't hurt to try that now.

Problem: Vampires are trying to kill me. Solution: My house is safe. My school is now safe thanks to Balthazar. I have to watch myself carefully anyplace else and minimize going out. Skye groaned inwardly as she realized she was, in effect, grounded. That was a small price to pay for staying alive, though. Maybe she could take up martial arts or something similar. Balthazar would always be the best at kicking ass when necessary, but she needed to be able to defend herself.

Problem: I can see the . . . psychic remnants of old deaths, all

*over the place. Solution: None. I can avoid most of the places I find,
but whenever a new one shows up, I'll just have to get through it
somehow.* That felt a lot harder to accomplish. When no answer
presented itself, she pushed herself on to the next issue.

*Problem: My ex-boyfriend and his skank girlfriend are all over
this school being judgy about me. Solution: None.* It wasn't that big
on her list of concerns at the moment, Skye admitted, but that
didn't mean it didn't suck.

*Problem: I never see my mom and dad. I know they need to
work hard—to have some space from our house and the family—so
that they can get over Dakota's death. But how am I supposed to
get over it? I need to talk to someone about him. I need to remember him sometimes. Solution: Find someone new to talk with.* Skye
wondered whether Madison might become the kind of friend
she could discuss these things with, but she doubted it. Clementine had been a rock to lean on last year at Evernight, but
she'd sensed when Skye was sad, or needed support; doing that
became much more difficult via text.

Nothing would really take the place of talking with her parents. They were the only ones who had loved Dakota the way
she had, who remembered the happy family they'd once had.
During the summer, Skye had been so numb that their distance
hadn't troubled her as much; plus, back then, she'd been able
to confide in Craig. She had believed that, in time, Mom and
Dad would come alive again. Remember her again. So far, they
hadn't.

Balthazar seemed like someone who would listen—

Problem: The guy I had a major crush on is now undercover as my substitute teacher, plus hanging around my house all the time, and I'm already liking him a thousand percent more than before. Also, he's a vampire, which makes this—complicated. How do I handle that?

A slow smile spread across Skye's face as she realized the one bright spot in this entire screaming mess that was her life.

Solution: Make Balthazar MINE.

Chapter Nine

BALTHAZAR HAD WALKED INTO VAMPIRE-HUNTER ambushes that filled him with less dread than walking into the Darby Glen High teachers' lounge.

"Well, *hello* there." A blond woman in a red skirt that was surely too short for teaching gave him an enormous smile. "Are you subbing for Sterling? Well, that's lucky. I mean, for you. Certainly not for him." She laughed a little too hard at her own joke. "I'm Tonia Loos. Anatomy and sex education."

Did she actually stress the word *sex*? Balthazar edged back toward the coffee and tea station. "Hello there—everybody," he said, making sure to include the entire roomful of people in his greeting. "Balthazar More. And yes, I'm filling in for Mr. Lovejoy. How's he doing, by the way?"

"That poor man," sighed a stocky guy in a colorful shirt and tie. "I'm taking him over some flowers after school today. Rick Bollinger, music, drama, and debate. Welcome aboard. This place isn't too bad."

"If you like suffering," said somebody who looked like a track coach.

"Don't scare the poor man off," said Tonia, as she ignored her own advice and stepped closer to Balthazar again. One of her fingers twirled a strand of her hair as she added, "Let's see— what do you need to know? Zaslow's not so bad if you stay on her good side. We've got an electric kettle, microwave, and hot plate in here, and we do a cake for the month's birthdays every first Friday. And if you're a smoker, the best spot to get a cigarette without the kids seeing you is right out this back way here."

With some wistfulness, Balthazar said, "I'm trying to quit, actually."

"Good for you," the track coach replied. "Stuff rots your lungs."

Not Balthazar's lungs, but he'd discovered that smoking had become incredibly annoying in the past decade. No smoking in theaters, on public transport, in most public buildings, even in bars: What was the point of that? The addiction, unfortunately, applied even to the undead, but he thought he could kick it. In the meantime, he kept chewing gum, patches, and an "electronic cigarette" at the ready.

Obviously worried that his attention was drifting, Tonia hurriedly added, "Well, we want you to feel really welcome here. If there's anything you need, Balthazar—you know, if you want someone to, um, show you the ropes—"

Was that a bondage joke? Please, let that not have been a bondage joke. Balthazar quickly turned his attention to Rick and said,

"Actually, I need a place to live while I'm here. I'm not . . . local. I was hoping for someplace out by the river, near the state land, maybe."

"You like your privacy?" Tonia gave him a low-lidded look perhaps meant to be sultry. Balthazar noticed only how thickly mascara had clumped on her lashes.

"I like hiking. Riding. That kind of thing." What he needed was to be close to Skye, the better to protect her, but that wouldn't go over well as a reason. As far as any of these people knew, he was an adult human male who should never, ever show any personal interest in one of his young female students, much less insist on living next door to one.

A gray-haired woman whose lunch was spread over an Algebra II textbook said, "The Macrossan house is for rent, if you want some space. Right in the center of town, but trust me, after the next big snowfall, you won't mind being closer to things."

"That's okay," Balthazar said. "I don't need much room; I don't have a lot." Also, he expected to spend very little time at whatever home he found—he'd be with Skye as much as possible. The new residence was mostly a place for Darby Glen High to send him his paychecks, because there was no way he was grading papers and taking attendance every day *for free.*

"It really is a tough commute when the weather gets tough," Tonia insisted. "And when you pull basketball duty during a blizzard—no fun."

Basketball duty, too? Great. Then again, just before he'd walked into Skye's homeroom, Balthazar had heard her talking to a friend about going to a game tonight. That was reckless of her, but he could at least be sure to be there. "Speaking of which, I need to take my fair share. There's a game tonight, isn't there?"

"Yes, but that's okay. Nola and I have it, don't we?" Tonia gave the track coach a rather fake grin; Nola didn't bother smiling back. These two clearly didn't even pretend to get along when a newcomer wasn't in the room.

"Take the night off," Balthazar said. "I'll go to the game, do my first shift."

Tonia's face lit up, and too late he realized that he'd sounded like he was flirting with her. "Aren't you sweet? Isn't he the sweetest thing?"

"Like a Snickers bar dipped in maple syrup," said the algebra teacher dryly, with an acerbic glance in Tonia's direction. "Good luck, More."

I'm going to need it, he thought.

During the day's classes, as the kids supposedly studied but mostly texted quietly, Balthazar reviewed some of what he'd be teaching this year. Ancient Civilizations: Well, that would take some work. He'd never been friendly with anybody from further back than about the eighth century AD. American Colonial History Honors Seminar, Skye's class: piece of cake, so much so that he didn't even bother flipping through the textbook. World War II Honors Seminar: Okay, doable. He'd just concentrate on the Pacific Theater, where he'd served his tour of duty. U.S. History, 1945–Present: been there, did that, had the T-shirt.

It was odd to look out at all the roomfuls of students and think that he was supposed to be an authority figure for them. They looked roughly the same age he looked most of the time, and the four centuries he'd walked the earth did nothing to change the fact that, deep within, Balthazar felt that he was a teenager. He always had, always would. Vampires never truly changed, after death—they gained experience, gained knowledge, and yet their souls remained, like their bodies, frozen in time.

And if there was any more proof that being a vampire was a form of damnation—well, Balthazar had never heard of a purer definition of hell than eternal adolescence.

His final hour at school was to be spent supervising an actual study hall in the library, which turned out to be Skye's study hall as well. As she walked in and saw him again, he had to turn his face away so as not to smile; it was going to be tough, pretending not to know each other every day.

But that didn't mean they couldn't communicate, as demonstrated by the fact that, about three minutes after Skye sat at her table with a friend, his phone vibrated to tell him he had a message.

He carefully slipped his phone in front of the Ancient Civilizations text he was reviewing to read: *OK, I've been wondering. Why didn't you just transfer in as a student? Then we could, you know, talk to each other during the day.*

NO WAY. I've tried real high schools several times in the past couple of centuries. They're all horrible. Unless another version of

Evernight Academy comes along, I'm done being a student forever. So I figured I'd try it on the other side.

Doesn't being a teacher suck even more than being a student? I mean, it looks like it would.

That's only because, most of the time, being a high school student is temporary, and being a teacher is permanent. In my case, that's reversed.

There was a long pause before Skye's next text; she clearly was holding on to her phone, but thinking hard, perhaps unsure what to say. Balthazar stole a long glance at her across the library—a bright room with pale gray scrubby carpet that was still soft underfoot, posters with various celebrities who thought everyone should READ, and bright orange movable bookshelves all around. Skye sat at the end of a long white table, sunlight painting warmth into her deep brown hair. She had a delicate face—more delicate than he'd realized before, more than he'd been able to see when she wasn't silent and still. Thick lashes visible even at this distance, pale skin that went rosy at her cheeks, and the elegant length of her throat—

—and that was just one more reason why he had a No Humans rule. Thoughts like that. Balthazar breathed out sharply as his phone vibrated again.

Are you really going to teach here every day until Mr. Lovejoy comes back?

Or until we get rid of Redgrave. Whichever comes first. Until then, I'm on faculty. I'm even sitting in on basketball duty tonight, so you can go to the game with your friend. Check with me about that stuff first, will you? I would've thought last night would make it clear that we have to be careful here.

I've been trying to get out of that all day! I wasn't going to go. I don't even want to.

Damn, Balthazar thought. Now he had Tonia Loos hanging all over him *and* basketball duty, for no good reason. *Obviously I'm the one who should've checked with you. Well, I'm stuck now. Can you go to the game anyway? I really don't want to leave you alone more than necessary at this point.*

Skye looked more depressed by this than he would have anticipated—it was only a basketball game, wasn't it? But she sent back, *Sure. That means I've got to hang out with Madison at Café Keats until the game starts, though.*

I'll make sure you get there safely, he promised.

Then her red-haired friend—Madison, presumably—began whispering to her, and their conversation was on hold.

Balthazar forced himself to stop watching Skye and to turn his attention to more critical matters. He was here to protect this girl; time to think less about the girl, more about the protection.

Now that he'd made sure he would be near Skye most of the time, he knew he was in a good position to stop Redgrave if he came after her. Now he needed to go on the offensive. To figure out what Redgrave meant to do with Skye, and the quickest, best way of stopping him, permanently.

Tailing Skye to Café Keats turned out not to be difficult. Baltha- zar was just one of several students and teachers who were headed toward the nearby Darby Glen town square; nobody would particularly notice that he happened to be about ten feet behind Skye and Madison at all times. There was a faster route to take to the center of town, a path that dipped into a small gorge but was perfectly walkable—but it was so severely ignored that he suspected it was considered uncool, somehow.

Apparently Café Keats was a coffeehouse. It looked inviting—bright turquoise walls, bright white tables and chairs, and some kind of stage in the back complete with a dark red piano. Students were crowding in, but others had already claimed the best tables. The place was packed. Skye would be safe there; no matter how bold Redgrave might be, he was nowhere near the point of trying an attack anywhere so crowded.

No, that would require getting Skye alone and Balthazar didn't intend to give him that opportunity.

For a moment, Balthazar watched Skye standing in line with her coffee, laughing with Madison, looking like the normal girl she deserved to be. He hoped she felt that way, at least for a while.

Then he took off. Before he devoted himself to Skye's protection full-time, he had one last logistical matter to handle.

"You're teaching at the high school?" said his new landlady, one Mrs. Findley. "My girl Madison's a senior there."

"I think she's in my first-period homeroom." Balthazar wrote the check out without worrying about the amount; investing well over the past few centuries meant money was the least of his concerns. "But it shouldn't be awkward. I keep to myself, mostly."

"And we'll let you do that, never fear. Madison's always out, and my husband and I let the tenants do what they like as long as we don't hear screams or see fire." Mrs. Findley obviously meant it as a joke, but Balthazar was uncomfortably aware that he couldn't rule either of those possibilities out. "Here's your key. Get yourself settled in, and let me know if you need anything."

His new home was a carriage house, located far enough back from the Findley home that Balthazar could scarcely see it through the trees. Good. He'd have his privacy. Although the interior wasn't of much interest to him, at least it was pleasant; the Findleys apparently normally rented it out to tourists who came to hike and sightsee in better weather, and so it was furnished with simple, older wooden furniture. Just three rooms—a small kitchen, a dated but shining clean bathroom, and a large bedroom with a gas fireplace and a huge four-poster bed. For honeymooners, he supposed. That bed was larger than their entire sleeping area had been in his childhood home.

For a moment, the memory flared brighter in his mind. He remembered the fields of grass, Fido's barking, the sound of Charity murmuring nonsense words in her sleep. He remembered the first time he'd seen Redgrave, and how suspicious he'd been. Yet not suspicious enough.

Balthazar tossed his few things onto the bed and went back out, taking stock of his surroundings. If he'd judged the area correctly, he was within half a mile from Skye's home—a distance he could cover quickly. He walked due south, past the Findley home and back into the woods, surer and surer that he was headed in the correct direction . . . then stopped.

Between the Findleys' home and the Tierneys' was a river.

No, not a river—a stream, but one large enough to still bubble with water despite the cold temperatures. Balthazar knew this because he could feel the deep, illogical and yet irresistible dread any vampire felt near running water.

I can't cross this, he thought—then immediately rejected that idea. He could cross it. If he had to, he would. It just wouldn't be easy. Crossing any kind of river or stream was, for a vampire, unpleasant at best, paralyzing at worst.

He imagined looking across the river and seeing her as he had that first evening, riding in the afternoon light. The sunset light now was much the same, and he could picture Skye perfectly: her alert gaze, the set of her shoulders, the outlines of her slim legs against the blackness of her horse. If she were over there, in trouble . . .

Yes. He could cross the water.

Resolved, Balthazar turned back so that he could begin the journey back to school for the basketball game. After a few steps, though, he realized that he wasn't alone.

Constantia stood among the trees, so tall that she seemed to belong to the forest, so ethereal and mysterious, he wondered if she was an illusion. He hated that he still felt a twinge of longing at the sight of her. She watched him quietly, hands in the pockets of her long coat, saying nothing. Instinctively he understood that she hadn't come here to fight him, that Redgrave's tribe had no interest in hurting him when he wasn't standing between them and Skye.

No, then their interest in him was far more insidious.

"Following me?" Balthazar said. "I thought you'd given that up."

"You're a bit of a bore." Constantia's voice held a curl of laughter; her eyes, as always, half mocked him, half devoured. "I keep waiting for you to start being fun, Balthazar. The first century or so, it was worth the wait. These days, not so much. Being near you is like trying to make wet tinder catch flame."

"Starting a fire requires a spark we don't have."

Her thin-lipped smile could be unspeakably cruel. "The first century and a half we knew each other—you didn't seem to think so."

Balthazar bit back a surge of anger. Constantia's selfish, thoughtless desires had led her to beg Redgrave for a toy. And he'd made her one—Balthazar himself. He'd been killed *for her*. His life, his mortality, perhaps his very soul: They'd all been destroyed to make her a young vampire plaything.

He tried to stay focused. "If you're not here to kill me, then why are you here, Constantia?"

"I'm here to explain how much easier it would be if you'd give up this—stubborn independence of yours and rejoin us."

"You can't seriously believe that will ever happen."

"You still don't see what the girl is."

This was his chance to find out what they wanted, though

he would have to be cagey about it. Asking her outright would only make her laugh in his face. "How do you know Redgrave isn't selling you more of his lies?"

"Lorenzo tasted her blood. Then he let us drink from him."

She said no more; she didn't have to. Between vampires, blood drinking was a way of communicating that went infinitely deeper than words—the taste of another vampire's blood let you experience his life, his emotions, even his pleasure. Balthazar had learned that by drinking Constantia's blood and tasting her desire for him, which had flowed into him until he had no choice but to desire her in turn. By sharing his blood, Lorenzo had made certain that every vampire knew Skye was worth pursuing. And Balthazar was still no closer to figuring out why.

She continued, "You're being given a chance, Balthazar. Redgrave doesn't give many second chances. Think long and hard before you waste it." Constantia began strolling away, her feet crunching in the snow, maddeningly confident. As she went, she called back over her shoulder, "By the way, 'ever' is a very long time."

Chapter Ten

ON GOOD DAYS AT CAFÉ KEATS, LOCAL BANDS would get up and jam for hours. On bad days, people who thought they were talented got up and proved themselves wrong. Skye and Madison didn't agree on which kind of day this was.

"How old is she? Like, eighty?" Madison rolled her eyes as she licked a bit of the whipped cream from the top of her drink.

"Probably. What does it matter?" Skye stole another glance at the white-haired woman sitting at the red piano, gently picking out a slow, melancholy version of "You Really Got a Hold on Me." It was an old song, but one she liked. "I mean, I hope I'm getting out and having fun when I'm her age. And she can really play. So why not?"

"I prefer music from this century," Madison insisted. After another sip of whipped cream, she said, "Listen, about tonight—the game—I only realized at the end of the day how that's kind of awkward for you. What with Craig and everything."

"I'll be okay." She kind of had to be, now that Balthazar was going there to guard her. Skye sensed it would be easier to sit through one of Craig's games with Balthazar as a distraction.

"We'll sit far away from that girlfriend of his. I can't stand her. She's just—vacant, you know? Like, the lights are on but nobody's home."

That was clearly an invitation to bitch about Britnee, but Skye didn't feel like it. Shrugging, she said, "I didn't really think about them as much today. Maybe I'm getting over him a little. I don't know."

Madison's face brightened with mischief. "I know. You were too busy thinking about our sexy new sub." Skye felt her face going warm, and she must have blushed, because Madison cackled with laughter. "You *were*! Somebody's hot for teacher."

"I'm not hot for—" That was a lie. But telling the truth was out of the question. "Okay, he's good-looking. I noticed. And so did you."

"True, true." Madison draped her legs over the side of the chintz armchair she was sitting in; they'd gotten the good table with the cozy chairs in the far corner by the poetry board. "Mr. More seems young. Like, really young. I bet he hasn't been out of college for long."

A few centuries or so, actually. "Looks that way."

"So that means he's only about four or five years older than us." Deep in thought, Madison licked the edge of her spoon. "If you ask me, that's close enough to date."

"But he's a teacher." *Plus he's a vampire, which I bet you would never be able to handle.* "That's against the rules."

"I never heard of that rule."

"Why would you hear about it? Who else are we going to date? Coach Haladki? Mr. Bollinger?" Skye made a face at the thought.

"Mr. Bollinger would be more interested in Mr. More than in us. We might have to fight him off if we want a piece." Madison gave Skye a hopeful look. "Do you think Mr. More's the kind of guy who breaks the rules?"

Laughing, Skye wadded up her paper napkin and tossed it at Madison. "Stop it."

"I'm *serious.*"

"You're not fooling anybody. And I'm going to write a poem."

Writing poems at the poetry board was a tradition at Café Keats. Most people tried to do something cute or funny; the occasional obscene drawing was quickly wiped by a barista. Every once in a while, one of the poems would actually be good, and that would get to stay up for a few weeks or even months. Skye, no writer, just wanted a few seconds where she wouldn't have to listen to jokes about Craig or Balthazar.

Though she did want to think about Balthazar—

He's my teacher now. Does that matter? The rules about the other teachers don't exactly apply to him. I mean, we were in English class together six weeks ago.

Skye understood that Balthazar wouldn't consider getting involved with any of the other students. But did she have a chance with him? There had been moments when she'd felt his eyes on her, known he was drawn to her . . . but only moments.

Briefly the memory of Bianca glimmered in her mind, aquamarine and ethereal, but it faded just as quickly.

No, whatever happened between Skye and Balthazar in the future wouldn't be about Bianca. It would be only about them.

Also, he's a vampire. Undead. Blood-drinking. Fang- . . . um, fang-having. What would that even mean for us, if we got together?

She wasn't at all sure about that. But she'd spent the last two and a half years surrounded by vampires, however unknowingly; for the most part, they acted like people. Arrogant, sometimes ruthless people, but still. Skye knew that if she'd learned Balthazar was a vampire when she'd first met him, she might never have wanted to get to know him better; now, however, this was just one more aspect of the supernatural strangeness surrounding her, one more quality he had that was as tantalizing as it was dangerous.

As she stepped up to the board, Skye disregarded the colorful chalk in its bucket and instead went to the poetry magnets, which were more her speed. Her fingers plucked the words from their jumble along one side, sliding them into place:

I remember
Soft rose fantasies

At Evernight she'd been Craig's girlfriend, faithful even in her imagination. Every time Balthazar had walked by her in the hallway, she'd drunk in the sight of him, then tried to go back to whatever she was thinking about before.

But at night in her dorm room, while Clementine snored in the next bunk, sometimes Skye's fantasies had demanded their due. She'd lie there all twisted up in her sheets, trying to think of the boyfriend she knew she ought to be thinking of, but instead remembering Balthazar: framed by the stone arches of Evernight's hallways; wearing fencing whites that outlined his muscular frame, mask tucked under one arm; ready with a gentle smile for everyone even though there was always something distant and melancholy in his eyes . . . something that made her want to take that melancholy away . . .

Skye felt a guilty flush of longing at the memory—*But why guilty?* she asked herself. *You're free now. And so is he.*

Except for the part where he's a vampire and everything.

With a sigh, Skye composed another line:

Us—caught between never and forever.

She decided she liked that, but before she could keep going, a man's hand pointed into her poem and slid out the word *remember*. He pushed it up so that it formed the phrase *remember me?*

Skye looked over at him, and in the first moment, she didn't remember him. It seemed impossible that she could have forgotten a man like this. He wasn't especially tall or short, but everything else about him was remarkable—the perfection of his profile, his gleaming dark blond hair, the warm hue of his skin, his piercing hazel eyes that almost seemed gold. More like the idealized sculpture of a man than any real human being. The crisp white collar of his shirt looked sharp enough to cut. He couldn't be a student at her school, because he was old enough to be one of the teachers—like Balthazar—

I've seen him with Balthazar.

Oh, my God.

Redgrave smiled. "Don't worry. You haven't hurt my feelings by failing to know my face." His accent was odd, not exactly British, not exactly American, hints of something else, too. Hard to place. "You saw me only in the dark, and only with human eyes. My question was sincere." He tapped his finger on the board, just beneath *remember me.*

"I'll scream," Skye whispered. It wasn't much of a threat, but it was all she had.

"That would be very silly of you. I'm not hurting you. I'm not even threatening you. I'm just a newcomer in town with an interest in poetry." Redgrave glanced over the board's current offerings and sighed. "Not that much of this is recognizable as poetry. I must bring Lorenzo here if I ever wish to punish him."

Skye wanted to run away, to bolt out of the coffeehouse as fast as she could, but surely that was what Redgrave meant for her to do. If she ran out, his vampire "tribe" would all be out there waiting for her. "What are you doing here?"

"Getting a coffee, strangely enough. And hoping to have a chat with you, now that your bodyguard isn't on hand." Redgrave's smile would, on any other man, have been stunningly beautiful. On him it was menacing. "Balthazar assumes that I won't attack you here, and he's absolutely right. I have absolutely no intention of spending so much as one day in the county jail or whatever picayune human lockup I'd be consigned to. So if we're going to talk, this is the place."

"We don't need to talk." Even getting those words out was hard; Skye's entire body had gone cold and clumsy, and she could hardly think anything besides the words *This man tried to murder me yesterday.*

"Nonsense, my dear. I see that you are not without resources. That you understand the nature of the supernatural. So I thought we might be able to speak like rational creatures, and perhaps strike a bargain."

"A bargain?" She made a sound that wasn't quite a laugh. "Okay, get out of town now and leave me alone, and I won't kick you in the balls."

Redgrave really did laugh at that. "You've got spirit. You see, I can work with you."

Her voice shaky, she whispered, "You're trying to kill me."

"I think we can come to a better compromise than that, if you're smart enough to see its value." He half turned, leaning against the wall next to the poetry board. Skye now thought that, even if she hadn't recognized him from the day before, she would have known by now that he was a vampire. Redgrave had that eerie grace and confidence familiar to her from the students at Evernight. All around them, the coffeehouse remained loud and bright; the piano music never stopped. "I don't have to kill you to get what I want. It follows, therefore, that your best chance at staying alive is simply to give me what I want."

Instinctively, she knew what that was. "My blood."

He shrugged. "People donate all the time, and for what? A sticker and a cup of apple juice. I can do far better than that."

"If I let you take any of my blood, you'll just take it all."

"Which would make a very entertaining evening for me, but no more than that. Whereas if you stay alive—if your body keeps creating and heating and pumping this miraculous liquid within your veins—I can enjoy your blood any time I please."

Skye had only a foggy idea of what he was suggesting; she didn't think she wanted to get a more precise picture. "I'm not your personal Coke machine."

"Aren't you curious, miss—forgive me, I don't know your name."

"Because I didn't tell you."

Redgrave tilted his head with a slight smile, acknowledging her right not to tell him. He looked so human then—so clever, so good-humored, so breathtakingly gorgeous—that Skye realized if she'd met him without Balthazar's warnings, she would have trusted him immediately. Completely.

He said, "A mystery within a mystery. And I'm being quite literal now. Within you lies a secret waiting to be discovered. If Lorenzo is to be believed, your blood has unique powers. Unique advantages. Don't you want to know what they are? Balthazar can't tell you. It's not in his nature to understand this. It is in mine." Redgrave leaned closer, so close they might have been about to kiss. "Only I can give you the answers you want. Only I can explain the line between life and death."

All the myriad deaths she'd witnessed through her visions over the past month flooded back to her, but one beyond the rest welled up in her mind—one she hadn't witnessed, but one that had haunted her for almost a year now: Dakota.

Skye jerked back, twisting her face away from him. "There's nothing I need badly enough to get it from you."

"As you like," Redgrave said. "But we'll meet again. One way or another."

Her legs shaky, she made her way back to the cozy chairs, where Madison was doing a not very good job of pretending to be absorbed only in her texting. "Sooooo," she singsonged. "Looks like you made a new friend at the poetry board."

"He's not a friend. He's . . . some old creep."

"Not too old. Not looking like *that*." Madison stared in wonder as Redgrave strode across the room, turning heads as he went. "Is it just raining hot older guys all of a sudden?"

"Forget it." Skye snatched up her backpack. "Let's head out. The game's starting soon anyway."

Her heart pounded. Her limbs trembled. But Skye kept taking deep breaths and telling herself she ought to have been relieved. Redgrave really wouldn't attack when she was in a public enough space. That gave her a lot of safety. More than she'd thought she had this morning. So that was good news, right?

But the questions he'd asked kept ringing in her mind. Did

he really understand what was going on with her? Could he give her answers? Was there a way to give him what he needed while keeping herself safe and alive?

As they walked out of Café Keats, Skye glanced over at the poetry board. Before leaving, Redgrave had changed his offering, sliding away the *remember* and the question mark and putting another word in its place.

Now the line read only *join me*.

"Hey, Big Blue, it's all up to you, so hey, Big Blue—PULL THROUGH!"

Cheers and clapping echoed through the gymnasium as Skye and Madison clambered up toward some seats with a group of people Madison knew. Though everyone was friendly enough, nobody went out of their way to talk to Skye, which meant she was soon sitting on the edge of the group, talking to nobody. That was fine with her.

She whipped out her phone to send a message, just as it chimed in her hand. The message was from Balthazar: *Good, you're here. I thought I remembered how boring this school spirit stuff is. Actually, I'd blocked it out, like any other kind of pain.*

Skye couldn't enjoy the joke. *Redgrave talked to me.*

What? When? Are you okay?

Fine. He came up to me in the coffeehouse and said a bunch of weird—can I just tell you this in person? It's going to take the whole game to type it.

Meet me by the concession stand.

"Be back in a sec," Skye said. Madison hardly turned as she waved her off.

While making her way back down the bleachers, Skye glanced at the actual game; there, in the heart of the defense action, was Craig. His hands were splayed wide, and his long limbs covered his hapless opponent like a spiderweb. His dark brown skin already gleamed with sweat—even this early in the first quarter, he was playing all out, going for broke, not holding back.

For one moment, her mind wasn't in the present. It was in the past—last summer by the river, with the August heat beating down on the two of them tangled, Craig's body against hers, skin gleaming with sweat as they came together for the first and last time—

Skye pushed the memory away. Already it seemed like something that had happened to somebody else. Or should've happened to somebody else.

The quickest way to the concession stand involved cutting under the bleachers. Teachers would stop students who tried, if they were seen, but since one of the teachers on b-ball duty was the person she was trying to meet, Skye figured she was safe. She glanced up to make sure she wasn't about to hit her head on one of the crossbars, then froze.

He stands on the framework, whole body shaking with fear. He doesn't want to do this but he doesn't see any other way out. Maybe this will make it better. Maybe it's the only thing that can.

Don't do it, Skye wanted to shout, but she knew it would

do no good. He'd gone through with it a long time ago. Her knowledge did nothing to diminish the overwhelming sadness and fear swelling inside her, pushing out her own feelings until she was nothing but a container for this boy's pain.

The noose is just some strips from his sheets, ripped off and braided together. He ties the knot, makes sure it's tight, and slips his head in. Their remembered taunts are louder now than his own heartbeat.

Skye's eyes widened as she saw him more clearly. This had taken place decades ago—his hair and clothes told her that much—but he looked so familiar. Though there was no relation, no connection, the boy about to commit suicide reminded her of Dakota.

He jumps. The noose tightens, tighter than he'd known anything could feel, and it hurts worse than he'd thought anything could hurt. His body, ignorant of bullies or cruelty or sadness, struggles to live—bursting blood vessels, tensing muscles, contorting in every direction. His neck is a vise of pain that wants nothing more than to open up enough to breathe, but it can't. It can't.

She put her hands to her own throat. Though nothing prevented her from breathing, her body wasn't doing it. Something in her begged her to surrender to the feeling, but she fought against it with every ounce of her will. Once again the boy's face appeared before her, and once again she thought, *Dakota.*

"Skye?" Balthazar's voice was distant. She couldn't see him. Couldn't see anything.

I take it back, the boy thinks. I take it back. His legs kick out wildly, seeking a place to stand, so he can get his life again; however broken or sad it is, it's better than this. But his feet can't find purchase, and everything in his brain is turning black—

Skye couldn't see. Couldn't think. She wasn't even sure how she knew she was falling.

Chapter Eleven

BALTHAZAR REACHED SKYE JUST AS SHE FELL, catching her in his arms in the moment before she would have hit the ground. A few people shouted and pointed—his calling out to her had drawn too much attention—but so far as anybody knew, this was nothing more than a student fainting during a ball game.

It might be far worse than that.

As he lifted Skye into his arms and began working his way back out of the bleachers—with faces from above peering down to get a look at what was going on—his fellow teacher on duty, Nola, shouted, "Everybody back up! Give her some air!"

"Skye? Can you hear me?" Balthazar glanced down at her; she wasn't entirely unconscious, but definitely dazed. One of her hands pawed feebly at her neck. "I'm getting you out of here. You'll be all right."

"Oh, my God. What's going on?" Madison Findley showed up, seemingly thrilled by the sudden drama. "Coach Haladki, what happened to Skye?"

"She fainted," Nola said, her voice then climbing to a shout, "which is what *happens* to kids who break the *rules*! Everybody get back to the game! Show's over!"

"It was like I couldn't breathe," Skye whispered. "That one was bad."

As they finally emerged from underneath the bleachers, Balthazar lowered her so that she could stand, but she still wavered on her feet. Nola shook her head. "Better get her to the nurse's station. No nurse on game duty anymore, thanks to the damn budget cuts, but this one probably only needs a box of juice and some quiet time. No more sneaking off under the bleachers again, all right, Tierney?"

"All right," Skye answered, her voice sincere. "I can swear I'll never walk under there again."

Madison appeared at their side. "Should I go with you? Keep you company?" Though obviously she was talking to Skye, Balthazar couldn't help noticing that Madison was looking only at him.

"She's fine," he insisted. "Skye will be back out soon. You can keep watching the game." Disappointed, Madison shrugged and stepped away from them.

Neither of them spoke again until he had her out of the gymnasium and they were in the silent, deserted halls of the school. "What happened under the bleachers?"

"Some guy from the seventies committed suicide down there." Her voice shook. "He wanted to take back what he'd done so bad, but he couldn't."

"Hey." Balthazar already had his arm firmly around her, but

he squeezed more tightly. "It's okay. You're past it."

"I felt everything he felt."

"What?" He used his key to the nurse's station, then edged her inside. A flip of the light switch revealed plain white cinder block walls and a simple cot, onto which Skye sank down gratefully. In the corner, a mini-fridge held a few boxes of orange and apple drink; Balthazar thrust the apple stuff at her. "Drink this. What do you mean, you felt everything he felt?"

"When he couldn't breathe, I couldn't either." Skye's fingers went to her neck again, and he realized that she was seeking the noose. "That hasn't happened before. Oh, my God. And the worst part—" She shook her head, denying the words. Then she started working on her juice box, her attention clearly turning within from shock.

"Stay with me." Balthazar brushed his hand along her arm, and her pale blue eyes turned back toward him. "If not being able to breathe wasn't the worst part, what was?"

Her voice small, she said, "He looked like my brother. Dakota."

"You mean—the one who died last summer."

Skye nodded. "It wasn't him. That's not how Dakota died, and—it just wasn't him. But it reminded me of him. That was bad enough."

Balthazar had always thought that if Charity had died in another way, he might have been done grieving for her by now. That eventually he could have accepted her death and moved on. Looking at Skye's devastated face, he wasn't as sure about that any longer.

Keeping his tone gentle, Balthazar said, "What happened to your brother?"

"He was spending his summer break in Australia with his girlfriend, Felicia. They went off-roading in the outback. His ATV flipped. He broke his neck." Her eyes had reddened with unshed tears. "So when I saw that guy beneath the bleachers, and he looked like Dakota, and there was all that pain in his neck, it was like—like I was feeling my brother die, too."

Skye looked away, apparently struggling for composure. Balthazar had learned over centuries that some grief could not be answered or consoled; the only service to give to people in that dark place was to bear witness. So he wrapped his hand around hers, accepting her sorrow, letting it flow through the space between them as her breathing slowed and became more steady.

After a few moments, Skye said, "We need to talk about Redgrave."

"I know." On top of all this, she still had Redgrave after her. How much would she have to bear? It was too much, and Balthazar felt a surge of anger—at Redgrave, at fate, at her brother for being such a daredevil—at anybody who had hurt Skye—

No humans, he reminded himself.

Skye then told him about Redgrave's latest stunt. Though Balthazar felt slightly relieved that Redgrave wasn't reckless enough to go after her in public—yet—the rest of it only made him angrier. "Don't listen to any of his . . . bargains, or compromises, or whatever else he's calling them. I did, once, almost four hundred years ago. I'm still paying the price."

"You mean—is Redgrave the vampire who—"

"He killed me. He turned me into a vampire." Baltha-zar realized his hand still clasped hers, and reluctantly pulled it away. It was difficult admitting this to her—to anyone. He disliked reliving their history even through the retelling. "Tech-nically, I agreed to the change. But only after he took me to a place where I would've done anything just to have the chance to die and end it."

Her face white, Skye nodded. "I don't trust him. I never will. But—he still knows something about me that we don't."

"We'll find out for ourselves."

It was an automatic response; anything was better than turn-ing to Redgrave and expecting answers. So it surprised Balthazar when Skye rose and went to the medicine cabinet. "Okay, then. Let's start."

When she turned back toward him, she held an empty plas-tic syringe, and he realized what she meant to do. "This is a bad idea."

Skye shook her head. Though she was obviously still weak-ened from her ordeal, having a goal made her focus on that and nothing else. "The only way we're going to understand what my blood does is for a vampire to drink it."

"I may have already done that."

"Wait—what?"

"After all that insanity at the gas station—right after Mr. Lovejoy crashed his car, I tasted a few drops of blood that were on the ground. I thought it might have been his, but . . . I felt strange afterward. So the blood must have been yours." Shameful to admit how much he had wanted that brief taste of human blood, but it had become too important not to talk about. But the intense hallucinatory experience that had followed—the almost total immersion in his own past—that couldn't be only about her blood. It was impossible. Or was it? "I can't be sure."

"You can be sure if you try it again, and you drink more this time."

"It's a bad idea." Getting used to the taste of her blood—it was so insanely tempting that Balthazar thought it would be better if he never, ever knew.

The desire to drink living human blood was the most inescapable part of being a vampire . . . more inescapable even than death. Living off animals was possible—Balthazar had proved that—but their blood lacked the full lifeforce that vampires craved past the point of reason. In the past century, the practice of blood donation had created ways to get even human blood without hurting people, but only a few hours outside the body robbed the blood of its most precious qualities.

Drinking human blood allowed vampires to continue to look human, to continue to use reason. Animal blood would hold the monster within at bay, too, but not for nearly as long. Trying to withstand temptation only led to madness—only brought the monster closer to the surface. To resist becoming nothing but a homicidal predator, Balthazar had to drink human blood from time to time. It was the governing irony of vampiric existence.

But to get hooked on the blood of one human in

particular—that was far more dangerous than not drinking blood at all.

Her expression only became more stubborn. "It's the only way to find out what they're after, so we're doing it." Skye hesitated as she looked down at the needle. "I never actually did this before, but it looks easy enough on TV."

"So does flipping over your car at a hundred miles per hour and not dying." Balthazar took the syringe from her. "I did some medic duty during the Korean conflict. I can handle this."

She was right, of course. They had to investigate, and there was no other place to begin than with testing her blood's true power.

But as Balthazar looked at Skye, he knew they courted danger. The vision he'd had before had been overwhelming; so real, he'd lost all control over the here and now. Bad enough at any time, but here—where he was being offered the blood of a living person, the human blood he so desperately missed and craved—in this small, private, closed-in room with a girl who drew him even more strongly than blood—

He slid the soft, plum-colored sleeve of her sweater up her arm. Her human skin was warm and silky against his. There was nothing handy for a tourniquet, so Balthazar simply clenched his fist tightly just above her elbow. A shiver ran along his body as she whimpered so softly he could barely hear, and the pale, fragile skin at the inside of her elbow seemed to streak with the blue of her veins, with the darkness of her blood.

The predator within him wanted to throw away the needle,

lower his mouth to her skin, bite in deep. His fangs burned within his jaw, eager for release.

Slowly, deliberately, he slid the needle into her arm, then pulled back the depressor. Brilliant red liquid filled the syringe. That shade of red had, as always, a hypnotic effect on him, and it was all he could do to keep going, to pull the needle out at the right moment and then bend her arm.

"You're good at that," Skye said. "It didn't hurt at all."

Balthazar couldn't look away from the syringe. He could feel the heat of her blood through the plastic. "I'm going to drink this now. If I act strangely—especially if I make a move toward you—get the hell out of here. Immediately."

Skye held her bent arm against her chest as if it might provide some protection, but said nothing. Balthazar angled the tip of the syringe into his mouth, pressed down, tasted warm, real, true human blood—

—and he was gone.

Massachusetts, 1640

"YOU CAN'T CATCH ME."

Though he couldn't see Jane, he could hear her giggling. Balthazar looked for her, but in the thickly wooded glade, with the still-thick leaves only just starting to turn to gold, she was just one of the many shadows.

Grinning, he said, "I can try."

He dashed in the direction of her voice and was rewarded

with a cry of laughter and a glimpse of her. Jane's favorite green dress would have made her invisible in the summertime, but now she was vivid against the gold, the one thing still living in a forest on the verge of its long sleep.

Although he could have caught her almost right away, Balthazar prolonged the chase as long as he could. It was wonderful to hear her laughter, to not worry about anyone overhearing or judging them, to just be in the moment—

—but even better to catch her.

His hands slid around her waist, and she pretended to push against his chest to escape, but she didn't push very hard. After one moment's hesitation, one moment where he wasn't sure he dared, Balthazar bent down and softly kissed her . . . hardly for a second. He'd never kissed anyone before.

Nor had she. He knew that when she pulled back and put her hand to her lips. Yet he could tell she was as delighted as he was.

"You shouldn't," Jane whispered, trying to sound scandalized. "What would the elders say?"

"The elders aren't here." If they were, Balthazar thought, they might order him put in the stocks for immorality, so people could throw rotten cabbages at his head. He imagined getting out of it by offering to marry Jane to preserve her honor. If the church elders agreed to that, his father couldn't stand in the way any longer, and he could have his own home with her.

A cool breeze rustled through the trees around them, and a fall of golden leaves showered down. Jane flung her arms wide and spun beneath them, her face turned up to the sky. "Oh, right now I feel like I could fly. Just like a bird."

"Come here, and we can both feel that way again." Balthazar caught one of her arms and pulled her close.

This time, the kiss lasted much longer, and by the end wasn't nearly as soft.

When they pulled apart, Balthazar combed his fingers through Jane's dark hair and smiled down at her—only to see her own expression crumpling, as if she was about to cry. "What's wrong?"

"We're wrong," she said. "Or so everyone around us believes."

"They're the ones who are wrong."

"We are Catholics." Jane spoke the words as though she had been over them in her mind many times before. "Your family are heretics."

"You know I care little for the church—"

"The churches care for us whether we like it or not. Where would we live?"

Balthazar fell silent. Throughout the colonies, a patchwork of religious beliefs and rules governed each settlement; the only true faith in one colony was forbidden and outlawed in another. Though the rules governing marriage were secular—at least, here in Massachusetts—nobody would allow either of them to remain here married to the other.

I could convert, he wanted to say, but the words died in his throat. To become a Papist would be to cast his parents, and Charity, out of his life forever; they would never even acknowledge him after that, and he could never reside permanently in Massachusetts again. He, like Jane and her father, would require special permission even to visit. Could he bear it? Yes, he could leave his parents—but not Charity. His dreamy little sister had no one else to understand her.

More than that, he'd heard sermons his whole life about the evils of the Roman Catholic Church. Although he could think for himself enough to judge Jane and her father as he found them, he knew he could never, in honesty, claim the Catholic faith as the truth of his heart. Without that, any conversion would be empty, and Jane would know it.

Jane stepped away from him, her earlier joy faded and blown away like the first fall leaves. "We shouldn't have come here today."

"Jane, don't. Let's enjoy what time we can."

"It will only make parting more difficult." He held out his hand to stop her, but Jane dodged him. "Let me go. Please. I can't think on this any longer now."

The gentle, mournful quality of her expression then stirred a memory in him of another girl—someone who reminded him of her. The name *Bianca* flickered in his mind, and it seemed to him it was important, but he couldn't hold on to it for long.

Jane hurried away, and Balthazar simply stood and watched her. The dreamlike quality of it all made him wonder if this could be really happening, but he found he didn't care. If it were a dream, let him get lost in it and go on dreaming, as long as he was able to keep looking after Jane, to keep her in his sights. That was worth anything.

"A pity, to see two young lovers parted," Redgrave said.

Balthazar startled; he hadn't heard Redgrave's approach. His cheeks burned as he thought of the private moment this peculiar man might have seen. "Sir, you should have made your presence known."

"As indeed I just have." Redgrave leaned against a nearby tree. He seemed a part of the golden grove around them—primeval, in some unfathomable sense—and yet unnatural, too. "Will you let her go so easily?"

"I'll see her again soon." Though, Balthazar thought with a pang, not for long: Within the month, they would return to Rhode Island, where Catholics, Anabaptists, and all sorts of freethinkers were tolerated.

"Yet the two of you think a parting is inevitable. That you could never marry, and of course you think marriage is the only way to truly be together."

The man presumed too much. Balthazar had tried to be friendly to these strangers for his sister's sake—she liked their eccentricities, and for their part they seemed to accept her—but something about the Redgraves had always unnerved him. Their money, which they blithely said came from "trading," seemed to outstrip even that of Governor Winthrop; Redgrave's ability to stare down the church elders and flout all kinds of rules was less inspiring, more unnerving. If Balthazar were to speak of such private matters with anybody, John Redgrave was the last candidate Balthazar would ever have chosen. "I can't see how it concerns you. It's improper to discuss it."

"Proper! You want to speak of propriety after such a

passionate scene." Redgrave laughed. Balthazar, who had never glimpsed even the knees or shoulders of a woman not his mother or sister, felt grossly violated by having been seen at such an intensely intimate moment—and Redgrave was vulgar enough to *laugh* about it. Just as Balthazar was ready to walk off without another word, Redgrave continued: "What if I told you there was a way to escape all the ties that bind you?"

To escape being a son? A brother? A citizen of Massachusetts Bay Colony? "Impossible."

"Very possible." Redgrave leaned closer, so close that Balthazar felt uneasier than before. "What would you be willing to do if it meant you could be with the woman you love?"

Balthazar considered the answer carefully before answering, "Anything but your bidding."

Redgrave didn't like that. The angry flash in his eyes threatened to shake his composure for the first time, and Balthazar felt a small thrill of triumph. How good it felt to deny this man his arrogance.

But Redgrave said only, "We'll see what you'll do. And I tell you now, Balthazar—you may be surprised."

Ropes around his wrists, blood trickling down his arms, Balthazar gasping helplessly as he looked at the knots holding him to the beam overhead as Redgrave whispered in his ear, "Are you ready to do my bidding yet?"

No, Balthazar thought, but already the world was slipping away.

Chapter Twelve

"HEY." SKYE SHOOK BALTHAZAR BY THE SHOUL-
ders as her mood shifted from merely concerned to deeply
freaked out. His eyes were all but shut, his face still, and he
swayed on his feet like a man in a trance. "Hey, come back.
Come back. *Balthazar!*"

She slapped her hand across his face, hard, and instantly his
fingers clamped around her wrist. His eyes opened wide, but it
still took him a moment to speak. "Skye."

"Yes. It's me. Where did you go?"

Balthazar slumped back, so unsteady that she wondered if he
was dizzy or ill. Was her blood some kind of poison? Skye braced
his shoulders in her hands, and that seemed to rouse him. Halt-
ingly, he said, "It was as if—it was like I was reliving my own past."

"Just memories?" Skye frowned; she didn't know what she
had been expecting, but not that.

"Not just memories. It's as if I'm really there. Every sensation, every sound—they're all perfect." As he spoke, he smiled,

but uncertainly, as if he were saying words he didn't dare believe. "And not just any memories, either. Skye, your blood takes vampires back to when they were alive."

She wasn't seeing any difference here. Why would vampires be mad to kill her merely to do the equivalent of looking through old photos? "So—just memories."

"You don't understand." Balthazar shook his head, impatient but not unkind. He took her arms from his shoulders and held her hands in his—only a gesture, she thought, but the touch still made this cold, sterile room feel as if it glowed with warmth. "Life has power, Skye. It has a . . . grace, and beauty, and vitality that nothing after death can match. Despite all our abilities and immortality, every single vampire longs, down deep, to feel the experience of life again. Some of us deny it, but each of us knows it. Life is irreplaceable."

"Except they can replace it through me." The impact finally sank in, and Skye felt a little dizzy. "Or are there other ways?"

"Your blood is the only thing I've ever heard of that would allow a vampire to truly feel alive again without surrendering our powers."

"Which means they want my blood really, really badly."

"Yeah." Balthazar breathed out, half elation, half frustration. "Skye, your blood is like a drug for us. The ultimate high."

"That's not good." Skye wrested her hands free from Balthazar's and began pacing the nurse's station; though she still felt shaken from the tumult earlier in the evening, she couldn't let the tension boil inside her. She needed to walk it out. "Is there anyplace in the world vampires don't go? Anyplace I can go?"

Grimly, Balthazar shook his head. "There aren't that many of us, but we're spread out. Besides, if Redgrave knows what you really are—and he does—he'll chase you as far as he has to. Even to the ends of the earth." He spoke as though from experience.

She put her hands against the wall, as if she could push her way through to escape. Only hours ago, Redgrave had stood by her side, polite and patient, while she composed a poem. "He said—he said he wouldn't kill me. Because they need my blood. So they won't murder me, won't even try—"

"That's not good news." He stepped closer to her, more fully present than he'd been since drinking that sip of her blood, every word urgent. "You have to trust me on this—there are fates worse than death. I've suffered some of them." Balthazar's broad hand closed around her shoulder. "You don't want to know what Redgrave would do to you, body and soul, to keep you captive."

Skye wanted to scream. She wanted to hit someone, but what was the point? That fury and fear had no place to go.

"Home," she whispered. "I want to go home." It was the only place Redgrave wouldn't come for her, she knew, but that wasn't as important as climbing into her own bed, pulling the covers tight, and hiding from the whole world.

From the way Balthazar squeezed her arm, she thought he understood. "Come on. Let's get you home."

As it turned out, escorting a sick student home was just the kind of thing teachers were on basketball duty for, and Coach

Haladki waved Balthazar off without even needing much of an explanation. Within ten minutes, they were sitting together on the crosstown bus, in the very back; the only other passenger was a man dozing in the front near the driver. Though there were lights within the bus, they weren't bright, and the road outside wasn't well lit or heavily traveled at this hour. Skye felt as if they were in a tiny shell of illumination and warmth, surrounded on all sides by endless cold and night.

Balthazar kept his arm around her shoulders, bracing her. Though his body didn't warm her the way another human's would have, the contact kept her own warmth close; it was like being wrapped in a blanket.

"I'll have to get a car," he said. "We can't rely on this."

"You don't have one?"

"I haven't owned one in a while. The past few years, I didn't bother; I was living at Evernight, so I couldn't have kept a car with me anyway. Time to remedy that."

"I should've bought one last summer. I'd saved up the money." All that lifeguarding at the pool. She'd earned enough for a clunker. "But I couldn't take it to Evernight, and Mom and Dad said they'd chip in so I could get something nicer if I waited until I was headed to college. I'll start looking for one right away."

"Not sure there's much point. Driving alone isn't that much safer for you than walking. But we'll think of something. Maybe you can work out a way to get a ride from Madison or some other friend."

Skye's phone chimed; she was so on edge that even that familiar sound made her jump. She lifted it to see a message from Clem: *Plz tell me ur quiet b/c ur making out with Balty.*

Hastily she sent back: *Will you SHUT IT b/c he's RIGHT HERE and he can read?!* Skye glanced over at Balthazar, who was paying no attention to her texts. Instead, he stared out the window into the darkness. She would've thought he was keeping watch if not for the deep sadness in his eyes.

Clem texted back: *Sorry!*

It's OK. Listen, lots of stuff is going on here. Crazy stuff. Will email 2nite or 2morrow and catch you up. Already Skye knew she needed a friend who could really talk to her about all of this; Madison might be fun to hang out with, but she didn't understand anything about vampires or ghosts, this entire vast supernatural world that hid within the cracks of everything else they'd ever known. Clementine, on the other hand, not only went to Evernight Academy but also grew up with a haunted car. She'd get it.

As she slid her phone back into her pack, she stole another glance at Balthazar. If anything, he was even more absorbed in thought than before. The motion of the bus rocked them back and forth in one rhythm. She said, "Are you okay?"

"I should really be asking you that question."

Her throat still hurt, but it was a dull ache now, like the sensation of trying not to cry. "I'm scared. That's all."

"That's enough."

"Definitely. But—something else is going on with you."

It was prying, and she knew it, but Balthazar obviously wasn't the type to talk easily about his feelings. If she wanted to know more, prying was clearly in order.

Balthazar didn't seem to mind, but he thought his answer over for a long time. "Those memories—of being alive—they're the best memories I have. And the worst memories I have. Living through that again brings a lot back."

"What did you remember?"

A small smile crossed his face. "My first kiss."

"Really?" That didn't sound so sad, Skye thought, until she realized how long ago it might've been. "When was that?"

"1640."

Skye tried very hard not to let her shock show; she'd guessed he was old, but somehow hearing him say it jolted her regardless. She said only, "Where?"

"Massachusetts Bay Colony. Just outside Boston."

It was such a simple answer, and yet she knew from the way he said it that Balthazar told very few people about his past. She wanted to hear more, but didn't want to push—to abuse the trust he was showing her. So she said only, "What happened?"

Balthazar shook his head. "One thing you can always be sure of—any vampire's life story has an unhappy ending."

Instinctively, Skye leaned her head against his shoulder— offering comfort and seeking it, all at once. Even as she did so, she thought, *This is too much. I shouldn't hang on him. Probably he isn't feeling what I'm feeling right now.*

But before she could pull away, Balthazar's arm tightened

around her, and his head rested against hers. Skye closed her eyes. She didn't know why she felt less lost now that she knew he was lost, too. Yet she did.

Balthazar walked her inside, all the way to her bedroom. As she wearily set down her pack, he went to the window and stared out into the darkness. "I don't think they're around tonight. Bianca's wraith show did the trick."

"That's something, anyway." She walked toward him, rubbing her sore neck. "Maybe I'll actually get some sleep tonight. But I doubt it."

"I could stay, if you wanted." Balthazar looked back at her, his fighter's frame outlined by the darkness.

"Stay tonight? In my room?"

"Yeah—oh. Or downstairs. Around. So you'd feel safer."

"I don't know."

Skye wanted him to stay as badly as she'd ever wanted anything. But right now it felt like she might do reckless things, without thinking, only to escape the fear beating within her like a second pulse.

"Are you okay?" Balthazar said. Only then did she realize she'd begun trembling again. She didn't know if that was from fright, tension, exhaustion, desire—all of them together—just that there was only so much she could take in a couple of days, and she'd taken it.

She reached out blindly with one hand, and Balthazar's arms went around her, enveloping her in his embrace. Skye didn't cry, didn't speak. Instead she gripped the lapels of his coat as she buried her face in the curve of his neck. He held her tightly as she breathed in and out, steady and slow, calming herself.

"We're going to get through this." He spoke as if they were truly in it together, as if she weren't the hunted and he the protector. "I'm not going to let them hurt you. Not ever."

Skye couldn't say anything. She pulled back to look at Balthazar, at the strong lines of his face so close to hers. The moonlight off the snow had painted him silver. Without hesitating, without thinking, she tilted her face up and kissed him.

It was the softest touch, only for an instant. Balthazar didn't move. The reality of what she'd done rushed over Skye, and she might have stepped away or even apologized—if Balthazar hadn't kissed her back.

This time she wound her arms around his neck, closed her eyes, and let the world fall away. His mouth was hard against hers, the kiss fierce enough to electrify. It was only a few seconds, but it felt like she'd escaped all the danger and fear forever.

When they broke apart, though, Balthazar took her arms from around his neck, shaking his head. "I shouldn't have done that. I'm sorry."

"Why not?" Skye gave him a look. "Because you don't like me that way?"

"What? No. That isn't—no." One of his hands stroked through her hair, a brief, simple caress. "It's just . . . I made a rule centuries ago, Skye. No getting involved with humans. It's dangerous for them, more than you can possibly realize."

"I'm already in danger," she pointed out, but she stepped away from him anyway. Although logically she thought she ought to have felt rejected, she didn't. Balthazar's eyes never left her face; his body remained taut from the tension of their brief kiss. And that kiss—

No, he wasn't rejecting her. He wanted her. He just wouldn't let himself have her.

Skye said, "You should go, I think."

"Yeah." Balthazar had obviously been expecting her to ask him to stay, or to try to kiss him again. Had he been hoping for that? Hoping she'd give him an excuse to give in? "I'll keep watch outside for a while, though. Make sure you're safe. So you can sleep."

She smiled at him crookedly. "Thanks."

Balthazar hesitated, clearly wanting to say something else. For a long moment they stared into each other's eyes, yearning to keep the connection. Then he was gone—not like a normal person, but vampire fast, as if he had flickered into shadow instead of walking out. She gasped, both from shock and from the pain of that sudden parting.

Every limb heavy with exhaustion, her brain fuzzy with sudden desire, Skye dressed for bed. Just before she put out the last light, though, she stood at the window for a moment, knowing the illumination from her lamp would outline her to anybody watching from below.

Tonight she knew Redgrave wasn't watching. Balthazar was.

"Good night," she whispered, before turning out the light.

Chapter Thirteen

BALTHAZAR PACED THE LENGTH OF HIS BARE carriage house; the sheets were rumpled from his brief, futile attempt to get some sleep. The early morning sunlight filtering through the curtains seemed to fall on his mistakes, making them clearer, and therefore worse.

No humans. It's a simple rule. How could you forget it?

His mind's reply didn't take the form of words; instead, he remembered Skye's face last night—drawn and pale, and yet trying so hard to be brave that his defenses had crumbled. The way she'd leaned against him on the bus, glowing with warmth like the last ember of a fire. The feel of her mouth against his.

Frustrated, Balthazar tried to push the memories away. Skye was a beautiful girl. He enjoyed spending time with her. He knew he was already committed to keeping her safe from Redgrave and his tribe. That was all there could ever be to it, though. Going any further than one impulsive, mistaken kiss would be unfair to her in the end.

But it had been so long since anyone good and decent had wanted him that way—and her silhouette against the window last night, looking for him in the darkness—

No humans.

As he got ready for the day, slicking back his hair and dressing as tweedy-preppy-conservative as he could manage with his wardrobe, Balthazar thought again of how fragile Skye had been the night before. Being pushed away after a kiss like that: That couldn't have helped her state of mind. How could he have gotten so carried away, been so selfish, as to pile one more thing onto the burdens she already had to bear?

He shrugged on his blazer and looked at himself in the mirror; his reflection was crisp and bright, no doubt thanks to the sip of Skye's blood he'd drunk the night before. Even in small doses, living human blood gave vampires a kind of vitality nothing else could. Not that he deserved it.

"You bastard," he said to the man in the mirror.

A knock on the door startled him. His first thought was Skye, but he hadn't told her exactly where he was staying yet. To find him here, somebody would have had to be following him.

Balthazar tensed. He walked to his small kitchen and looked in the knife drawer; nothing in there was larger than a ten-inch carving knife, but the blade seemed sturdy. It would do. Palming the handle so that the knife lay flat against one arm, he put one hand on the doorknob, took a deep breath, and opened it—

—to see Madison Findley on his doorstop, a coffeemaker in her hands.

"Madison!" He put his hands behind his back, the better to conceal the knife. "Good morning."

"Sorry to intrude, Mr. More." Madison didn't look sorry; her eyes darted around the bit of his carriage house she could see, the gesture of the perpetually nosy. "My dad remembered last night that the coffeepot in here broke and we hadn't gotten around to putting in the replacement." She hoisted the coffeemaker a little higher in her arms. "Meet the replacement."

"Oh, thanks. Some caffeine would be good around now." Balthazar didn't respond much to caffeine; he just needed something to joke about, so he could laugh to cover the sound of his sliding the knife onto his table.

"They said you took Skye home last night. Is she okay?"

"Fine, I think. It can get hot in the gym, and just after you come in from the cold—you know." Which made no sense, but hopefully Madison would skip over it. "Just dropped her off at the house. She should be in class this morning."

"That's good. Hey, want me to set this up for you?"

She'd taken one step inside before Balthazar's hands were free to collect the coffeemaker from her. "That's okay, Madison. I've got it. But seriously, thanks for bringing it by."

"Well, okay." Madison hesitated a moment before stepping back out again. "See you in class!"

"Don't be late!" he called cheerfully as he shut the door. That was a teacherish sort of thing to say, right? At that moment he was too relieved to worry about it much.

It never occurred to him to wonder whether Redgrave and

the others would really have knocked on the door if they'd come intending to do violence.

He suspected they wouldn't knock on his door the night they came to kill him.

Balthazar walked into his first class just before the bell, so all the students were in their seats. Though he gave the room a glance he hoped was professional, his eyes searched for Skye first of all—

—and found her. Instead of looking crushed by last night's events, as he'd feared she would, she gazed back at him evenly. Serene, almost. As if she didn't have a care in the world. And she'd dressed accordingly.

That skirt . . . that cannot possibly pass the dress code.

Skye's outfit wasn't outrageous; her sweater was slightly oversized, even, and the colors were all blacks and dark grays and plum-colored tights. But he could see a whole lot of the tights, almost all the way up her thighs, because that skirt . . .

Drooling over one of the students in front of the rest of the class is definitely not professional, he told himself, pulling it together as best he could. "Good morning, everybody. We'll be diving into chapter one today—though I haven't had much time to review, I'm afraid. Had to catch the game last night."

"Where the Weatherman kicked their butts!" somebody said, and most everyone started cheering and clapping. A few people patted the shoulders of a tall, handsome kid in the front row, who hung his head in not entirely false modesty. Balthazar glanced at the seating chart to see that this was WEATHERS, CRAIG . . . Skye's ex, he realized. Not that he should care one way or the other.

"Okay, everyone, settle down." That was definitely a teacherish thing to say. "Basketball is over, and Colonial History Honors Seminar has begun. Let's see, what do we have here, chapter one is . . . freedom of religion?"

"It's, like, about the Pilgrims?" said a cute Asian girl seated directly beside Craig. "And how they came to America so they could create freedom of religion for everybody?"

"Well, that's not true," Balthazar said. "Seriously, does it say that?"

Everyone in the class seemed to be glancing around at one another—except Skye, who was now hiding a smile behind her hand. Madison Findley piped up: "Yeah, it does. I mean, that was the whole point, right?"

"No. That was—as far from the whole point as it gets." He started flipping through that first chapter, which had been written by someone with more patriotism than common sense. "This is wrong. And that's not—Good God, it's *all* wrong. Completely and totally wrong."

The Asian girl (whom the seating chart called FONG, BRITNEE) said, "Then why did they come?"

"The reason the Godly—wait, let me back up. The Puritans didn't call themselves Puritans; that was a nickname given to them by people who disliked them—in other words, everyone who wasn't a Puritan." Though he'd fallen into the trap of using it himself, in the centuries since: The present always exercised a kind of tyranny over the past, all-knowing, invariably right. "The reason nobody liked them was because they were convinced they knew the only true way to God, the only true way for people to live. They didn't come to the New World to create freedom of religion; they came to create the kingdom of God on earth. They could worship as they chose, but anybody else who came to that territory—or, in the case of the Native Americans, anybody who lived there already—was going to have to worship in the same way. Even other Christians weren't welcome. Roman Catholics in particular."

Some of the students had started to smile, but in a good way, as if they were actually sort of interested against their will. Balthazar decided to go with it. He shut the idiotic book and just went to the board. If the best way to handle this class was to talk about what he already knew, fine.

"The Puritans called themselves the Godly," he said, jotting it on the board. All around him, students started taking notes. Skye looked down last, though. Their eyes locked for an instant, long enough for Balthazar to realize how good it felt to know at least one person understood that he was telling his own truth.

By the study hall at the end of the day, Balthazar was feeling pretty good about the whole teacher thing—at least until Skye walked into the library, and how could that skirt possibly have become shorter since homeroom? It had to have. There was no way she could've walked around like that for hours without being spoken to. Or possibly arrested.

Balthazar realized that was partly the old-fashioned side of him talking—her skirt was short but not indecent. The obscenity of it wasn't the length of the hemline; it was the thoughts that hemline inspired in him.

Skye texted him first: *I'm going straight home after school. Madison asked me over, but I told her I still feel weird. You didn't tell me you were living over there!*

Haven't had much chance. Listen, are you okay?

Yeah. The vision in Ms. Loos's class today was intense, but since I fainted yesterday at the game, she was actually nice about it for a change. I think everybody thinks I'm epileptic or something. I should be transferred out of there by the end of the week, though.

Balthazar raised an eyebrow at the realization that Tonia had been giving Skye a difficult time, but that was hardly the most important subject for them to discuss. *I just need to say—I'm sorry. About last night.*

For what?

For going further than I should've gone.

I was hoping you were going to say, for leaving too soon.

The idea of lingering longer in Skye's bedroom flickered in his mind, invitingly, but Balthazar pushed it away. *I think you're amazing. You know that. But I meant what I said. Getting involved with humans—it's a line I don't cross.*

There's a first time for everything.

He glanced up from his phone to look at her the precise moment she did the same. As their eyes met across the library,

Skye recrossed her legs, giving him another glimpse of just how long and slim and toned they were.

A bold move—but her eyes told the true story. There he could see her uncertainty, her vulnerability. Whatever it was, that mixture of flirtation and fragility struck deep within him.

Balthazar's response was as much a reminder to himself as to Skye: *We can't be anything more than friends.*

I hear you, Skye sent back, which seemed surprisingly reasonable—until the next line arrived. *But nobody said I had to make it easy for you.*

He should have been exasperated. Concerned. Something like that.

Instead, it was all he could do to keep from smiling.

Madison walked as far as Skye's house with her, so Balthazar followed them at a distance. It was easier watching Skye when she was wearing a long puffer coat that hid those legs. Yet as they wound their way through to her house, Balthazar began to sense it—that faint energy in the air, thick and ominous, like the coming of a storm.

A vampire was near.

Balthazar moved a little faster; better to be seen following Skye than to leave her exposed. Yet the vampire didn't close in, didn't give chase. The presence lingered until a few moments after Skye and Madison had gone inside.

That was when he heard Redgrave's voice: "It doesn't bother you?"

"A lot of things are bothering me right now." Balthazar resolved to get a meat cleaver or something to keep on hand. Anything that would equip him for an impromptu beheading. "Which one are you referring to? The fact that you're stalking one of my friends?"

"'Friend.' How courtly of you." Redgrave appeared from the underbrush, his elegant clothes still perfect. That camel-colored coat probably cost thousands of dollars; the crocodile leather shoes shone as if the slush and ice couldn't touch them. His maddening ability to remain polished, no matter what, was just one of the things Balthazar loathed about him. "I mean, the fact that the young lady has a haunted house. The wraiths are no greater friends to you than they are to us. How have you conquered your fear? Or tell me, Balthazar—have you conquered the wraiths?"

That was uncertainty in Redgrave's voice—the only uncertainty Balthazar had ever heard from him. The ancient terror of the wraiths among vampires was especially strong in Redgrave's, for reasons Balthazar had never been allowed to know; perhaps, two thousand years ago when Redgrave had still been new, still calling himself by the name his mother had given him, violence between the twin forms of the undead had been more common. At any rate, his fear of the supposed haunting within Skye's house was very real . . . which meant Skye remained safe when at home.

Small as this victory was, Balthazar had learned to cherish any win against his oldest and worst enemy. "Let's just say I have friends in the strangest places."

They faced each other then, without weapons, without other vampires. Balthazar tried to remember what it had been like before Redgrave. For the centuries since his death, Redgrave's shadow had stretched across Balthazar's years, drawing away the light.

Redgrave said, "Teaching school. How droll. And dull, I'd think."

"You're not going to hurt Skye."

"Skye." His voice caressed the word in a way that made Balthazar's gut clench. He'd been fool enough to give Redgrave her name. "I don't intend to hurt Skye. Didn't she tell you about our chat?"

"She did. And your definition of *hurt* and mine are a long way apart."

"Have you drunk from her yet?" Redgrave's eyes grew hungry, as if he wanted to live vicariously through Balthazar. "She'd let you, of course. It's written all over her." He took a deep breath, as if scenting the air, then sighed. "You *have*."

"I tasted her blood to see what it is you're after."

"And now you know what she's really worth."

"I know that better than you ever could." Balthazar decided to try to talk some sense into Redgrave; selfish and corrupt as he was, he was usually logical. "Those memories are tempting. Too tempting. They make the existence we have now seem—pale and meaningless. If you drink Skye's blood, if you try to make a habit of it, you'll turn yourself into an addict. Nothing more than that. You'll only keep trying to escape into the past more and more until you've lost yourself completely. Is that really what you want?"

"You never understood the power of giving in to pleasure, did you? The Puritan in you never did entirely die." Redgrave seemed to mull it over, genuinely weighing Balthazar's words, but as if trying to decide how they could best be twisted for his amusement. "I could of course take her only out of spite."

"What reason could you have to spite a girl who's never done anything to you?"

"Not her, Balthazar. To spite you. To take her from you the same way I took Charity, and your precious—ah, what was her name? Yes. Jane." Hearing that monster speak her name sickened Balthazar, and he wished again for a blade. Redgrave continued, "Someday you'll understand: There's nothing and no one you can love that I can't destroy."

"I don't love Skye," Balthazar said.

Redgrave laughed, and then he disappeared—melting into the shadows almost instantly, leaving Balthazar standing there alone.

His words seemed to hang in the air: *I don't love Skye.*

He wanted them to be a lie, for her protection even more than for his.

I don't. I couldn't.

And yet no matter how many times he said it, no matter how many ways he put it, it never sounded entirely true.

The Time Between:
Interlude Two

New York City
July 14, 1863

A BOTTLE SHATTERED AGAINST THE WALL JUST
beyond the window, sending shards of glass spraying against the
frame. Some of the people inside groaned, but Balthazar and
Richard shushed them. It was vitally important that they not
be heard.

Outside this warehouse, a violent riot was taking place—the
worst New York City had ever seen, or would ever see. Anger
over the severe Union losses in the Civil War had boiled over
into bloodshed unleashed upon African-Americans, whether
former slaves or free men of color. Some anti-war elements had
seized upon the idea that the war was being fought for blacks . . .
and that blacks should somehow be made to pay for all the thousands of young men dying even now on the fields of battle. The

great victory at Gettysburg had done nothing to encourage support for the war; all the rioters knew were that more men had been drafted, and so would be sent to die. They preferred to do their killing here, for no purpose, Balthazar supposed. For his part, he would rather have been a soldier with honor, but he no longer claimed to understand humanity.

Richard's dark face shone in the light of the one lantern he held. "They're powerful close."

"They're all around us. It doesn't mean anything." Balthazar hoped he was speaking the truth. If the rioters found this place—and the dozens of black families huddled inside—the repercussions would be deadly. And he would feel obligated to defend those hiding here, by any means necessary . . . no matter how unholy his means might be.

"Thought the rain last night might've cooled them off."

"No such luck." Already the summer heat beat down on the city, punishing and heavy with humidity, enough to drive the sanity out of more stable men than those gone savage outside.

This was Richard's mission, Richard's rescue; he was the one who had mobilized late last night after the first day's ugliness and had gathered the others together. That was the hard part. Balthazar knew he played only a very small role in this by offering a warehouse he owned as a hiding place. But if the rioters realized who hid here and broke through the door, his role would expand into violence. Only his full vampiric strength would allow him to fight off so many attackers. The people huddled in this warehouse would then realize that Balthazar was something other than human. The semblance of a normal life he had painstakingly carved out for himself here in Manhattan would shatter in an instant.

If that were to be the price of keeping these people alive, then Balthazar would pay it. But he would not pay it gladly. Whatever shadow of a life he had, he hoped to keep.

Richard whispered, "I don't like the sound of it out there."

"Me either." Balthazar didn't say what he'd *seen*, rather than heard: the two bodies hanging from a makeshift gallows, dying slowly, the ropes too short to allow for broken necks and merciful swift deaths. The sight of a suffocating man's feet kicking—that wasn't for sharing. "When it's quieter, I'll go out. See what's happening."

"Appreciated," Richard said. Their eyes met, sharing a glance of the darkest humor. To the fools outside, who looked no deeper than a person's skin, Richard was somehow suspect, and Balthazar—the murderer, the monster—would be trusted.

The warehouse had fortunately been all but empty of cargo; only a few barrels sat stacked in the corner. This left more room for the dozens of people—African-Americans, some escaped slaves but mostly free people whose ancestors had lived here for generations—to hide from the marauding hordes in the streets. They huddled together, some of them families with small children, desperately silent in contrast to the ugly yelling from outside. In the past day, more than one hundred people had died—far more, Balthazar suspected. Some of the slain had been the friends, neighbors, or family members of those who hid here now.

Balthazar took a deep breath as he realized, yet again, the fragility of human society. When you thought it was set, it shifted; when you thought it was safe, it changed. He'd spent most of the past century on his own, more or less—wandering for a couple of decades before realizing that the hustle and bustle of New York City was the best place to disguise his own unearthly nature. For the past thirty years, he'd made his home in lower Manhattan, shunting from neighborhood to neighborhood as needed to make sure that nobody noticed he didn't age. A handful of individuals had even gotten to know him; they'd all observed and commented on his peculiar habits, even Richard, who swore that Balthazar must live on air and sunshine like a flower, since nobody ever saw him eat. But in New York, it took more than that to count as "weird," and so he was accepted. Some of these people Balthazar would even dare to call friends, the first friends he'd had since his death.

He loved it here . . . or he had, before this violence beneath the surface had finally boiled over. Now Balthazar saw the ugliness beneath the chaos that had hidden him so well.

Richard whispered, "They're coming closer."

"Only a few." Balthazar's sharp vampire senses told him that the people walking closer to the door were no more than six or seven in number. He could take that many humans easily, as long as they were not Black Cross. And what would Black Cross be doing here now?

And yet when he lifted his face to sniff the air, he could scent nothing. The people approaching were oddly without smell, as if they were scrubbed without soap, or as if they were . . .

His eyes opened wide.

"Balthazar?" Richard whispered. "What's going on?"

"The people coming here—" *They're not people.* Balthazar wanted to say this but couldn't. "They're dangerous."

"Like I couldn't have guessed that for myself," Richard said. His dry humor normally amused Balthazar, but not today.

In the far distance came a roaring sound, as if some great firework had been set off, or something had exploded. God only knew what the rioters were doing to this city. But the rioters had already become second on Balthazar's list of concerns.

First were the people approaching this place, closer and closer. Something within him stirred, signaling to him: Other vampires were near.

Balthazar rolled up the sleeves of his loose cambric shirt and took the gas lamp in his hand. Resolutely he climbed the steps to the door, set his hand upon the iron lock, took a deep breath, and opened the door.

Outside was chaos. The street was all but deserted, but along the ground lay evidence of the day's mayhem: scattered debris, crumpled leaflets, an abandoned shoe, various bottles and trinkets and trash tossed aside by the fleeing. The twilight dark had begun to cast shadows, but not so deep as to obscure the group of people standing at the far end of the square. Balthazar had known, even before leaving the warehouse, that he would find vampires here.

But he had not expected to find Redgrave . . . or Charity.

They stood together, side by side. Behind them was Constantia, as beautiful and deadly as ever. Her dress was silk, deep red, the color of blood. Her dark eyes narrowed as she recognized him, and he could sense both anger and unwilling desire as they glimpsed each other—or was that only what he felt himself? Lorenzo, too, remained with the tribe; he was clothed in the latest fashions for men, plaid trousers and stovepipe hat, and he would have looked ridiculous but for the crazed, feral gleam in his eyes.

Worst was seeing Charity—even more broken—still by Redgrave's side. She wore one of the hoop-skirted dresses that were all the rage, lavender and ivory, all frills and lace except for the ragged, dirty hem and sleeves. His little sister's wide, dark eyes took him in, and he could see no joy, no relief. Even anger would have been something for him to cling to. Instead there was only mute, numb unknowing.

"The prodigal," Redgrave said, his smile white amid the dusky gloom. Not a speck of ash or dust marred the black sheen of his suit. "How we've missed you, dear boy."

"I haven't missed you," Balthazar replied, hating the false bravado in his voice but not knowing how else to answer. "Move along. Nobody wants you here."

"Nobody wants us anywhere." It was Constantia who answered him, her voice commanding in a way that sent chills coursing through him—some good, some bad. "That's why we go where *we* want."

Redgrave cocked his head. His profile might have been

carved of ivory, perfect and cold. "Shouldn't you be on the battlefields?"

"Shouldn't you?" Balthazar shot back.

"We have been, of course. This is a fine war for wounded. Minié balls shatter the bones so brutally, and yet leave the soldiers gasping there for hours. Delicious. Don't pretend you haven't sampled. We saw your tracks at Second Manassas, you know."

"Bull Run," Balthazar corrected, but bickering between Union and Confederate names for battles was a puny attempt at distraction. Yes, he'd drunk his fill of human blood during this war. It was a mercy, he told himself—and that was true, because the shattered, dying men he killed welcomed a swifter, less painful death. But he did not do it as an act of mercy. He drank because he wanted blood. When he had left the war to return to New York City last year, he had done so primarily because he was afraid of what he was becoming.

"Balthazar?" Charity whispered. "Is it really you?"

How the childlike sound of her voice broke him. Balthazar could hardly bear the sight of his little sister standing among her captors as soiled and ineffectual as a broken doll. "Yes. It's me. Come here, Charity."

"Go nowhere, Charity." Redgrave put his hand out to stop Charity, his palm resting against her abdomen in a gesture of indecent ownership. Charity stopped in place, her eyes meeting Redgrave's as if they knew nowhere else to turn. "Balthazar. Who is it you're hiding in there? Should we investigate?"

The chill that swept through Balthazar's bones nearly paralyzed him. His own fate—what did it matter, damned as he surely was? But the people inside this warehouse still owned their own lives and their own souls. They had to be protected . . . no matter the cost.

Balthazar swallowed hard. "Do you want me to come with you?" Every syllable was bitter in his mouth. "I will."

Charity's childlike face lit up. For a moment, he saw his wretched future—as Constantia's plaything, as Charity's companion and brother only in silence—and Balthazar forced himself to accept it. If that were the price of innocent lives, it would be paid.

"How good it would be to have you with us again." Redgrave stepped closer. The nearby gaslights made his aristocratic silhouette sharp despite the increasing darkness. His golden eyes glittered as he brought his black-gloved hand to Balthazar's chin and grasped it, turning his head from side to side as though he were inspecting a horse he hoped to buy. The leather was cool and soft against his skin. "But you turned on us once. What guarantee would we have that you wouldn't do so again?"

"You have a hostage," Balthazar said, his voice as low as a growl. "As you well know."

"But I'll never hurt little Charity. Not in any way she doesn't enjoy being hurt. She remains my favorite toy. So that doesn't work, you see?" Redgrave's hand dropped, and Balthazar sensed the increasing danger. "We can't trust you again, I fear. I know you won't hunt us, for baby sister's sake, but beyond that—no one could say what you might be capable of. Least of all your-self." That bloodless smile leered too close to Balthazar's face. "If you ever awoke to your full potential, you might be a creature to reckon with. But you're too busy grieving for what you lost. Too busy pitying the weak and wishing to be human."

In the distance, another great crashing sound echoed through the streets, as well as a fresh wave of screaming. Far-away firelight glowed orange behind the outlines of buildings. This heat, this riot, this horrible moment—they seemed as if they could never end.

Balthazar tried to catch Charity's eyes, hoping she might take this moment to turn against Redgrave—they weren't strong enough to beat him, not even together, but they might be able to get away if they worked in tandem. Instead she was playing with a strip of lace that had come loose from the sleeve of her dress, as thoughtless and unconcerned as a child.

Could he leave her here? Abandon her once again to Red-grave? Balthazar knew he had to, but it was no easier the second time.

Lorenzo strode forward, past Balthazar. "I say it's time we find out what's behind this door, don't you think, Redgrave?"

"No!" Balthazar shouted, but too late; Lorenzo had ripped the warehouse door from its hinges. The other vampires swarmed after him, and Balthazar ran inside, too—to see that the build-ing was empty, the back door still ajar.

Richard took his chance, Balthazar thought with a rush of relief. He'd spoken of hiding them in the nearby post office basement—too obvious, Balthazar had said. While he'd been arguing with Redgrave, Richard had silently herded the group into their new place. The uproar outside had muffled the sounds.

Redgrave breathed in deeply, nostrils flaring. "Many. Afraid—ah, deliciously afraid. Gone . . . but not far. Shall we follow?"

Balthazar was the first to reply, by slamming his fist into Redgrave's face.

It was only the second time he'd dared to attack his sire, and even with more than two hundred years' strength and experience, Balthazar knew he was still no match for Redgrave. But he could hold his own now. He could cause the bastard pain.

They fell to the plank floor, a loose nail head cutting into Balthazar's back even as he grabbed Redgrave by the ear and jaw and slammed him down alongside him. Redgrave shoved him so hard that Balthazar went skidding across the floor; splinters jabbed into the skin of his side, arm, and face as he slid. He hit the wall so hard that a couple of his ribs broke—they'd heal quickly, but that didn't make it hurt any less.

As Balthazar groaned, he heard Constantia call out gleefully, "This way! Come on!"

Redgrave grinned down at him, clearly understanding that murdering the people Balthazar had been helping to protect would be more hurtful to him than any further physical punishment. He was gone in an instant, the vampires leaping through the back door faster than Balthazar could get to his feet.

But he pushed himself upright and ran after them, ignoring

the blood trickling down his face and the stabbing pain in his side. They reached the door only a few seconds before he did, but long enough for them to pull it from its hinges—a great tearing sound of metal, a shriek that rang out over the bedlam surrounding them—and leap inside. Balthazar shouted out, a wordless cry of anger and helplessness, and hurtled inside after them . . .

. . . to face the cold.

"What the—" Balthazar's voice choked off as he realized the basement stairs on which they stood were far colder than could be explained by being inside or underground. It was more than the absence of the sweltering July heat; it was as cold as January, as though they had stepped inside an icebox.

And though no torches burned, and no lanterns were held aloft, the room glowed with an eerie blue incandescence.

Richard, like those he had brought with him, stared up in mingled worry, anger, and confusion. His eyes clearly asked the question, *What's happening?* Balthazar could not answer.

Then he glimpsed something he had always longed to see on Redgrave's face—pure fear. But it gave Balthazar no comfort, because he heard Constantia whisper, "*Wraiths.*"

Wraiths. Ghosts. The spirits of the slaughtered dead, lingering on earth because of their unfinished business—or so Redgrave had always said. He had spoken of wraiths with the deepest terror and loathing, swearing they were the sworn enemies of vampires, the only creatures on earth who found it easy to harm them, and steering them far clear of any building rumored to be haunted. Although wraiths occasionally terrorized human beings, they chose to manifest seldom—if at all—to mortals. However, the mere presence of a vampire could drive the wraiths to spectral phenomena as spectacular as they were dangerous. Constantia had once whispered to Balthazar, as their heads lay on one pillow, that the whole reason Redgrave had asked them to endure the voyage to the New World was because he thought a land so desolate would harbor fewer wraiths.

But the New World wasn't so new any longer, and as blue light burned brighter and nausea gripped Balthazar's gut, he knew that all Redgrave's fears had been justified.

The wraiths were the only creatures unholier than he was himself.

The pain lashed through him—through all of them—like being stabbed with a sword of ice. Balthazar crumpled along with the rest; they collapsed atop one another in a heap. Charity fell beside him, and for one moment their eyes met.

Still, two centuries later, she was more afraid of him than of Redgrave or the wraiths.

Wraith light swept down again, agonizing and swift. Redgrave somehow summoned the strength to lunge back up the steps and out the door the way he had come; his tribe followed, Charity among them. Although Balthazar tried to clutch at the hem of her skirt, pain had weakened his grip, and the fabric simply brushed his fingertips for a moment before she was gone.

Now the wraiths had only one vampire to torment—Balthazar himself—and the attacks grew more blinding, more terrible. His body twisted in response to the assault, fangs jutting from his jaw as if this were an attacker he could fend off. He could hear the screams of the people inside, horrified by what they were witnessing even if they didn't understand it. As Balthazar pushed himself toward the door, he looked up once to see Richard . . . and in his old friend's face was more revulsion than compassion.

Richard had never seen this—his monstrous true form. It could never be unseen. Although he could not have guessed the full truth, Richard must now realize that Balthazar was not human. One small refuge, one fragile friendship, was broken. With it went Balthazar's ties to the human world.

He pushed himself out onto the street, falling into a mud puddle. As Balthazar spat dank water from his mouth, he looked up to see that Redgrave, Charity, and the rest were gone; no doubt they'd fled this place as fast as they could.

As the fire-reddened sky overhead churned and faraway screams split the night, Balthazar thought, *They've left me here in hell.*

Chapter Fourteen

THE NEXT DAY, REDGRAVE DIDN'T COME. HE didn't approach Skye at school, didn't stalk her house, anything.

Or the next day.

Or the day after that.

During study hall on that third day, Skye texted Balthazar, *Did you actually scare Redgrave off? Or talk him out of it?*

I doubt it. I just can't believe it's going to be that easy.

Balthazar had told her about his altercation with Redgrave, and that he'd basically given him the equivalent of an antidrug speech. There was something else he hadn't told her about what Redgrave had said or done—she could sense Balthazar holding back about it. Regardless of what that might be, Skye didn't think one serious talking-to was going to be enough to save her.

She typed, *So what's he waiting for?*

I don't know. He can be patient, when he wants something. He knows how to bide his time.

That sent a shiver down her spine, and she sank back in her

library chair. This place seemed so ordinary, so cozy—like if anything as terrifying as Redgrave walked in here, he'd turn to dust or burst into flame, the way vampires in movies did when they walked into a sunbeam.

And yet he could appear at any minute.

"Who do you keep texting?" Madison said quietly, though not quietly enough; people at nearby tables—and Balthazar—would've been able to hear her.

"Shhhh! It's just—a friend of mine from my old school." Skye couldn't resist a small smile; after all, she was telling the absolute truth.

Somebody at a nearby table muttered, "In other words, a friend she thinks actually counts."

Madison flushed so deeply with anger that her freckles seemed to disappear. Skye snapped back at the other girl, "The only person in this room who doesn't count is you."

"Ahem." Balthazar rose from his desk and strolled toward them. How was it he could look that hot while wearing glasses and a blazer? But the glasses did something to his face—made his cheekbones look even more cut, maybe—and there was apparently no piece of clothing that couldn't be rendered hot by being draped over those shoulders. "Study hall is for studying, young ladies. Not for arguing. Let's keep it down, okay?"

Skye had to look away from him to keep from laughing. As he went back to his place, she quickly texted, *Young ladies?*

I'm trying to talk like a teacher! Too much?

You're hilarious. But I think they're buying it.

She stole a glance at him at the same moment he was stealing a glance at her. Though she would've thought that would make it harder to keep from laughing, it had a very different effect. As their eyes met, she remembered their two hungry kisses—the way it had felt to be held in his arms—and she knew, beyond a doubt, he was remembering that, too.

Quickly she looked away, turning back to her books, though calculus had never seemed less interesting. Madison whispered, "Is it just me or is he getting even better looking?"

"It's not just you." With determination, Skye kept her eyes on her calculus.

"Now I need to change panties."

"Madison!" Skye started giggling despite herself.

Her phone chimed again. *Let's keep it down, young lady.*

Which only made her laugh harder. But she kept it quiet.

As the days went on, and Redgrave didn't come, Skye and Balthazar began to fall into a pattern. He watched her get on the bus in the mornings, from a distance; they never saw each other then, never spoke, but she knew he was there to guard her if needed.

They saw each other for the first time each day in her homeroom, where he took her name and tried to act official . . . and, when she wore one of her skirts, tried very hard not to look at her legs. Skye supposed she could have worn jeans a little more often, if she wanted to make things easier on him; they were definitely warmer, which counted for something in upstate New York during January. But she didn't. All those years of riding had given her great legs—they were her best feature, she thought—and she liked the warmth that rushed through her every time she caught Balthazar stealing a peek.

History class was less fun, because Balthazar took history seriously. "So are we still going to use the textbook?" Madison asked one day as Balthazar handed out these enormous packets of photocopied material.

"No, we're not." Balthazar sounded extremely satisfied about that. "You won't need it until Mr. Lovejoy returns, and frankly, you'd be better off without it even then. For a genuine perspective on the colonial period, you need to go back to original sources."

Flipping through the packet, Skye saw that their materials were now old legal deeds and diaries and other documents from the colonial era. Not excerpts, not interpretations, not commentaries: just the original stuff. The rest of the class started to groan, and she was mostly grateful she had access to the ideal tutor.

"I know this doesn't look good," Balthazar said, though he remained cheerful. "But I'm here to help you as much as you need. If there's anything about this era—anything at all—ask me, and I'll explain." Britnee's hand shot up. "Already! Okay. What is it, Britnee?"

"Mr. More? I was wondering? Whenever you read old stuff like this, people's spelling is weird, and they use an *f* when they mean an *s*? And I don't get why that is? Did they actually say it differently back then?"

Balthazar could only stare at her, nonplussed, for a long second. Then he managed to say, "They didn't pronounce it differently. The spelling was just—a convention of the time. Which I admit doesn't make much sense, but there are things we do today that are just as strange." He took a deep breath. "Moving on!"

The rest of her school days were never as much fun, at least not until study hall. She finally got her transfer out of anatomy, because the risk of suffering the janitor's heart attack the same way she had the suicide victim's hanging was just too much to think about. The school filled her free hour by letting her work as an aide to Mr. Bollinger, who was super nice but didn't have a whole lot for her to do.

Sometimes Skye felt herself falling into a rut—going only the places she knew were safe—but with vampires after her, a routine seemed like a good thing. She'd deal with the impact her psychic visions would have on her life more when this crisis had passed.

Her routine involved capping off each day with study hall, normally the most boring hour in school. Now study hall was the good part. That was when she got to text Balthazar some more.

She braved Craig's basketball games when Balthazar had to supervise, though she never, ever cut under the bleachers. Usually she went with Madison and her group of friends, which meant they could sometimes sit near Balthazar and even talk and joke with him in the stands. Though Skye was careful never to speak to him directly when there were so many people around to see, sometimes it was nice just being close to him. Nicer to see how his gaze followed her while she joked around with Madison, Keith, Khadijah, and the rest of the gang.

Best of all, though, was when they were alone together.

"You're really good with Peppermint," Skye said, watching Balthazar riding beside her. While she was on Eb, he sat astride the mare from her stables, who was fairly old and fairly cranky. As a result, she wasn't ridden often—which meant she'd gotten a little fat. However, Balthazar handled her smoothly.

"I've always done best with mares. Not sure why." Balthazar patted the reddish shoulder of his horse; Peppermint responded with a whicker. "She's a steady girl."

"With you, she is." Maybe the old horse had never needed anything but kindness and patience. "The only other rider she was ever as good with was Dakota. He was gentle with her, like you."

For a moment she thought of Dakota as he had been one short year ago—riding ahead of her on Christmas break, coaxing stubborn Peppermint swiftly uphill, while she and Eb followed behind. The forest seemed to ring with their lost laughter.

"You don't speak about Dakota often," Balthazar said. His voice was even, inviting her to talk if she wanted to, but clearly not pushing the matter.

Skye knew she wanted to talk about Dakota, but it didn't feel like the right time. Then again, it never seemed to feel like the right time. Maybe she should take the chance. "He was—the brave one. The free one."

"You seem pretty brave to me."

"You didn't know Dakota." She realized then that Baltha-zar and Dakota would have liked each other. They weren't alike, exactly, but they would have gotten along. It was one more cruelty to her brother's early death—one more friend-ship and experience he'd been denied. Skye stared down at the reins in her hands. "He wasn't a rebel—Mom and Dad were never around enough to rebel against—but he did his own thing. Made up his mind about everything. I wanted to be as fearless as he was someday. But I always knew our parents needed me more. So I kept doing the safe thing, the right thing, for them."

"You sell yourself short," Balthazar said. His tone was so ten-der that Skye didn't dare look at him. "But your brother sounds like an amazing guy."

"He was." And then Skye banished the memory as quickly as it had come. "Let's ride."

They were on the high ridge about thirty minutes' ride from her house. After that first terrible attack, it had taken her awhile to go out on Eb again; even with Balthazar by her side, it seemed too scary. Mrs. Lefler rode Eb often enough to make sure he had adequate exercise, so it wasn't a necessity. But ultimately, she missed it too much. Letting Redgrave take that part of her life from her was too cruel.

Besides, the woods had their own stark beauty in winter— and Balthazar had proved to be an enthusiastic rider.

"Don't get me wrong," he said as they looked down on the valley, with the bare-branched trees silvered with frost. "I love cars. I bought my first one in 1912. But I miss horses, sometimes."

She appreciated his willingness to change the subject. "Did you ride a lot when you were—well, when you were alive?"

"Sometimes. Usually we used him to pull the wagon, though." Balthazar stared out at the horizon and the small bit of town visible from here, no more than a few houses and one church steeple. "But I had a horse purely for riding by the eighteenth century. Bucephalus. He looked like a wreck—bony no matter how much you fed him—but that horse could *run*."

"Why did you call him something crazy like Bucephalus?"

"That was the name of Alexander the Great's horse," he said, as if that were a logical reason. "Which was kind of a joke, based on how scruffy he looked, but how did you come up with Eb's name? It's unusual."

"Oh." This was embarrassing. "Well, I got him when I was twelve. And back then I thought it would be cool and romantic to call a horse . . . um . . . . Ebony Wind."

Balthazar didn't laugh. "Why not?"

"It sounds a little silly now. Besides, even within the first week or so, I was already calling him Eb."

"So you knew his name from the start."

Balthazar's smile made Skye feel as though something within her was melting, going deliciously liquid and soft. She could have leaned over to him—their horses were that close—could have kissed him, right then, and she *knew* if she did, he would respond.

But she didn't. The next time they kissed, Balthazar was going to have to be the one who made the move; Skye was determined on that point. Though it was hard to remain firm. Why did he have to possess so much willpower?

He said, "It's good of you to come to the basketball games, but you really don't have to. Even with me there, going home is safer for you."

"Also more boring for me."

"Yeah, but—I know it's tough for you." Balthazar shifted in his saddle, slightly awkward in the way he was when he thought he had to do something for someone's own good. "With Craig being there. Britnee, too."

Skye shrugged. The cold wind whipped past them, stinging her cheeks and making her tuck her scarf in more snugly around her neck. "It's not as hard seeing them together as it used to be. I mean, I'm still angry. But . . . I don't want to be with Craig anymore. I guess I've moved on."

"Ah." That was all Balthazar said, but Skye knew he was happy to hear it.

Because she believed that someday, probably soon, Redgrave would be back, Skye also used that time to learn how to defend herself.

She learned from the ideal teacher, of course.

"Okay, keep a wider stance." Balthazar wore ordinary street

clothes; Skye wore yoga pants and a camisole. They were in the basement of her house, an unused "family room," which was almost bare of furniture and thickly carpeted and thus ideal for use as a sparring ring. "A wider stance is a steadier stance."

Skye planted her feet farther apart. "Now what?"

"You want to protect your throat. Technically a vampire could bite you anywhere, but we tend to go for the throat—for the jugular or the carotid. It's a powerful instinct." Balthazar's eyes were locked on her bare neck, which Skye figured she should have found unnerving, but didn't. His black T-shirt fitted his broad chest and taut abdominal muscles like so much body paint.

"And how do I do that?" As Balthazar began lifting his hands, apparently in demonstration, Skye shook her head. "Don't show me. Make me do it. That's the only way I'm going to learn."

"You mean—"

"Yeah." Skye tossed her hair as she met his eyes. "Attack me. Don't hold back."

Faster than she could see, almost faster than she could think, Balthazar pounced on her, his body slamming against hers so hard that it took them both to the ground. Skye flung her arms up to block her throat in the instant before he brought his mouth to her neck.

For a long moment, they paused there, motionless. Balthazar's lips were only inches from her hands—his legs straddling hers, his enormous body blocking her on every side. "Good," he said, his voice low. "That's good."

"But not enough." Skye tried to keep her voice from shaking and her mind from wandering. This was vitally important. "If Redgrave did this to me, he wouldn't stop here. What would I do next? What are a vampire's—I don't know, vulnerable spots?"

Balthazar remained above her, his arms framing her shoulders. He never took his eyes from hers. "There are only two ways to kill a vampire," he said. "Fire or beheading. It's possible that a blade dipped in holy water might do it, but I'm not sure about that, so it's not worth risking your life to try."

Fire or beheading. Check. Horror-movie details swam in her mind again, and she had to ask: "What about a stake through the heart?"

"A stake can paralyze, but not kill. In a situation like this one, it's fine to settle for staking. You might have a chance to come back and burn or behead the vampire later; even if not, you'll definitely have a chance to get away. Anything wood will do, but it has to pierce the heart."

Skye nodded slowly. "What if we're—if I'm like this, and I can't grab something to use as a stake?"

"Then a vampire's vulnerable spots are the same as a human being's, more or less. The windpipe is useless—we only breathe from habit—but a blow there hurts. You can always try to go for the eyes." Balthazar then looked slightly sheepish. "With a guy vampire—well, strike at the obvious."

She jerked her knee up between his legs, stopping just short of hitting him someplace that would've hurt a human male a *lot*. "Like this?"

Eyes wide, he said, "You've got the idea."

The final element of her daily routine was the end of the day, when Balthazar left her. Although Skye knew he entirely trusted Redgrave's fear of the wraiths to protect her—and she trusted it in return—she sensed that he would have preferred to remain in her home to protect her. But, he said, they never knew when her parents would start spending more time at home, and they had to keep up the student/teacher facade.

My parents will start hanging out at home exactly never, Skye could have told him, but she knew that wasn't his real reason.

The reason he left every evening was the same reason she didn't want him to leave. Because if he lingered in her house late at night—in her room—the tension simmering between them would finally boil over.

As much as she wanted that, Skye knew it would only lead to heartbreak. If Balthazar kissed her only when he was carried away, he would eventually take it back. That had hurt too much last time; she was in no hurry to go there again.

No, the next time they kissed—she wanted it to be their choice. Their decision. Something neither of them would ever take back.

Not everyone agreed with this point of view.

"You sound better," Clementine said.

Skye stretched across her bed, propping her ankles up on the footboard as she adjusted her phone's headset. "Not being repeatedly attacked by vampires really helps your mood."

"Well, yeah. I still can't get over that. I mean, we were surrounded by vampires all the time at Evernight, and none of them ever tried to hurt us. Except that one time you and Courtney Briganti wore the same dress to the Autumn Ball."

"Do you think Courtney was a vampire?" After she thought that over for a second, Skye finished, "No, wait, of course she was."

Clem continued, "Anyway, as soon as we found out vampires were real—I don't know about you, but I figured they weren't all bad."

"Some of them aren't." Skye sighed heavily as she glanced at her most recent packet of history readings. "But some of them definitely are."

"Speaking of the ones who aren't—when I said you sounded better, I didn't just mean, you know, not freaking out all the time." By now Clem sounded almost smug; it was as if her satisfied smile could shine across the cellular connection. "I mean, you sound happy. Especially when you talk about Balthazar."

"Nothing else has happened."

"He kissed you!"

"Once. And I kissed him once. That's it."

"You need to jump his bones."

"Clementine!"

"You know you do!"

"No," Skye said, trying to sound more firm than she felt. "Chasing a guy like that only gets you hurt. Any guy who really cares about you should want to be with you. Once he knows how you feel, he should step up."

"And you feel like Balthazar's not stepping up?"

Skye pushed herself up onto her pillows, trying to think about how best to say what she really meant. "He looks out for me every single day. He's my protector. He's my friend. So it's not like he's treating me badly, you know? Nobody's ever treated me like this. Like I . . . mattered more than anything. Not since Craig when we first got together, and even then, it wasn't like the way Balthazar treats me."

". . . but . . ." Even that one word was enough to make Skye envision her friend's teasing face at that moment.

"But he won't make a move. I guess he has his reasons." Breathing out in frustration, Skye said, "I hate his reasons."

"I say jump him now and ask his reasons later."

Skye would have told Clem to shut up about jumping Balthazar if she hadn't been laughing too hard to get the words out.

She was still thinking about Clementine's advice the next Saturday, when she and Balthazar went riding again.

"The sky looks like snow." Balthazar stared out toward the horizon, where the clouds were a low, even, pale gray. "Good thing we're riding today. It'll be a week or two before we could take the horses out again."

"You've gotten to like this as much as I do." Skye could tell by the lift of his chin, the way a smile played on his face, just beneath the surface.

He patted Peppermint's neck. "You're right. Riding out here—it's reminded me of so many things. Moments I'd let myself get too far away from."

"You mean, memories of your life?" That short time was all the life he'd had . . . only one year more than her. Everything else, all the centuries in between—whatever they were, they weren't living.

"That's part of what I mean," Balthazar said. Then he hesitated, as he if he knew he shouldn't say any more.

Skye thought of everything else he might mean—what else he might have gotten too far away from in all those years alone, and the pleasure they took in riding together—and suddenly it was hard not to shyly look away.

But she didn't. She kept her eyes on Balthazar's face, and she could see the struggle inside him, though she couldn't tell whether he was fighting to speak or to stay silent. The cold wind picked up, whipping past so briskly that her cheeks stung and her ears felt numb. Skye would have remained there all day, though, if it meant that Balthazar might finally take a stand for her—

—until Eb suddenly reared back, dumping her off her saddle.

"Skye!" Balthazar reined in his horse, which was also shifting unevenly, then swiftly dismounted. "Are you okay?"

"Fine." She adjusted her helmet, more embarrassed than anything else. Though she'd landed hard on her butt, that was a pretty standard risk when riding horses. "Eb, what got into you? That's not like you."

Balthazar's hand cupped her elbow as he helped her up. "Take it easy," he said, looking down at her. Suddenly that one small touch didn't seem as simple, or as innocent. And that warm concern in his eyes—like she mattered more than anything—

"Your horse knows when you're in danger."

Skye and Balthazar turned together to see a figure approaching from the thick underbrush near them: Lorenzo. His eyes were unfocused, almost glazed. The rustling behind them told her he wasn't alone.

"Redgrave said—" She felt stupid relying on anything Redgrave had ever said, and yet— "He said you wouldn't come after me."

"I'm tired of what Redgrave says." Lorenzo took another step toward them, his eyes only on Skye. "Make me feel alive again."

Chapter Fifteen

THEY'VE REBELLED, BALTHAZAR THOUGHT. THE idea of anyone else rebelling against Redgrave shocked him—he'd done it, but so far as he knew he was the only one, ever—but that vanished as he saw Lorenzo's hunger.

In an instant, he was a hunter. Free to kill.

Balthazar leaped forward, straight for Lorenzo. But Lorenzo was equally as fast and far more prepared; he dodged so swiftly that he seemed to vanish. As Balthazar scrambled for balance on the icy ground, he shouted, "Skye! Get out of here!"

Just then Eb whinnied, and Balthazar saw he hadn't had to tell Skye what to do; she was already mounted again, working to control her uneasy horse. Just as Lorenzo clutched her arm, she drove her heels into the horse's side, and Eb took off at full gallop. Peppermint followed just behind. Which left him on his own, but he could defend himself.

Balthazar grabbed the closest weapon—a heavy, fallen tree branch—and swung it at Lorenzo as hard as he could. Lorenzo went down, but that would last only a moment, and the branch was too thick to be used as a stake. Worse, he could hear that the other vampires weren't joining their fight. They were pursuing Skye.

He jumped with all his strength, not toward Lorenzo but into the treetops. Once he was high enough to be above the fray, Balthazar moved forward, leaping from tree to tree, not knowing if Lorenzo was behind him and not caring. Skye was all that mattered.

Where is she? Please, let her be on her horse, let her have a chance—

Even in the heat of pursuit, Balthazar knew he shouldn't be this scared for Skye. That he ought to be thinking of keeping her secure, not held safe in his embrace. He'd been too captivated by her to sense the other vampires' approach—had that taught him nothing? No time to question himself now, no time to do anything but fight.

As he launched himself into a taller tree—some forty feet off the ground now—he finally saw her. Skye still clung to Eb's back, her horse's dark coat stark against the frosty ground. Though they raced at full gallop, the vampires were closing. How many were there—three? No, four, because Balthazar knew he hadn't delayed Lorenzo for long. He'd catch up soon.

The others he didn't know. That meant they were probably young, a hundred years old at the most. Younger vampires were weaker. Balthazar intended to use every one of his four centuries against them.

Balthazar jumped from the tree, letting himself plummet downward, a long streak of black against the gray sky, until he landed solidly in front of one of Skye's pursuers. The impact would've crushed a human's legs; Balthazar felt the pain of it but still stood. The vampire nearly skidded into him, off-balance, which made it even more effective when Balthazar smashed his fist into the vampire's face.

The vampire staggered back. Balthazar hit him again, aiming not for his nose but a place about four inches behind it, deep in the skull. At impact he heard the sound of crunching bone, felt the hot, wet smear of blood against his hand; the vampire went down solidly. For a human, the blow would have been fatal. For a vampire, it was a delay, no more. Balthazar grabbed a stick nearby—firm, not too thick—and stabbed it through the vampire's chest.

Instantly, the glow of knowledge faded from his eyes; the grimace of pain disappeared from his face. What lay before Balthazar now was a dead body, no more. He wouldn't awaken until someone removed the stake. Hopefully that wouldn't be before Balthazar could come back and cut off the worthless creature's head.

For one moment, Balthazar felt a grim satisfaction—but then he heard Skye scream.

He turned and ran as fast as he could toward her, so fast no earthly being would have been able to see much of him, but he knew he wasn't going to make it in time. Lorenzo had not only caught up, but he'd also managed to intercept Eb and pull Skye down to the ground, just on the riverbank. She was in the fighting stance he'd taught her, holding him at bay—but with three other vampires surrounding her, too, she'd only be able to buy herself seconds.

Balthazar pushed himself harder, desperate to reach her.

But somebody else made it there before him.

At first all Balthazar saw was a golden blur, but then Lorenzo was flung backward, bodily, until he slammed into a nearby tree and fell. The blur went still, took the form of Redgrave.

"How dare you?" Redgrave didn't sound as angry as he looked; his voice, as ever, was polite, almost cool. He might have been scolding Lorenzo for going out in the cold without his hat. "Were my instructions not clear?"

"You know what she is!" One of the vampires said, almost pleading.

"You know I intend her to be mine," Redgrave replied. "That should be enough for you. As it isn't—let's try a reminder."

Constantia appeared as if out of nowhere, her long, blond hair whipping around her, her gray coat swirling behind her like a cape, to clutch one of the other vampires around the throat. Her grip was so fierce that even at a distance Balthazar could hear the crunch of cartilage. Choking a vampire wouldn't kill, but he knew from experience that it could hurt like hell.

Skye had the sense to start running—away from Redgrave, away from all of them—over the next ridge. Eb must have gone that way, too. As much as Balthazar would've liked to use the melee to take a crack at Redgrave—hoped for a momentary distraction that would give him a chance to crush his sire's skull—he thought he'd see whether Redgrave's own tribe might take him out. That would make a nice change. He turned to the side, ready to dash after her, when he came face-to-face with another of Redgrave's loyalists and enforcers.

She stood a few feet from him, silent as a cat. Instead of the heavy coat even vampires would want in this bleak chill, she wore only a short-sleeved white dress that stopped far short of her knees. Her legs were bare; she wore high heels that might have glittered back before they were so dingy. Balthazar knew better than to assume she couldn't run in them. Her fair, curly hair hung loose, halfway down her back, and a few tendrils blew across her face. She'd washed it recently—rare, for her. Her eyes remained locked with his, as if she were as startled to see him as he was to see her.

He could manage nothing louder than a whisper: "Charity."

"Hello, dear brother." Charity smiled at him, guileless and sweet—for only one instant. Then her face twisted into a grimace. "Still saving everybody's life but *mine*."

Guilt and shock froze him only for a moment, but it was a moment too long. Charity swung something into his head; he hadn't even seen that she had something in her hand, but whatever it was, it was metal, heavy, and long. She swung again and again, stunning him further with each blow, and the more his head hurt, the harder it was to defend himself or even to think.

Once again she struck him, and he stumbled backward on ground that sloped sharply. Balthazar fell, rolling over and over, at first only grateful that for a moment Charity wasn't beating the hell out of him.

Then he realized that the only ground sloping sharply beneath him was the riverbank.

If there was one thing vampires hated more than trying to cross running water—it was being submerged *in* running water.

Balthazar grabbed desperately for something to hang on to, anything, but it was too late. He fell from the riverbank, fell through the air for one terrible moment, and then plunged into the ice-cold rapids.

He sank like a stone.

Chapter Sixteen

SKYE RAN AS HARD AS SHE COULD. HER SIDE cramped and each breath was cold and ragged in her lungs, but she kept pushing. Eb stood not far away, quivering with fright, but if she could calm him enough to ride, she could take advantage of whatever insane vampire battle was going on to get out of here.

But where was Balthazar? She'd seen him just seconds ago, before Redgrave appeared, but not since. They couldn't have hurt him, could they? Or would they have staked him, beheaded—

Her terror for Balthazar outweighed her fear for herself, and Skye turned to look for him. Within seconds, she sighted him—being beaten, brutally, by somebody who appeared to be a bedraggled middle-school girl but must have been another vampire. He fell backward onto the riverbank, sliding along the loose rocks and brush there, then tumbled into the water.

Could he swim? There was something about vampires and running water, something bad. Skye couldn't remember; she couldn't think straight with her heartbeat pounding and her whole body already aching. All she knew was that Balthazar wasn't able to save her. Instead, she'd have to save him.

Skye ran the rest of the way to Eb, who stood still but remained jittery. Even amid her panic, she knew she had to make sure he was steady to ride; the only way to make her situation worse would be to wind up thrown or trampled by a frightened animal that weighed half a ton. "C'mon, boy," she murmured as she ran her hands reassuringly along his side. "Good boy. You want to get out of here, don't you? Let's get out of here. Okay, Eb? That's my boy."

He seemed good—not great, but enough, she thought. Skye hooked her foot into the stirrup and got herself into the saddle. Eb stamped his feet a couple of times, but he remained steady. Grabbing the reins, she urged him forward so that they galloped downstream.

The tide pool, she thought. She and Dakota had played down there as children before their parents caught them at it and forbade it—after which they played down there only slightly less. They'd discovered that almost anything tossed into the river upstream (Frisbees, canteens, various Nerf sporting goods) eventually washed into the tide pool. If Balthazar couldn't swim, or was too dazed to do so, he'd probably wind up there. Certainly it would be her best chance to retrieve him.

But then she heard the sound of someone—multiple someones—crashing through the trees behind her, and knew Redgrave hadn't stopped all of her pursuers.

Skye spurred Eb harder, wishing she didn't have to do it, and maybe she didn't; her horse wanted out of there as badly as she did. As she steered Eb down the slope leading to the tide pool, Skye looked around desperately; almost right away, she saw what she'd sought. A tree nearby had lost a few branches during the last hard ice, and one hung amid the lower limbs, almost as thick around as her arm and twice as long. Skye tugged it free and clutched it close to her side, end out.

But then Lorenzo sprang out, running toward her at that blurry vampire speed. Almost without consciously deciding to do it, Skye drove Eb forward, toward Lorenzo rather than away, leaning forward with her makeshift weapon leading the way.

Maybe she'd meant to frighten the vampire; maybe she'd meant to knock him aside. Skye wasn't certain. She *didn't* mean for the branch to stab Lorenzo through the chest—but it did.

He just . . . fell. One moment he was an insane killer; the next he was a corpse, nothing more. The branch jerked out of her shaking arm as he tumbled limply to the ground.

For a moment she could only stare, and think, *I needed that!* But pulling the stake out was a bad idea; Balthazar said that would allow the vampire to awaken. Lorenzo was out of commission only as long as she left it in.

Skye wheeled Eb around, clucking reassuringly for him, to look for another branch. Her gaze swept across the tide pool, and she gasped as she saw something roll just beneath the surface—something that looked like a dead body—

Which is what Balthazar is, right now, and he's going to stay that way if you don't do something about it.

She dismounted and combed through the underbrush, looking for another branch; soon she found one less sturdy but perhaps long enough to work. Carefully she picked through the icy edges of the tide pool, her leather riding boots making only the slightest imprint in the frozen mud. As the ice cracked around her feet, she took a deep breath and leaned forward.

There, beneath the murky water, she could see Balthazar's face. His features were still, his eyes open. Though she'd never seen a drowning victim, she knew now what one looked like, and it sent a chill through her that had nothing to do with the bitter cold.

If he was conscious and could see her, he wasn't able to act or even to give her a sign. Skye leaned forward and reached out with the branch to snag the shoulder of his long coat; it wasn't nearly sturdy enough to drag him, but the tide pool's current kept the water roiling. Maybe just getting him to drift closer would be enough.

It worked, or well enough. Balthazar floated closer to the edge, lying flat just beneath the surface, like a male version of that *Ophelia* painting. Skye hesitated only a second before ripping off her leather gloves and thick coat; they'd do her more good later if they weren't wet.

Then she stooped down and plunged her hands through the thin ice, into the frigid water, to grab Balthazar.

But, oh, God, he was heavy. She hadn't realized how heavy dead weight could be—and even if Balthazar had been in any

shape to help her, he was at least six feet three and heavily mus-
cled. Did he weigh two hundred pounds? More? Skye knew she
had more upper-body strength than most women, thanks to her
many years handling saddles, but it took all her might to tow
him from the tide pool.

Even after she'd dragged him free of the water, Balthazar
didn't revive. Teeth chattering, Skye pulled her coat on over
her damp sweater and clumsily attempted to replace her gloves
for a moment before giving up. The other vampires were probably after them—unless Redgrave had stopped them, but that
would only mean that he was in pursuit instead. How was
she going to get out of here? Eb could carry them both, but
there was no way she could get Balthazar on the horse. With
her white, numb fingers, she shook his shoulder. "Balthazar.
Balthazar, wake up!"

"He won't be able to hear you for a while yet." Redgrave
strolled into the clearing near the tide pool, his slicked-back,
golden hair unmussed, and his usual carefree smile upon his
face. "Hours, I'd think. If he doesn't get blood soon—days.
And since our mutual friend prefers animal blood to human, I'd
count on days, if I were you."

Skye remained crouched by Balthazar's side. As badly as she
wanted to think Redgrave was lying, she knew he wasn't.

"You look as frightened as a fawn separated from its mother.
As fragile, too." He fixed her in his glittering hazel gaze, and she
understood how he might captivate—or hypnotize—someone
just with his eyes. Then he glanced over at Lorenzo, who still lay

crumpled on the ground with the branch jutting from his chest. "You're not, though, are you? Here, let me see to that."

While Redgrave bent over Lorenzo, Skye wondered if she could run, but it was impossible. Redgrave was faster, Eb was several feet away, and leaving Balthazar behind probably meant leaving him for Redgrave to shove back out into the river—or worse. No, she'd have to think fast. Could she bargain with him for her blood? But what was the point of bargaining with him for something he'd soon take by force? Soon he'd unstake Lorenzo, and the two of them would be after her at once, and there was nothing she could do about it.

Redgrave took something from his jacket—something that glinted silver in the pale winter sunlight—and swung down hard. Lorenzo's head lolled to one side . . . no, it was rolling, rolling free of his body.

Lorenzo, now beheaded and finally, utterly dead, decayed in an instant. His skin curled up and blackened like paper in fire; his flesh crumbled to dust, the bones following. What rolled to the river still looked a little like a skull when it sank through the slushy ice and vanished. Skye gagged.

"There, there. The worst is over. For now, I mean." Redgrave walked closer to her, his hands clasped behind his back. "You'll want help getting Balthazar on your horse, won't you?"

She remained motionless, staring up at him. Her voice cracked when she finally spoke. "You're just—letting him go."

"Letting both of you go. Unless, of course, you choose to stay with me. Which would be both charming and sensible of you." Redgrave's grin would have been blindingly handsome, but for the fangs.

"Why would you do that?" There had to be a catch.

Redgrave sighed as he stooped by her side. Their faces were once again close, and she felt the intensity of his presence. "I don't want to brutalize you, Skye. I want to convince you that joining me is the right thing for you to do. The only thing."

"I don't trust you."

"Balthazar's been poisoning your mind against me, hasn't he?" His fingers brushed through the damp curls of Balthazar's hair, almost fondly. The gesture reminded her of a father with his little boy. "He has his grudges. And his reasons, I suppose. But you must have learned by now that, when it comes to the world of vampires, good and evil can become rather . . . relative."

"You broke in my house!"

"To *talk*," Redgrave insisted. "You don't believe me, of course. Well, let's strike a deal. I'll help you hoist the formidable Mr. More onto the back of your horse and let you both depart, safe and sound. In his case, also frozen, but don't worry. He'll thaw."

Skye hesitated. "What do I owe you in return?"

"One conversation. You and I, with nobody else present— and that includes Balthazar. And instead of spending all your time talking about what a blackguard I am, you'll listen. Really listen." He leaned still closer, and two of his fingers curled around one tendril of her brown hair that had shaken free from the helmet. "Is that so unfair?"

There had to be more to it. She knew that. But what could she do?

"Hurry, Skye. You can't yet hear the others approaching, but I can. Perhaps it's Constantia and Charity, who are loyal to me and won't touch you without my permission—but perhaps it's not."

"Well—when do we have this talk? And where?" She was stalling now; it was obvious that he knew it.

Teasingly, he singsonged, "I will choose the time, and I will choose the place. And for once you'll be a good girl and hear me out. Are we agreed? Choose now, before I change my mind and my offer."

Skye swallowed hard. "Agreed. Now help me."

"Bossy little thing, aren't you?" But Redgrave scooped his arms around Balthazar and lifted him as easily as he could have done Skye herself. She went to Eb and took the reins, soothing him through the placement of the heavy, unfamiliar burden on his back. Balthazar lay unconscious, stomach down, behind her saddle before Redgrave stepped away. "Until we meet again, Skye, I'd like you to remember one thing."

Hands still on the reins, Skye said, "What's that?"

"You were in grave danger today, and it wasn't Balthazar who saved you."

Redgrave took one step back, and then seemed to melt into the underbrush—running away so quickly, so inhumanly fast, that his afterimage seemed to linger after he did. Skye didn't stay to find out who else might approach; she swung up into the saddle instantly, thinking only of Balthazar and home.

Peppermint had already found her way back to the stables and stood there outside the door, blinking sleepily.

"You saved your own butt pretty quickly, huh, fatso?" Skye said "fatso" as fondly as it was possible to; she'd been half convinced the old mare had been devoured by frustrated vampires and was grateful to see her. Peppermint had been Dakota's, after all. Skye wanted to keep something of his safe. Maybe she should nail a couple of crucifixes up in the stables.

She managed to haul Balthazar down well enough. He was beginning to regain consciousness. Though he couldn't speak, and still didn't seem to understand her, he tried to balance on his feet as she guided him to the nearby garden bench. As soon as she let go, he slumped back again, but she now knew she could get him upstairs.

Quickly Skye guided the horses into their stalls, grabbed her cell phone, and begged Mrs. Lefler to come over and see to them. Family emergency, she claimed. Fortunately, Mrs. Lefler didn't ask, just promised to be there within five minutes. Skye stroked Eb's nose in apology for leaving him wet even for that long, then went back to Balthazar.

Once his muscular arm was draped around her shoulders, she could guide him through the house. By now he had started to talk . . . sort of.

"Redgrave."

"That's right. He was in the woods." *He came after us*, she wanted to say, but that wasn't the truth, was it? And Skye couldn't bring herself to say, *he saved us*, even though that appeared to be the case. "Come on. We've got to warm you up."

She brought him to her room. Although her parents weren't expected back until after midnight, as usual, the one time they'd get home early probably would be when she had a semiconscious man laid out on the sofa. Once they were up there, Skye wasn't sure what to do until she glanced at the door of her bathroom. "Let's get you undressed."

"Wait." Balthazar pushed away her hands. "Shouldn't."

"I'm not *molesting* you. I'm putting you in a hot shower. You can't do it yourself." Skye tugged off his wet coat, then got to work unbuttoning his shirt. The damp fabric stuck to his skin. "I've seen a naked man before, you know. I'm not a virgin. My eyes aren't going to fall out in astonishment or anything."

Balthazar didn't argue any further, but as she got down to yank off his boots (cold river water dribbling out of them), she noticed that he clumsily saw to his own belt and jeans. But as he stripped them off—

Okay, she thought. *Deep breaths.* Yeah, she'd seen Craig naked, and Craig was a hot guy, but Balthazar was—like a statue, something else perfect—

Skye managed to tear her eyes away long enough to get the shower running. The water ran hot right away, clouds of steam billowing around her, and her red, raw hands stung at the mere presence of heat. Really, she needed a hot shower, too, but climbing in with a naked Balthazar—that would definitely undo her "no molestation" promise.

Balthazar stumbled into the bathroom, still so dazed that he hardly seemed to care that she was there to see him. Skye guided him in; he was still frighteningly weak. As water ran down him, like glass against his bare skin, she tried to keep her eyes averted while still hanging on to his arm so he could stand.

"Is it helping?" she cried, when she couldn't take the silence any longer.

"Don't—don't know." Balthazar's head leaned against the white tiles of her shower. He didn't seem any better than he had outside.

Her thumb brushed against something on his bicep, and Skye looked—she couldn't help it—to see a nicotine patch. His vulnerability moved her more than his beauty.

"Come on," she said. Leaving the water running, Skye guided him out of the shower; his skin was now warm, but the shock of being in the river still stupefied him. Carefully she walked him to her bed and tucked him in. The sheets and heavy quilt would dry his body.

While he lay there, stunned, she stripped off her own wet things and jumped into the shower. The hot water burned her only for a moment; then she breathed in the steamy air, feeling truly alive for the first time since the vampires had attacked.

It's okay, she told herself as she leaned her arms against the tile, water pounding onto her back. The bruises she'd earned with her fall already hurt; tomorrow she'd be black-and-blue. *You made it.*

Thanks to Redgrave, said another voice inside her, one she chose not to pay attention to.

Skye shut off the taps, toweled herself off, and walked back into the bedroom. Balthazar lay there, as motionless as he'd been when she first tugged him from the river. His eyes were shut, but she still walked into the closet to slip into her T-shirt and yoga pants. As she wriggled into her soft nightclothes, relishing the feeling of warmth in her body, Skye wondered what her next step should be. Redgrave had said it would take days for Balthazar to return to normal. Those were days that left her vulnerable, not to mention days her absentee parents might possibly glance into her room and notice the naked man there. Balthazar needed to be back in action as soon as possible. Preferably now.

By the time she walked back into her bedroom, towel-dried hair hanging around her face and soft cotton next to her skin, she knew what she had to do.

Skye pulled back the covers of her bed and slid in next to Balthazar. He turned toward her, still dazed, but instinctively seeking her. Slowly she wrapped her arms around him. He responded to the heat of their embrace, and one of his heavy hands curled around her slender rib cage, then found the small of her back. Despite the shower, his body felt cooler than her own, and she began to shake—partly from cold, partly from something else that was difficult to name.

As they curled closer to each other, Skye wound one of her legs around his. He rolled nearer, nestling his head against her chest. She wriggled so that his face nuzzled the curve of her neck.

With him lying half on top of her, responding to nothing

more than instinct, Skye whispered, "Drink."

Balthazar didn't bite her. But he didn't say no. He continued caressing her, moving in slow motion, as if he hardly understood what he was doing but knew he wanted to touch her. She hoped like hell there was an instinct to stop drinking that was just as powerful as the instinct to bite.

Skye arched herself against him, and Balthazar's hand tightened around her shoulder. He made a low growl deep in his throat, a purely animal sound that made her shiver. His lips brushed against her neck . . . not a kiss. A test.

"Drink from me," she said. How could he not feel her heart beating? It was about to pound out of her chest. Surely her pulse beat against his lips—surely he could hear it, because she could. "Bite down."

Balthazar clutched her close, fingers digging into her skin so hard it hurt, but Skye didn't cry out until his fangs sank into her throat.

Chapter Seventeen

AT FIRST IT ALL SEEMED TO BE HAPPENING AT once.

Balthazar was underwater, an experience as horrifying as death. The currents flowed around him, freezing him, confusing him, turning the entire world inside out and upside down.

Balthazar was in Skye's arms, her lithe body pressed against his, and he could sense nothing but the warmth of her flesh and the scent of blood just beneath the surface.

Balthazar was in the barn, Redgrave's trance holding him fast, listening to the screams from his house as his parents died.

"Drink," someone said. The need for blood filled him, the only need that his numb, blind body understood. His prey lay within his arms. Balthazar's fangs slid from his jaw, slicing open his tongue. The taste of his own blood did nothing. But human blood—living blood—that was different. Necessary.

Balthazar tried to reach the surface of the river, but he was too stunned to move. The water seemed like a cyclone around him, winding about his body and binding him like a shroud.

Balthazar tried to pull free of the ropes, but they bound his wrists too tightly, and the vampires laughed as they pulled it taut against the rafter and tugged his arms over his head so that his feet barely touched the ground. Only hours ago he'd had no idea that such creatures existed. Then the vampires were on him, their teeth tearing his flesh, and the world paled and chilled until he was surrounded by a whiteness darker than any black.

Balthazar tried to hold back, but Skye was so close, so beautiful, and the longing he'd rarely acknowledged was now his whole world.

The whisper came again. "Drink."

He stopped fighting it. Stopped remembering why he even wanted to fight. He rolled Skye over and bit down, feeling the hot rush of blood in his mouth. Then there was nothing but the pure animal pleasure of feeding.

Then there was nothing at all.

Massachusetts, 1640

IT WASN'T LIKE WAKING UP.

First all Balthazar felt was pain. His flesh had been torn open all along his neck, arms, torso, legs—everywhere. The ropes had long since cut through his wrists, and the weight of his body hanging from them had gone from agony to numbness and, now, back to agony again. There was an odd silence—a stillness within him, rather than without—that he didn't understand.

He didn't remember what had happened to him. He didn't

not remember. Instead he was in a place beyond memory or thought. Balthazar was nothing but pain—pain and something else—

—hunger.

"There he is." Redgrave's voice was smooth and soft again. "We thought you'd never join us. Constantia here was wondering if we'd have to dig you a grave."

Smooth, feminine arms wrapped around his waist. Balthazar managed to open his eyes and take in the scene. His familiar old barn was now smeared with gore. The tattered remnants of his shirt and jacket lay on the floor with the straw. Constantia clung to him the way Charity liked to carry around her dolls. "Isn't that better?" she said, smiling at him. "You'll see."

An image welled within his mind: his mother and father, drained of all blood, lying broken and dead upon the floor. He thought he remembered screaming when he saw that, but none of it seemed to matter any longer.

Balthazar tried to speak, but his throat was dry. "I'm— I'm hungry." Why wasn't he getting angry or fighting back or demanding to know where his sister was? Down deep, he knew all those things were more important, but he'd never been hungry like this. It was as if he'd never eaten, never in his life, and if he didn't have something right now, he'd die.

Only then did he realize what the stillness within him was: the lack of a heartbeat.

Redgrave seemed to know what he was thinking. He gave Balthazar a silky smile. "I apologize for the unpleasantness last evening. But your father's accusation made things rather difficult for me and for your sister, and it was obvious that you wouldn't be willing to assist us. And Constantia here was so fond of you."

Your father's accusation. Memories exploded inside Balthazar's head like gunpowder in a keg. Charity had kept slipping away, more and more often, and they had all thought it more of her silliness until two days before. Mama had found Charity and Redgrave on the riverbank, and though it seemed he'd done no more than steal a kiss, it was obvious that he meant more by it. Redgrave was not a man to content himself with a young girl's kiss.

Charity had sworn he used some black magic on her, made her submit to him though she didn't wish to, but even those who believed in black magic didn't believe her.

Papa had denounced Redgrave to the elders—there was talk of making him and Constantia leave town, rumors even that Constantia was not his sister, though they lived together—

—and then last night.

I want to explain myself and beg your pardon, Redgrave had said at the threshold of their house. Papa had slammed the door in his face.

Then they had burst through the door.

"They're dead," Balthazar said. He pulled at the ropes, pulled harder, desperate to be free, to kill Redgrave, and to eat. More than anything, he needed to eat.

"Your parents are indeed with us no more." Redgrave leaned against the wall of the barn, his arms folded in front of him. "Your sister is still breathing, though she's less pleased with her liberation than I would have expected. And she's all too reluctant to take the next step."

Balthazar pulled harder on the ropes, and they shredded. For the first time in what felt like months, he had his weight back on his feet where it belonged. Dust and splinters rained down on him as he lowered his aching arms. Constantia stepped back—not in dismay, though. Her expression was more amused than anything else.

Redgrave confided, "I really dislike forcing the issue. We did with you; it's made Constantia so happy. The things I do to please her. But Charity—her I meant to persuade. She's not easy to persuade."

Charity was alive. That was good. Balthazar took some encouragement from that, but it was hard to focus. He needed something to eat—or drink. Needed it desperately. He looked in the horse's troughs—he was hungry enough to eat oats, or straw—but no, that wasn't right. What did he need?

"So, we're going to play a little game," Redgrave said. Constantia hurried outside, like someone about to bring in a surprise. "Glutted as we were last night, both Constantia and I fed this morning. I tried to show Charity how easy it could all be, but it seemed to—traumatize her. Constantia paid her attentions to a visitor to your home, someone who was concerned because you hadn't been seen this morning. I should warn you: Constantia's the jealous type."

The barn door opened again, and Constantia pushed two girls into the barn so hard that they tumbled to the ground.

Their hands were bound, and both of them were disheveled, crying, and streaked with blood—

Blood.

The thought of it filled Balthazar's mind, a tide that turned his whole world red.

But—Charity. His little sister had never looked more like what the townspeople called her: a madwoman. Though tears streaked her face, her expression was vacant; she lifted her tied wrists so that she could tug at the ends of her curls, hard enough to hurt, though she never flinched. Her whole body shook.

Jane was steadier. Terror was in her eyes, but she righted herself into a sitting position and was obviously working hard to stay calm. On her cheek was a smear of blood. Balthazar imagined licking it off.

Then he could hear everything. The stamping and snuffling of the horse and the cow—the wind through the high grasses outside—and the beating of Charity's and Jane's hearts. The rushing of blood in their veins.

Blood. That was what he needed.

His jaw began to ache. Fangs slid through the flesh.

"You need something to eat," Constantia said. "So you can have one of them."

"Have?" Balthazar didn't understand.

Then he did.

He launched himself at Redgrave, shoving the man back against the wall and tearing at his face—only to be thrown back with such force that he slammed against one of the stable stalls and splintered it almost in half. Before Balthazar could even get to his feet again, Redgrave had grabbed him by the hair and punched him in the face, again, three times, until only his own blood (not enough blood) clogged his nose, ears, and eyes.

Seemingly at a great distance, Jane and Charity screamed and screamed. It made no difference.

Only when Balthazar was too weak to stand did Redgrave stop. "That was unpleasant, wasn't it?" He sounded unconcerned. "You're only one day old, boy. I've got centuries on you. If you fight me, you'll get more of the same. Except next time, I'll make you watch me beat them first."

"Balthazar, what's happening?" Jane said. Her eyes were red, her voice hoarse. "Who are these people? Are they demons?"

Charity rocked back and forth in her little crumpled heap on the floor. Before she had seemed shattered; now she seemed utterly disengaged. "Ring a round the rosy, a pocket full of posies—"

Redgrave stepped forward. "One of these girls will become a vampire—and you will be the one to do it. They've already been bitten; oh, trust me, I drank deep. That means they're prepared. All you have to do is drink her blood until she's dead."

"I won't—" The words froze in Balthazar's mouth. He could only think of the phrase *drink her blood*.

"Do you think your refusal will save their lives? It won't. But I want you to do it, Balthazar. I want to see the pleasure on your face as you make your first kill. And I relish the chance to make you choose which one to murder—your sister or your love?"

Jane tried to rise, but Constantia shoved her down again. Charity's voice was even softer as she sang, very slowly, "Ashes, ashes—"

She's mad, Balthazar thought as he looked at his sister. *She always was, a little, but now she's broken. She'll never be right again.*

"Which one will we bring to you, Balthazar?" Constantia said. "Choose quickly, or we'll have to start making them beg you to choose. You don't want to see us do that."

Jane shook her head, increasingly desperate. "Don't let them do it—hold on, someone will come—"

Balthazar had never been so enraged, and yet the ever-increasing hunger within him was even stronger than his anger. He couldn't think, couldn't speak. This was what it meant to cease being human; this was what it meant to be a monster. Even the sound of heartbeats was driving him mad.

The part of his mind that remained his own rationalized: *Charity's broken. She'll never be right again, never be sane again. Jane is the stronger one; she can endure this. It's already too late for Charity.*

His eyes fell on his little sister. For one moment he remembered her as a small child, playing in the meadow. She used to pick wildflowers by the armful and drop them in his lap.

Then he closed his swollen eyes, and all he could hear was the rushing of blood in her veins for one final, fatal moment.

Charity whisper-sang, "We all—fall—down!"

Balthazar snapped. He leaped at the sound of her voice,

heard her start screaming (*"No! No! Don't, not you, don't, please don't!"*), and bit into her throat. Charity's scream rose in pitch, and she beat at him desperately with her other hand, but there was no stopping now. He didn't want to stop. This feeling—fangs in human flesh, human blood filling his mouth, his body growing stronger with every swallow—was the most glorious, satisfying sensation he had ever known.

Her punches grew weaker, then ceased. Her body became heavy in his arms. Her pulse went as soft and uneven as the beating wings of a butterfly, until finally it stopped.

Balthazar dropped her body onto the stable floor. At first he felt nothing save the desire for even more blood—but no, he was sated. Only then did it hit him that this was his little sister, dead by his hand. She looked like a broken porcelain doll. Balthazar pulled back from her, recoiling from what he'd done, but there was no leaving this behind.

"Isn't that better?" Redgrave said. "Don't be too glum. She'll be with us again at the next sunrise. A bit peeved with you, I'd expect, but still. Awake and immortal."

Slowly, Balthazar lifted his head to look at Jane. The revulsion on her face seemed to hold up a mirror to his soul.

She can go on from here, he told himself. *She'll be scared, and she'll hate me until she dies—but Jane can bear this.* "Let her go," he said. "You made me choose. I chose. We're done here."

Constantia helped Jane to her feet and brushed off her gown. Jane shook so that she could barely stand, but her expression was resolute.

✤ 219 ✤

Then Redgrave said, "I made you choose which one to turn into a vampire. I never said what would happen to the other one." He grabbed Jane by the neck and twisted it the way someone would wring a chicken. Bones snapped. The light in her eyes went out. Constantia stepped back as Jane fell to the floor, dead.

Balthazar stared at her. He should have been outraged or nauseated, or at least overcome with grief, but it was as if he could feel nothing else—like any capacity for normal emotion had finally been drained from him. For the last time, he gazed at the girl he had loved. Jane's hair was dark against the hay.

"Waste of a good meal, if you ask me," Constantia said.

"Go ahead," Redgrave replied. "It's still fresh."

Balthazar came to with a start. More shocking than finding himself back in the here and now was the realization that he lay in Skye's bed—with her in his arms.

She still dozed, and unlike him she was fully clothed—thank God he hadn't totally lost control—but he could make out the small puncture wounds on her throat. The marks were healing fast, the way vampire bites always did, but the mere sight sickened him.

Then he heard a woman's voice in the hallway: "Skye, honey, are you awake?"

Skye stirred, smiled drowsily at him, and called back, "Sort of. What's up, Mom?"

Balthazar started to scuttle from the bed, but Skye kept him in place.

She whispered, "She only talks through the door. If she hears somebody in here, though—all bets are off."

The better part of valor was obviously staying in bed with Skye. Though in every other way it felt dangerously unwise.

"Can you order in some groceries for us, be around for the delivery tomorrow? We're running out of oatmeal again. You know what to get."

"Sure thing," Skye replied. Apparently this was the only sort of conversation daughter and parents ever had anymore. Her pale blue eyes looked up at Balthazar with nothing but trust, and for a moment—lying naked next to her, feeling her warmth, seeing the dark fall of her hair against the pillow—he saw everything he could have with her. Everything he wanted.

But the bite on her neck, and the memories he'd just relived, made it clear that none of it could ever be.

"We brought back some of that fudge you like," Mrs. Tierney called from the hallway, over the hiss of a hairspray can. "You'll find it on the kitchen counter."

"Thank you!" Skye sighed, then whispered, "Sometimes there are presents. It makes them feel better about not being here."

Balthazar couldn't reply. He remained far too aware of— many things he didn't need to be aware of at all at this moment. Like how long it had been since he'd been in bed with a girl.

"Have a good day, honey!" called a man, who must have been Mr. Tierney.

"You too!" Skye said. As footsteps pounded down the stairs,

she rolled to face Balthazar, so that they were only a few inches apart. Just after the front door slammed, she murmured, "Feeling better?"

"Yes." He started to throw off the covers, remembered again that he was nude, and looked around the room. "Ah, you should probably bring me my clothes."

Skye shrugged. The smile playing on her lips was exactly the kind that could drive him wild if he let it, which he wouldn't. "I've already seen everything. So don't be bashful on my account."

Fine. Balthazar got out of bed, grabbed his pants, and started getting dressed. He could see that Skye looked hurt—she'd been happy only moments before, and Balthazar knew he was being unforgivably cold to someone who had just saved him. "Thanks for yesterday," he said, hating the clipped, tight words. "We have to get to school."

"I know, but—Balthazar—I thought we—"

"Let's get one thing clear. Nothing happened between us last night, and nothing's going to happen." Balthazar found his shirt hanging on a doorknob; the fabric was still damp. "I know I've let things get—confused, between us, but that's my mistake."

Skye sat upright, bracing her hands behind her. "Excuse me? *Confused?*"

He had to be even more brutal. He had to do more than slam the door; he had to nail it shut. "I don't love you. You should be glad I don't. The only woman I ever truly loved died because of it."

That made her go pale, but she didn't drop it. "When you

drank this time—what did you see? What's done this to you?"

"I remembered the last moments of my life, and the first hour of being a vampire." Balthazar's damp coat felt like ice, but he shrugged it on anyway. "I remembered murdering my little sister. I killed her myself. Drank her dry." There. Now Skye would know what a monster he really was.

Skye's jaw dropped, but after a moment, she said, "So, you hate yourself so much that you're punishing *me* for it."

"Don't pretend like you understand me."

"I understand enough." She rose from the bed, then winced—the onslaught of heightened senses that followed a vampire bite were no doubt hitting her now. "You used to be a vampire like Redgrave and the others. You did some terrible things. Then you started leading a good life but still treated yourself like a bad person."

"When you're dead, you don't get to leave your past behind."

"Guess what? Nobody does!"

He bit back the impulse to continue the argument. "I'm going. I'll watch you on the way to school."

"Watch," she retorted. "That's all you'll ever do."

Balthazar stormed out, slamming her bedroom door behind him. She didn't follow.

If she understood, he thought, *if she knew how . . . unclean I am, how poisonous to everything I love—*

Which was the first moment he knew beyond any doubt that he loved her—the same moment he walked out of her house, intending never to return.

Chapter Eighteen

SKYE MANAGED TO GET READY FOR SCHOOL AS
though it were any other day. Her body went through the
motions, while her heart kept breaking on the inside.

She'd been rejected. Well, that happened. She'd liked Jason
Mulroney in middle school, and he'd never looked twice at her.
So she would cope.

*Liking a boy in middle school is nothing like finding a guy you
can share everything with, someone who knows where you hurt and
what you've lost and still cares about you—*

So, like losing Craig. She'd survived that.

*Craig went to bed with you once, and after that he just walked
away without a backward glance.*

Maybe you're just an easy girl to leave.

And she had never wanted Craig as badly as she'd wanted
Balthazar this morning. That was something she'd never understood until now—how she had sex with Craig more because she
longed for closeness and comfort after Dakota's death. She'd

learned about real desire only when she woke up in the arms of a guy she couldn't have.

Skye grabbed some tissue to dab at her eyes. Then she kept on getting ready as if it were any other day—except she used the waterproof mascara. The tears were probably going to keep coming.

Being at school made the situation even worse. Every noise seemed deafening to her, and even the pale sun that crept through the constantly falling snow was too bright, as were the fluorescent lights in Darby Glen High. And was it her imagination, or was her hearing better than before? Tennis shoes squeaking on linoleum, the metallic slam of locker doors, Florence and The Machine in someone's earbuds: All of it flooded through her, leaving her overwhelmed.

"Hey," Madison said, falling into step with her as they walked into homeroom. "Whoa. What happened? You look like crap today. No offense."

"None taken. I feel like crap." Skye let her books drop onto her desk, then winced at the sound of it.

"Oh, my God, are you hungover? You're totally acting like you're hungover."

"I just slept badly." Skye cast about for any additional way to explain this, then came up with something. "Plus my horse threw me yesterday afternoon. I wasn't injured or anything, but it shook me up, and I'm bruised everywhere."

"Poor you." Madison leaned across her desk, mock

confidential. "What if I told you something guaranteed to make you feel better?"

"School's canceled forever?" Skye was too tired to think of a better joke. Craig and Britnee walked in, hand in hand, and she had to close her eyes.

"Like I'd be here if it were. Listen, you know the Valentine's Dance is coming up. And you're gonna have a date. Guess who's asking you? Keith!"

Skye had to work to remember exactly who Keith was—one of Madison's friends, of course. He was actually pretty cute, though in a blond, catalog-model way that had never much appealed to her. "Oh."

"Oh? That news only gets an *oh*? Keith's about the hottest guy in this school." Madison paused before adding, "Except, of course, for a certain homeroom teacher."

Balthazar had just walked in. Skye glanced up at him to see him looking at her; his expression appeared as desolate as she felt inside. They broke the connection at the same moment, and after that she could only stare at her desk and be glad about the waterproof mascara.

Madison whispered, "He's acting as weird as you."

Skye shrugged. She didn't trust herself to speak.

Somehow she made it through homeroom and history class; for the first day ever, it was dull. Balthazar was obviously phoning it in, and it was a very small consolation to know that he felt rotten, too.

It could have been so different, if he'd just turned to her this morning.

When the bell rang, louder than ever before, Skye hurried out as quickly as she could. Mr. Bollinger's room felt like the only safe haven at school, even if he did make her polish the triangles again. But as she walked past Ms. Loos's room, she felt it:

Pain shooting up the arm, circling the chest. Knowing the doctor said to be careful but not really believing death was possible, not until now—

"Oh, no," she whispered. Never before had she been able to sense the death if there was some kind of barrier between her and the place where that person had died. But her senses were heightened today—*all* of them.

She started running away from the room, hurtling down the hall much faster than was allowed or safe. Some people swore as they ducked away from her, and she could hear cranky Coach Haladki yelling for her to slow down, but she didn't. All that mattered was getting farther away from that death—

Then she slammed into someone so hard that she stumbled and her victim fell.

"I'm sorry!" Skye gasped as she bent to grab her books, and only then did she see who it was she'd knocked over. Britnee Fong stared up at her, a little angry but more shocked.

"Are you, like, in trouble?" Britnee didn't say it like she thought Skye could possibly be in any real trouble. "Because you were going really fast? And I'd hope you wouldn't knock anybody down on purpose?"

"I said I was sorry," Skye said curtly. She would've apologized more to anyone else on earth, but not this girl. Not the one who stole her boyfriend.

As if he'd heard her thoughts, Craig appeared at that moment to help Britnee up. "What is your problem, Skye?"

"My problem? *My* problem?" If only she had just one problem to deal with. "Forget it, okay?"

"No," Craig said. "We've got to talk. Britnee, tell Ms. Loos I'm—sick or out or something."

"Um, okay?" Britnee looked as startled as Skye felt when Craig took her by the arm and steered her toward the art room, which was empty during second period.

"Don't grab me!" Skye threw his hand off.

"Don't make me say all this in the hall," Craig retorted.

Skye, who had already had enough of people at Darby Glen staring at her like she was some kind of freak, followed him into the room. Besides, it would feel good to unload on somebody. Anybody. The fact that it was Craig—faithless, cruel—was a bonus.

As soon as she shut the door, he said, "Where do you get off attacking my girlfriend?"

"It was an accident, Craig. I wasn't looking where I was going. Is that a crime?"

"An accident. Right. You *hate* Britnee. You laugh every time that bitch Madison Findley jokes about Britnee being 'fat' or 'stupid' or any other insult she can throw at her."

Which—was true. And not exactly cool of her to do, even if Madison was only making those jokes to cheer Skye up. "Don't call Madison a bitch. She's my friend."

"If that's the kind of person you want to hang around with,

fine. You've changed, Skye. I used to think we could be friends again someday, but there's nothing in you but hate."

"If I hate you, don't I have a reason?" Skye's voice was getting louder. She tried to keep her voice down, so that the entirety of Mrs. McCauley's Algebra II class next door wouldn't hear every word. "You slept with me and then you dumped me."

"Months after that!"

"How could you do any of that to me after Dakota died?"

Her words were shrill even to her ears. The anger drained out of Craig in an instant. Wearily he leaned against the drafting table, bowing over as if from the weight of it all. "Skye, don't you get it?" he said. "If Dakota hadn't—I was going to break up with you at the start of the summer. Face-to-face, like I know I should've. But after he died, I couldn't."

"What?" She'd never dreamed that was possible. Craig had been there for her every second of that time, and she'd been too lost in her own grief to notice that his thoughts might have been far away, too. "But—why?"

"There wasn't any reason why. We'd been at different schools for two years. You came home talking about all these people I didn't know and events I hadn't been to, and when I talked about being here, it bored you, too, and—we were just growing apart. It happens. I knew I cared about Britnee, but I never asked her out—never even touched her—and finally it got to the point where I had to break up with you or turn into a cheater. I don't cheat. I was honest with you. So why do I have to be the bad guy?"

Skye's anger returned. "Well, now because you slept with me knowing you were going to dump me."

Craig ran his hand over his stubble-short hair. "I shouldn't have. I know that. But—it was your idea, remember?"

It had been. She'd felt so empty, so alone, after Dakota's death. Craig had been her lifeline and her comfort that summer, and she'd thought—maybe if they took that final step, she'd finally feel alive again. Feel *anything* again. But she'd never dreamed that it wasn't something Craig wanted, too.

"My idea." Her eyes were welling with tears now. "Well, thanks for humoring me."

"That's not—oh, crap. I know it was a mistake, all right? I know. But I was mixed-up, and I thought maybe it would change things for us. That was stupid. I'm sorry." Craig's voice wavered a little; this had upset him as badly as it had her. What right did he have to be so hurt?

And yet, the part of her that remembered being in love with him hated to hear him so broken up. That flicker of feeling—no longer love, but still powerful, still real—upset her as much as anything else she'd been through that day. She didn't hate him, not down deep, and she wanted to, just because hate was easier. Simpler. Knowing that about herself was hard.

"You shouldn't have done it," she repeated, but quietly this time. "You should've told me the truth."

"I couldn't leave you after Dakota." While she was dating him, Craig and Dakota had become friends. They used to shoot hoops out in the driveway of the old house. How had she forgotten that?

"All you did was put the pain off until later." Skye wiped at her eyes. "It didn't hurt any less."

Craig looked as guilty as she wanted him to feel. She'd always thought it would help to see him feeling like the scum of the earth. It didn't.

He said only, "If I had it to do over, I'd do it differently."

"Whatever. Let's just drop it, okay? And for the record, knocking Britnee over really was an accident. I didn't see her. Tell her—tell her I'm sorry." Skye pulled herself together and hurried out, hoping none of the hall monitors would see her.

When she got to Mr. Bollinger's room, he was busily leafing through sheet music. "There you are! And here I thought you must have called in sick today." His voice trailed off as he saw her face. "Uh-oh. What's the matter?"

Skye tried to turn it into a joke. "Boys are stupid."

"Don't I know it." Mr. Bollinger sighed. "Sit down and take a load off."

Instead of making her work through the period, he set up the A/V screener and let her watch thirty minutes of *Singin' in the Rain*, which as far as she was concerned made him the best teacher ever.

So, ur just ditching study hall?

It's not ditching, Skye typed as she elbowed her locker shut for the day. *If ur a senior, u can sign out up to 2x a week. This is the 1st time I've ever signed out. Y not?*

Clem replied: *B/c vampires r trying to KILL U and staying close to ur bodyguard might be a good idea!*

Redgrave's not going to kill me anytime soon. He could've done that yesterday if he wanted to. He didn't.

Other vampires tried to kill u too. Maybe they got the smack-down, but doesn't mean they won't try again.

Clementine had a point. *I just can't be around Balthazar right now.*

I get that. But u have to b careful.

She walked through the front doors of the school, where it was still snowing thick and heavy, with big, fat flakes blanketing down so abundantly that the whole world got fuzzy about two hundred yards in the distance. The snowfall hadn't stopped since last night; the drifts were at least seven inches deep by now. This softening of the world—the muffling of sound, the dimming of light—helped soothe her overwrought senses. This was just what she needed: deep, endless snow.

After rewrapping her muffler around her neck, she sent back, *I'll go to Café Keats. I'll even take the shortcut nobody uses. Madison can meet me there after school.* It was weird that Madison hadn't wanted to sign out with her, and Skye would have appreciated the company, but if somebody wanted to actually study in study hall, so be it. *Even vampires won't be out in the middle of this.*

I guess, Clem replied. *But txt me when u get there. Besides, we have to talk more about ur date to the dance!*

Skye sighed. Keith had asked her at lunch period, so

offhandedly that he either didn't care if she said yes or not, or wanted her to think he didn't. It was a huge turnoff, but since the alternative now seemed to be sitting at home and crying about Balthazar, she'd said yes. *Sure thing. Next text within 10 minutes, I swear.*

Tromping through the drifts was vaguely satisfying; the cornstarch crunch of her boots in the snow was virtually the only sound she could hear, and even her enhanced senses didn't overreact to that. Skye curved around the school grounds, grateful that the staff had thoroughly salted the paved path and steps. All she had to do was cut through Battlefield Gorge, and she'd be at Café Keats within seconds. The only reason she couldn't already see it was the blinding snow—

He's scared, he doesn't know what to do, war isn't like this in the books or the prints Mama showed him. There are no straight lines, there is no one telling him what to do. There are only men running at him to kill him, and he has to kill them or else. Why did no one tell him how sad he would feel to kill someone?

Damned musket! The whoreson thing won't reload and the damned frogs are on him now!

The bullet through his head feels like a blow—like his mother boxing his ears—but he doesn't die right away. He has time to put one hand to the side of his head, or where the side of his head used to be, before the real pain begins and turns the world black.

Skye staggered back, assaulted on every side by the visions of soldiers (in red coats, in blue, some Native Americans in homespun) shooting, being shot, knifing, being knifed, screaming in pain that shot through her in waves.

Battlefield Gorge, she thought. She'd known it her whole life and never thought about it twice. Never once had she wondered how it got that name.

The paths of the bullets through her body were bright, hot lines of pain. The terror and fury and agony of the dying rose up inside her, a thousand times worse than anything else her powers had ever shown her.

Skye couldn't see, couldn't think. She was neither conscious nor unconscious; her mind no longer belonged to her. She didn't even have the strength to keep herself from toppling over into the thick snow. The flakes fell faster, it seemed, the better to cover her forever.

Chapter Nineteen

"YOU OWE ME ONE FOR THIS, MISTER," RICK BOL-
linger said as he took over study hall from Balthazar.

"Name your price." Balthazar kept a smile on his face, but
all he could think of was how badly he needed to get out of this
school now, right now.

"How about, oh—hmmm—chaperoning the Valentine's
Dance?" Rick suggested, mock innocently.

"You drive a hard bargain."

"That's me. The consigliere of Darby Glen High."

"Fine. I'll do it. Thanks again." Balthazar managed to leave
the library and let the door shut behind him before he broke into
a run.

The shortcut, the shortcut—that had to be the gorge. None of
the kids went that way because it wasn't cool or something like
that. That meant nobody would be there to help Skye, as if they
even could. It was up to him.

He didn't even tug on his coat until he had dashed halfway

down the walk leading to the gorge. The cold didn't matter; he didn't care if he froze. But he needed his hands free to fight for her.

As he stood at the edge of the gorge, though, he realized that no other vampires were near; he hadn't felt them. Then his sharp eyes picked out a patch of color amid the nearby snowdrifts—the sapphire blue of Skye's winter coat.

Balthazar ran toward her, the scene unveiling slowly before him because of the snow: Skye lay unconscious (*not dead, please not dead*) just off the path in the hollow of the gorge. He saw no blood, nor any sign of a struggle. It was as if she'd simply fallen over—fainted dead away.

Someone must have died nearby, and died horribly enough for it to have overwhelmed her. Balthazar reached her, went on his knees, felt for her pulse at her throat. Skye was alive.

Relief washed over him, not enough to submerge his fear but enough to focus him again on action. Balthazar swept her up in his arms and ran with all his speed toward his car. He needed to keep her with him. To keep her safe.

Skye remained unconscious the whole way back, even after Balthazar had placed her on his bed and started the fire, but her breathing was deeper and more even. He thought now she was more asleep than knocked out, and that her body probably needed the rest.

After shaking off his snow-wet coat, Balthazar reclaimed his phone and called the person who had warned him that Skye was in danger.

"Balthazar?" Lucas sounded tense. "Did you find Skye?"

"Found her. She hadn't been attacked; it was another of her visions, I think. Skye's still unconscious, but I think she'll be all right after she warms up and rests a little." Balthazar breathed out heavily. The need to sigh didn't go away with the need to breathe.

"You sound shaken up. Sure everything's okay?"

"I'm not sure of anything. But—she took a risk today. Because of me, I think. If she'd gotten hurt today, or if she'd—if anything worse had happened, it would be my fault."

"Mea maxima culpa, huh?"

Balthazar frowned. "Since when do you speak Latin?"

"I did go to Evernight for a while, remember?" Now Lucas sounded more amused than anything else. "It's just interesting how much you're beating yourself up about this."

"I told you. It's my fault." He looked at Skye as he spoke, thin and pale on his bed, the firelight burnishing her dark brown hair.

"You seem worried about her. Real worried. Deeply concerned. Are things getting interesting for you two?" Lucas was downright smug by now. "If you keep it up, my girlfriend's gonna get jealous."

"I don't get involved with humans," Balthazar said.

"You sound pretty involved to me," Lucas replied. "And why no humans? What's wrong with us? On behalf of my species, I object."

"It doesn't end well." He remembered Jane lying on the floor of his parents' barn, a broken shell of the girl he had too briefly loved. "For a mortal, being with someone supernatural is dangerous. You ought to know."

"Don't remind me." Lucas had already died and been resurrected once; he spoke from weary experience. "But speaking as a mere mortal—sometimes it's worth it. Danger and all."

Balthazar didn't want to hear this. Shortly, he said, "The only thing that matters is keeping Skye safe. We need to figure out how to stop the visions."

"Let her catch her breath first," Lucas said. "Listen, I need to call Clementine back. She was half frantic when she called me to say Skye hadn't checked in; by now she's probably pulling her hair out. Keep us posted, okay?"

"Will do."

"And Bianca says hi."

"Oh, right. Hi." Balthazar snapped off the call. Weird to think he'd forgotten to send a message to Bianca.

As he did, Skye stirred on the bed. He hurried to her side. "Hey. Don't sit up too fast."

"What the—where am I—oh." Skye's eyes widened as she took in her surroundings, and saw him. "What happened?"

"I was hoping you could tell me. I found you out by the gorge, unconscious."

"Oh, my God." Memory had obviously just come flooding back. Skye grimaced as she put her fingers to her temple, then slowly pushed herself upright. "It was awful. Turns out they call it Battlefield Gorge for a reason."

"You didn't have to run out there like that," Balthazar said. "Study hall—we would've been okay."

It was as much of an opening to talk about their argument this morning as he could offer, but he thought it would be enough. To his surprise, though, Skye didn't go there. "Hundreds of men died out there. It was like I was feeling them all at once—and sharper than before. I think my power must be getting stronger. Just walking by Ms. Loos's room today was worse than being in it was before."

"Maybe it's getting stronger. It might just be the aftermath of . . . of the bite." *My bite. When I bit into you in your bed and drank the blood you gave me to save my life, and then yelled at you to leave me alone.* Shamefaced, Balthazar continued, "After you're bitten by a vampire, your senses are enhanced for a while. The powers become longer lasting, maybe permanent, with subsequent bites. It's a small taste of what being a vampire is like all the time."

"I'll pass, thanks." She didn't even look directly at him; instead she gazed into the firelight. "That was too close, this afternoon."

When he'd told her that his decision not to be with her was final, she'd accepted it. Balthazar hadn't realized until now that he was counting on her to push back—to tempt him, to keep inviting him places. To offer all the pleasures of her company and her adoration, without being able to expect anything from him in return. Was he really that selfish? That stupid about his own desires?

He said the first thing that came to mind: "How does Clementine have Lucas's number, anyway?"

"They used to sit next to each other in English," Skye said absently. Then she sat up straighter, as if newly resolved. "We have to go back."

"Back—where? You can't mean the gorge."

She shuddered. "No. I can't face that again. Not ever, I don't think. It's too much. I—I'm glad you found me." For one moment, her eyes met his, and against his will, Balthazar found himself remembering the moment he'd awakened with her in his arms, and how warm she'd felt, how her legs had brushed against his.

"Don't run off like that again." His voice sounded rough and unsteady, even to him. "No matter—no matter how badly I screw up."

"I won't. I promise." Skye looked away from him again. "So come with me now."

"Of course. You must want to get home."

"No. I'm going back to school."

"It's—" Balthazar glanced over at the old-fashioned brass clock on the mantel. "After four thirty. Nobody's going to be there now."

"Which is the whole point." Cautiously she stood, tested her steadiness, then took her coat from the chair where he'd dumped it and began shrugging it back on. "I've run from these 'death visions' every time I've encountered them. And I haven't learned anything that way. It's past time to face them down. You've got a key, right?"

"Yeah, but—Skye, that's incredibly dangerous for you. You've nearly died before."

"I've *felt* like I nearly died. It's time to find out exactly what happens to me afterward. I know it's risky, but that's why you're coming along." She tossed him a challenging glance over her shoulder as she headed for the door. "You are coming along, right?"

"Right." He had no choice now but to follow where she led.

Chapter Twenty

SKYE WRAPPED HER COAT MORE WARMLY around herself as Balthazar drove through the winter storm on their way back to Darby Glen High. The snowfall had, if anything, only increased; the true winter of upstate New York was now well under way. All around them cars crawled along, cautious on slush-slick roads.

"Are you sure about this?" Balthazar said. His handsome face looked almost brutish in the harsh dashboard lights of his old beater car. "We could try later. Another day, maybe, when you haven't had such a rough time."

"If I wait, I'll chicken out. Let's just do this." Skye tucked a lock of her hair behind one ear. On the radio, some guy sang about sadness and loss, and how they kept you up at night. "I'm not feeling the . . . enhanced senses, or whatever they are, so much anymore. So it probably won't get to me until I'm in Ms. Loos's room."

"Wait—that's right. You said that today, you could sense it

even outside her room. It enhanced your psychic senses, too?"

It. The bite. The moment he'd pulled her close in her bed, and she'd felt herself surrendering completely. They were just going to call the bite "it" from now on. Fine. "I guess so. It made me a little crazy—went running off through the hallways, and evil Coach Haladki was screeching at me—"

"Nola's not that bad. Just cranky."

"I knocked Britnee Fong down in the hallway, which led to a whole screaming match between me and Craig. Today's been awesome all over."

Balthazar hesitated before saying, "Screaming match?"

"Well. Not screaming. Neither of us wanted the entire school to hear. But we had it out about our breakup." The taste of it was still sour. "It was a good thing, I guess. We talked about how weird things got after Dakota died, and how we—" Did she want to say this out loud to Balthazar? What the hell, she decided. After a guy had bitten you while naked in your bed, privacy pretty much flew out the window. "How we never should have slept together. We weren't going to be together long. Craig already knew it, and I . . . I guess I should've known, too."

Even Craig admitted it was his mistake. That ought to have helped her more than it did. Maybe it would in time.

"You couldn't have been thinking clearly that soon after your brother's death," Balthazar said. "He shouldn't have done that to you." She could see him clenching and unclenching his jaw in the dim light, as if he were biting back something else to say. Her face flushed warm as she realized that he was jealous—that the thought of her with Craig got under his skin.

Even one day ago, that jealousy would've made her incredibly happy. Now, however, Skye didn't see how it mattered. So what if Balthazar wanted to be with her, if he refused to do anything about it?

Slowly she said, "If a guy wants to be with you, he should be. If he doesn't, he should keep his distance."

A pause followed before Balthazar said, "I guess maybe he had his reasons."

"Or maybe he was too chicken to face the truth." Skye turned the volume up on the radio, so that the sad song was even louder. For the rest of the ride, it was the only sound in the car besides the slap-slap of the windshield wipers pushing away the snow.

Darby Glen High became a lot creepier after dark.

Skye had been here at nighttime before, of course, but always for a dance, ball game, or recital, which meant that the parking lots were filled with cars and a few people were always milling around. Now the place was deserted, so eerily silent that she could hear the echo of their footsteps on the tile and Balthazar's keys jangling in his pocket. The flashlight Balthazar held provided their only illumination.

They reached the door of Ms. Loos's room and stopped. Neither made a move. Skye breathed in and out, keeping the rhythm regular and slow.

"Is it getting to you already?" Balthazar stepped closer to her.

Once again she remembered how much bigger he was than her, with his dark outline looming overhead. "We should go back."

"No. I don't sense anything, I'm just—"

"I know." His hand hovered next to her shoulder for a moment before he dropped it again, denying them both the touch.

After one more deep breath, Skye put her hand on the door-knob and turned.

When she first walked in, the room looked like any other classroom. Written on the dry-erase board in all caps were the words *UTERINE CYCLE*, which made her profoundly glad she'd dropped out of Ms. Loos's class when she did.

"Anything?" Balthazar kept glancing around the room, like he expected a ghost or vampire to appear at any second. At least they would have known how to fight those.

"It usually takes a few minutes." Skye sat on the edge of one of the desks—the one where Britnee Fong used to sit. She hadn't really thought about Britnee since her fight with Craig; she'd hardly had a chance. Now, though, she realized that if Craig was telling the truth, Britnee wasn't the schemer Skye had believed her to be. Craig wasn't off the hook with Skye yet—not by a long shot—but maybe she'd try being more polite to Britnee in the future. Or at least get Madison to quit snarking on her so much.

Then she saw him: the janitor, always unaware, always defeated looking, as he wheeled his trash can into the room again. "Here we go," she said, stepping backward until she half sat, half fell into the chair. Balthazar came nearer, but already it was harder for her to see him. The world was taking shape in a new way. She was seeing through a dead man's eyes.

Pain curls up his arm, lances into his heart. It shallows his lungs, blurs his vision. For one moment he can taste metal, as if he were about to be struck by lightning. His heart, he thinks, and there's nothing scarier than the feeling that a time bomb is ticking in his chest, and someone's just pressed the detonator.

"Skye!" Balthazar had seized her shoulders and was trying to shake her out of it. But this time she didn't let him. Instead of struggling against the visions—which she'd always tried to do before—Skye exhaled and let go completely. It was like swimming in the river and allowing the current to take you under. Like giving in.

The pain clamps around him, a vise squeezing tighter and tighter. His tongue feels thick in his mouth, his eyes too large for their sockets. There's no pain worse than this. There can't be. This is every cell in the body screaming for air, devouring itself, total immolation inside and out.

She was vaguely aware that she'd collapsed, that Balthazar had her leaned against his chest and was saying something—pleading with her—but that was too far away to pay attention to any longer.

The pain builds, and builds, beyond any endurance, beyond any imagining—

Until it turns inside out.

The cells stop screaming. There's no need for air anymore, or for blood. No need for anything. He's complete as he is. He let go so

the pain could stop, and there's nothing more joyous than that sur-
render. The contentment he feels in the death of his human body is
the same he might feel when cuddled within a very snug blanket—
warm and enveloping, but not any part of him, really.

That makes it easy to throw the blanket aside.

Skye opened her eyes. She sat on the floor, legs twisted up, leaning against Balthazar. He kept saying, "Stay with me, stay with me, stay—Skye?"

"Yeah." She breathed in, and the mere movement of air in her lungs was inexpressibly sweet. *Life is irreplaceable*, Balthazar had said, and now she thought she understood some fraction of what he'd meant.

"We have to get you out of here. It's too much for you."

"It's over." Shakily she coughed once—how did even that feel good? Her pulse seemed to hum throughout her body. The high, silvery sound of her nervous system chimed like a rolling cymbal. "I'll be okay now."

And from now on, she thought. Although she knew that there was no telling what other deaths might do to her—she couldn't begin to imagine facing Battlefield Gorge again—she understood instinctively that this death, in this room, wouldn't overcome her in the same way if she ever returned.

"You weren't okay a minute ago," Balthazar insisted. Still he held her close, and she realized one of his hands was stroking her hair.

Skye jerked back from him. The fast movement dizzied her, but only for a moment. Balthazar seemed to realize what he'd been doing, and he pulled back, scooting farther away on the floor.

She said, "I mean it. The trick is—the trick is giving in."

"Giving in?"

"Surrendering to the death."

Balthazar scowled, his heavy brow furrowing. "Surrendering to death sounds like a bad idea. In any situation, but especially this one."

"I know how it sounds. But somehow—somehow it was the right thing to do." Skye braced herself against one of the desks as she shakily got to her feet. "I'll know better what to do next time. It won't destroy me."

"I don't like the sound of this."

Skye shrugged. "It's not your choice to like or dislike."

"Skye—do we have to be like—"

"We're okay," she said, and tried to mean it. Her feelings were too raw for that, really, but she didn't want to turn into a teary mess with two guys in the same day. "Just take me home, all right?"

He took her home.

The drive to her place went even slower than the journey there. The snow had finally outstripped the plows' ability to keep up with it, and the scant few cars still on the road were creeping along. Balthazar's car was no four-wheel drive, but he kept it steady anyway. He was as good with automobiles as he was with horses.

"I should call Mom and Dad," she said, just to break the

silence in the car. "They won't be able to make it back tonight. Their organization usually springs for a hotel room in Albany when that happens."

Balthazar said, "I'm sorry if I hurt you this morning."

Skye stared over at him. "That's not what we were talking about."

"It's just a relief to have you talking to me," he admitted. "I mean it. I shouldn't have been as—rough on you. Or as rude. And I shouldn't have bitten you."

He didn't regret walking away from her, Skye decided. He only regretted letting her get close at all.

She said only, "You're here to protect me. That's it. I understand now."

"All right." He sounded as if he didn't entirely believe her. Fair enough, she figured; she didn't entirely believe herself. "Hopefully we can still hang around—"

"I don't think so." Riding together in the snow. Sparring in her basement, flushed and sweaty and enjoying every touch. Texting each other throughout study hall. Did she have to give it all up? Yes. Skye knew she had to be ruthless for her own sake. "You're still here, and I appreciate that—you'll never know how—anyway. But we should move on."

"Move on," Balthazar repeated, as he finally steered the car into her driveway.

"You'll do—whatever you'd do otherwise. I'll hang out with Madison more. Study at home, even. It's not like it would kill me. I'm even going to the Valentine's Dance with Keith Kramer.

So—yeah. Moving on."

He gave her a look—oh, God, why did he look his absolute hottest when he was crazy jealous? The absurdity of any guy as amazing as Balthazar being jealous of cardboard-cutout Keith would've been hilarious at any other time. As it was, it stung almost as badly as his rejection had that morning.

"Thanks again," Skye said as she got out of the car. "Good night." She walked inside and shut the door behind her without a backward glance.

Moving on, she repeated to herself, meaning it. *That means you don't get to think about the fact that you've made Balthazar jealous. That can't be why you go to the dance.*

Though I guess you can enjoy it a little *bit.*

The Time Between:
Interlude Three

Philadelphia, Pennsylvania
October 1918

FOR A VAMPIRE, ONLY ONE CALAMITY PROVIDED
more abundant feeding grounds than wartime: plague.

That made 1918 a very good year for the undead.

Although the war had not yet ended, it was clearly in its
last gasps; armistice was expected any day. With the conclusion
of the bloodiest conflict in history near, Philadelphia ought to
have been cheerful and bustling with activity. Instead, Balthazar
found himself walking along deserted streets.

In the past few weeks, a deadly wave of the Spanish flu had
swept through the city with the same virulence with which it had
killed millions from the Arctic Circle to South Africa. Victims—
oddly, usually the youngest and strongest—began coughing and
complaining of earaches or headaches. Then came the fevers,

scorching hot. The pulses of the sick quickened so that Balthazar could hear them, fast and tremulous as the hearts of rabbits
before the kill, from far away. Death seized them through the
lungs, infecting and swelling them so that air could no longer
course through the body. The sufferers turned blue-black with
suffocation before their terrible deaths.

Sometimes he could spare them that. Their blood tasted
foul to him; viruses could not poison vampires, but this one was
so wretched that it spoiled even the pleasure of drinking from
humans without guilt. But if providing a merciful death for a
few sick people was the lone service he could provide for humanity, then he would provide it.

In Philadelphia, the Spanish flu epidemic was so severe that
city officials had ordered trenches dug for mass graves. Some
undertakers, taking opportunity of rising demand, had raised
their fees; others told survivors they'd have to dig loved ones'
graves themselves. Doctors and nurses were in desperately short
supply.

Which was why a suspiciously young-looking man could
describe himself as a medical student from "out west" and get
away with it.

Balthazar wore a cloth mask over his face as he walked along
the street making his "rounds." Although he of course could
not contract the flu—death provided the only absolute immu-
nity—he would have attracted too much notice by not wearing
it. Everyone wore the masks now in a futile effort to keep the
epidemic at bay. Now he looked the part in his dark brown suit,

high-collared shirt, and low-brimmed hat; a long coat and a pair of wire-rimmed glasses allowed him to look a few years older than he was. A police paddy wagon farther down the road took a small bundle wrapped in a sheet and tossed it unceremoniously in the back; that would be a young child, dead in a city that no longer had the wood for coffins.

Witnessing the devastation of the influenza had made Balthazar wish desperately that he could do something beyond providing a merciful death for the sickest among them. When he'd been alive, medicine had been little more than guesswork; anything approaching an actual drug had been condemned as witchcraft. But in the twentieth century, maybe he'd have the opportunity to learn more. Maybe someday he could be a healer instead of a bringer of death.

For now, though, death was his only gift.

As he approached the house he sought, he saw a young nurse walking along, white headdress falling past her cheeks, a basket of food for the sick clutched in her hands. She was the first legitimate medical professional he'd seen in days; the few who weren't ill were too busy to leave the clinics. Balthazar raised a hand to her in greeting, but she stopped in her tracks as if startled.

Above her mask, he recognized Charity's eyes.

The first words Balthazar could find were: "Where's Redgrave?"

"France." She said this in her tiniest, most childlike voice.

Of course he would still be on the battlefields. Balthazar relished the spoils of war, the way any vampire had to, but crossing the ocean merely to feast on the dying was too much for him. Not for Redgrave. "Are you alone in Philadelphia?"

Charity shook her head. "Constantia's here, too. The others stayed with Redgrave."

Disappointing that she wasn't entirely alone, but not surprising: Balthazar could tell just from the cleanliness and appropriateness of Charity's disguise that someone had helped her with it. Still, this was the closest to freedom Charity had come since the day of her death—and Balthazar's best chance to help her.

She hadn't attacked him. Hadn't turned away in anger. Was it possible his sister was finally ready to be helped?

"Let's go," he said. "You and me. Come with me now. Right away."

"Go where?"

"New York. Toronto. San Francisco. It doesn't matter. Someplace far from here, where Redgrave can't find us."

Balthazar reached his arm out, meaning to stretch it across her shoulders and lead her off, but Charity shrank back as if he were going to strike her. The old fear still lingered inside her, and Balthazar knew that was his own fault. "I can't," she whispered. "He'll find out. He'll find me. He always does; you know that."

So she had tried to run away before, and failed. His heart ached at the thought of his little sister's long captivity—and his own wretched inability to protect her. Now, though, things could be different. He had to make her see that. "Look around you," Balthazar said, gesturing at the deserted streets. "Nobody will stop us."

"Constantia would."

"She's not Redgrave."

"She's just as bad. Worse, maybe. You've never seen that, but I have."

Charity was talking nonsense—who knew Constantia Gabrielis's bag of tricks better than he did?—but Balthazar persisted. "Where is Constantia now?" With his luck, she'd come storming out of the nearest house, stake in hand.

"She's at the house up the hill, the one we took. Everyone inside was sick, so they couldn't fight us off. Well, the old man wasn't sick, but he couldn't fight us off either." Charity's pink tongue darted to the corner of her mouth, as if she were licking her chops at the memory. "I don't like this flu. It makes everyone taste funny."

"Charity, concentrate. If Constantia isn't here, then she can't stop us from going." Could it really be as easy as this? It seemed impossible, and yet nothing stood in their way. Wild hope Balthazar had thought long dead sprang up inside him. They might flee this ghost town and start over somewhere. He could show her how to exist among humans without causing harm. How there were a few friendships to be had, a few deeds worth doing. That sometimes, just sometimes, their time on earth could feel like it mattered.

His sister furrowed her brow, deep in thought; it was the first time he'd seen her so focused on anything since well before her death. "She'll know. She'll figure it out."

"Only that you're gone!"

"We can't leave her behind to tattle." Charity's dark eyes lit up with glee. "We'll have to finish her off."

Balthazar had never slain a vampire before—though not because he hadn't wanted to. There had been nights he'd been unable to sleep because his thoughts were too full of what he could do to Redgrave: beating his smug, porcelain face until it cracked. Slicing through his neck and watching him turn to bones. Setting him on fire and lingering long enough to hear him scream. Before Redgrave, Balthazar hadn't even known it was possible to hate that much.

Constantia . . . he hated her, but not like that. Not enough to enjoy killing her.

But he would do what he had to do.

The plan was mostly his, in the end; Charity could hardly focus on anything past telling him where the house was and what time to come. Just at sunset, she said: Constantia liked the anonymity of the streets after dark and would often go out prowling. During the day, she'd almost certainly be sleeping.

That seemed unlike the Constantia he remembered— Balthazar recalled her minding sunlight less than any other vampire he'd ever encountered—but he hadn't shared her bed for 140 years or so. Habits could change.

Wasn't he proof enough of that?

He dressed as if for a fancy party; she'd see it as a compliment. Then he went to the address Charity had given. Evening shadows falling across the stricken, eerily silent city, Balthazar made his way up the steps and simply rang the doorbell.

It took a long time for anyone to approach. His sensitive ears picked up the swishing of skirts, the click of her boots against wood. Balthazar leaned close to the door. If Constantia breathed in deeply, she would recognize even his scent. Already he recognized her. For a few moments, he simply remained there motionless while she did as well; he knew they were aware of each other, poised only inches apart, at the intersection of wrath and desire.

Finally Constantia opened the door. She stood there, blond hair down and loose as if she'd just risen from her bed. "Balthazar," she said. "My God. Charity told the truth. With her, you never know."

He'd told Charity to inform Constantia that he was in town. That he was lonely, regretting his isolation from other vampires. That he'd been excited to learn they were without Redgrave. Lies were always strongest when mixed with the truth: Redgrave had taught him this much.

"Constantia." He managed a smile for her; it was bent and uncertain, but that was all right. She wouldn't have believed an overly enthusiastic welcome. "May I come in?"

Instead of welcoming him, Constantia merely stepped backward. Balthazar walked into that space and shut the door behind him. They stood very close. She was the only woman he'd ever known tall enough to look him in the eyes.

"Where's Charity?" he asked, as if he didn't know.

"Wandering the streets, as usual. She can hunt on her own now. Quite well, in fact. You'd be proud of her."

Proud wasn't exactly the word. Still, his sister had followed the plan. She was away from the house, away from any potential blame should he fail. Already he could see that her description of this place had been entirely accurate; she could focus better than he'd realized before. Celadon paper wreathed with white vines covered each wall, and the home possessed newfangled electric lighting and a broad stairwell just next to the door. That meant the room he could barely glimpse upstairs was the bedroom Charity and Constantia weren't using . . . the one his sister would have hidden the stakes in.

All he had to do was get Constantia upstairs.

To judge by the quick rise and fall of her breath as she looked at him, Balthazar thought he could manage.

"You're finally done with Redgrave," he said.

"We don't always travel together. You know that by now."

"I realize that. I meant it as . . . a suggestion."

Constantia cocked an eyebrow. "You don't want to come back to Redgrave's tribe. You want us to start a tribe of our own."

"You and me and Charity. A good place to start, don't you think?" Balthazar leaned forward, slid one hand along her waist. Apparently she'd joined the fad of doing without corsets; only thin fabric separated his skin from her flesh.

She whispered, "You hate me."

"I hate Redgrave. You—you I miss, from time to time."

A lie mixed with the truth. He hated his old desire for her; that didn't meant it wasn't still a part of him.

"You wouldn't want us to hunt the same way."

"There are other ways to hunt, Constantia. Ways that let us lead lives almost like normal."

"Since when did we care about normal?"

"You can't like existing this way," Balthazar insisted. "Always on the fringes. Always in the dark. Always coming and going at Redgrave's command. Take control, Constantia."

He came closer still to her, so close that their lips almost touched.

Balthazar finished, "Take me."

Impossible to say who kissed whom first, or where the lies ended and the truth began. For a few moments, he knew only that Constantia was familiar to him, darkly beautiful even now, and how good it had felt to drown his soul in her night after night.

But even as he backed her toward the stairs, Balthazar reminded himself, *I'm about to kill her.*

Conscience pricked at him, but not as much as the need to finally rescue his sister. He could finally do it—set them both free. Constantia had helped imprison them to begin with; now she had to pay the price.

They found their way into the bedroom and fell together on the bed. Balthazar cupped her face in his hands, kissing her deeply even as he opened his eyes to look for the bedside table on the right. That was where Charity would have hidden the stakes. Once he'd staked Constantia and paralyzed her, he could burn this house down.

He pushed her back, not roughly, but an old signal he

thought she'd recognize. Sure enough, Constantia began to shrug off her dove-gray dress, laughing throatily. Her perfect body could still move him. "You haven't learned any new tricks these past centuries, have you?" She grinned at Balthazar as she scooted across the bed, the better to undress. "I see I still have a lot to teach you."

"I'm ready to learn." Taking off his shirt gave Balthazar the cover he needed for the swift movement toward the bedside table. In a flash he opened the drawer to find—nothing.

He looked up to see Constantia sitting still on the other side of the bed. Where the drawer of the bedside table on the left was open. And where she'd no doubt found the stake now in her hand.

Her eyes were almost sad. "Do you know, I'd hoped Charity was lying?"

She betrayed me, Balthazar thought in the split second before the stake slammed into his chest.

The rest was a kind of darkness that couldn't be seen, a silence that couldn't be heard. Balthazar knew he was not dead, but he knew nothing else. At times his stunned senses delivered a signal—the sight of Charity standing above him, triumphant and proud, or the smell of burning wood—but his mind could not process the information. It slipped in and slipped out, unheeded and barely remembered.

Until the moment a great weight fell upon him and dislodged the stake.

Balthazar screamed. The stake now jabbed through his

chest, if not his heart, with the full pain of a deep stab wound. He sucked in a breath and found his lungs filled with smoke; when his eyes would see again, he realized that Charity had fulfilled his plan to the letter—she'd simply turned it against him instead of against Constantia. He was the one now trapped in a burning house, half a smoldering timber across his gut searing his skin, only seconds from oblivion.

Charity, why?

But he knew why. He had killed his sister. She was returning the favor.

Despair settled over him, heavier than the beam that pinned him down. It would be easy to just lie back and let it happen. And yet he couldn't. Maybe that made him a coward. Maybe the instinct to survive outlasted death itself.

Using all his remaining strength, Balthazar shoved the fallen timber off his body. His remaining clothes were singed, his skin blackened and blistering. The tips of his fingers stuck to the stake he yanked from his own chest, peeling away from his flesh. He staggered toward the nearest window and threw himself through it; glass stabbed into him, just one more layer of pain to mingle with all the rest.

The fall hurt, too; the bones in one forearm snapped as he hit the ground, but somehow he managed to stifle a shout of pain. Balthazar crawled away from the burning house, expecting Constantia and Charity to arrive at any moment to finish him at any cost.

But no one was there. In Philadelphia during the influenza

epidemic, even firefighters weren't risking their lives for anyone else. And apparently Charity and Constantia had already written him off.

Balthazar found his way to the edge of town, to an abandoned building where rats dwelled and made for easy eating. He remained there long after his burns and broken bones healed. Long after the flu epidemic ended. He spoke to no one. He let his beard grow. He spent long days watching a rectangle of light from his room's one window crawl from one side of the room to the other as the sun rose and set.

Dozens of days.

Hundreds of days.

Without human blood, he felt himself changing: his flesh hung more loosely on him, and his fingers increasingly curved into claws. The monster was taking over, but the monster could feel no pain, so Balthazar accepted it. Filth matted his hair and beard, and his torn clothing turned into mere rags. When vermin scurried close enough to be caught, he devoured them. He was as low as he deserved to be; that was as much as he thought about the matter, when he bothered to think of anything at all.

One evening, though, as he lay on the floor halfway between stupor and slumber, he heard a low, guttural laugh. "Lookit this. Some damn hobo."

"Trash, if you ask me."

"Might have something in here, though."

"Not this guy. Lookit him. He don't need a squat. He needs a grave."

"We can take care of that, can't we?"

Balthazar breathed in, smelled human blood, and the monster had killed and devoured them both long before his mind told him he'd even been in danger.

He stood over the corpses of his victims for nearly an hour as he tried to process his return to human consciousness. Already Balthazar could feel his body restoring itself, taking on the muscular form he'd had in life. His tangled beard disgusted him now, as did the grime coating his body, but he'd have to clean himself later.

First he had to figure out just how long he'd been in this place.

One of the dead men was at least close to his size, so Balthazar put on his shirt, coat, and shoes before venturing outside. It was late at night—but that was all he recognized. The entire neighborhood had been rebuilt around him. The roads were repaved, and no horses and carriages were to be seen; instead, automobiles rolled past, faster and more contained than they'd been before.

Buying stock in General Motors was a good idea, Balthazar thought. But his portfolio wasn't his main concern at the moment.

Moving more naturally and decisively now, Balthazar went to a nearby trash bin and pulled out a crumpled newspaper. The headlines blared unfamiliar information—*Depression, Dust Bowl*—and one unexpectedly familiar phrase—*President Roosevelt? Again?*—but he'd read this and absorb the contents later. Right now he cared about only one thing: the date.

April 26, 1933.

Almost fifteen years gone, and he hadn't even noticed them going.

He would have to return to Evernight Academy and enroll again. There he could find out what the world was like these days and start to adapt. Balthazar hated the process of starting over, but he could do it when he had to.

And he would this time, too, though his weary heart still held only the thought of his sister, and the knowledge of pain.

Chapter Twenty-one

BALTHAZAR KNEW HE SHOULD BE RELIEVED AT the news that Skye had a date. It was a definite sign that she was willing to walk away from—whatever it was that had been building between them. She was no angrier than his bad manners deserved; she wasn't going to cry or carry on like a woman scorned. They could cooperate in figuring out her powers; they could work together to ensure she remained safe from Redgrave. She wouldn't ask anything else of him. That was exactly what he should hope for.

Instead, as he drove back to his home through the winter storm, he kept thinking about Skye in Keith Kramer's arms.

Keith Kramer. A mere boy. And not even a particularly intelligent, dynamic, or kind one. One who turned in history papers late, and despite repeated corrections kept confusing *your* and *you're*. He was handsome in a generic sort of way, though, and apparently a football star—some girls went for that, but Skye? Not her. She was special. There was nothing ordinary about her.

Keith was the definition of *earthbound*.

Damn, but he needed a cigarette. His resolution to quit had never been as difficult as it was right then. He wanted to light one up, suck it in, blow out smoke that could kill other people. Such as Keith Kramer. How could she even think of going out with that . . . blond lump?

She can think about it because you cast her aside, he reminded himself. *You don't have the right to control who she sees.*

Yet the mere thought of Keith's hands on Skye's lithe body made Balthazar furious with jealousy.

For one moment, he couldn't see the road in front of him, even his hands clenched on the steering wheel. All he saw was his dark vision of Skye lifting her face for someone else's kiss—

And that was the moment someone walked into the road in front of his car.

He shouted in wordless horror at the thump of his car striking flesh and bone. Even as he slammed on the brakes, sending his car careering into the thicker snow alongside the road, the body was flung up onto the hood, onto his windshield, limp and in tatters. For a moment he could only stare, aghast, at the crumpled form that lay in front of the windshield. Then, slowly, his victim lifted her head to stare through the glass at him.

"Gotcha," Charity said, before bursting into peals of laughter.

Balthazar slammed his fists against the steering wheel in frustration. "Jesus, Charity! You scared the hell out of me."

She grinned at him, wriggling with pleasure as if she were a little girl telling riddles again. "Just think! If it had been a human, you could've eaten it! And no guilt about biting that one at all."

"Your idea of guilt and mine are very different."

Her expression darkened. "They are, aren't they?"

Balthazar got out of the car. His feet sank in loose, powdery snow almost up to his knees. The darkness around them was nearly total, and by now almost nobody else was foolish enough to be out on the road. He and Charity were alone. Her white dress and pale hair made her appear to be part of the snowstorm around them.

"You've gone back to Redgrave," he said. "Thought you had your own tribe."

"I do. They're with me. But you never forget your first love, do you?"

Once again he remembered the barn where he'd drawn his last breath as a living man, and how slick with blood and gore it had been when he'd finished murdering her. No moment in his existence had greater horror than the one when he'd seen Charity dead by his hand—lying next to his first love, the woman he'd tried to save by sacrificing his sister. Tried and failed.

Charity was thinking of it, too. Her high, youthful voice shook, as if from the cold. "Why do you never choose me? Why am I never the one you want to save?"

"Why do you always choose to go back to Redgrave? How can you be on his side after what he did to both of us?"

"Redgrave only killed *you*," she spat back. "*You're* the one who murdered me!"

They'd had this argument before—hundreds of times, over hundreds of years. This was Balthazar's cue to retort that he'd been given no choice, that she knew how it was, that she would have died one way or the other before that night was through. Would she rather be poor Jane?

But this time was different. Because this time, he'd been back there. He'd relived it, as vividly and immediately as he had experienced those events the first time. This time, Balthazar finally understood.

Charity wasn't asking him why he hadn't somehow managed to save them all from Redgrave's clutches.

She was asking why he hadn't done her the mercy of allowing her to be the one who died.

Jane had a chance, he'd told himself. *Charity didn't.* Charity's spirit and soul had already been broken.

But that was why he should have killed her. Had Jane been a vampire—maybe she would've been a killer like Redgrave, because the change transformed people in every possible sense, but maybe she would've been like Balthazar or the other vampires of Evernight. Sane. Reasonable. At any rate, her choices would've been her own.

By turning Charity into a vampire, Balthazar had ensured that she would remain trapped in the labyrinthine chambers of her own insanity for all time.

Balthazar said, "I'm sorry."

"You always say—"

He sank to his knees in the snow and looked up at her. The gesture silenced her beyond any words he'd ever spoken.

All the same, he spoke. "Charity, if I could go back, I'd do it all differently. If Redgrave told me again to choose one of you to turn, I'd walk to you and snap your neck myself. I'd let you go along with Mom and Dad. I'd let it be over. I would set you free. What I did to you I live with every single day, and even though you don't see it, I swear to God, it's as bad as the fate I made for you."

She only became angrier. "You can't go back! There's no wishing for it, because I wish and I wish—" Charity wiped angrily at her face with the back of her hand; it was the first time Balthazar realized she'd begun crying. "We're vampires now. Both of us. We always will be. So there's no such thing as 'Redgrave's side' or 'our side.' We're on the same side, forever. Thanks to you."

Balthazar didn't rise. The snow was already thick on his shoulders and the front of his coat. His car's headlights showed him that Charity's feet were bare and raw. "It's not as simple as that. What Redgrave is—that doesn't have to be what we are."

"What we are is vampires. You just play-pretend you're a human." Charity's eyes narrowed. "Is that why you got yourself another girlfriend? A simple, stupid human girl filled up with the best blood of all—"

"You don't get to judge her. Judge me all you want. You've got the right. But not Skye."

She bent over, bringing her face not far above his. Despite her disheveled appearance and singsong voice, her eyes were shrewd. "Or are you saving her for yourself? Make her your girlfriend, and then you can have all the blood you like and never, ever share."

If only he could answer that he'd never drunk Skye's blood.

Instead, he rose from the snow, forcing Charity to stand, too, until they faced each other again. Balthazar repeated, "Not Skye. Don't let Redgrave set you on her, Charity. Don't do to her what he did to me or . . . or what I did to you."

Charity said nothing. She never moved, even as he got back in his car and drove away. In the rearview mirror, he could see her remaining there, utterly still, until she was erased by the snow that surrounded her.

The next few days were . . . awkward.

Skye was as good as her word. She didn't text him during study hall, didn't exchange glances with him during history class, and spoke only to answer "present" during the homeroom attendance roll. It wasn't that she froze him out; in every way, she was calm and polite.

Balthazar managed to remain polite, but he wasn't at all calm.

There she was, walking down the hallway with That Lump. Or exchanging notes with Madison in study hall, Madison all giggles; probably they were talking about Keith, or the dance, which he already profoundly regretted agreeing to chaperone.

The next weekend, she wanted to go riding again, but suggested evenly that it made more sense for him to be at something of a distance, the better to scout around for intruders. "That way I won't be a distraction," she said, as if everything about her wasn't maddeningly distracting.

He kept guard over her house at night, which he felt was in no way like stalking. Except, that was, for that moment every evening when she walked to the window, just before turning out her light. It was her silent way of affirming that she knew he was there—her only acknowledgment of the bond between them that survived their silence. The silhouette of her body against the bedroom light always stayed with him throughout the long hours before dawn.

Teaching at Darby Glen High began to feel like a job. Watching her began to feel like a mission. Countless little details distracted him (Tonia Loos's endless flirting in the staff room, Madison Findley's numerous questions about her impending term paper on John Alden), but nothing ever took his mind away from Skye.

Balthazar was beginning to think that nothing ever would—that even if he walked away from her in Darby Glen after the immediate crises were resolved, Skye would always claim a part of him.

One night, after hours of tossing around in bed and trying desperately not to think of Skye, he finally fell asleep—and dreamed of her.

They were back at Evernight Academy, though no longer strangers to each other as they had been then. Together they rode on the grounds, which were green and warm as summertime:

"You're too slow," she called, glancing over her shoulder. Her deep brown hair, free from the helmet she always wore, framed the curve of her face. As Skye urged Eb onward, she said, "Catch up!"

"I'm coming!" He spurred on Bucephalus, thinking idly that it had been too long since he rode him. Why didn't he take this horse out every day? Bony and awkward he still looked, but he was fast. Fast enough to catch Skye.

She and Eb vanished into a glade of trees, and Balthazar followed, eager to find her again. When he found her, he'd take her into his arms and kiss her again. This time nothing would stop them. Nothing would get in the way.

Once they entered the clearing, he saw Eb standing still, bridle aside, so he could munch on the grass. Balthazar dismounted, expecting to see Skye somewhere nearby. Perhaps she was hiding, turning this all into a game. He felt himself starting to smile. "Skye?"

"Find me!" Her voice rang out joyfully from deeper in the glade, and he dashed toward the sound. The branches seemed incredibly thick—and the sunlight was dimmer here, less steady than it had been but moments before—yet it didn't matter, not if he were about to find Skye.

Finally he pushed aside the last branch and saw a small grove. In the center stood Skye, her ruffled sundress fluttering in the sudden strong breeze. Her bare feet were pale against the vivid grass.

She simply stood there, waiting for him with a smile on her face, and Balthazar took a step toward her—

—just as Redgrave appeared behind Skye, and slipped his arms around her waist.

"Only her friend," Redgrave whispered as he stroked Skye's hair away from her face. She simply glanced back at him, as eager to be with him as she'd been for Balthazar a moment before. "Only her protector. And yet you dream about her dancing for you barefoot in a meadow. How incredibly pathetic, Balthazar. Your erotic imagination might at least have become a bit more creative in the past few centuries."

This wasn't right. It couldn't be. Why wasn't this real anymore? "Let go of Skye," Balthazar said. The words were difficult to force out. "She doesn't want you."

"I'm the master of this dream now," Redgrave said as he traced his fingers along Skye's bare arm. "So I think she does want me. Don't you, my dear?"

Skye's response was to turn to Redgrave and kiss him, as passionately as she had ever kissed Balthazar. But Redgrave wasn't pushing her away the way Balthazar had. Instead he was responding to her, delighting in her, and the sight was sickening to behold.

This isn't real, Balthazar thought. He knew that, didn't he? He attempted to step forward and break this up—to fight for her if he had to—but his feet wouldn't move. Glancing down, he saw that he stood in mud, or quicksand . . . something dark and liquid that had begun to drag him down.

Redgrave's laughter made him look up again. "I've half a mind to make you watch this in real life, Balthazar. It could be even more enjoyable. And you know I can do it, don't you?"

Balthazar awakened with a start. Panting, he leaned against his headboard and put his face in his hands. The fact that his sire was invading his dreams again to torture him was bad enough.

Worse that Redgrave knew what Skye really meant to Balthazar—and had figured it out faster than Balthazar himself had.

"I hate this hellhole," Nola Haladki said.

Balthazar gave her a sympathetic glance. They stood on the sidelines of the auditorium, which was now draped with various pink and red decor, while Snow Patrol blared from the DJ's booth and couples did that weird twitching thing that for the past forty years or so had passed for "dancing." He missed the waltz. "By hellhole, do you mean Darby Glen High in particular, or the Valentine's Dance in particular?"

"Both." Nola took a swig of the sherbet-and-Sprite punch from her blue plastic cup. "I've been getting my certification for physical therapy online. This summer I'm doing the hands-on part of the training, and then I am so out. Of. Here."

"You're going after what you really love," he said. "Good for you."

Nola gave him a sidelong glance. "Listen, kid. You're fresh out of college. You probably still think you can 'inspire students' or some crap like that. But I'm telling you now, if you think it's going to be all Freedom Writers all the time, you're living in a dream world. This business sucks. Get out while you still can."

As gravely as he could, Balthazar said, "I doubt I'll be doing this for the rest of my life."

"What's that you won't be doing?" Tonia Loos came skittering up on her high heels, which, like her skintight dress, were brilliant red. "Balthazar, you look amazing in that suit. Too bad you can't wear it to school so we could enjoy the view every day. . . . Oh, hi, Nola."

"You both look wonderful tonight, too," Balthazar said. Which was true: Although Tonia's getup was a little loud for his taste, she was undeniably attractive in it, and Nola had abandoned her usual fleece track jackets for a gray satin sheath that gave her a classic elegance.

Nola gave him a grin and a nod; Tonia draped herself on his arm. "You're a smooth talker, you know that?"

"I'm gonna see if any of the kids got around to spiking the punch yet," Nola said, with the definite implication that, if they had, she'd help herself to a glass before making the students dump it out.

"You know," Tonia said, looking up at him from beneath a veil of thickly mascaraed lashes, "later on, when the crowd's started to die down, sometimes the teachers dance."

"I doubt they'll play many songs I know."

"You're always so mysterious! Never talking about yourself. Like, for instance, what kinds of music you enjoy. What songs would you know?"

Balthazar considered Tonia carefully before answering. "If

I answer one of your questions, will you answer one of mine?"

"Ooooh, a guessing game. I love games." Tonia's grin widened.

"I tend to like older music," he said. "Classical, mostly, though I have a soft spot for fifties stuff. Elvis, rockabilly, that kind of thing."

"I bet the DJ would play some Elvis. At least the remixes." Tonia was obviously very fixated on the idea of their dancing together later that night. Balthazar resolved to have something very important to do at the end. "Okay, your turn. What do you want to know?"

Balthazar kept his voice very gentle, because he suspected that, with her, the words would have to be harsh: "Why is a woman as attractive as you so insecure?"

Tonia didn't answer at first. Then she raked her nails through her hair, as if that could calm her down. "Wow. You're—blunt. Really blunt."

"I'm trying to be honest."

"If you're not interested—or there's someone else—there is, isn't there? Should've known the women of this country wouldn't let you wander around unattached."

Balthazar nodded and tried not to think of Skye. "Will you tell me why?"

"You only see the final result. But in high school—really, my whole life up to now—I didn't have this." She made one gesture that seemed to take her in, head to toe. "Do you know, I lost fifty pounds the year before I came to Darby Glen? I thought it would change things. But nothing ever changes."

He was too familiar with loneliness not to recognize it in another. "You're not the person you were before. I'm not talking about the weight; I mean—you get to change. Mature. Grow up." It was a journey Balthazar would never be able to take; no matter how many centuries he lived or how much wisdom he acquired, his heart would always be young. "Trust the person you've become. Take pride in it. And see who chases *you*."

Tonia finally smiled a little. "Maybe you should be a guidance counselor instead of a history teacher."

"You never know." Before fate was done with him, who could guess what else he might have to become?

The song shifted to something slower, almost mournfully sweet. The lights dimmed slightly, and the room filled with a rosy glow and dozens of tiny white scattering beams reflected throughout. For one brief moment, even the high school auditorium seemed to be beautiful.

Laughter echoed from the doors as another group of students came in. Balthazar turned, knowing even as he did so that he would see Skye there.

She stood at the edge of the group, tethered to them only by Keith's meaty hand around hers. Skye wore a more elegant dress than the showy stuff most of the girls favored; in this light, her dress appeared to be some delicate shade between champagne and rose, made out of filmy stuff that left her shoulders and most of her legs bare while wrapping her body in soft petals. Her dark, burnished hair was gathered into an artfully messy tail that fell to one side of her neck. There was no pretending that she wasn't the most beautiful girl in the room.

Skye's gaze locked with his. In that instant, he saw just how much she didn't want to be with Keith . . . how she'd dressed for him, so that he would see her and want her.

And he knew she saw how badly he wanted her.

The moment between them was broken when Keith towed her out onto the dance floor. Within seconds, they were only one of the many couples shuffling along awkwardly out there, Keith half talking to his friends over her shoulder as if she weren't even present.

Balthazar remembered seeing Skye waltz with Lucas at Evernight Academy's grand Autumn Ball a few months ago. That was the place for a girl like this, not some crepe-papered auditorium. And the guy who should be with her . . . the one who should dance with her . . . God, anybody else but Keith Kramer. She was so much more graceful than her lump of a partner would let her be.

But he didn't mean that. He didn't want her to be with "anybody else." He wanted her to be with him.

The rest of the dance was torture. He had to confiscate some cigarettes from a few juniors out back, and summon the willpower to toss them away unsmoked. Tonia Loos had finally gotten the picture, but a couple of students, including Madison Findley, asked him if he was allowed to dance with them even though he was a teacher. Balthazar instantly said no. One of the final couples to arrive was Craig Weathers and Britnee Fong, which made him want to somehow shield Skye from the sight. She didn't seem overly troubled, but not long after they came, she let Keith lead her off the dance floor and out of the auditorium.

Probably they were going out back to talk. Or make out. Or to Keith's car. A guy could get a lot done in a car.

"Balthazar?" Nola said. "You need to take five? You're looking glazed. Besides, this thing's wrapping up."

Don't go after her unless you're going to follow through, he told himself. *Don't put her through it. If you stop her from being alone with Keith, you're stopping her from moving on. You can't do that unless you're ready to go the whole way.*

Nola repeated, "Balthazar? You want to take off? Tawdry, I mean, Tonia and I can wrap up here."

"Thanks," he said, straightening up. "There's somewhere else I need to be."

And someone else I need to be with.

Chapter Twenty-two

IT'S GOING GREAT, SKYE TAPPED OUT ON HER phone as she stood in the back hall of the auditorium. *We're having a good time.*

I call bullcrap on that. Nobody ever took time to text their friends in the middle of an actual fun *date.*

Clementine had a point, as usual. Skye said, *You have to start somewhere, right?* Then she glanced up and added, *Keith's back. TTYL.*

"Hey, Madison and Phillip figured out how to jimmy the library lock," Keith said. "We're gonna get the six-packs out of the trunk. Come on."

"We can drink those later, right?" Skye glanced backward at the doors that led to the auditorium, through which music faintly played. "We're at the dance, Keith. We ought to dance."

"But all the guys are in the library," he said, like the whole point of going to a dance was to hang out with as many of your friends as possible, as far from the actual dancing as possible.

Evernight's Autumn Ball would have been lost on him. "What, you don't drink or something?"

"It's not that. It's just—" *Forget it*, she decided. "Go ahead. I'll catch up with you in a few minutes." By which she meant, never, if she could swing another ride home.

Keith said, "Sure thing!" as he started jogging back toward the library. Obviously he was completely unconcerned whether she stayed with him or not. Why shouldn't he be? She didn't care any more than he did. For him, she was just his excuse to come to the dance; for her, he was just proof that somebody out there might eventually want her, even if Balthazar didn't.

Balthazar did want her, though. She knew that. The memory of the two hungry kisses they'd shared rippled through her. Skye had thought if she pulled back, she'd stop longing for him, but her longing had only become sharper. She wanted him to ride beside her, to make dry comments in study hall, to spar with her until she was breathing fast and her heart pumped wildly— Skye missed both everything they'd had and everything they *should* have had.

Give me More, she thought, but the joke fell flat even in her own head.

She wanted to walk back onto the dance floor. Being watched by Balthazar was hotter than being held by Keith. And she'd chosen this dress, these nude shoes, her hair, her makeup, everything, thinking only of how Balthazar would feel when he saw her.

But her walking back out there alone would look like she

was begging him to notice her again, or to take that next step, and she wouldn't beg. Also, she'd be all by herself in front of Craig and Britnee; she was doing better with that, but not better enough to let them see her apparently ditched by her date for the evening.

Maybe she could just walk through quickly, go to the door, and snag a ride with somebody who was leaving, like couples were starting to do . . .

Someone tapped her on the shoulder, and Skye turned to see Redgrave standing next to her. "Shall we dance?"

She gasped and started backing away, but Redgrave made no immediate move to follow. He was as debonair as ever—dark gold hair immaculately slicked back, his suit a deep tan that matched his skin. His attire was appropriate for the occasion, complete with elegantly knotted cream silk tie at his throat. His hazel eyes looked less like those of a human and more like those of a wolf.

"I'll scream," Skye managed to say. "Someone will come."

"Someone will. One of your dear school chums, I suppose. It makes no difference to me, because whoever runs through that door first will be the next person I kill. Do you really want blood on your hands?"

"You won't kill them if it's Balthazar. He's here." Though she knew better how to defend herself now, she also knew exactly how much of a chance she stood against Redgrave on her own.

"I realize that. But we don't want to drag him into this, do we? Or take the chance that he won't be first through the door?"

He smiled at her gently and gave her a quick, courtly half bow. "I only asked for a dance, my dear. And, of course, for that conversation you owe me. You don't seem at all the type to break her word."

Skye had made that promise to save Balthazar's life, but she'd envisioned Redgrave finding her in Café Keats again or some other neutral ground. Not here, in a half-lighted hallway, when she was all alone.

Balthazar's on the other side of the door, she reminded herself. *Stay here so that if anything happens, you can scream or run for it. This is as good a place as any to get this over with.* "All right. If you want to talk, talk."

"I also want to dance."

"I didn't promise you a dance."

Redgrave laughed softly. "But you want to dance, too, don't you?"

The strangest sensation settled over her—not real emotions, but a weird sort of echo of love and desire. Skye could almost feel the weight of it, light but inescapable, like a shroud. She found herself lifting her arms into dancing position, and Redgrave smoothly slipped into her unwilling embrace.

"What are you doing to me?" she managed to say.

"A very few of us can do this. It takes a thousand years or so to age into the gift, but when it comes, ah, everything becomes so much easier. The effect doesn't usually last long—so don't worry, you'll be repelled by me again soon enough." Redgrave began to sway back and forth with her. "Evolution works for all creatures, you know. Not just the living. And nothing says 'survival of the fittest' like the ability to hypnotize your prey into remaining still just long enough to be bitten."

He's going to bite me! Skye wanted to pull away, but her body didn't obey. She just kept dancing, a marionette to his will. "You get one conversation. Use it."

He ran his cool fingers down her spine, pausing just long enough to dip his fingers in slightly beneath the back of her dress. "You should join me. If you don't, you'll regret it. I mean that sincerely. You've proved to be a resourceful and courageous girl—and quite a lovely one, if I may say so." Redgrave dropped a kiss on her shoulder, which made her want to shove him away with all her strength. His hold on her remained fast.

At least she could still speak the words she wanted. "One, I'm not joining you. I don't want to be a vampire. And two, get your hands off me."

"After this dance," Redgrave promised, as his hands shifted lower on her back and pulled her close so that their bodies were pressed against each other. "I told you before, my dear. Joining me doesn't mean becoming a vampire. There's no saying whether your miraculous blood would still have its power after the change, which means I'm not willing to take the risk."

"So, what, then? I pay my membership dues, get the secret decoder ring?"

He chuckled slightly. "I want you to agree to come with me. To remain by my side, under my protection, and to give me or any vampire I choose a taste of your blood when we wish it. I promise you, if you do that, we'll never take so much as to make you ill or weak. Scarcity is half the value, you know. You'll have all the trappings of wealth. My tribe will serve you as ardently as they serve me. If you liked, we could make this a very pleasant arrangement—" His hands settled on her hips, making it clear what he meant by that. "But if you wish to keep matters on a professional basis, you may have whatever companions you wish. Except Balthazar, of course. He's a rogue. A menace to his own kind. That won't do at all."

"Why is it so important to you that I join you if you're just going to take me anyway?"

"Easier, for one," he said. "More agreeable, also, and I like things to be agreeable and easy. Despite what Balthazar might have told you, I'm actually rather generous as long as I get my way." *As if that was some great virtue*, Skye thought. "Besides, there's a particular sweetness in bending someone's will that mere force cannot possess. The deaths of the More family? A night's entertainment. Slowly turning Charity into my most devoted progeny? Unending bliss."

"Is that supposed to be your sales pitch?" Already she could begin to feel some of her will returning to her; the ghostly shimmers of false pleasure she'd felt at Redgrave's touch had started to fade. "There's nothing I want more than to be rid of you. Forever. I'm not coming with you, no matter what."

"You say that before I describe the alternative." Redgrave's hands went to her hands around his neck and seized them both; the pressure was hard, crushing. Meant to hurt. He pushed her back—dance over—but kept her in his powerful grip. "You will come with me, Skye. By your will or against your will. As I've said, I'd prefer it if you chose this path. And much less trouble than keeping you captive. But if I have to build you a cage, girl—I will."

"Let me go," Skye said. Finally her body returned to her, and she jerked back as hard as she could, but it wasn't enough to break his hold. "I'll never do it."

"I could do so much for you, Skye. Why don't you choose a man who really wants you? Who knows what he is and doesn't run away from it?"

The reminder of Balthazar's rejection stung, but not enough to distract Skye from what she had to do.

"I would never choose you." With that, she kneed Redgrave between the legs as hard as she could.

Somehow Redgrave still held on to her, but she had the satisfaction of seeing his face contort in pain as he half doubled over. As he swore, Skye kept trying to tug herself free of him, and at least managed to tow them a few steps closer to the door before he recovered himself, gasping, "That wasn't nice."

"Let go of me, you son of a bitch!"

"Why are you carrying on so? I'm not going to hurt you tonight. Nothing's going to change tonight, nothing at all. This is merely your chance to learn more about what will happen." Redgrave's expression betrayed his smoothly handsome face; at last she could see the monster within. "Let me tell you what your life's going to be like in the cage."

✤ 286 ✤

Skye jerked back again—just in time for Redgrave to be flung bodily away from her, into the wall.

Balthazar stood there—in from the side hallway, silent as a cat, so that she hadn't heard him approaching. His hands were clenched into fists, and again it hit her just how enormous a man he was. "Get out of here," he said to Redgrave, reaching into his pocket and revealing a stake. Was he keeping that on him at all times? Not a bad idea. "Get the hell out of here, now."

Redgrave rose, attempting to collect himself. But the eerie light in his eyes was more inhuman than ever. "Why so furious? I only came here to talk—that's all."

"You were *touching* her."

Something deep in Skye's chest fluttered, turned over.

Redgrave began backing away, but he said, "It's too late, Balthazar. The others are coming. They know about Skye. They're eager for a taste. And what won't they do to get it?"

"You sound like a drug dealer," Skye snapped.

Balthazar's eyes widened. "Oh, my God. That's it. You don't want her blood for yourself at all; you want others to do your bidding in order to get it."

Redgrave grinned. "I expected you to catch on before now, Balthazar. You've always been clever—clever enough, at least. How you went on and on about Skye's blood as a drug, without ever realizing the possibilities. I realized them as soon as Lorenzo let me drink from him. Virtually any vampire on earth would do anything . . . *anything*, if it meant they could feel the experience of life again."

It was too much at once, but Skye kept trying to put it all together. "You—you said scarcity was half the value. That's why you'd only bleed me bit by bit. You want my blood to be hard to get, so the others will have to come through you."

"As indeed they will," Redgrave said. "Think of the potential, Balthazar. It's been more than a century since we last had a prince. Don't you think we're overdue?"

Balthazar backed closer to Skye, his arm out, as if attempting to shield her from even the idea of this. "You want to start the old wars over again. Claim absolute power for yourself."

Redgrave said, "I waited as long as I could. This really is easier if you cooperate, Skye. But the word has spread. The messengers with the shades of Lorenzo's blood have traveled far and wide—beyond this continent, almost across the world. They all know where to find you."

Skye clutched at Balthazar's shoulders. He'd just barely managed to keep her protected from half a dozen vampires; no matter how strong or how fast he was, or how hard he tried, he couldn't protect her from hundreds.

"You see it now." Redgrave put his hands behind his back; his old polish had been restored to him, as if neither of them had landed a blow on him tonight. "You're a vital resource, Skye. One I intend to exploit. And that's why you should join me— because I have the ability to think long term. To plan ahead. That's why I see the wisdom of keeping you alive. Most of the other vampires who will mass here within the month? They'll want nothing more than to drain you dry."

"They won't all follow you," Balthazar said. "Some are too decent to do it. And others will fight you. Soon the wars won't even be about her blood anymore."

"The noble ones are harder to marshal now than they were before, aren't they? Without Evernight Academy to bind them together, they're more truly lost souls than ever. And Skye's blood will give me power beyond any other. Loyalty beyond any other." He took a few steps back, becoming part of the shadows farther down the hall. "It's too late to stop it, Balthazar. But it's not too late to join me, even if she won't. Bring her to me and save yourself."

Balthazar threw the stake so hard and fast that Skye didn't even recognize it until after Redgrave dodged it—but only barely. A bright red line welled up along his high cheekbone, though the blood didn't flow out. Because his heart didn't beat, Skye supposed. Balthazar said, "You'll die for this."

"Doesn't matter if I do," Redgrave pointed out. "They'll still come." Then he melted into the dark and was gone.

Skye breathed out, half a sob, and put her hand to her chest. "Oh, God. Balthazar, what are we going to do?"

"I don't know." He remained tense, at the ready, like he still hoped for a chance to kill Redgrave with his bare hands.

"Will it happen like Redgrave says it will?"

"Probably." Balthazar's frustration was palpable—he kept clenching and unclenching his fists, rocking on his feet, like he needed to beat the hell out of something but didn't have anything handy. Skye could recognize that feeling, because she had it herself.

"What am I going to do?"

"You should leave town. Get away from here—from me, too. Someplace where Redgrave won't know to look for you."

"I can't leave my parents."

"They've already left you."

The harshness was one thing more than she could bear. "Don't say that! They need me to be strong for them! They already lost Dakota—"

"That's why they can't lose you, too," Balthazar said. "Please, Skye. If anything happened to you, I couldn't bear it." He glanced at her over his shoulder, and in his eyes she saw raw fear, raw need. She knew that she'd meant to keep her distance from him, but that seemed absurd. As if she could ever be parted from Balthazar—he was always in her, always a part of her.

Down the hall, someone—Coach Haladki?—yelled, "Hey, is somebody back here? We're closing this place up!"

"They shouldn't see us," Skye whispered, looking around quickly for some kind of exit, but Balthazar found it first.

"Come on," he murmured, pulling both of them into a nearby closet and softly pulling the door shut behind them.

Now they were hidden—and they were face-to-face, only inches apart, in a small and very dark space. Skye put her hands against his chest, though she didn't know whether it was to keep them slightly apart or to touch him however she could.

"Hello? Being locked in until Monday morning isn't going to be any fun!" Coach Haladki's footsteps echoed in the hallway outside. Then, in a normal voice, she said, "Jesus, what is this?

A tent peg or something? Are they *camping* in here? Somebody's getting suspended."

So quietly it was barely a sound, Skye said, "You found me."

"It took me too long. I shouldn't have let you out of my sight—I went after you when you walked out, but I only saw Keith and followed him—then I had to bust Madison and the rest of them for drinking in the library, which was idiotic, but I was stuck."

"Will you come on?" Ms. Loos's voice came from farther down the hallway. "Nobody's here."

"I thought I heard voices!" Coach Haladki protested.

Ms. Loos replied, fake-sweet, "Maybe it was the echo of your amazingly loud voice that never stops talking."

"Fine. If they were here, they're gone. Let's lock up." Coach Haladki walked off, her footsteps becoming fainter with each step.

Balthazar's hands covered hers. She realized only at his touch how icy with shock her fingers were; he was the one warming her. "Redgrave didn't hurt you, did he?"

"No." That dance didn't count, she decided, disgusting though it had been. "Did you see him come in, or—or sense that he was here?"

"No. Usually we can sense one another if we're not distracted—vampires, I mean—but I was. Distracted." He sounded like he wanted to cut that part of himself away, that if he could take a knife to himself and do it, he would.

Skye whispered, "Then how did you know I was in danger?"

"I didn't." Dark though the room was, he was close enough

now for her to see his eyes.

"Why were you distracted?" She lifted her face to him. "Why did you come after me?"

Balthazar paused one moment before confessing, "Because you were off with some other guy. I couldn't stand it. Skye—"

He didn't finish what he was going to say. He crushed her to him as his mouth closed over hers.

This time he didn't pull away after two kisses, or five, or ten. This time his hands brushed over her hair, outlined her back, traced her entire body. This time she didn't have to come to him. She could get lost in the wild tide that swept over them both, demanding that she touch him, kiss him again, breathe him in.

When his broad hand slid up her skirt to cup her thigh, she gasped—in delight, but it shook him out of the trance. "Home," he said, hoarse and ragged. "I need to get you home."

She knew what would happen if she went home with him. They were about to take a step they could never undo, go so far that there would be no turning back.

Skye kissed him again before whispering against his open mouth, "Yes."

They tangled up in each other all the way down the hall, all the way to his car, and at every stoplight on the way to his house. Then everything blurred together—the moment she took down her hair, the feel of his chest beneath her palms as she pushed off his shirt, the way their bodies looked together in the firelight—all one long, delirious dream from which she never wanted to wake.

Chapter Twenty-three

BALTHAZAR HAD FORGOTTEN HOW THIS COULD feel. Lying next to the girl you loved, knowing that she loved you in return. The simple pleasure of waking next to someone and watching them sleep. Or what it was like to be still together for a long time, talking of nothing in particular, being silly just to make her smile.

Not that they had much time to waste on silliness.

That Saturday afternoon, after he'd taken her back to her home, they hung out in her bedroom. Her bed was still made—for the moment—but she lay across it with her head on his thigh. "Would they try to take my parents hostage?"

If they could find *them*, Balthazar thought, but he'd never been as grateful for the absenteeism of Mr. and Mrs. Tierney as he was this weekend. "I can't rule it out, but I suspect not. They see you as prey. The only one who would try to negotiate with you as an equal is Redgrave, and taking your parents captive . . . it's not the kind of thing he does."

If Redgrave wanted her parents dead, they'd be dead already. Balthazar knew that from his own nightmarish experience. If he told her that, though, it would scare Skye too badly. He didn't want her more frightened than she already was.

"I don't want Mom and Dad to lose another child. Losing Dakota was hard enough on them," she said. He brushed his thumb along her cheek. "I have to stay here. For them." Her voice trembled, but when she glanced up at him, her blue eyes shone with faith. "But you'll be with me."

It seemed to him that he'd never forget anything about that moment: the way she managed to smile for him, the pattern of the soft blue quilt on which they rested, or the slant of winter sunlight through the window that painted rich shades of red into her dark hair.

He hated to shatter that serenity, but he had to: "Not always."

"What do you mean?"

"I'll protect you as long as you need it. Forever, if that's how long it takes." With Redgrave's vampires spreading the word far and wide, "forever" wasn't a rash promise; it was a realistic estimate. "But, Skye—as much as I care about you—you know we can't always be together."

She pushed herself upright. "What? Why?"

"Because you're alive, and I'm not." Such a simple way to phrase such a complicated truth: Speaking the words was no easier than thinking them had been that first night they spent together, when he held her in his arms and wished in vain that they could always be like this, that nothing would ever have to change. "Someday soon you'll want to go to college. You'll have other friends, human friends, and you won't be able to explain me to them."

"What couldn't I explain? You look like any other guy—well, any other massively hot guy—"

"I look like I'm a couple years older than you. I can pass for a few years older than that. I can't go any further. Could you explain me when I still look nineteen and you look thirty? Forty?"

Skye blinked; obviously she'd never considered matters in that light before. Maybe it was rash of him to be thinking so far ahead—but he could imagine loving Skye that long. Even longer. She tried to rally. "I'll tell them I'm a cougar."

"And you won't ever want to get married? You won't ever want to have children?"

"Do you seriously think that's the only way a woman can ever be happy? You really are from the seventeenth century, aren't you?"

"You can't know now what you'll want someday," Balthazar insisted. "What you can know, what you have to know, is that being with me long term has a price. A price you shouldn't have to pay."

They stared at each other for a long moment. The tranquility of their afternoon had been shattered, and he wondered whether Skye would choose to separate herself from him now rather than continue a relationship that ultimately had to end.

Then she said, "I don't think you've thought this through."

"Skye, I've had centuries to think about what it would mean for a mortal to get involved with a vampire."

"You're not listening to me." She tucked a lock of her hair behind her ear; her pale blue eyes met his steadily. "Balthazar, Redgrave and his tribe want to enslave me for my blood. Hundreds, maybe thousands, of them are coming here. Hasn't it occurred to you that maybe—maybe the only way to stop them—is to change my blood forever?"

He didn't understand. Or did he? But no. She couldn't mean that. "What are you saying?"

"It's possible the only way to change my blood so that Redgrave can't use it is to change me." Skye's voice shook slightly, but she continued on, resolute. "To turn me into a vampire, like you."

"Absolutely not." Balthazar could see the logic of the idea, but it was distant, far behind all the many emotions that told him to refuse her. "You don't know what it means to be a vampire, Skye. You don't know what it means to die."

"Do you think I want to die? I don't. But you're not the only one who can look into the future and see hard choices." Breathing out sharply, Skye looked away from him for a moment; when she turned back, there was a fierceness in her gaze that took his breath away. "Well, we agree on one thing. We need to seize the moment."

Then she kissed him, more hungrily than ever before, and within seconds he had pulled her down onto the bed, willing the world to go away for them both.

The rest of the weekend was one long blur of her lips against his. They didn't argue about their different ideas about the future, at least not explicitly. Instead they focused on how best to keep Skye alive and in Darby Glen, for her parents' sake and for her own.

This involved some serious tactical thinking. Balthazar had already emailed Lucas and Bianca to talk about who could help protect her, or how best to dissuade the vampires from searching for her. Apparently Bianca's parents were spreading a counter-rumor that Skye was only an illusion Redgrave had planted in Lorenzo's mind, and the stories about her were all another of his well-known, elaborate tricks. This was now being whispered through all the gathering places that served similar purposes to the fallen Evernight Academy—small, secluded schools, retreats, and centers where the undead came together, including a rehab center in Arizona. This was a good first step, but it could only help so much, Balthazar thought. The vampires who went to these places were, by definition, the more civilized among them, the ones who wanted to live among humans without causing undue harm. What they had to worry about were the wild ones. The ones who never came near Evernight Academy, who cared less about appearing human and more about taking prey wher-ever they could find it.

And even the civilized vampires might miss the old days of the wars, the days when they had a prince . . . but that was something to worry about later. Skye's dilemma was all he could concentrate on now.

Lucas had come up with the idea of notifying Black Cross about the coming vampire incursion in Darby Glen. As much as Balthazar disliked the idea of relying on a band of vampire hunters for any reason, he had to admit—the surest way of scattering a pack of vampires was to set an even larger pack of hunters on them. Lucas was going to attempt to reach out soon, which meant Black Cross would be on the scene, in force, before long.

Balthazar wasn't sure how long he could remain out in the open once Black Cross arrived. They never allied with vampires, ever; to them, all vampires were merely animals. But he'd face that when the time came. Whatever it took to remain with the woman he loved, he would do.

They never parted once until Monday. That morning, at dawn, he ran with Skye toward his car, the better to get her home to change for school.

As she bounced onto the passenger seat, she said, "I don't know how I'm going to keep a straight face during homeroom."

"You'd better. I don't want to be arrested for indecency."

"After this weekend, you could be arrested many times over." Skye beamed at him.

"I don't want to take advantage of you," he blurted.

She gave him a look. "It's a little late for that. Besides, I'm legal, consent-wise. You knew that, right? The 'arrested' thing was just a joke."

Balthazar, who had grown up in an era when women Skye's age were usually married and giving birth to their second or third child, had other things on his mind than some arcane legal limit. What mattered went deeper than that. "Skye, I don't want you to look back and feel like you . . . didn't have any choice. Like you were only with me because of the intense situation you're in."

Skye leaned over and kissed him, long and slow, mouth open. When their lips parted, she whispered, "I want to be with you, too. I know that, absolutely."

"Okay," he said, a smile spreading across his face.

As Balthazar put the car in reverse, he thought he saw a flicker of movement at the corner of his eye and turned sharply to look at it—but it was nothing. Maybe the reflection of a bird on one of the Findleys' windows, or the swing of a curtain. Redgrave was nowhere near, and it felt for a moment as if they had time for everything in the world.

Homeroom was indeed tough to get through, but he managed to get the class talking among themselves about *The Crucible*, which meant he was at least relieved of the burden of having to say one thing while his brain was thinking another. Particularly given what his brain was thinking.

Balthazar knew he was doing a bad job of not looking at Skye; it seemed impossible not to watch her, to see her long dark hair and remember how it had felt against his skin, or to fix his gaze on her lips and remember kissing her. Fortunately the class was too preoccupied in trying to derail the conversation from school topics to notice, he thought.

"My, you're in a good mood today," Tonia said to him in the

teachers' lounge. "I'll let you out of dance duty early again if it makes you this happy each time."

"*You* let him?" Nola said, stirring a cupful of creamer into her coffee.

"I left about twenty minutes early, that's all," Balthazar insisted. The coffee in the lounge was crap—the coffeemaker purchased by the school board was of no brand he knew, or wanted to know. And yet today the brew seemed to taste great. "Besides, why can't I just be in a good mood?"

Rick put one finger to his cheek, pretending to consider it. "Because it's mid-February, and the sky is the color of the stuff that clogs up drains, and we're in the dead center of a semester that seems like it's never going to end?"

"And yet I'm feeling fine." Balthazar shrugged. "Can't help it."

"Freak," Nola said good-naturedly as she headed out into the halls.

"Hey, since when does honors history do *The Crucible*?" Rick said. "That's my turf, buddy."

Balthazar took the joke as it was intended. "You could always do *Rent* instead."

Rick sighed. "I wish. When it comes to doing any play that's even the slightest bit 'risky,' this school board has its head up its—well, let's just say, the same location where I think they got this coffeemaker."

Balthazar had to laugh, and for the first time he realized he'd miss being here . . . well, a little bit.

As he headed into study hall at the end of the day, he was

already weighing the merits of spending the hour texting Skye with various plans for their evening versus brainstorming a way of living in Darby Glen without having any public presence Black Cross would be able to detect. That would have been easier if he hadn't spent the past month and change as a schoolteacher; going underground, usually simple enough to do, would be complicated now. But he'd manage somehow, if that was what Skye needed—

"Hey, you." Rick met him at the entrance to the library, cutting off that train of thought. "I'll take this shift, okay?"

"What do you want me to chaperone this time?"

"You catch on fast. Actually, though, Zaslow wants to see you."

Balthazar frowned. "What about?"

"Didn't say. She's got on her grumpy face, though, so brace yourself." Rick waved good-bye before he retreated to the safety of the library.

While Balthazar walked toward the principal's office, he wondered if leaving the dance early, even with permission from the other chaperones, was definitely against the rules. He wasn't too worried about it in any case; it was difficult to get too anxious about your boss's opinion when you were undead.

Nothing about it bothered him much until he walked into Principal Zaslow's office and saw Skye sitting in one of the chairs, tears in her eyes.

Even before Zaslow said a word, Balthazar thought, *Damn it. They found out.*

"Mr. More, I'm afraid a student has come forward with some troubling allegations," Zaslow said. She folded her blue-framed glasses on the desk in front of her. "Miss Tierney, you may go. I've already spoken to your parents; they're on their way home."

Oh, great, now *her parents show up.* "Is everything all right?" Balthazar said, keeping his voice steady but looking appropriately concerned.

"Good-bye, Miss Tierney," Zaslow said, firmly dismissing her. Skye walked out without looking back at Balthazar once—exactly the right way to play it, he thought—and he didn't stare after her.

Already Balthazar's mind was racing. He had spent so much time worrying about the supernatural obstacles they were up against that he'd never seriously considered the more literal road-blocks they could face. If Skye's parents chose this inconvenient time to become present in her life again, remaining near her would be even harder. If people were now watching him around Skye, or if he was fired before he had backup on the scene at school, it would make it that much more difficult to protect her—just as things had become much, much more dangerous.

"Now that we're alone, Mr. More," Zaslow said, "let's cut to the chase. Are you sleeping with Skye Tierney?"

"Of course not," he lied. He would have to lie. *I'm not really a substitute teacher; I'm a vampire* was not a great defense.

"Another student reported seeing you together leaving your house in the wee hours of the morning."

Madison, he thought, remembering that flicker at the window.

"That student is mistaken. I admit—I, ah, did have some company this weekend. Female company, I mean. And I must not have been as discreet as I needed to be." Balthazar tried to look merely sheepish, rather than horrified. "Come to think of it, she's around the same height, same coloring—I can see how someone might be confused if they saw us together from a distance."

Zaslow didn't seem convinced, but she didn't dismiss his explanation entirely. "Miss Tierney said that the two of you do spend some time together outside of school."

Skye didn't have as much experience as he did at these things, unfortunately—she'd cracked a little—but he knew what she must have told Zaslow. It was as clear as if she'd whispered it into his ear. "We both enjoy riding, so we inevitably end up running into each other on the trail. I've even rented one of her stable's horses a few times. And we do talk." Once again, a lie was stronger when laced with the truth. "You might know that she lost her brother almost a year ago. Well, my younger sister died tragically, too, and I know what it's like to need someone to talk to."

Because he'd admitted to going slightly over the line, he could see Zaslow was considering the idea that he was being honest. "You realize how easily that could be misconstrued."

"Well. I do *now*." He ran one hand through his hair, allowing the curls to show; the younger he looked at the moment, the better. "I'm sorry, Principal Zaslow. I'm new at this, and I guess I'm still figuring out where to draw the boundaries. But I'd never abuse her trust." *Yours, sure. I'm abusing that right now.*

Balthazar didn't like that, but he knew better than to attempt to share any part of the truth.

"She said your friendship was just that. Friendship." Zaslow sighed. "I'm inclined to believe you both. You haven't done anything damaging—yet. But I can tell that girl thinks the world of you, which is why you need to back off. If you don't, you're going to have a brokenhearted teenage girl on your hands at best, a lawsuit by her parents against the school district at worst."

"Never," Balthazar said. He wasn't sure exactly what her parents would be able to sue him for but devoutly hoped never to learn.

Zaslow looked more relieved than frustrated. "Listen—I want you to go in and talk with the counselor for a while. She's ready for you, and she'll be dealing with Skye for the next few weeks. I just need to be able to write this up to the satisfaction of Skye's parents, and to clear your record so you won't have any trouble getting hired in this state again."

How quickly could he get that over with? An hour, Balthazar figured. Skye was smart enough to get home immediately and stay there until he came for her. "Okay. Sounds like a good idea."

"And I meant what I said," Zaslow said, leaning forward over her desk. "We don't need a situation on our hands, and we don't need gossip. Stay away from Skye Tierney."

"I will," he replied, thinking only of how quickly he could get to her again.

Chapter Twenty-four

IT'S BEEN SUGGESTED THAT YOUR RELATIONSHIP with Mr. More may be inappropriate for that of a teacher and student.

Principal Zaslow had been so calm when she spoke—kindly, even—but Skye still felt like she wanted to throw up. Balthazar was only the second guy she'd ever been with, and to have the principal asking questions about it like it was something gross or dirty—it popped the happy bubble she'd been in since Friday night, and all those feelings of being trapped on every side were rushing back.

Skye's phone rang as she crossed the quad, gravel crunching under her feet. Had to be her parents—though her phone didn't recognize the number. Maybe they were calling from some office phone in the capitol building. "Hello?"

"Why, hello there," Redgrave said. "Am I calling at a bad time?"

She froze in her tracks. "How did you get this number?"

"You put it in the public information on your Facebook profile. Which is an enormously stupid thing to do, by the way. Everyone knows there are all sorts of predators on the internet." Even over the phone, it was obvious he was smiling. "So, I was wondering if you'd come to any final answer for me."

"I told you I don't want to have anything to do with you." Her voice shook, and she wished it didn't.

"But now that you know what's at stake—what your alternatives really are—I was hoping you'd have changed your mind. We could have such wild times together."

"Both alternatives have me as your slave. No thanks."

Redgrave made a tsk-tsk sound with his tongue. "As you say—it's going to happen one way or the other. You've chosen the other. So be it. See you soon, my dear."

The call disconnected. Skye stuffed her phone in her bag and dashed toward the nearest bathroom. She definitely needed to rinse her face off with cold water; she might need a little while to cry alone in a stall.

See you soon. She could just imagine the leer on Redgrave's face as he said it. Never had she needed Balthazar's presence so badly. Forget the protection he offered—she only wanted him to wrap his arms around her and comfort her. But she couldn't go to him now. For at least a couple of hours, she'd have to brave it on her own.

As she walked into the bathroom, she was breaking down her options: *Okay, I can take the bus home. Once I get inside my house, I'm safe. Mom and Dad are probably coming home early—and, hey, I can use this, make it seem like all the gossip is why I want to leave school. Why I have to. So Balthazar and I can still get out of here in a few days—*

Then Skye realized that somebody else was in the bathroom with her: Madison, who was touching up her blush in the mirrors.

"Oh," Madison said, her voice a flat parody of its usual enthusiasm. "Hey, Skye."

"It was you," she replied. There was nobody else it could have been. "You told Principal Zaslow that I was—was seeing Mr. More."

Madison turned toward her, a fake sympathetic look on her face. "I was only thinking of your well-being. He shouldn't take advantage of you. It's so wrong. Khadijah and I were talking earlier about how he's probably, like, brainwashed you or something."

"You were only thinking of my well-being." Skye's voice was shaking again, but now from anger instead of terror. Anger felt better. She embraced it. "So you decided to spread your little stories throughout the entire school. Because you were thinking of me."

"It's better to let it all out." Madison shrugged, cooler than ever as she turned to continue fixing her makeup. "Secrecy just makes it seem like you should be ashamed, when he's the one who did something wrong."

Flushes from the other area of the bathroom told Skye they weren't alone—and if everybody didn't already know thanks to

Madison, they all would soon. Her last day or two at Darby Glen High would be her absolute worst.

Eyes narrowing, Skye said, "You were jealous."

Madison glared at her. "You don't know anything."

"I know you always talked about Mr. More and tried to get him to notice you and took stuff over to his house. You're angry because you think he likes me instead of you. How pathetic can you be?"

"You're one to talk," Madison retorted. "I saw you this morning on your walk of shame."

"You didn't see anything!" It was a lie, but Skye didn't care. It felt good to yell. "You don't know anything! You're just a jealous, small-minded loser."

Madison folded her arms. "And you're just the slut who slept with a substitute teacher."

"Don't mind her, Skye?" Britnee Fong walked out to wash her hands. She smiled at Skye as she went to the sink. "Madison's just freaking out? You know, because you were the last person at this school who didn't think she was a total jerk? And now you're onto her, too? And also, Madison, *slut* is a sex-shaming word? Plus antifeminist? So maybe don't say that?"

"I don't have to take this from the school whore and the fat pig." Madison threw her blusher in her purse and stalked out of the bathroom.

Skye and Britnee stood staring at each other for a long minute. At first there was no sound but the water pouring from the faucet, unattended. Then Britnee said, "Do you need a ride home or something?"

"I'm okay," Skye said. "I can catch the bus. But—thank you."

Britnee shrugged, obviously unable to think of anything else to say, and went back to washing her hands. Skye got out of there without even rinsing off her face.

That was the longest bus ride home she'd ever taken. Skye leaned her forehead against the window, stared at the royal-blue plastic seat in front of her and tiredly wondered which part of her school day was the worst.

Finding out Madison wasn't even a real friend? Bad.

Finding out Britnee was actually an okay person? Bad and good at the same time, but definitely embarrassing, considering how many times she'd snickered at Madison's mean jokes at Britnee's expense.

Having Principal Zaslow ask her about her sex life? Extra super bad.

Getting a phone call from Redgrave telling her that her time was up? Yeah. That one was the worst.

She ran as hard and fast as she could from the bus stop to her house, and her hands shook as she worked the keys, but within seconds she was inside, her back to the front door she'd just slammed. Skye breathed out in relief. At least Balthazar and Bianca had made sure this place was safe for her. If she hadn't been able to have one safe fortress, one place she knew nobody could harm her, she thought she would have self-destructed weeks ago.

Skye went to the kitchen, ate a couple of restorative cookies, and went upstairs. Almost without realizing it, she went into her closet and looked at the suitcases she had stored on a high shelf. Balthazar wanted her to stay so she could lead some TV-commercial version of the ideal life that he seemed to believe in. Skye knew better than that; maybe it was too easy to romanticize life after you'd stopped living it. Logic told her that while her life might not be better if she fled Darby Glen now, odds were it would at least be longer, and at this point, that seemed like more than enough reason to go.

But Mom and Dad—losing her within a year of losing Dakota—what would that do to them?

For the first time in months, tears of grief welled in her eyes. She'd thought she had cried for her brother so much in the months right after his death that she never would again, but the wound could still open up, raw and painful as ever. Probably it always would. Skye flopped onto her bed and opened the bottom drawer of her bedstand; there, in the very back, were the photos of Dakota she'd stowed there last summer. It had been too painful to look at them then, but she could never, ever have thrown them away.

The picture she'd grabbed showed the two of them together, white-water rafting a couple of years ago. He was always the true adventurer. She was always the wannabe.

Dakota was probably the one person in Darby Glen to whom she could ever have told the whole truth about Balthazar. Sure, he would have flipped out—but he always had an open mind, and stood by her no matter what. He never tried to fit people or relationships into tiny, neat little boxes. More than anybody else Skye had ever met, Dakota had been truly free.

He died doing what he loved, her mother had always said, and for the first time, the thought didn't make Skye want to scream. Dakota had taken his own wild chances. If he'd known he would hurt them all so badly and lose his own life, no, he would never have gone off-roading. But he hadn't known. He had just been rushing out into life's adventure, arms flung wide.

"I'm having my adventure now," she whispered to the image of his smiling face. "And it's a whole lot scarier than yours. But I'm going to have better luck. I know I will, because you'll be looking out for me."

Downstairs, she heard the front door open and shut, and two sets of footsteps coming toward her room. Skye rolled her eyes. Mom and Dad, finally on the scene, when she least needed them to be. "I hope you guys didn't freak out," she called. "The principal was totally off base, I swear. It's nothing."

"Oh, it's something," said Redgrave as he pushed open her bedroom door.

Skye screamed and flung herself backward, but there was nowhere to run. Charity was with him, and two other vampires, three, four—oh, God, how many were there? "How did you get in?" she cried.

"Once our dear Miss More joined us, and finally learned what was keeping us from paying you another call, she was kind enough to tell us that certain charms can repel the wraiths. Apparently her last, brief stay at Evernight Academy was highly instructive." Redgrave lifted a chain from around his neck, from which dangled a copper key. "The wraiths loathe certain metals. Won't come near a surplus of them. So we came with a surplus. But don't worry, we'll be leaving shortly. And you'll be leaving with us."

He stepped closer, and once again she felt that shroud descend over her—the one that wouldn't let her move except as he wished. Skye could only stand still as Redgrave stroked her hair and said, "I did warn you, my dear. You've made your choice. And now it begins." He leaned so close that his lips nearly brushed her cheek. "You're mine."

Chapter Twenty-five

BALTHAZAR DITCHED THE COUNSELING SESSION as fast as he could while appearing cooperative; the last thing he needed was for Zaslow to decide he should be questioned some more. As soon as he walked out, he heard the final school bell, and the hallways and quad were instantly flooded with students. He hurried through them as quickly as he could, heading toward his car. Reaching Skye as soon as possible was his only goal.

Even as he reached into his pocket, though, he noticed that several of the students—mostly the girls, but several of the guys, too—were looking at him in ill-disguised fascination, or whispering about him as they passed by. In the clamor of school letting out, he wasn't sure what they were saying, but he had an idea . . . and was pretty sure Madison Findley got it started.

Gossip wasn't his biggest problem at the moment. He picked up his cell to see that he had a message from Skye, sent a while ago: *Redgrave called me. He was talking like whatever it is he's going to do, he's going to do it soon. Tomorrow, maybe. Let me know as soon as you're free.*

Quickly he texted Skye, *I'm out of there. Are you all right? I'm headed your way.*

Just as he pressed Send, someone stepped in front of him, blocking his path. Balthazar looked up to see Madison Findley standing there, all innocence, made-up and smelling strongly of perfume. "Mr. More?" she breathlessly said. "I just wanted to let you know—what people are saying—well, I for one totally believe in you."

He gave her a look that showed more of his true power— more of his nearly four hundred years on earth—than he normally showed any mortal. She couldn't have understood what that really meant, but her face paled slightly. "What *are* people saying, Madison?" Balthazar leaned slightly closer, the predator in him close to the surface. "Since you seem to know."

"I didn't mean to—well—it's not my place to say," she finally managed to get out.

Did she think she was fooling anyone with that act? He said only, "I'm leaving now, Madison. Excuse me." Then he stepped past her, giving her distance, as if she were a pile of trash to be avoided.

When he looked down at his phone again on the edge of the parking lot, he saw that Skye hadn't responded.

It had been a whole two to three minutes, at most.

Skye wouldn't fail to answer instantly today unless—unless something was preventing her from answering.

Or someone.

Balthazar swung into his car and gunned the motor. If any students got in his way while he drove out, he'd just fulfill Nola Haladki's dream and run a few over.

As he tore through the streets of Darby Glen, tires squealing on the asphalt, Balthazar kept glancing at his phone, as if somehow he'd missed its chime. It never blinked. No messages.

At one stoplight, he hastily typed, *Skye? Did you get my last message? Are you OK?*

She didn't reply to that one either.

Balthazar drove even faster, almost blind to the road or anything else—which is why it shouldn't have been so surprising when he zipped into an intersection at the same moment another car did.

For one split second it rushed toward him—this looming mass of metal—and then the shattering power of impact. The world turned into the sound of tearing steel, and glittering shards of broken glass.

After that, for several long moments, it was hard to say exactly what happened when. Balthazar knew that his car flipped and rolled. He knew that he was suspended upside down by his seat belt for a few seconds that still lasted too long. Although he could taste blood in his mouth, the wreck had done nothing very severe to his resilient vampire body.

But the other driver—

Jesus Christ, Balthazar thought, coming back to himself as he struggled to open the door with it upside down. *I wanted to*

get to Skye, but I didn't want to hurt some innocent person. Or kill
them—please, not that.

He managed to push his way out onto the days-old snow, which had turned black from dirt and soot along the roadway. The intersection wasn't a busy one, at least; only the two cars were damaged, though both of them appeared to be nearly totaled. Each of them was now a twisted, smoldering hulk on the side of the road. His Ancient Civilizations text lay in the dead center of the intersection, open to an illustration of the pyramids. The only structure nearby was a junky bar farther down the road that looked as if it had a shady clientele; though most bars wouldn't have been open yet at this hour, neon signs in the window proclaimed different beer brands as the best. Nobody had ventured out to see what the ruckus was, though; the wreck must have been distant enough not to be heard inside.

All of this flooded into Balthazar's mind unfiltered, slightly disjointed. He must have struck his head—not badly, but enough to shake him for a second. As he struggled to his feet, he saw someone walking toward him—the other driver, it had to be, thank God she was okay—

Then he saw who it was.

"Constantia," Balthazar said. He realized that he hadn't had a stop sign at the intersection; he'd done nothing wrong to cause the wreck. "You rammed me."

"It looked like the only way to get you to stop. I had to do some wild driving just to catch up with you." She smiled at him, maddeningly confident despite the bloody scratches across her cheek, or the splinters of dashboard glass scattered across her jeans and olive-green coat. "In a hurry?"

"Where's Redgrave?"

Constantia's smile became even more smug. "Where you'd most like to be, I think."

That meant, *with Skye.*

His car was beyond driving, now or ever again. He'd have to run the rest of the way. But he was within a mile of her house—it wouldn't take long. "Get out of my way," he said.

"I think it's past time for me to be in your way," Constantia said.

Balthazar reached inside his jacket—no, he'd lost the stake at the Valentine's Dance. So he'd have to improvise. He snapped a short branch off a nearby tree, never dropping eye contact with Constantia. "It's past time for us to settle this."

She laughed at him. "Think about it, would you? You're so desperate to reach Skye in time. Well, it's too late for that. Redgrave has her. What you need to know is what's going to happen next. I'm willing to tell you."

Did he believe her? To his horror, he did. At times like this, Constantia didn't bluff. "Are you saying you'll help me?"

"And all it will cost you is one drink." She nodded toward the bar. "C'mon, Balthazar. For old times' sake."

As if the old times had been any better than these. But if Constantia was telling the truth—and he suspected she was—getting more information was probably the best thing he could do. "Five minutes," he said. "Tops."

"Ten minutes, and you buy the drinks."

"If it's ten minutes, you're buying."

"Fine." Constantia laughed again. When she was happy, and thought herself in control, she could be such a beautiful woman. "Ten minutes and the booze is on me."

The bar was even more decrepit on the inside. Avocado-green linoleum on the floor seemed to have been laid down in the 1970s, which Balthazar suspected was also the last time it had been mopped. Only a handful of other customers were in there, all men, all reeking of tobacco, alcohol, or other, more highly controlled, substances. Eighties heavy metal blared from the jukebox; no wonder nobody had heard the wreck. A few of the men gave Constantia hungry looks, but as soon as she looked back, they seemed to understand that it was time to turn their heads and study something else.

Constantia spoke to the bartender, ample breasts snug on the bar, a bill folded between two of her fingers; all of this guaranteed his attention. "This guy usually prefers red wine, but here, I think he'd like . . . a scotch. Straight. I'll have a shot of tequila."

"You've changed your drink," Balthazar said.

"Good absinthe's not as easy to come by, these days. They finally sell it again, but they've stripped the hallucinogens out. So what's the point?" Constantia smiled at him, warm and inviting, the same way she'd looked at him countless times in the centuries between them. Despite her cruelty and her petty need for vengeance, she was beautiful, vital, and witty. Had she not orchestrated his murder, and Charity's, Balthazar might have truly cared for her.

As it was, he said only, "You never give up, do you?"

"On you? I'm glad to see you have enough ego to assume my only possible motivation could be jumping your bones again." The bartender slid her shot in front of her, and she gulped it back in one smooth motion. "I've moved on to bigger game now."

Balthazar was wild to reach Skye, to find out what was happening to her, but he knew the only way to get that information was to let Constantia play it her way. "And what's that?"

Constantia leaned closer to him, and in the avid, hungry gleam of her eyes, he could see flickers of the Teutonic warrior-woman she'd been in the thirteenth century. "Redgrave. It's time to finish him. My suggestion? We take Redgrave on together, like you suggested back in 1918. I knew you didn't really mean it then, and that's why I didn't listen, but you were righter than either of us realized. That wasn't the best opportunity, though. This is."

It was only one of many shocks he'd received that day, but in some ways it was the greatest. Redgrave and Constantia had been together when he met them; their alliance had continued from centuries before Balthazar's birth to now. Constantia turning on Redgrave was like the moon turning on the sun. "You can't mean it."

"I do."

"How?"

"He's right about Skye," she said. "As soon as I tasted Lorenzo's blood and knew what he'd experienced through her, I

✤ 319 ✤

realized the potential. The vampires are already massing. They'll do whatever they have to do just for a taste."

"So how do we stop it?"

Constantia stared at him. "We don't. We use it for ourselves."

Incredulously, he stared at her for a long moment before he could speak. When the bartender put his scotch in front of him, Balthazar found his first words, "Give me the whole bottle."

As it slid across the bar to him, Constantia said, "Don't reject it out of hand."

"If you think I'd ever put her through that—"

"What would you be putting her through, Balthazar? She adores you. Skye's sweet teenage putty in your hands. Just get her to give a pint every six weeks. Standard blood donation. That would be more than enough for you and me to claim power over Redgrave. Over anyone. Skye won't even mind, not if she's doing it for you." Constantia gave him a sidelong glance. "And I promise not to be jealous. Though maybe you'll let me watch occasionally? For old times' sake."

He had to stretch this out a little longer. Besides, he truly wanted to know: "Why would you ever turn against Redgrave?"

"You're not the only one who got murdered, you know." Constantia stared into the distance for a moment before throwing back another swallow of her drink. "Did that ever sink into your self-absorbed mind? Some of us hide our resentment better than you do. You were always a guy who wore his heart on his sleeve, Balthazar. Me—I take my time. I choose my moment. And the moment is now. He's never played for higher stakes; that means he's never been more vulnerable."

Balthazar let his inner turmoil show on his face, the better to weigh his words with the proper reluctance. "It seems inevitable—with so many vampires after her, they're going to get her blood one way or the other. I just can't believe this is the only way out. But it is, isn't it?"

"I knew you'd see sense!" Constantia leaned closer. "Or is it just that you're past ready to slice off Redgrave's head and throw it in the nearest river?"

"That would be a side benefit."

She laughed—a rich laugh, husky and sensual. "They're taking her to Redgrave's hideout. You'll never guess where—I'm sure you looked—well, it's the old church on Holland Avenue."

"A church?" Churches repelled vampires; Balthazar couldn't have searched the churches in town even if it had ever occurred to him. "How is that possible?"

"Desanctified." Constantia's grin widened. The unsteady light from the television above the bar painted her face and blond hair in different shades, second to second. "Something ghastly happened there—I'll spare you the details, since you were always the squeamish type. Anyway, it's about as holy as a McDonald's. Let's go there. You explain to Skye how we're going to handle this. Sweet-talk her. You know how. And we take Redgrave out forever, claim Skye for ourselves."

Balthazar tilted his face toward her—not suggestively close, but not far short of it. "Just one thing, Constantia. Which part of this do I need you for?"

"If you could take Redgrave out on your own, you'd have done it by now. So would I. Together, we have the chance neither of us had alone. After that? You'll stand by the bargain, because that's the kind of sap you are."

Drifting still closer to her as his fingers closed around the scotch bottle as if to pour again, he said, "You might be right." Then he smashed the bottle into the side of her head.

Constantia collapsed, unconscious. "Hey!" the bartender yelled. This place didn't have high standards, but apparently knocking women out during happy hour was beyond the pale. "Hey, what are you trying to do?"

Balthazar went for the door, pointing at the bill Constantia had left on the bar. "Keep the change."

As soon as he was out, he took off—pushing himself into a run, faster again, then faster, as hard as he'd ever driven himself, praying against hope that he'd reach Skye in time.

Chapter Twenty-six

SKYE WALKED OUT OF HER HOUSE WITHOUT THE vampires laying a hand on her.

Redgrave had her, utterly, completely. In whatever spell he could weave that controlled her actions, he pulled her forward. With one hand on the banister, she carefully descended the stairs, the vampires behind her mocking her powerlessness. She struggled with all of her strength—and yet she remained trapped within the meek, pliant shell Redgrave had sealed her in.

As she walked, she could hear her phone chiming—she had a text from someone, probably Balthazar—but she was as unable to answer it as she was to do anything else of her own free will.

The effect wore off once she was in the van, but by then it was too late. Vampires sat on either side of her, their clawlike hands clamped around her arms, and the one behind the wheel was taking them toward the highway.

"Where are we going?" she demanded.

"My dear, does that matter?" Redgrave rode shotgun. He

carelessly yanked the copper key from around his neck and tossed it into the tray between the two front seats. "Soon it will make very little difference to you where you are. Or who you are. It's enough to say that we're going to a stronghold of mine only a few hours away. Once we're there—you'll see."

Skye imagined a cage—a literal cage of steel bars—and fought back the sudden, throat-clenching urge to vomit. *I'll fight*, she thought. *I need to surprise them. That's the only chance I've got. What I need is the right opportunity and the courage to go for it.*

She looked out the windows, trying to get her bearings. Though the fear racing through her and the van's speed threw her off for a moment, finding their location wasn't that difficult for her in the town where she'd lived her whole life. They were taking the longer but better-known route to the highway, which meant they were going to lead her right by . . .

Could that work? No telling until she tried it.

The vampire closest to her was Charity, whose beauty and height made it clear that she was Balthazar's sister, even if nothing else about them was the same. As Charity yanked off the copper chain she wore, breaking the links with no thought of using it again, she said, "Why can't we start now?"

"Charity." Redgrave's voice held a note of warning, despite his undeniable fondness. "You know the rules."

Charity stomped her foot on the floorboard of the van. "I *hate* rules."

Redgrave chuckled. "You've been a good girl lately, haven't

you? Coming back when you were called, telling us how to battle the wraiths: all very useful. I suppose we do need someone else to spread the news of what Skye can really do, now that Lorenzo is gone."

"May I? Please? May I?" Charity's eagerness had taken on a gleeful edge that made Skye's skin crawl.

"Just one sip," Redgrave said, and Skye's gut tensed so hard that she thought she might vomit.

Charity turned to look at Skye with eerie eyes that seemed to penetrate her. They were not unlike Balthazar's eyes, but— unfocused, somehow. Even as Skye tried to push herself away, in vain, Charity lifted Skye's arm and bit in just below the elbow.

Skye cried out more in revulsion than in pain, though that was bad enough. Just the sight of Charity, lips curled back, fangs sunk deep in her flesh as red blood welled—it was utterly repulsive.

"Charity! That's enough!" Redgrave's polite mask had again fallen; he reached behind to grab Charity by the neckline of her dress and forcibly pull her away from Skye. The pulling away hurt even worse than the bite, and Skye folded her arm against her chest with a cry. Charity didn't even seem to notice. Her eyes had a glazed, uncertain look.

The mere scent of blood had never been so distinct to Skye before. It seemed to fill the van. All the vampires breathed in deeply, and she could almost see the ripple of excitement that went through them.

All of them except Charity: She remained lost in that far-off place—in her long-lost life, Skye realized. Her jaw was slightly slack, and blood smeared her lips, yet Charity looked more sane . . . more alive . . . than she ever had before.

"From now on, nobody touches her but me," Redgrave said. "Nobody ever drinks from her without my permission, and nobody takes one drop more than I allow. When she's herself again, Charity will be reminded of the price of even momentary disobedience." The other vampires nodded, willing to do anything if it meant they had a chance at her blood.

The van took a turn onto a road Skye knew well. She pushed Charity away from her, as if she were too disgusted to bear having her near. Now they were past the old Crouther house—now the Hanna place—

As soon as she saw the intersection she sought, Skye brought both knees to her chest and reached for the door on the other side of Charity. When the other vampire tried to seize her, she kicked him soundly in the jaw with both feet. Her sweaty fingers slipped on the door handle—but she had it. The door swung open, and Skye shoved toward it with all her strength. Both she and Charity fell out onto the side of the road.

The impact slammed into her gut, robbing her of breath, but Skye pushed herself to her feet immediately. She had to stumble over Charity's inert form; Charity kept staring upward, as if at the stars, taking no notice of what was happening near her. Once she was up and clear, Skye ran as fast as she could down the side street. If she could just reach it—

Behind her she heard the squealing of brakes, the slamming

of doors. Redgrave and the others were behind her, gaining fast, and Skye didn't dare look back.

A weather-beaten FOR SALE sign marked her target, though Skye would have known it anywhere. The yellow paint, now faded, the dark green shutters on the windows: Her childhood home was as she remembered it. She took the front steps two at a time, the way she used to when she was racing Dakota to see who would get the first brownie fresh from the oven. The lock had never been the best, and she kicked the door just beneath it, the same way she had when she got mad about Dakota stealing her Padmé Amidala action figure. Just as it had then, the front door gave way, and she ran into the empty house.

"I'm here!" she called. Her words echoed amid the empty rooms. It hurt to see the place like this—cobwebs in the windows, every room bare and lonely—but there was one thing Skye knew hadn't left. It couldn't leave. "Help me!"

More steps thundered on the front stoop. Skye bolted toward the back door, just in case this didn't work, though if it didn't, she would be buying herself a few more seconds of freedom at most. She'd take it.

"Do you really think you can escape?" Redgrave said. His voice echoed, too; the vampires were inside. Her hands shook as she placed them on the back doorknob. "Silly girl. Don't you understand?" He was half growling now, his words more like those of a demon than a human being. "You belong to me."

Which was when the light began to flicker.

Not the electric lights: Those remained as dead as they

had been a year ago when her family moved out and cut off the power. No, this was an unearthly light, a sharp blue-green that sliced through the darkness in flickering waves not unlike sunlight against the bottom of a swimming pool. The air chilled around her in an instant, as if she'd opened a refrigerator door. Skye's rapid, panicked breath made small clouds in the coldness around her.

She knew what this was. This was what happened when a ghost became angry.

And Skye had always known that her childhood home was haunted.

Sleet began to fall, thick, frigid sheets of it, appearing out of nowhere, and behind her she could hear the vampires begin to screech in astonishment and fear. Balthazar had been right: Most vampires hated ghosts and feared them so much that they couldn't bear even facing them—and the talismans they'd brought to ambush her in her own home had been discarded in the van. They were powerless against ghosts now. And her ghost—the ghost she'd known as a child, the one she had never feared, always welcomed—was striking back with all its might, saving the little girl it had once cherished.

The vampires scrambled back the way they'd come, not quite out the door but close. She could stay in here, remain safe . . . but no. She didn't have her phone or any other way of contacting Balthazar, which meant the vampires would have plenty of time to think about how to flush her out. They could set the place on fire, for instance; if she'd thought of that within five seconds, the vampires would think of it soon. She had to use this chance, this momentary disorientation, to get as far away from Redgrave as possible.

"Thank you," Skye whispered as she yanked the back door open and ran into the night.

The cold air hit her harder than it had before, when she'd been entranced by Redgrave. He hadn't done her the small kindness of allowing her to grab her coat, and so she wore only her skirt, boots, and a violet sweater that did little to ward off the intense chill. Snow had begun falling again, tiny, sharp flakes that blew sideways with the fierce wind.

Hang on, she told herself. *You're not far now.*

Soon the vampires would escape from her childhood house; not long after that, they would pursue her. But Skye thought she'd bought herself a few minutes, and that was all she needed.

It seemed to her that her childhood ghost remained with her—a helpful little shadow trailing behind. Skye could picture her more vividly than ever now: the small girl by the fireside, who wore a long nightgown and hugged her knees to her chest.

But, no. It wasn't just a picture. The ghost truly was with her—communicating, perhaps, through Skye's connection with death.

Skye thought, *Why didn't I feel your death, too?*

The reply was an image rather than words: the little girl in an old-fashioned hospital, sick from something the doctors didn't understand. Her tiny hands above the blanket, clutching and pulling at it in her pain, until finally she let go. That was where she had died, not at home. But the death remained unnatural and wrong.

You were poisoned, Skye realized. *By who? And why?*

The child had never known. Her parents? The strict nanny? Something horrible, though—all those images were immersed in a depthless kind of evil that felt like oil against Skye's skin.

Skye grabbed at the branches of the trees around her as she took the steep slope down to the riverbank. The wind had never seemed more brutal, and the edges of the water were thickly overlaid with a crust of ice. Still, she knew what she had to do.

Quickly she stripped off her sweater, boots, and skirt, until she wore only her underwear and camisole. The cold was almost unbearable, but she knew that trying to swim in heavy clothes would drown her, and wearing wet things after she got out of the water would freeze her faster than anything else.

And she had to swim. To cross the river. It was the one way to hold the vampires off long enough for her to reach Balthazar. On the other side of the river was the high school, Café Keats, lots of places—and her running naked and wet into Café Keats would be the gossip of the year, for sure, but that was fine by her.

No matter what the cost, Skye was going to win. She was going to live.

She took a deep breath and jumped into the river.

The freezing water felt like a thousand razor blades slicing into her at once. Skye surfaced and screamed in pain, but she also started kicking as hard as she could, fighting the current to take herself to the far shore.

The cold had its own will, it seemed, and within seconds her limbs seemed almost too heavy to move. Skye kept kicking, though, reaching out with each arm even as her teeth began to chatter. Water splashed her face, stung her eyes. She could feel the droplets beginning to freeze on her skin and hair within moments.

Her ghost seemed to surround her again, but it felt different this time—like she was being shown something. Another way.

A door.

Gasping, Skye's hand broke through the ice on the far shore of the river. She managed to stumble out, and her wet body felt as if it were freezing to the ground. Shaking so hard she could barely move, she crawled up the riverbank toward the grove near her school.

The door opened near her, around her. It was as if she had no choice but to fall through. Skye collapsed onto the frozen snow, unable to move any longer. What was happening within her body had become a thousand times more important than what was happening around her.

Someone was reaching through the door to her. Someone who loved her.

Her lips formed the word she no longer had the strength to speak: "Dakota."

And that was when she knew she must be about to die.

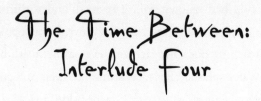

The Time Between: Interlude Four

June 12, 1978
Los Angeles, California

DONNA SUMMER CROONED OVER THE SPEAKERS as the dancers moved on the discotheque's illuminated floor. Balthazar—decked out in the polyester slacks and open shirt the era's fashion required—moved among them, grateful for the crowd and the thick wreaths of cigarette smoke that caught the whirling blue-and-white lights overhead.

All of these would help hide him.

Finally, amid the swirling figures around him, at the very center of the dance floor, Balthazar glimpsed the people he sought.

Redgrave, slick in a dark red suit and shiny pink shirt, dancing with Charity—she who had been so sweet, so innocent, so lost—now wearing a sheer white top and hot pants that barely covered her childish body. Sparkly shadow coated her eyelids all the way to the brows, and the thick, creamy blush so in vogue now made her look as artificially rosy as a porcelain doll.

They were having fun. Even Balthazar could recognize that.

The thought of it pricked through any semblance of sanity he'd restored to himself over the years. Rage swept through him—at Charity, at fate, but most of all at Redgrave, who had created them all in his own murderous, soulless image.

Well, Redgrave was the one he'd come to kill. Charity could break her heart crying for him if she wanted. Balthazar told himself he didn't care. What happened to his faithless baby sister didn't matter. Nothing mattered but finally ending Redgrave.

The others weren't here tonight; he'd taken care to watch them for a long time, to track their movements for months, before making his move. Lorenzo wasn't currently with the tribe—off on one of his solo jaunts, from which he inevitably returned blood-fat and overly satisfied with himself, a new, terrible poem in hand. Constantia and the others had set out in a black Trans-Am, to hunt or to party, assuming they saw any difference between the two.

And finally—after weeks of Balthazar's waiting and watching, the moment he'd wanted had arrived. Redgrave and Charity were out in public, and therefore vulnerable, all on their own.

Balthazar grinned as he maneuvered his way through the dancers, more eager for this kill than he'd ever been for human blood. For the first time ever, he was going to murder someone and enjoy every second of it.

As he approached, Charity whirled around in a circle beneath the glittering ball that hung overhead. The lights painted her blue, white, blue again. Redgrave laughed as he danced closer to her, his movements half obscene. For the first time, Balthazar didn't care; anything that distracted his prey was welcome.

He slipped one hand into his back pocket, where the switchblade's handle found his fingers. It wouldn't be easy beheading someone with this, but good luck getting an ax into a nightclub.

Besides, if he had to saw harder to get the job done, that was just more fun for him.

The music shifted to something even louder and faster as Balthazar finally made his way to their side. Before Redgrave could even turn his head to look at him, Balthazar brought his free hand to the man's neck, gripping him with all his strength.

"Say good night, Charity," Balthazar said, swinging the blade up to slice through Redgrave's neck.

Charity screamed and jumped onto them, and they sprawled on the dance floor in a tangle of limbs.

He'd expected a fight. Balthazar smashed his fist into Charity's jaw—the first time he'd ever really struck her, and it hurt as much as he'd always expected. All around them, people began screaming, skittering away from the fight on their platform boots and wedge heels. As she went down, the blinking lights beneath the floor outlining her prostrate body, Balthazar turned back to Redgrave, and this time he managed to get the blade in.

"What are you—" Redgrave's voice cut off in a gurgle of blood. God, it felt good to shut that bastard up.

"The hell is going on?" A bouncer made his belated appearance, but Balthazar easily threw the guy across the room before turning back to his messy work. The bouncer could pick himself up later. If the cops came, he could hurl them back easily enough, too. Balthazar had a job to do.

He sawed deeper. Deeper again. Redgrave kicked and struck at him, but already his strength was beginning to fail. Balthazar finally had enough centuries, enough power, to stand against him. The golden eyes darkened with panic, and Balthazar rejoiced to see it.

And then he smelled the smoke.

Balthazar turned and realized that the loudening screams within the room had nothing to do with the fact that he was murdering Redgrave in front of nearly a hundred witnesses. They were mostly about the fact that the disco was now on fire.

There was never one moment's question about who was responsible, but all the same, he had to stare at the sight of Charity standing atop the bar, right behind the wall of fire. "They're all going to die!" she shouted, pointing at the people desperately cramming the few exits they could reach. "And it's your fault like always!"

Instantly Balthazar knew he had a choice: He could finish Redgrave now and let the innocent humans around him pay the price, or he could save them and let Redgrave go free.

Swearing violently, Balthazar rose to his feet, kicked Redgrave once in the face to make himself feel better, and ran toward the nearest exit. Some people were trying to get out, but they were crammed into the door so tightly that they were crushing one another; others, dazed and frightened, simply stood on the edges of the dance floor as if numb. He'd seen this in humans before—an almost animal response to danger, freezing still as if to keep a predator from seeing them. That same instinct could kill them now.

Balthazar vaulted over the crowd, seizing one of the light arrays suspended over the dance floor to hang slightly above eye level. From there he could reach down and rip the door away from its hinges; although he banged it against several people and heard them cry out, the most important thing was that the exit was now clear. People began rushing out in earnest, and even the stupefied ones reacted once they saw clearly what they needed to do.

He looked up through the smoky air—still striped with the colors of the rotating lights upon the ceiling—and searched for Redgrave and Charity. They were nowhere to be seen.

"Redgrave!" he shouted, furious at the lost chance. But already he could hear fire engine sirens wailing—probably the police, too, if anybody had reported his attack before Charity turned to arson—and it was time to get the hell out.

The scene in the parking lot was chaos. By now the discotheque was ablaze, tongues of orange fire leaping into the sky. Balthazar ducked through the crowd, hoping the soot that now coated his skin and hair would mask his appearance somewhat. Although he'd been willing to suffer the consequences of killing Redgrave in public—up to and including years in prison, execution in the electric chair, and the long, messy process of digging himself out of whatever pauper's grave they'd have buried him in after—he didn't want to go through all that while Redgrave still lived.

He'd done his best. Taken every risk. And he'd failed.

Wearily he walked to his red Mustang GT Fastback to find a note on the windshield, tucked beneath one of the wipers. He knew who it was from and was only mildly surprised to realize that they'd been able to determine which was his car. Probably he shouldn't have left a pack of cigarettes on the dash. Or at least he should've switched brands.

The handwriting was in Redgrave's elegant script, each letter flourished the way it would have been in a note penned centuries ago:

Balthazar—
As long as you wish to be human, you will never be able to defeat me.
When you finally accept that you are a monster, you'll no longer wish to defeat me. You will again become mine.
Charity sends her love.
Redgrave

Balthazar crumpled the note and let it fall to the asphalt. Behind him, the nightclub burned, and somehow the music played on and on.

Chapter Twenty-seven

BALTHAZAR HAD RUN AS HARD AS HE COULD TO the church Constantia had described . . . only to find it empty. There were signs Redgrave's tribe had been here not long ago (empty vodka bottles, cigarette butts, a tattered bit of lace he knew could only have come from a dress of Charity's), but they were gone now.

Constantia had lied. Even when she was trying to take him in as a partner, she'd lied. In retrospect, he didn't know why he hadn't understood that to begin with.

He needed to go back to the last place he thought Skye had reached safely: her home. From there he could track her. At least the Tierneys' house wasn't far from the church. Within minutes he'd run to her door, only to see that he was too late.

The front door had been forced. "Skye!" Balthazar shouted as he ran inside, though he knew she wouldn't answer. Despite the darkness, he could see the few telltale signs that she had made it home and not left of her own free will. Her backpack was slung on the bench in the front hallway; wet footprints along the carpeted stair showed that at least four vampires had come after her.

He ran up to her bedroom; he knew he wouldn't find her there, but he couldn't help himself. In her room was her phone—still blinking to tell her about texts she'd never read—and her coat. Balthazar's fist closed around the collar of her coat, clutching it close to him as if it could somehow stand in for her.

Where would they have gone? He had to think. There was only the one main highway out of town; ultimately Redgrave and his tribe had to travel that path if they were leaving Darby Glen, and Balthazar felt sure that they were. If he hurried, he might be able to cut them off—but how could he get there in time with his car a torn wreck on the side of the road?

He could saddle up Eb—or ride bareback to save time, if Eb would submit to it—but even the fastest horse in the world couldn't make that trip with the speed Balthazar needed to save Skye.

Just then he heard a vehicle pulling in to the driveway. Skye's parents, finally coming home too late? Constantia out for revenge? Balthazar went to the window, preparing to jump to the earth below and circle around, hopefully in time to steal whatever car had just pulled up while the driver was inside the house.

Then he heard the voices from below: "Skye? Are you here?" That was Craig Weathers.

"Hello? We thought we would check on you?" And that was Britnee Fong.

Balthazar weighed the possibilities, made his decision, turned around, and started downstairs, just as the lights came back on.

Craig stood near the door, his hand on the light switch. Britnee was a few steps ahead. Both of them gaped when they saw him descending the stairs.

"Oh, my God?" Britnee said. "I thought Madison was just making stuff up?"

Craig's face hardened with anger; in one instant, he went from looking like a handsome boy to a formidable man. "What have you done? Where's Skye?"

Balthazar held up his hands, a gesture that he too late realized might have been more effective if he hadn't been holding Skye's abandoned coat. "Skye's in serious trouble. We have to find her, now, and I need your help."

"The only trouble she's in is because of you," Craig said. "You're our teacher. You're not supposed to . . . mess with any of the students."

"I'm not a teacher," Balthazar replied, giving them as much of the truth as he could while sounding credible. "I've been pretending to be one, but I'm not. She's known all along. Skye's been in danger since before this semester started, and I came to Darby Glen to protect her."

Both Craig and Britnee stared at him, clearly caught between surprise and disbelief. Britnee finally said, "That is so not where I saw this conversation going?"

Balthazar descended the final few steps so that he and Craig were face-to-face. He said, "Skye's been kidnapped. If we don't stop the people who took her before they get out of town, I don't know if we're ever going to get her back. I don't have a vehicle. Are you going to lend me yours or not?"

Britnee raised her hand, as if they were still in history class. "Maybe we should call the police?"

"This isn't a situation the police can deal with," Balthazar said. *Especially not the handful of rent-a-cops in this small town*, he left unspoken.

Craig's glare only became more intense. "Why should we trust you?" he demanded. "How do we know you didn't hurt Skye?"

Balthazar's patience, already frayed, began to break. "Let's *find her* and then you can *ask* her, okay?"

Although he could tell Craig wasn't convinced, Britnee put one hand on Craig's arm and said the first sentence Balthazar had ever heard from her that didn't sound like a question: "I believe him."

Craig breathed out sharply, then said, "I'm not giving you my car. But I'll drive you wherever you want to go."

"That's a bad idea." Balthazar didn't want to drag any more humans than necessary into this.

"No way," Craig insisted. "If you're going anywhere in my car, we're going with you."

Every second they spent arguing here was a second Skye didn't have to spare. Balthazar yanked the car keys from Craig's hand and said, "You're coming with me, but I'm driving."

"Watch it!" Craig yelped as Balthazar swerved around another, slower vehicle; they were traveling at nearly a hundred miles per hour despite the high winds and light snow.

"I've got this," Balthazar said. This was definitely not the time to mention that he'd already totaled one car today.

"Can you describe the car the kidnappers are in?" Britnee sat in the backseat. "We could call it in as a possible DUI? So the cops would at least stop them?"

That would've been a good idea under different circumstances. "If the police try to pull them over, they won't be able to help Skye. We'd probably just get the cops killed."

Craig said, very quietly, "Could that really happen to the police? To Skye?"

What awaited Skye was so much worse that Balthazar couldn't bring himself to think about it, much less describe it to Craig and Britnee. "This is as dangerous as it could possibly be," he said. "Which is why, when we find them, I want you both to stay out of it."

"I could help," Craig said. Balthazar shook his head once, a swift no.

Britnee said, "I think I would probably be more of a hindrance in this situation?"

"Exactly. Stay in the backseat. That works."

For a moment, they were all silent; the main noise Balthazar could hear was the roar of the car's engine. His fear welled up to fill the spaces where their conversation had been. All he knew was his own wild terror that he'd lost Skye.

Don't be stupid, he told himself. *Even if . . . even if Redgrave has her, even if he's drunk from her, you know he won't kill her. You'll still be able to save Skye. She's strong. No matter what she's been through, she'll fight to stay alive.*

The thought failed to reassure him. Every other time Redgrave had tried to take something from him during the past four centuries, Redgrave had succeeded. Anger pent up from those old treacheries, his countless defeats, burned within Balthazar until it pushed the fear out.

Before, Balthazar hadn't thought beyond retrieving Skye and making sure she remained safe and well. Now he knew he couldn't rest until Redgrave was finished once and for all.

As they took the next curve, Craig said, "This is around where Skye used to live." He obviously said it just to fill the silence, but the idea caught fire in Balthazar's mind. Instantly he knew what Skye would have done.

"Show me where," Balthazar said, turning in the direction that Craig pointed. Even as he did, he saw the black van, the vampires around it—and Redgrave.

They looked dazed, as though they stood on consecrated ground. No doubt they'd encountered the wraith within Skye's house . . . and she wasn't with them. Maybe she was barricaded inside.

Balthazar stepped hard on the brakes, tires squealing, and shifted Craig's car into park so fast he could feel the gears grinding. "If I go down, get the hell out of here. If they come after you, go however far you have to go to lose them. Out of town, out of state, whatever you have to do. Got it?" Quickly he popped the trunk.

Craig began, "Wait a second—" But Balthazar was already out of the car, slamming the door.

He went to the trunk of the car even as Redgrave said, "You again?"

Balthazar took out the crowbar he'd found there, marched toward Redgrave, and said, "Me again," just before swinging the iron rod into Redgrave's face.

They were all on him within seconds, but none of them was at their full strength, and he'd never been angrier or more vicious. More deadly. Balthazar pounded at their guts, their groins, their heads, swinging so savagely that none of them could even reach him. Nothing held him back now: not worrying about being seen by humans who would misunderstand, not fear of capture, not any sense of sentimentality, nothing. He might even have been able to hurt Charity, if she'd been with them. The monster within him had never been so free. Causing pain had never felt so good.

Redgrave staggered backward, falling to his knees. Through bloodied lips, he spat, "You know—this won't—stop us. So why—do you bother?"

"It'll slow you down enough," Balthazar said, beating back one of the others. "And then I'm going to find out if it's possible to behead you just by ripping your head off with my bare hands. Never tried that before. But you know what? I bet it works."

Redgrave leaped up, but he was slower than a human now, and Balthazar threw him back like so many rags. As his sire fell in the snow, a pathetic wreck of his old self, Balthazar heard him say, "You're killing Skye even now."

Balthazar hit him again, so hard he heard the collarbone snap. As Redgrave doubled over in pain, Balthazar shouted, "Where is she?"

"She flung herself in the river," Redgrave panted. "Better to freeze than to bleed, I suppose. Skye's drowning or freezing to death right now . . . and you can't be bothered to save her. This time, we both lose. Skye's just like Charity—another pretty toy we broke between us."

Once more, Balthazar smashed his crowbar into Redgrave, this time into the side of his head. His old foe went down, unconscious, and the other vampires weren't trying to stop him; they were inching back, hoping that Balthazar would forget them.

He almost had. Without Redgrave, they were merely vermin. Let Black Cross handle them when they arrived in town. But it was Redgrave he had to kill, Redgrave he had to punish for everything he'd done—

—but every second he spent here was one he wasn't using to help Skye.

As long as you wish to be human, you will never be able to defeat me, Redgrave had said. But keeping his soul human—human enough to love Skye and to save her—was more important than anything else. Even killing Redgrave.

Balthazar bolted for the car, leaving Redgrave behind. Craig and Britnee were still there, though both of them stared at him as if he'd grown another head. He slid into the driver's seat, letting the crowbar fall to the floorboard, as he said, "Tell me the fastest way to get to the other side of this river. When we go over the bridge, you'll have to hang on to the steering wheel."

As he put the car in reverse and backed out, burning rubber, Britnee said, very quietly, "Mr. More? What's going on?"

"We're getting the hell out of here." Balthazar put the car in drive as Craig mutely pointed forward. "And we're going to save Skye."

His anger had left him. He didn't even glance backward at Redgrave. All Balthazar could think was, *Please let me get there in time.*

Chapter Twenty-eight

SKYE UNDERSTOOD NOW.

The visions weren't merely visions. They weren't some kind of cosmic punishment inflicted on her; they were signs showing her the path. Every death was a doorway.

"And you can walk through," Dakota said. He sat next to her in the snow, his forearms resting on his bent knees. She still lay on the riverbank, shaking, but the cold and the pain were very distant. Her body might have been no more than an old nightgown she'd tossed aside.

Although she would have loved to embrace her brother, that was impossible the way they were now—spirits untethered to the physical world. It would have been beside the point, too. They were more fully together now—more fully aware of their love for each other—than they'd ever been before. "What—what is this?"

Dakota ran one hand through his scruffy hair; he still looked just as he had the last time she'd seen him, with his skater gear T-shirt and cargo shorts, braided necklace around his throat, and Teva sandals. "It's only the gate. You go through, and you're on the other side. Afterward it seems simple."

Skye remembered the phone ringing late at night, and how she'd known, even before anybody answered, that it meant something horrible had happened. The sound of her mother sucking in a sharp breath as she heard, and the long silence that had followed before she could speak to tell them. The first time she'd seen Dad cry, and how old he looked, as if the tears had etched his wrinkles deeper. The funeral, with Dakota's girlfriend Felicia trying to talk about how great a time he'd been having on the adventure that claimed his life. How Mom and Dad had buried themselves further in their work, hardly even acknowledging the other child they had, maybe because she reminded them too painfully of the one they'd lost.

Skye realized more fully than she ever had before that Dakota wasn't the only one who had died that night; their family, as they had known it, had died, too.

Quietly she said, "The afterward isn't easy for the rest of us."

"I know. I'm sorry."

Although Skye didn't know if he was apologizing for behaving so recklessly, or simply telling her how badly he felt, it didn't matter. Dakota was here—as much with her as he had ever been—and that was enough.

Dakota said, "You know you can't stay here."

"With you?" The thought of leaving her brother again, when she'd only now found him, felt horribly wrong. "I don't want to leave you."

"You can find me again anytime, now that you know how," Dakota said. "You're the path, Skye. The gateway between our worlds. You can always talk to me; you can always talk to *any* of us. And trust me, there's a lot of guys over here who are dying to talk to you . . . okay, maybe that wasn't the best choice of phrase. Ready and waiting, let's say."

"I can talk to the dead now?"

"The dead who have something to say. And I don't mean like some crappy TV psychic, you know? This is going to be the real deal."

"Am I supposed to—make people feel better? Solve murders or something?" Well, now she had something original to speak up about on career day. "Where is this gift supposed to take me?"

"Wherever you want to go, sis. But none of that matters if you cross over for good now."

If she froze to death, he meant. Skye became aware of her physical body again—still at a distance, but enough to feel the dangerous numbness claiming her limbs. "Do you promise I'll be able to find you again?"

Dakota gave her that lopsided grin that always made her want to smack him, and yet smile back, too. "Oh, you're never gonna get rid of me now."

Skye laughed. It seemed to her that she'd gone from a place of ultimate fear to a place where fear didn't even exist. If the only danger was death, that was no danger at all, not in the end. "I love you, Dakota. I always felt like I never said it enough."

"Love you, too. And yeah—nobody ever says it enough.

Nobody in the world. But I always knew you loved me. Except maybe that time you stole my skateboard." His expression was half tenderness, half exasperation. "Will you save yourself already?"

"I'll go. I'll get out of here. But I'll come to you again soon."

"Count on it," Dakota said, as if he knew much more about it that he wasn't saying yet.

Her body closed around her again, and Skye transformed from the liberated spirit she'd been back into a creature of blood and bone. The cold hit her, and she gasped, almost unable to catch her breath.

Clumsily she pushed herself to sit up and take in her surroundings. Dakota had vanished; nothing of his presence remained. It was stranger than it should have been to realize that he had left no footprints, no impression in the snow. She was alone in the underbrush, her wet underclothes freezing around her shaking body; the tips of her hair were already becoming icicles. An incredible sleepiness hit her, as if all she needed to make herself feel better was to lie down and take a long nap.

That was hypothermia talking: Skye knew the signs. So she fought the urge to rest, braced her hands against the trunk of the nearest tree, and shoved herself upright until she could stand.

Where am I? Okay, not too far from the area with all the shops—but she understood now that it was farther than she'd be able to walk, suffering as she was from shock and exposure. She'd just have to make it to the nearest road. It was well after dark now, and in this weather few people would be out, but she only needed one car to stop and help her, or even just to call the police. Though her legs shook and she felt weak, Skye began moving toward the road. One step. One more. That was all she had to do, keep going.

As she got closer to her goal, Skye saw a pair of headlights drawing near. Could she make it in time to wave at them, get their attention? Her red, numb feet wouldn't move much faster. But she didn't have to get to the road; the car pulled over anyway, and she heard the slamming of doors.

Skye opened her mouth to shout for help, then thought, *What if it's the vampires? What if it's Redgrave?* They'd had a van before, but they might have a car at their disposal, too; she didn't know. Fear returned to her—not of dying, but of living as a captive. That was the only thing worth fearing.

Then she heard a voice call out, "Skye?"

"Balthazar!"

He emerged from the inky blackness, long coat billowing behind him as he ran toward her, his handsome face bruised and cut. Never had he looked so beautiful to her. Skye managed a few steps on her shaky feet before he closed the distance and pulled her fiercely into his arms.

"God, I thought we'd lost you," Balthazar murmured, between rough kisses against her cheek. "Are you all right?"

"Just—just cold." Her teeth chattered so much that it was hard to get the words out. "I'm so glad you found me."

Two more figures came toward them, indistinct amid the swirling sleet until one of them called, "Did you find her?"

Incredulous, Skye said, "Craig? Britnee?"

Sure enough, her ex-boyfriend and his current girlfriend were coming toward them; Britnee even held Skye's coat in her hands. As Skye yanked it on gratefully, Craig said, "We dropped by to check on you, and Mr. More was there and he told us some people were after you, or something like that—I didn't know what to think until that weird crew showed up at your old house. Anyway, now I realize he was telling the truth. I'm glad you're okay."

"I'll be okay when I'm warm," Skye said. "But . . . thanks, guys."

Britnee raised her hand. "Mr. More? The way you were fighting those guys back there? You were, like, super fast and stuff? So I was thinking in the car—well—are you a ninja?"

It took Balthazar a moment to answer. "No. I can't explain all of this, guys. I wish I could, but—it's better if you don't know. Let's just get Skye home so we can get her warm."

Skye leaned heavily on his shoulder as they made their way toward the car. She murmured, "You didn't tell me there were ways for vampires to repel ghosts."

"Redgrave found out about that? How did he—Charity. Of *course*." Balthazar grimaced. "I should have realized as soon as she rejoined them that they'd catch on."

"Don't beat yourself up about it. Once he was ready to get me, he was going to get me one way or another." Skye realized that Redgrave was still too close. "What are we going to do now?"

"Get you to safety and worry about the rest later." There was so much unsaid there: What was safety for her now? Did "the rest" mean that Balthazar still held on to his illogical belief that she could go on to a normal life after this—a "normal life" meaning one without him? All that ran through Skye's mind as Balthazar continued, "But first we have to make sure you're not freezing to death."

Shivering, she said, "Sounds good to me."

But as they got within ten feet of the car, more headlights appeared, and Skye's stomach dropped as she realized it was the black van. Redgrave and his tribe had found them.

"It's those guys," Craig said, putting a protective arm in front of Britnee. "How are they up after you beat them down like that?"

"Because I didn't finish the job," Balthazar said grimly. "Stand back, all of you."

Redgrave appeared at the head of them—six vampires, all men. The finely drawn, debonair features of Redgrave's face had been battered almost past recognition; his lips were split, his eyes swollen, his golden skin already purpling with bruises. Nor did he wear his usual smug smile—only a snarl. He finally appeared as monstrous as he truly was within. "Fool," he said to Balthazar. "You gave up your chance to kill me in order to save her—all so I can take her away from you again."

Balthazar let go of her, and she had to struggle to stand on her own. "I've got more than one chance to kill you."

"But you're not armed now, are you? And we are, this time."

Skye realized it was true. Balthazar glanced toward the car, where vampires were waiting. As good a fighter as Balthazar was, he didn't stand a chance against this many vampires when he was unarmed and they all carried stakes. Redgrave was battered, probably still not at his full strength, but the ones Balthazar had spent less time beating down already appeared completely undamaged again. Skye was in no condition to fight, and even if she were, she couldn't have been much help against these odds. Craig and Britnee had no idea what they were dealing with.

There was only way to avoid becoming Redgrave's servant forever.

"Change me," she whispered.

Her eyes and Balthazar's met for one tortured moment. Skye hated to ask him to kill her—hated the thought of becoming a vampire—but if this was her only way to escape, then she would take it.

Balthazar's expression told her that, even loathing the idea as he did, he would have changed her if he could—but he shook his head. *No time*, she realized. *No chance.*

Just when she thought the situation could get no worse, another figure stepped closer: Charity. She was almost as white as the snow that surrounded them, her dress, skin, and hair all the color of frost. Only her lips were dark, still stained with Skye's blood. In her hand was the largest, most lethally curved knife Skye had ever seen.

"Charity," Balthazar said, and his voice sounded broken. "Don't watch this."

"You think she wouldn't want to watch your final destruction?" Redgrave's exhilaration creased his battered face into a smile. "I think Charity's been waiting for this a long time."

"I remember now," Charity said. "Yes. A very long time."

Then she swung the blade savagely upward. In one lightning-swift move, she sliced straight through Redgrave's neck.

Britnee screamed, and Craig jumped. Skye clutched Baltha-zar's arm, but all he could do was stare as Redgrave's head and body both tumbled toward the snow—then dissipated into so much ash.

As the clouds of what had been Redgrave settled around her feet, Charity brought up her blade and screamed at the other vampires, "*Nobody* kills my brother but *me*!"

They scattered. Whether it was from the fall of their leader or the sheer homicidal insanity in Charity's eyes, the vampires had lost their nerve. Within a few moments, their small party stood alone except for Charity. Her eyes were locked with her brother's; her blade was still at the ready.

She repeated, in a whisper, "I remember now."

Balthazar said, "Are you going to kill me next?"

Charity let the blade drop to her side. Like a petulant, bored child, she said, "I don't feel like it tonight."

The glance that brother and sister shared was confused and even angry, but loving, too. "Um, I was wondering, what in the hell is going on?" Britnee asked.

"We'll talk at the house," Skye said. The cold she'd nearly for-gotten during their confrontation with Redgrave had returned. "Let's go home."

Chapter Twenty-nine

BALTHAZAR WAS REALLY TOO LARGE TO RIDE IN the middle of the backseat, but he did anyway. This meant that he could fold Skye into his right side, his arm around her shoulders, as the car's heaters and his own shelter warmed her from the terrible chill. Though she still shivered, he could see her strength returning to her. Despite everything, Skye was going to be all right.

This seating arrangement also meant that he could keep Charity on his left. She sat quietly, hands in her lap as neatly folded as if they were over a linen napkin instead of the blade she'd used to kill Redgrave.

His sister had done it. She'd really killed him. As badly as Balthazar had wanted his own vengeance, he would never have denied that Charity deserved that kill as much as he did. The main thing was that Redgrave was gone, forever.

"I drank her blood," Charity said. Although Balthazar realized what she meant, Skye held out her arm, revealing the two small pink marks that lingered there, for proof. "I went back to before."

"What did you go back to?" he said gently. He had not spoken to her this way since they were both alive.

"The day I put my bonnet on the cow to make you laugh."

Balthazar had almost forgotten that. How ludicrous the cow had looked, and how silly they'd been about it. "That was funny, wasn't it?"

"It was." Charity leaned her head against his shoulder, the way she used to when she was little and they sat in front of the fire. "We used to have lots of fun, didn't we?"

"Yeah. We did."

That was why she'd murdered Redgrave. The sip of Skye's blood—the tool Redgrave had thought would make any vampire his minion forever—had instead reminded Charity of who she was when she was alive. At the moment, she was more his sister . . . more truly herself . . . than she'd been since becoming a vampire. He let his head rest against hers, just for a second.

From the front seat, Britnee said, "So, I couldn't help hearing the comment about drinking blood? Are we talking about vampires here?"

"Don't be ridiculous," Craig said.

"Yes," Balthazar said. "I'm a vampire. So is my sister, Charity."

"I'm not," Skye added sleepily. "I'm just a psychic. I can see deaths suspended in time, and use them to reach through and speak to the dead." When Balthazar glanced over at her, she said,

"I'll explain later. That last trip over the river told me a lot."

Britnee said, "Our next substitute is going to seem so boring?"

Craig shook his head from side to side. "This night had better not get any weirder."

Once they reached Skye's house, she was able to take the warm shower she needed to heat herself up; Britnee found a tin of cocoa in the kitchen and set about making some for everyone, with Craig's help. Balthazar remained downstairs with Charity.

She clearly hadn't spent much time in a normal human home anytime recently; Charity's curiosity led her to pick up the remotes and punch multiple buttons at once, then to trace her fingers around the sides of the unfamiliar thin plasma-screen TV. Balthazar let her do what she wanted as long as she didn't cause any harm; for tonight, at least, he thought she was safe to be around.

In the meantime, he checked himself out in the front hall mirror; it had been too long since he'd properly fed, because the image was hazy. Still, he could see that the cuts on his face had already healed, and the bruises were almost entirely gone.

"Looking good," Skye said.

Balthazar glanced up to see Skye standing at the top of the stairs. She wore a simple white cotton T-shirt and jeans; her hair had the slightly windblown look that told him she'd just finished with the blow dryer, and her face was clean-scrubbed, still somewhat pale. To him, she had never appeared more beautiful.

"Come here," he said, opening his arms for her as she came down the steps to leap into them. She smelled like fresh soap and lavender. When they kissed this time, he buried his hands in her warm hair, opened his mouth, and pretended they were all alone.

When they finally pulled back from each other, Skye said, slightly breathless, "Well, I'm heated up *now*."

"You're sure you're all right? If you need to go to the hospital—"

"I'm fine," she insisted. "I'm warm again, and you're with me, and we're safe. I've never been better." Her eyes flicked over to Charity. "I can't believe I just said we're safe, considering . . . but we are, aren't we?"

"For now."

Eventually, Charity would become monstrous again. But Balthazar now knew—no matter how terrible she became, no matter what she did, he would never be the one to destroy her. There had been times, over the past few years in particular, when he'd attempted to find the will to kill her. Charity was a murderer countless times over. She was unstable, manipulative, and cruel. Right now she remembered their love for each other as brother and sister, but she'd probably forget it again.

Someday, someone would have to stop her. Balthazar accepted that. But he also knew that he would never have the right. He'd killed her once; that had been more than enough to damn them both. No matter what she became, Charity was his sister—in life, in death, always.

When he turned back to Skye, her sad smile told him that, somehow, she knew exactly what he was feeling; she understood him more than he'd ever thought a human could. Perhaps more than he'd thought anyone could. "I saw Dakota," she said. "While I was on the riverbank. Brothers and sisters . . . the bond doesn't go away when you die."

"Or long after death," Balthazar said. "What did you see?"

Before Skye could answer, Craig and Britnee entered the room, Craig with a tray of steaming mugs in his hands. "Okay, who wants hot chocolate?" Britnee chirped.

Skye went straight for it; she needed the heat. Though human food had little taste for Balthazar, he wouldn't mind some himself—vampire bodies were slower to chill but also slower to warm again. When Britnee cheerfully handed a mug to Charity, his sister stared down into it suspiciously, as if they might have spiked it with holy water. But she held on to it, and he could see a small smile of pleasure as a few curls of steam wafted past her face.

While everyone settled in, Craig said, "Let me see if I've got this straight. Skye's got psychic powers, and that does something amazing to her blood, so a vampire was trying to capture her and make other vampires follow him just to get some of the blood for themselves. But now that vampire's dead, so everything's okay?"

Balthazar had been feeling better before Craig said that. "The first part is right. But Redgrave's death doesn't make everything okay. Not by a long shot."

"They're still coming," Charity confided. Good God, she

was actually trying to be helpful. He could see her struggling to be clear, to behave well. "So many vampires. They won't know what to do without Redgrave, but they'll look and they'll look."

"And Black Cross is on the way," Balthazar added. Charity startled; Craig and Britnee looked confused. To explain to them both, he said, "Vampire hunters. Armed and extremely dangerous. Our old friend Lucas used some old contacts to send them this way. They'll take out any vampire they find, present company included."

Britnee said, "Are we about to be in a vampire war or something like that?"

"Are all the vampires going to come after Skye?" Craig said. Charity nodded, almost gleeful, before apparently realizing that wasn't the right reaction and sobering herself.

Skye and Balthazar looked at each other; in her eyes he could see the mirror of his own dismay. They'd long known this crisis was coming, but he'd always believed Redgrave would be in charge . . . which, ironically, had given him a false sense of security. With Redgrave claiming power, the other vampires would have been held in some kind of check. There would have been some chance to control them, to guess what the dangers might be and when they might fall.

With Redgrave gone, everything changed.

Every vampire or tribe that came to Darby Glen would be independent, seeking Skye for its own use. They would make wars on one another. Form alliances and betray them. There was no saying when or how they would attack. This town would be more than endangered; it would become a battleground once again, just as it had been during the French and Indian War. Except now the battles would be between the dead—with untold human beings at risk as well. The only way to prevent that catastrophe was for Skye to leave.

Quietly, Balthazar said to Skye, "You can't stay here."

"I can't leave Mom and Dad," she insisted, as stubbornly as she always had. "Not after they lost Dakota. It's too cruel, Balthazar."

"Too cruel," Charity agreed, in such a singsong tone of voice that Balthazar at first thought she was simply parroting words she'd heard, as she often did. But then she continued, "Crueler if they die because of you."

That got through to Skye as nothing else had, Balthazar realized. She paled at the thought. Redgrave would have spared her parents because it suited his absurd ideas of his own nobility and fairness; the other vampires descending on the town would have no such qualms.

Craig suggested, "Take them with you."

"Mom and Dad?" Skye considered this for a moment. "You mean, tell them the truth about all this?"

"Maybe they could handle it?" Britnee said. "I mean, we're kinda catching up?"

Craig nodded, deep in thought. It occurred to Balthazar that, as Skye's ex-boyfriend, Craig probably knew the Tierneys better than anyone else in the room besides Skye herself . . . and his view of them might be less clouded by guilt and grief.

"I know they've been acting weird since Dakota—well, since Dakota," Craig said. "But this stuff you're dealing with is too big for you to carry alone, Skye."

Balthazar could imagine it now. Spiriting Skye and her parents somewhere out of the way, an unknown location where they could still lead regular lives. He could make sure they remained safe—perhaps allow himself the luxury of remaining with Skye a while longer before letting her get back to being the normal girl she deserved to be.

At that moment the front door opened. Balthazar went for Charity's blade, now in his own coat, but the new intruders weren't from Redgrave's tribe. They were people he'd never seen before—

"Mom! Dad!" Skye's eyes lit up as she put down her mug and rushed into her parents' arms. "We were just talking about you."

"Honey, we came as soon as we could," Mrs. Tierney said. "The bill's up for a vote tonight, but we just said, screw it."

"Your mother means that we knew we needed to be here." Mr. Tierney was the one his daughter took after, with the same dark hair and pale eyes. "We need to talk to you about this business with the teacher."

Said teacher, still sitting on the sofa, now felt acutely embarrassed. Before Balthazar could begin making any kind of explanations or excuses, though, Mrs. Tierney gave them all a big smile. "Well, hello, Craig! Good to see you again. And you've got all your friends over, honey."

"They're trying to make me feel better," Skye said, "because all that stuff about the teacher is just Madison Findley's gossip. Ask Principal Zaslow yourself tomorrow."

Craig grinned, at ease with people he must have known well for years. "Hey, Mr. and Mrs. Tierney. I see you guys still keep hot chocolate on hand for the needy."

"We try," Mr. Tierney said. Their jokes seemed a little hollow to Balthazar—as if her parents were trying hard to come across as happy and easygoing, but couldn't quite pull it off. Still, he would try to cut them some slack, now that he saw how comforted Skye was to finally have them near. "Why don't you introduce us to everyone else?"

Skye said, "Well, this is Balthazar. He's . . . in history with me." Balthazar hoped he looked much younger with his glasses off. "And that's Craig's new girlfriend, Britnee, and—and that's—um—that's Charity."

Charity looked cornered; she knew she needed to come across as a perfectly normal teenager, but clearly had no idea how to pull it off. She was casting around for something to say; God alone knew what she would come up with. Before Balthazar could start talking and cover the awkward moment, Charity blurted out, "I love Justin Bieber."

"Oh, I remember that feeling!" Mrs. Tierney chuckled as she patted Charity fondly on the arm; Balthazar could see his sister resisting the urge to bite. "For me it was Shaun Cassidy. I used to sleep with his LP under my pillow."

Mr. Tierney said, "As good as it is to see all of you, I think we need to talk with Skye for a while."

"We're going," Balthazar said, rising to his feet and taking hold of Charity's arm; her gaze toward Mrs. Tierney had only grown more pointed, and he gave her his best *don't eat the nice people* look. "Skye, I'll talk to you soon."

"Soon," she repeated. The night hadn't scarred her; her cheeks were rosy again, and her smile had never been as bright.

Craig and Britnee offered them a ride, but Balthazar refused it. As they drove off, he and Charity walked into the forest; the driving sleet of earlier had turned into light, gentle snow.

"Where will you go?" he said.

"I don't know. I always used to find Redgrave when I didn't know what to do. Now . . . I'll find out." Though she still spoke in a childlike tone, Charity made more sense than she had in a long time. Balthazar wondered if—just possibly—Skye's blood had been powerful enough to work a permanent change in his sister. If she remembered enough of her living self, of the girl she'd been before the savage attack that killed them, she might be different from now on. Maybe that was too much to hope for, but for the first time in nearly four hundred years, he dared to dream.

He warned her, "Constantia's still out there. She's going to try to take over."

"Should we stop her?"

"I think we should avoid her."

"I don't like her," Charity said. "She pulls hair."

"Among other things." Balthazar realized, with increasing

concern, that Constantia was the most likely candidate to become the head of the vampires coming to Darby Glen. And she would be a formidable enemy—one capable of predicting Balthazar's moves, who knew many of his hideouts and habitations as well as he did. One capable of rallying most of Redgrave's tribe to join her instantly. One who already knew Skye's face and would never, ever forget it. Tonight's victory, sweet as it had been, was only the beginning of a longer battle.

Charity gave him a brittle look. "I'm still going to get you back someday."

"You'll *try*."

She laughed, as if it were now all one great game between them. Perhaps, from now on, that was what it would be. "You'll see!" Then she ran away from him at full speed, a zephyr of frost in the woods for one split second before she vanished completely.

Balthazar didn't chase her. The truth about whether or not Charity had changed would come only when she chose to find him again.

Chapter Thirty

SKYE KNEW THE DANGER WAS FAR FROM OVER, but she couldn't think about that yet. Right now she just wanted to be where she was—on her living room sofa, between her parents—and who she was—the daughter they had forgotten, remembered at last.

As she took the last swallow of her hot cocoa, she watched her parents, both of whom were checking their phones . . . which was kind of annoying, but the bill *was* up for a vote tonight. What mattered most was that they'd finally dropped everything to return to her. Between this and seeing Dakota earlier, it was as though she'd gotten her entire family back tonight. Skye couldn't stop smiling.

"Ohhhh-kay," Mom said, finally putting her phone on the coffee table. "Now, what's up with this teacher?"

"Nothing," Skye insisted. By now, in her head, "Mr. More, the history teacher" was just a fictional character Balthazar had played; it was as easy to deny this as it would've been to deny that she'd had a hot affair with Harry Potter. The real Balthazar—the one she loved—was someone else entirely. "He never did anything inappropriate. He just let me talk to him about things. About . . . about Dakota."

That was the first time she'd spoken his name to her parents since the day after the funeral. Their faces went slightly rigid, as if there was no way any real emotion was going to get to the surface, ever. Seeing that made Skye's heart ache for them, but she wasn't going to pull back, not now. It was time to talk about this. Eventually, when they learned she could still speak to Dakota, they'd be so grateful.

"His sister died when he was about my age," she said. "So he understood about Dakota. About how—how you try to push the person you lost away, but you can't. You have to hold on to them, on to how much you loved them. Because you don't lose someone when they die. You only lose them when you forget the love you had together."

There was a moment of silence before her father briskly folded his glasses and tucked them in a case. "It's a relief to hear that nothing problematic is going on," he said. "We always thought you were far too sensible to get mixed up in anything like that."

"I told you we should have stayed in Albany," her mother said to him, and he shrugged, like, *Score one for you.*

And that was it. They hadn't even acknowledged that she'd said anything about Dakota. They were sorry they'd come home for her at all.

"Dad. Mom. Come on." Skye felt sure she could get through to them. Okay, so it would take a little work. She couldn't expect them to change completely in an instant. "Aren't we ever going to talk about Dakota again?"

Sharply, her mother said, "Nobody's forgotten your brother, Skye. But we all handle things in our own ways. We've tried to respect your grief; you have to respect ours."

When had they ever tried to respect her grief? When had they ever done anything but expect her to handle this the same way they did—by pushing her brother into the darkness of the past?

Dozens of images from the past year flickered in Skye's mind, illuminated differently than they had been before, and finally in true focus: Her father glancing away from the photos of Dakota in her room—away from Skye herself—until the day she gave up and put them in the drawer, away from sight. How they'd gone about business as usual the afternoon following the funeral, and how Skye had felt bad for crying when they could be so "brave."

How they'd expected her to care for herself from now on, leaving her alone day and night to bury themselves in work. How she'd accepted that absurdity as something she could do for them. And for a month or two, maybe that wouldn't have been so wrong. They had come home tonight, after all; it wasn't as if they didn't love her. Skye knew perfectly well that they did.

But now—now she realized her parents were so deep in denial that they would never get out.

And they expected her to go on denying her brother's death with them, forever, even though that also meant denying his life.

Skye slowly rose from the couch. Neither of her parents looked up; Mom already had her phone back in hand. She said, "I've had a long day." Which was putting it lightly. "I'm going to go up to bed."

Her father gave her a distant sort of smile. "You're a good girl, Skye." *We're so pleased with you for dropping the subject. See how easy denial can be?* "Sweet dreams."

Once she was alone in her room again, Skye started work.

She pulled out her largest suitcase, stared at it for a minute, then put it back up and grabbed a pack for long horse trips instead. Into it she tucked only a couple changes of clothing, a few toiletries, and the picture of Dakota and her on their white-water rafting trip.

Then she saw her phone, still sitting where she'd dropped it hours ago. Balthazar's text messages were all hours old by now, but there were several from Clem: *R U there?*

OK, I know u r busy but srsly txt me back. I'm freaking here. Skye?

Quickly Skye sent a few words back: *I'm safe—but barely. Will tell u the rest l8r.* She paused before adding, *Luv u.* That was kind of sappy for her and Clementine, but tonight Skye felt like she'd rather say too much than not enough. Like Dakota had told her, you could never say those words too often.

She glanced around her room, saw an equestrian trophy, and

snapped a photo of it with her phone before tucking the phone into her coat pocket. At least that way she could still look at it.

Then she stood at her bedroom window, knowing that the light would silhouette her to anyone watching from the darkness.

To Balthazar.

Skye turned off the lights and waited. Within a few moments, she heard scraping on the bark of the tree outside, which made her breath come a little faster just in case it wasn't—but it was. Balthazar appeared outside her window, clinging to the tree branch with unearthly grace, and she slid the pane upward to allow him to climb in.

He whispered, "Downstairs, the lights are still on."

"They're probably talking with their cronies at the state house, finding out how the vote is going." Skye didn't bother to whisper. Even if they could hear, they weren't listening. "Balthazar, you were right. I have to leave Darby Glen."

He studied her for a moment, no doubt weighing how serious she was about this. She knew that he understood her; he would see right away that she meant it. But he asked, "Your parents didn't believe you?"

"I never got as far as telling them the truth. The minute I started speaking about Dakota, they just . . . shut down, same as always." Disappointment welled up inside her, but she fought back the urge to cry. She'd been through too much tonight to give in to it now. "If I'm ever going to find the courage to learn how to deal with this gift I have, and be able to find Dakota again—I'm going to have to do it on my own. I can't do it while I'm with them. They won't let me."

Balthazar's hand brushed against the side of her face, his thumb tracing the line of her cheekbone. "Are you sure, Skye? I think you're right, but—it's not about what I think. If you aren't absolutely positive, you'll come to regret this."

Skye nodded. "I'm positive. I mean, I'll let them know that I'm out there and I'm okay. But somehow, I doubt worrying *too much* is going to be one of their problems."

"I'm sorry," Balthazar said, and she could hear in his voice how deeply he meant it.

"Me too," she confessed, but then she turned her thoughts to the matter at hand. "So. For my sake, and the town's sake, I need to get out of Darby Glen as soon as possible. That means tonight. I packed what I need in a saddlebag. We can ride over to the Findleys' place, pick up whatever you need there. And I bet we can make it to Reardon Falls by sunrise. There's campgrounds there. A lodge. It'll work in the short term."

Balthazar looked at her in surprise. "You want the two of us to ride out of here?"

"Well, I'm not leaving Eb behind." That was all there was to it. The vampires might have taken her home away from her, but she'd be damned if they'd get her horse, too. "There's plenty of places we can go with two horses—you'll have to be on Peppermint, of course. We'll be able to rent a trailer to take us where we need to go, eventually. Out west, maybe. Someplace with a lot of open sky, and nobody to be too nosy about us—and end up revealing where we are to people who shouldn't know."

"It's good thinking, but—" His voice trailed off, and she knew what weighed on his mind. Throughout all of this, he'd expected their relationship to have an expiration date; he'd wanted to get her someplace safe, but in Balthazar's mind, "safe" meant "far from him."

Which was crap, and it was high time she said so.

"Listen to me." Skye wrapped her hands around the edges of his coat, drawing them closer together. Balthazar's face was only inches from her own. "Don't start with me about how I need a 'normal life.' After this, I don't get to be normal. Not ever. I'm always going to have these powers. I'm always going to have vampires after me." Unless and until she herself was changed into one of them—but she couldn't begin thinking of that now. "If you walk away from me, you're not saving me from anything. Do you understand? If you walk away from me, it's because you want to. If you stay with me, it's because you need to." Her voice trembled slightly as she said the last: "I hope you need to."

Balthazar's only answer was to pull her against him in the longest, deepest kiss they'd ever shared. As she opened her mouth beneath his, Skye allowed herself to get lost in the feel and the taste of him, to rest against his broad chest and imagine that nothing in the world could ever touch them.

Maybe it couldn't, as long as they stood together.

When their lips parted, Balthazar roughly whispered, "I need you. I love you. The only way I could ever have walked away from you was for your own good—because of *how much* I loved you, not how little. Do you understand that?"

Skye nodded. She'd always known that, deep down. "But you want this?" The path she was asking him to walk down wasn't any easier for him than it was for her: always on the run, always at risk, with predators from his past forever on their trail. "It's not much of a life."

"Don't you see? It's the first life I've had in four hundred years." Balthazar cupped her cheek in his hand. "With you—in the only way that matters—I'm alive again."